Please enter at your own risk. There are no refunds.

Conditions may include low light, no light, strobe effects, Y reality, beats, alcohol, flowers, broken glass, broken bones, broken dreams, exhilaration, disorientation, ecstasy, self-knowledge, and death. Flash photography is permitted.

Remember to be aware of your surroundings. Your surroundings are aware of you.

Welcome to Dark Factory.

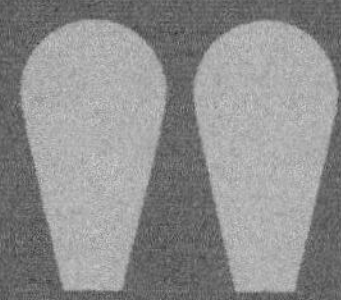

"Koja crafts the future that the ravers of the 1990s dreamed of in this immersive and propulsive cyberpunk outing. . . . In breathless, careening prose, Koja captures minds that see a thousand worlds at once, lives lived at 150 beats per minute, and the complicated, messy reality that lies beneath the endless search for the perfect night out. This is sure to delight fans of Jeff Noon and mind-bending speculative fiction."
PUBLISHERS WEEKLY

"Visionary. Stunning. A near-future vision of clubbing culture that takes us beyond virtual reality but, at the same time, presents an intimate look at the life of artists. Koja proves once again that she is a master of her craft."
ALMA KATSU, author of *The Fervor* and *The Deep*

"You don't read *Dark Factory* so much as slam dance your way through its glittering labyrinth of art, tech, danger, and lust. Meticulously envisioned and impeccably performed, this book lives and breathes far beyond its pages, providing an experience more akin to experimental theater than traditional literature; once again, Koja drags fiction kicking and screaming into the future, where it belongs."
MARYSE MEIJER, author of The *Seventh Mansion* and *Heartbreaker*

"Some writers are born to spin tales from the shadows. Kathe Koja is one such author. *Dark Factory* is a unique and esoteric experience. A journey into the throbbing heart of creativity itself. Where we find kisses and cuts. A fantastic story."
S.A. COSBY, NYT bestselling author of *Razorblade Tears* and *Blacktop Wasteland*

"Koja writes like she's an entire collective of artists, senses in overdrive, voracious for the next hit of art that will push them—and us—over the edge. This is pure energy, a glow-in-the-dark vision of a new kind of writing."
DANIEL KRAUS, NYT bestselling author of *Bent Heavens* and *The Living Dead*

"Koja has redefined the possibilities and limits of literature with *Dark Factory*—a thunderous, all-consuming tour de force executed by one of our finest and most skilled creators. This is not a book. This is an unforgettable and transformative experience."
ERIC LAROCCA, author of *Things Have Gotten Worse Since We Last Spoke*

"There isn't anywhere I wouldn't go with Kathe Koja, and the seams of reality are no exception."
SARAH MILLER, author of *Caroline* and *The Borden Murders*

"*Dark Factory* is a wickedly original and wild book—a steadily evolving mystery, an ecstatic search for beauty and reality, a confrontation with our need to tell and be told stories—all borne of Koja's endless curiosity and dexterity."
LINDSAY LERMAN, author of *I'm From Nowhere* and *What Are You*

"'You can dream while you're awake.' She's done it again: with *Dark Factory* Kathe Koja spins a nighttime world fully realized and revelatory, all while reaching new linguistic highs. And how many books have you read that made you want to dance?"
TOM CARDAMONE, author of *The Lurid Sea*, *Green Thumb*, and *Night Sweats: Tales of Homosexual Wonder and Woe*

"*Dark Factory* reminds us that Kathe Koja is not only a great writer, but an important one. Bolstered by inventive audiovisual supplements, the book is both intimate and epic, an ensemble genre-bender that envisions new possibilities for the novel as narrative form. This is a daring work of multisensory and multimedia immersion, an exemplar of Koja's career-long commitment to dissolving boundaries—between genres and delivery systems, between body and mind, between story and reader, between virtual and real. This is a propulsive, wickedly funny literary party; enter the Factory, lose yourself, and dance."
MIKE THORN, author of *Shelter for the Damned*, *Darkest Hours*, and *Peel Back and See*

"*Dark Factory* is quintessential Kathe Koja, and duly represents her style, tastes, choices, wit, and unparalleled skill. In a career brimming with immersive fiction, here, now, a novel about immersion itself. Nobody could've told this story but Kathe Koja. *Dark Factory* is written with the appetite and buzzing of a debut novel, but the sureness of a modern master. Each sentence takes a stand, makes a joke, reveals a truth, so that halfway deep, the reader is wholly and truly immersed."

JOSH MALERMAN, NYT bestselling author of *Bird Box* and *Daphne*

"As onetime gatekeeper to some of New York's most legendary nightclubs, I can assure you there has never been one quite like *Dark Factory*. Situated in an imminent, perhaps even parallel time, this is a club Philip K. Dick might have envisioned, designed to provide the ultimate heightened user experience. Here virtual and altered reality mix and combust to create a new kind of collective Dionysian ecstasy, sensually intoxicating and potentially transgressive. Behind this *Dark Factory*, Ari Regon is the creative alchemist looking to push boundaries of what a club experience, if not life itself might be. Meta-author Kathe Koja builds a hyperdetailed, tangibly peopled, noirish world around Ari's own world-building mission with all its challenges, foibles, and loves. But this world doesn't stop there; it continues with you, because *Dark Factory* isn't merely a book; it's an ongoing interactive 'club' experience that you may, indeed are encouraged to enter, revel in, expand and transmutate with. It's an explosively unpredictable scene, so if you're adventurous, limitlessly curious, and a bit crazy put on your 'tiara' and enter *Dark Factory* at your own risk and delight—you're on the list."

JORGE SOCARRAS, singer and writer, and former staffer at New York's Danceteria, Area, Palladium, Tunnel, MK and Big Haus

Praise for THE CIPHER:

"Those of us who have been around awhile remember the impact Kathe Koja's *The Cipher* made on the scene when it first appeared in 1991. It was like a perfect onyx jewel wrested from Hell: gorgeous, hideous, and terrifying. We'd never seen anything like it before. Its return to print is something to be celebrated by anyone who loves brilliant horror fiction. *The Cipher* is a stone-cold classic."

NATHAN BALLINGRUD, award-winning author of *Wounds* and *North American Lake Monsters*

"This entry into the body-horror canon carries with it the kind of fatalism horror readers prize—it's going to end badly, for sure, but just how badly?"

BOOKLIST

"Koja has created credible characters who are desperate for both entertainment and salvation . . . this powerful first novel is as thought-provoking as it is horrifying."

PUBLISHERS WEEKLY

Praise for VELOCITIES: STORIES:

"*Velocities* is prime Kathe Koja, with all that that entails: supercharged, dense as hell, oblique, glorious. Every story is a lesson in how to write faster, more intensely, from angles other people never seem to think of: industrial poetry, word mosaics like insect eyes, multifoliate as the insides of flowers, every image a scattered, burrowing seed, spreading narrative like a disease. I've loved her work since long before I ever aspired to produce anything like it—in fact, I'm still not sure anyone else is capable of doing what she does, of coming close, let alone hitting the mark. But damn, it's equally so much fun to admire the result as it is to even vaguely try."

GEMMA FILES, award-winning author of *Spectral Evidence*

"An impressive collection of stories unafraid to explore bleak topics like death and despondency."

KIRKUS REVIEWS

"A modern genius of weird and dark fiction, Kathe Koja once again proves with *Velocities* that she's adept at plunging the reader into strange and unexpected places. One of my favorite collections of the year."

JEFF VANDERMEER, NYT bestselling author of *Dead Astronauts*, *Borne* and the *Southern Reach trilogy*

"Koja's stories are at their most superb where they study the strength in bodies perceived as delicate or fragile . . . Koja explores the misunderstood and the dark in twisting and often experimental prose."

BOOKLIST

ALSO BY KATHE KOJA

The Cipher
Bad Brains
Skin
Strange Angels
Kink
Extremities: Stories
Under the Poppy
The Mercury Waltz
The Bastards' Paradise
Christopher Wild
Velocities: Stories

DARK FACTORY

PRESENTED BY

KATHE KOJA

Meerkat Press
Asheville

ISBN-13 978-1-946154-75-0 (Paperback)
ISBN-13 978-1-946154-76-7 (Ebook)

This is a work of fiction. Names, characters, businesses, places, events and incidents are either the products of the author's imagination or used in a fictitious manner. Any resemblance to actual persons, living or dead, or actual events is purely coincidental.

Author Photo by Rick Lieder
Cover design by Tricia Reeks
Book design by Tricia Reeks
Foxglove drawing © Sofia Ajram
Emperor logo and Silver Landings poster © Rena Hopkins

Stock photos and composite imagery from AdobeStock.com, Twenty20.com, and Pexels.com

Printed in the United States of America

Published in the United States of America by
Meerkat Press, LLC, Asheville, NC
www.meerkatpress.com

The Dark Factory project combines Kathe Koja's writing and her immersive event creation, for a new fiction experience online and on the page.

This book contains bonus content that can be read along with the story as it appears in the book (dark background), or afterward: there is no "correct" way, whatever works for each reader is best. Bonus content is highlighted on the Contents page.

Readers can also interact with the posts at DarkFactory.club, follow Dark Factory on Instagram and Twitter and Facebook, make Dark Factory art, and go as far into this world as the party takes them.

DarkFactory.club

CONTENT

"KATHE KOJA IS A SPHINX, A GI
THE RAREST OF TALENTS
JOSH MALERMAN, AUTHOR OF
BIRD BOX AND MALORIE
DARK
FACTORY

01

"Ari! Hey Ari, how's it going?"

"Hey," his nod to the skinny DJ on the bench opposite Jonas's office, blue glass walls half-covered with overlapping Dark Factory posters, the effect is like peering into a paper aquarium. "It's going good. Tight."

"I just got in from Chromefest, I played some crazy great shit," the DJ digging into his bag, a dangle of fake gold giveaway charms, too many stickers, TOOT SWEET, U DONT REDLINE U DONT HEADLINE, pulling out a mix stick. "You got a minute?"

"Got a meeting," with a shrug, a smile, his public smile—

—but inside the office no Jonas, only his spoor: empty NooJuice cans, Causabon trainers still new in the box, a white dinner jacket hung on the hulking recliner, and between the tilting piles on the blue glass table that is Jonas's desk, two burner phones, both vibrating like wind-up toys: Ari takes up one, then the other, neither are numbers he knows. Also on the desk is a flat delivery box stacked with t-shirts, a new streamlined design, and "Y makes the logo move," Jonas at the door, slamming the door, Jonas wearing last summer's t-shirt, black and sleeveless beneath a clear plastic wrap jacket; with his hair sheared at the sides he looks like a brand-new cleaning brush, Ari hides a smile. "Lee thinks it's too subtle. What do you think?"

"Not if it moves," an answer and a parry, Jonas likes to test everyone, Ari most of all. "Chockablock thinks of everything."

"And overcharges for everything too. Wear it around, see what people say," and as Ari drapes a shirt around his neck, "I know it's your day off, but I need you in the box tonight."

"Just me?"

"You and whoever else I stick in there. Be good, or it'll be Lee."

"I don't have a problem with Lee."

"That's not what she says."

"Then that's her problem."

"True. Got a smoke? Darcy's after me to quit," as Ari offers one of the black blunts he gets from the boys in the clubs, Jonas rooting in the desk's mess for an ashtray, and "Lee said," Jonas's shrug half-annoyed, "some woman gave birth on the floor last night? To an actual baby? What a mess."

And Ari laughs—"The Factory's first natural-born citizen"—and after a moment Jonas laughs too: "Your brain, Ari, your fucking brain," pulling out his real phone, a quick dictating bark, "Lee, find those baby people, give the baby free admission for life. Tell Media to make a big deal out of it—"

—as Ari exits in a puff of smoke and a flutter of posters, past the still-waiting DJ, and two runners toting scent canisters like oversized silver bullets, another runner wrangling a wobbling rack of boxed NooJuice, provided to the production in exchange for ad placement, another of Ari's ideas that Jonas approves, Jonas drinks half a dozen cans of that swill a day. Lee drinks it too, though Ari knows she hates it; sometimes he catches Lee studying him when she thinks no one can see.

In the performers' lounge he slips on the new t-shirt—a little loose across the chest, he likes his shirts tighter—smooths back his hair, then heads for the NOT AN EXIT sign over the loading dock doors: a delivery van rolling out, another just backing in that he sidesteps, out to the street, Neuberg Street . . . A teenager, the first time, he came here to drink cheap lager and fuck and dance to loud music with boys—he still fucks and dances, but Jonas has taught him something about wine, so he drinks that instead, chilled and white, it pairs nicely with the blunts—sixteen then and wide open, new to the scene, new to joy: his look changed, his slang, even his walk, more swagger, more aware of his body as he roamed past the schnapps bars and phone stores and crumbled brick alleys, the corner charging stations shaped like top hats where the boys hung out, flirting and sparring in the noise of sidewalk speakers and the whirring purr of the trains, the muezzin's call floating over avenues of beech and linden trees and the black-washed façades of the remodeled industrial flats, cafés hot with espresso and frothing oat milk, and the clubs' 4 a.m. aroma of lager and latex and Club-Mate, dancing panting bodies, moisturizer and tobacco and tears. And now these streets are his streets, he lives in one of those expensive flats, he has everything he wants in this world, almost everything.

The October sky is overcast as a tarnished mirror, heat still radiating from the pavement, he stops at a Kaffee Kart for an iced espresso and "Your shirt's really cool," says the freckled barista, as Ari records her reaction for Jonas's eventual benefit. "Dark Factory! I'd go every weekend if I could, it's like the world if the world was perfect. You go a lot?"

"I go every night. I work there."

"You *work* at Dark Factory? Oh cool! What do you do?"

And Ari smiles, because there is no name for what he does, what he is, what Jonas needs most, what Lee for all her stats and apps and 24/7 devotion can never be: the bridge between the Factory and the world, a native of both because "I'm the ambassador," he says, and lifts his cup to toast—the barista, the Factory, his job, himself—as a sudden gust of steam surrounds him, like a saint's silver halo, or a personal storm.

###

"Where are the other masks?" Max asks, foraging behind the salvaged kitchen table that serves as a production desk, through cut burlap squares and twiggy detritus, little plastic bags of dusty white quartz, a drift of unused Bitter Lake flyers. "Teresa, where—"

"In here—Oh," Teresa tipping a water-stained cardboard box to show less than a dozen inside, heavy black waxed paper with fake fur ears. "Is this all we have? It's a good thing no one's booked today."

"That's not a good thing—"

—as the door opens on Mila in a sleeveless hoodie, soft braids the brown of leaves in winter water, carrying a paper sack filled with "Seedpods," she says, "moth's bane, look," showing Teresa who smiles, Max who frowns: "You came all the way out here just to drop off seeds?"

"Katya drove me. They should be planted right away, but I have a class. Will you do it?" setting the bag to the desk as he follows her out, to share a kiss, then hangs back from Katya's car and its burst of dust, Katya accelerating down the graveled access road, away from him and the isolated copse that is Bitter Lake.

No signage, no way to be sure where the production begins or ends, every action taken must be a conscious choice, Max's choice to enforce full participation in this experience, his experience: on a fully booked day there could be forty people on these paths, wearing those masks, dancing with Mila, splashing through the stream, picking the apples carefully tied onto the trees, tasting the honey Teresa adds to the papier-mâché "hive," he had envisioned a real beehive and apple tree but *Bees are a liability*, Teresa had warned, *what if someone gets stung? And we can't book at night, without artificial light they could fall, maybe get hurt—*

There's this thing called the moon.

We just can't afford the risk—

—because the production has no money, last week the only day booked was Saturday, and only for five people, how long can they keep on? But still—as he tramps down that half-gravel track, the dividing line between the real world and his own—still he is made to make worlds, he believes that, quixote or not . . . Last week Adam Kaiser had invited him for a lager at Apostles', *How's it going at Bitter Water, still spinning those windmills? I've been meaning to stop out there.*

Bitter Lake. Bring your students, maybe they'll learn something.

My students? All they talk about is Y subsuming MR—

Good luck with that. And you shouldn't use that term, you shouldn't let them use it either. There's no such thing as "meat reality."

Did you see Ari Regon's Q&A for Storyboard? They loved that.

Fuck Dark Factory. And fuck Ari Regon. Especially Ari Regon—

—but he had had to leave for work then, refusing Adam's treat for the drinks, though his café wage has no room for a splurge. Adam and Teresa, shepherds of creativity, they each would say so: Adam the art professor, Teresa the former theater manager, the property owner who replenishes the apples and the farmers' market honey, picks up stray trash on the paths, keeps the lights on—

—Teresa leaning now from the doorway, paper sack in hand: "We just got a booking! A school outing, a teacher and twelve students, upper-level art students—"

"Good. When?"

"Thursday afternoon."

"Good," again, even though Thursday is one of his workdays, he needs every single day's pay, but "I can do a Q&A afterward, with the teacher too. And I—Where are you going?"

"The seeds. Mila said they needed to be planted right away—"

"Masks," taking the sack from her, leading her back inside. "We need to make more masks."

Bonus Content

Make Your Night: How Dark Factory Gets It All Done

by Jake Ulrich

reprinted from *ForwardFast Magazine*, Issue 251

With his mad scientist's hair and model's smile, Ari Regon is the face of Dark Factory, some would say the heart of it. Like Alice down a strobing rabbit hole, last night I followed Regon into the cavernous cacophony of that megaclub's reality, and learned that a business model built on human magic can be both efficient and enjoyable.

The club and its brand were originally conceived by entrepreneur Jonas Siegler, whose background in behavior studies is an unlikely but canny springboard into the entertainment world. The name itself is taken from another arty hustler's enterprise, Andy Warhol's late 20th century venture called the Factory. But, as Regon notes, the difference is that "Dark Factory is a total nightlife experience," so what gets made will not be something to hang on a wall, but each user's definition of a perfect night on the town, aided by a small army of Y reality technicians, dancers, performance bartenders, and roster of DJs.

Do you want to "go bare" and sip punnily-named cocktails like the Nuts & Bolts, and dance to DJ beats that are engaging if not especially transcendent? Do you want to take a step further, put on the customizable tiara (comfortable to wear, and with a stall-free interface), and explore the three floors of bars, pocket bars, and dancefloors, and make your mark on the Graffiti Room where messages, mostly of the come-on variety, fill the walls with neon, all the while interacting with the sexy denizens created by the Y technicians? Do you want to take yet another step, and purchase the expensive power user package, to access even more haptic-enabled interface moments with those characters, both Y and real? Or do

continued on page 008

02

Half-waking to the sound of the rain, no not rain, the shower? then waking fully, remembering, knee-high vinyl boots and a ginger quiff, the nightcap treat he picked up at the Playpen . . . His night had begun in the box, soundproof and all-seeing, the techs with their headphones and smudged steel vacuum bottles and bags of half-eaten licorice, and *Hi, Jake Ulrich,* in business-style jeans and horn-rimmed glasses, *I'm doing a Dark Factory piece for* ForwardFast, another one of Jonas's tests, why not just say I want you to talk to a journo? But *Absolutely,* his public smile, starting the spiel: The name inspired by a famous art collective, *Dark Factory is a total nightlife experience, anything and everything you see and hear and feel—*

"Make your night," right, I've already got the press packet. But your media person said you could give me the real intel—

—so a walk-through of the building, an edited journey since no visitors are allowed in material or shipping areas, or anywhere near Jonas's office, Ari pointing out the other kind of hot spots—*Here's the mixologists' lab, we're launching a new drink, the Nuts & Bolts, it's got a cashew liqueur base, want a taste? This is where the dancers rehearse, they're getting one-on-ones with Barrie Bless, she came straight from her tour to work with us. And here's the costume shop, our costumes have full haptics capability, transmit too, want to try? Feels wild, right? For patrons we have the onbody interactives, the*

continued from page 006

you just want to sit in the comfort of your own flat and stream your way to beats and bliss? Having those options available makes Dark Factory "unique," according to Regon, an assertion that is fully debatable—many clubs follow the same template, though admittedly with less success—but Regon's own enthusiasm for the Dark Factory brand and experience is uniquely irresistible.

And his input on its content is palpable. While none of those technicians, dancers, or crew were made available to speak on the record, a thoughtful scan of their MePages and other social accounts testifies to Regon's role as content curator. His experience running smaller clubs and wild warehouse events has made Regon seemingly the perfect foil for Siegler's take no prisoners business model: what could come off as marketing bombast seems, from Regon—whose self-stated role and mandate is "I'm here to make things happen" because he's "all about parties"—to be a special invite into a flashy world you're already eager to join. If the Red Queen and the White Rabbit were even half as engaging, Alice would have fired up a tiara, grabbed a drink, and stayed in Wonderland for good.

intensity's multi-customizable and fully adjustable, you want to feel more, you can—watching what caught Jake the journo's attention, made him take a picture, make a note, make a smile; always looking for the trigger.

And then the plunge and merge onto the floor, not the busiest night, two-thirds capacity and only eighteen power users onsite, but still plenty to see, several hundred intersecting realities, exploring, dancing, drinking, fucking the evening's partner or partners of choice, three floors of visibly satisfied customers—

—but Jake the journo went hard for the contrarian snark: *Some people claim Dark Factory's just a warehouse party dressed up with high-end Y instead of inflatables and confetti. You used to run warehouse parties, didn't you? Some fairly dicey ones, at the Holy Roman Empire?* But he was ready for that too, no snark back, just a friendly shrug: *Sure, I'm all about parties. But once you experience Dark Factory, you know that it's unique.*

Experience it onsite, you mean? Don't the streaming patrons get their money's worth?

Have you tried our streaming platform? I can code you in. It's tight, there are users there from all over the world—

What about the power users? I see they get special headsets, so do they have a better experience?

Power users have spatially enhanced tracks. And their individual experiences are gated, but anybody can be a power user—

What happens if I just take this off?

Go bare? You can, the drinks are still amazing and so are the DJs. But the parameters change, a lot of content has to drop off the menus—

What exactly is your input on that content? Who really calls the creative shots here, you or Jonas Siegler?

And he gave his brightest, most public smile—*I'm here to make things happen, Jake. Why don't we grab a drink? Mikey Trouble's set is starting on three*—and he kept that smile, kept Jake moving, even a little spin together on the dancefloor in the rose-red DJ TRBL lights, synced rose oil scent drops, rosy floating glitch balloons that popped to reveal more and tinier balloons that popped too, like dancing in a sea of pink champagne bubbles, until *Thanks a ton, Ari,* Jake's somewhat sweaty handshake at the door. *I'll send the link as soon as it's up.*

Then he left too, out into the last hours of darkness, a yellowish rumor of moon, down to the G line clubs, the Playpen where in the first five minutes he had a Modska shot and found the ginger, shiny boots and careful French quiff, uncut and with an ass like a trampoline—

—who stands toweling off now beside the bed, just as hot as last night though the quiff has wilted from the wet: "Redhead bedhead! Want to grab some brunch?"

And his own yawn from the pillows—"Brunch for me is a smoke"—but the ginger says he is a huge fan of the Factory, he has a performer's loop to share, between that and a farewell fuck it takes almost an hour to get him out the door. By then Ari's phone is tinging, Jonas embroiled somehow with ***Darcy, way upset***—Darcy the Brussels trophy girlfriend, Darcy whose tantrums are increasingly disruptive—***go do script w/Lee, check in w/me after.*** But why does he have to be physically present to Lee if Jonas is elsewhere? why not just upload the fucking cheat sheet? This requires hard caffeine—

—and sipping at a triple espresso as Lee waves from the door of the performers' lounge, not a greeting, not smiling, wearing the new black-on-black t-shirt, of course she is, and "Jonas said you were on your way," she says, as if he is unforgivably late. "Let's begin."

"Yeah, let's. . . . Any births or deaths to report?" trying to get comfortable in the spindly metal chair, why are the chairs in this lounge so shite? while Lee clicks her clipboard through the floor script, everything of note that happened the night before—

"The performers' door feed went down for four minutes, maintenance will change out the camera again—You can't smoke in here, you know that."

"Mmm."

"The Nuts & Bolts is testing very poorly. One of the bartenders quit—"

"Which one?"

An extra click: "David Corollo."

"Oh, Rollo. No surprise there, he's been hacked off for a while."

"If you knew that, you should have flagged him for HR retention." Ari says nothing, rolls the unlit blunt between his fingers, how many blunts would it take to make Lee bearable? as Lee clicks on: "Security ejected nine patrons, four for intoxication—two of those were a repeat drug issue, door staff needs a Safe Scan review—two for fighting, and three for lewd conduct."

"'Lewd conduct'? *Lewd?* What exactly qualifies as—"

"They were having sex in the candle room. Three women from a, what was it, a bachelorette party."

"And?"

"It was bare sex, they were—messy. And extremely offensive to other patrons, there were multiple complaints—"

"Did we get footage?"

"It isn't funny, Ari."

"Yes it is. Did we get footage?"

"Security footage."

"Maybe Media can use it for the new sizzle reel."

Without Jonas slouched on his ergonomic throne, interjecting questions and rude non sequiturs, they finish in less than half an hour: "Unless you have something for me," Lee already up from her chair, as if Ari could have nothing useful to add, so "Just this," thumbing her the link to last night's interview, he has been reading while she checked through her checklist. Now he watches her read, too—with a certain satisfaction, Jake the journo not so snarky after all—until "This," her brittle half-frown. "Media can't post this, it's clearly off-message."

"Yeah? How so."

"That lede—'With his mad scientist's hair and model's smile, Ari Regon is the face of Dark Factory, some would say the heart of it—' The *heart*? Dark Factory belongs to Jonas."

"Oh for fuck's sake—"

"Has Jonas seen this?"

"Why don't you ask him? Interrupt his Darcy-time, I'll wait," turning the knife just a little, if Lee hates him she hates Darcy even more, what Darcy represents, any shift of Jonas's attention or allegiance to the world past the Factory walls. "Or you can just tell Media to approve the link. You know Jonas is the one who set up that interview—"

"I do know that. I told him—" then stops herself, a visible stop, and "There's more to you than Jonas sees, I've told him that, too. One day he'll realize it for himself."

"I'll take that as a compliment—"

"Don't."

"—but Jonas doesn't need you to 'realize' anything, Lee, or me either, Jonas could operate just fine without either one of us," not believing what he says, believing she may be recording this little spat, she has done that before, not to him but she has done it before. "So we're done here."

"I'll never be done here," with her dry coral lipstick smile, inside that armored business façade Lee is a true believer, but what does she get out of the Factory besides a paycheck? Her salary is confidential, Jonas keeps that information to himself . . . Jonas would smile if he saw them now, like spiders circling in a jar, Jonas the hardcore behaviorist: *Humans are just a walking set of triggers, everybody's got them, I don't care who it is, the president of Europe or some tourist from Long Island. And once you know where those triggers are, you can pull them and get results, every time. All the rest is just lighting and liquor* . . . What are Jonas's triggers, Darcy and money? the never-ending thrill of pulling other people's triggers? and what are Lee's? What are his own? as "Dark Factory," Lee says, "is so much bigger than you, Ari—"

"Well jesus, I hope so," his smile the opposite of hers, toothy and dazzling—*model's smile* is nice but *mad scientist's hair*, ugh, he obviously needs a haircut, he sends a quick message to his stylist, ***got time 4 me 2day?***—looking up again, he sees Lee has left the lounge.

The salon is halfway across town, on a rapidly gentrifying avenue lined by heat-browned lindens and a few maples slowly going gold, next door to a still-open fetish jeweler—STEEL & SKIN, he had bought earrings there once, black chrome hoops he never wears—and above a grungy coffee bar called Cuba: briefly tempted on the stairs by the whiff of café cubano, but he is already late, so "Thanks for squeezing me in, Beatriz," he says to the stylist, a tall beauty with cinnamon locs who briskly swirls and rinses his mop of hair as "Squeeze, you know it," Beatriz says, "we can barely turn around in here. Good thing they're expanding," massaging some unguent into his scalp, its fragrance of clean mint and rosemary, his eyes close briefly with bliss—

—as on the floor below, Max stands in the doorway of a crowded storage room that reeks of old coffee and ammonia, where the manager shares the bad news that the café space has been sold: "The salon upstairs is putting in some kind of spa, and—Wait, wait," as the baristas erupt in protest, Max too, he cannot, cannot afford to lose this job. "Our lease runs to the end of November, but there's a bonus for getting out early. So if you want to work late tonight—"

"I'll stay," he says at once, rubbing grimly at his forearm, his black Mayan cat tattoo, and "At least," snipes one of the other baristas, "*you* have another job, Max, you have Bitter Lake," and he does not laugh, he can do that, can shut his mouth and let that cat howl for him.

Leaving at last—late, shoulders aching, needing a wash, needing to be alone with his thoughts—he almost collides with Mila, waiting on the sidewalk with a takeout bag from Nudel's: "Dirty spaghetti, I thought maybe you are hungry after such a long day. We can have a picnic—"

"A picnic? Here?" then realizing Mila means all the way out at Bitter Lake, oh god—but finally he nods, and they take the train then the bus then walk the rest of the way, in the rustle of the trees, the stream's voice louder, everything here is different at night. Teresa always leaves a light on in the garage, the ghost light she calls it from her theater days, it shines a lonely yellow—

—and inside, the pasta puttanesca is congealing, there is only one usable fork, but "This is so nice," Mila handing him a Vino-2-Go, too-sweet red wine, popping open one for herself. "We should add this into Bitter Lake."

He sets the can aside. "We can't have people here at night."

"In the daytime, I meant."

"Food costs money, Mila," but of course she knows that, her money bought this food, the money she earns at TanzStudio teaching giggly older couples to samba and slide, a kind of denial of her formidable gifts as a dancer but *People like to dance*, she always says, which though true is not the point . . . He first saw Mila in a video bar some Kunstfarmer had told him was amazing, it was not, but she was: astonishing sylph in a thigh-length white t-shirt, when she saw him watching her she smiled, until finally he smiled back, tried to engage her, keep her attention, buy her a drink, broke as always but somehow she had guessed that, had led him up the street to a two-for-one dive, but gracefully, so gracefully he had barely noticed, Mila does everything that way, with grace.

It was Teresa who suggested that Mila might come and dance at Bitter Lake: *That Mila is magic. And she's a teacher, she knows how to work with people, get them to play along—*

"Play along"? Bitter Lake's not a game.

I know, but—

It's not a game.

Though Mila is magic, he feels it himself, though he cannot find the words to tell her so. See her now, setting aside the empty food containers to bundle an old afghan into a pillow, and unfold a long crackle of blue tarp, speckled with dry mildew but clean enough for them to stretch out together, to kiss and cradle and cry out, Mila bare and rocking above him, damp-skinned as a river maiden, unbound hair to curtain her closed-eyed breathless smile, then curling close—"Rest, Max, for a little"—as he lay with her tight in his arms, a sudden ache in his throat, held by the quietude, solitude of Bitter Lake, as if it truly is the world, his world, his answer, there has to be an answer somewhere to all the dark factories.

Though Bitter Lake was almost nowhere, Teresa not the first landholder he approached but the only one who had returned any of his messages, who smiled when he described his vision, there at Apostles', he had paid for the lagers that time, borrowing to do it, tense and wary of fresh defeat: *Imagine if the Garden of Eden was real, a real place, right now. And instead of being the first humans, we're the last. So the site needs to have trees—apple trees would be ideal—and be isolated from traffic*, to bring Teresa's immediate nod: *I have a little property off the Bergen bus line, it has trees.*

And there's a storage garage, and a stream! eagerly. *Could you use a stream?* with its urgent, rising splash—

—and waking to Mila splashing in the tiny lav, drying off with a twist of brown towel, then "I have to go," she says, buttoning her skirt. "I'm on schedule to open, and I need to sleep first. Did you have enough sleep? You look so tired."

"I need to tell you something," rubbing his face with both hands as she waits, his gainfully employed girlfriend who shares a clean and modest flat with her friend also gainfully employed, Mila will be nothing but kind when he tells her the café is closing and his job is gone, how can he tell her that? so instead "We're going to have a bunch of students here Thursday afternoon. If you can come—"

"Max, that's wonderful! I have contact mambo on Thursdays, and private classes at four, but I'll ask if Katya—"

"We can talk about it later," dressing, rinsing the crusty fork, checking his proudly primitive phone. "The early bus is coming—"

"The moth's bane," Mila pointing to the crumpled sack, "you didn't plant it?"

"—we need to go."

On the path out, he almost stumbles, she catches at his elbow: "Careful, a big root there," and "I see it," he says, snaps, she lets her hand fall, she cannot see him bite his lip. Then the looming green light of the bus, the brakes' short wheeze, she waits for him to board behind her but "My bag's in the shed," he says. "Go on, you'll be late," as the doors flap closed, she seats herself by a window, mouthing something—is it "you," see you? love you?—then she is gone, and he is walking purposefully up the access road, in case she looks back—

—but his bag is not in the shed, his bag is still in the storage room at Café Cuba, he needs to be back in three hours for another ten hour shift; but for now all he does, all he can do, is walk the paths of Bitter Lake, avoiding the roots, avoiding all thoughts of the future, head down and alone as the sun rises, pale lemon and indifferent through the scattered rowan trees.

03

The last dark before true dawn, Ari reaches for the water glass beside the bed, a headache warm behind his eyes, a body warm beside him, too warm, the linen sheets are wound around them both, and stifling. Naked to the kitchen island, pumping water from the filtration unit, ice cold with the faint tang of minerals, he drinks the glass down, fills it up again.

The man in the bed is gorgeous, and a gorgeous dancer: last night, the first floor DJ working "Hurry Up," *hurry up hurry up, get it get it now!* that man had stepped deliberately into his path, cheeky little beard and shiny with sweat, *Wow, you're Ari Regon, you're famous! Want to dance?* And though he usually avoids pickups straight from the floor—it seems unprofessional, hooking up with random guests—this one felt inevitable, why? It was only once they were back at his place, when the fucking was over, that the answer struck him: Carlos, this man's name, his muscled dancer's legs, he is a sideways mirror of Karl.

Karl had announced the night they met that that he was born to be a dancer, Karl appearing out of nowhere like some fugitive god of the night, at the Blue Balloon where Ari was working—fresh from failing out of first year uni, disappointing his father, disappointing himself by even going to uni, he had slept through most of it, rebellious, hungover and bored—working his self-created job selling lager and vodka shots by having the most fun, the best time, keeping the clientele lingering and buying more drinks, so they could have the best time too. And he did have a good time there, he made friends, he met men, he was chased, he was a prize.

But Karl was different, Karl was distant, that slow green blink like a cat's, a breathtaking ass; Karl's rare smile lit that dim little bar and expanded his own heart in a way that was first alarming, like falling off a cliff he had not known existed, then exhilarating, crazy-making, as if Karl somehow owned him by simply showing up at the Blue Balloon, Ari calling it the Blue Balls Saloon to make Karl smile; he did a lot of things, anything, to make Karl smile.

Yet Karl had continued distant, some part of him resolutely untouched, no matter what Ari did to make him smile, make him come, make his life into the life he claimed to want. Karl had a part-time gig as a leisure therapist, and Ari's own puzzlement, *What's a leisure therapist do?* roused Karl's coldest shrug—*Ari, you shouldn't care what I do unless I do it to you*—but he did care, he introduced Karl to dancers he met, to producers who hired dancers, scouting clubs and shows and performances, curating all the best ones, the most enticing, the ones that might be good enough for Karl.

Until *Time to wish me luck*, Karl said, taking one of Ari's cigarettes on the curb outside the bar; it had just rained, a cold December downpour, the slick streets were nearly deserted. *I'm heading to Basel tomorrow.*

Tomorrow? What for?

For good, blowing smoke. *I just got a great position at a wellness resort,* some members' only Xanadu where he would make three times what he was making now, would meet clients from all over, wealthy men, but when Ari had asked *What about dancing?* Karl took a long flaring drag and *Don't you mean "What about us"?*

And his pulse had started pounding, in his chest, his temples, a feeling worse than pain, closer to panic: *I mean, you want to dance, don't you? You always say—*

Here's some wisdom, as Karl ground out the cigarette and took up his bag, cheap leather and brass fasteners, they shone like fool's gold in the bar sign's reflected light. *People always do what they want to do. Always. Like you'll always be a hustler, you don't really believe in that place, you just like to dance. Now give us a kiss,* with a smile that at the time seemed grotesque, that in memory seems even worse; they could have been happy together, Karl could have danced at Dark Factory every single night . . . Now he rubs his aching head, lights a blunt, cranks open one of the windows to sit angled on the concrete sill until "Hey," from the sheets, a shadowy smile, "I'm up too," but "You need to go," he says. "I have to work."

"Right now?"

"Sorry," naked and aloof, staring into the street that is already waking with the calls of unseen birds, two arrow-swift bike commuters, the corner café's lights springing on as Carlos dresses, leaves, closes the door on a last word, what did he say? see you? fuck you? as Ari heads back to bed, pillow clamped around his head, the expensive programmable pillow that is supposed to help him sleep. When Karl decamped to Basel, he had left behind not only a blank numb hurt but a ferocious insomnia, as if taking all dreams along with him; it took months of work and drinking and serious anonymous fucking for Ari to exhaust himself back to baseline, or whatever baseline had become.

And somewhere in that timeless time, he replaced the cigarettes with blunts, found a different flat on a busier, noisier, more interesting street, found himself one night stepping into the Skidmore Revue: third rate DJs and dancers, vodka cannons, 3D projections—the owner, Jan, so proud of those shitty projections, insisting that their unreliability was part of their charm, *You're not sure if they're there or not, they're like a fantasy—*

They're like a game from five years ago. You should upgrade, it wouldn't have to cost that much.

And because Jan was so demonstrably inept, he demonstrated, he found a distributor willing to let go of obsolete projectors, and a slouchy freelance tech to program them for cheap, immediately improving the Skidmore Revue's overall ambience and its ability to attract paying patrons. And because Ari had so many good ideas and so much time on his hands, because he was sick of the Blue Balloon and its landmine memories of Karl, he allowed Jan to hire him—though Einar the owner was left bereft, shocked unhappily into speech: *You made this place better than it's ever been, Ari, how can you just walk away? Is it the money? Because I could try to match*—But it was never the money, though more money made life easier, kept him in blunts and Benito shirts, kept him from ever having to call his father; what truly lured him was the growing sense of what a club could be, or become, what a night's experience could do for the people who came there, not that he had those words for it, not yet.

So he took the jump, he traded up, vodka shots for vodka cannons, a roomful of amiable regulars for a much bigger room full of people expecting actual entertainment with their booze, *How can you call it a revue, Jan, if you don't have any real acts?* He culled out the dancers and DJs to hire better ones, ones he had met while trying to woo Karl, he created a creative team—that projections tech, a rebel choreographer fresh out of uni, a frustrated playwright turned passable sketch writer, a dour workaholic stylist—and made Jan give them a working budget, *They'll make it back for you in three months, two!*—he used everything he had learned to make that club the center of the universe for as long as a night could last. And as he did those things, he felt his own talents stir, the surges and peaks of intuition, the guesses that turned out to be genius, sometimes he surprised himself with what he brought to life in that room.

And that room, that work, became his own truest center: back alone again and again in the mornings to his bed, he fucked and fucked but never dated, never cared for any of the men he met at Skidmore, or in the G line clubs, or at the Holy Roman Empire, that variable posse of dancers and artists and coconspirators. More

than a few wanted much more from him—the bondage costumer who decked him in combat boots and scratchy black tulle, the lovesick suburban twins drizzling chocolate down his bare back, the criminal lawyer and his glorious balcony blowjobs, the pining woman from London, what was her name? Elfreda, Dodi's friend, who swore they were lovers in a previous life—but his answer was always a smile and a shrug, *See you later,* content to be wanted, wanting nothing more from them than what he took.

And then he met Jonas, or Jonas met him: alert on the Skidmore floor, backstage like a heat-seeking missile, Jonas with a business haircut then, but the same hard dominating handshake: *I'm Jonas Siegler. And you're Ari Regon, I've been watching you.*

What for?

This, waving an arm, *what you've got going—It's good, that laser dance stuff, people really like it. But this place?* with the shrug that he would learn later, it seemed to heighten every flaw in that flawed room. *You don't belong here. Come work for me, we'll make something big happen.*

He had felt himself stand up straighter, felt as if something was coming, like ocean rollers headed for the shore. *Big like how?*

As big as it gets. You in?

And *What are you doing here?* Jan in his baggy blazer, alarmed and bristling to break it up, whatever it was. *Why are you backstage, who the fuck are you?*

Who the fuck am I? Jonas had not even bothered to lie. *Your competition.*

What, some pirate? And you think you can just stroll in here and poach my producer? Ari, tell him you already have a job, while Jonas stood arms crossed and waiting, still smiling, as if all this was just a formality, as if he and Ari already knew what would happen next—

—as his phone fully wakes him, tinging and tinging, highest priority tone: Jonas, but not at the Factory, Jonas in the midst of some furious personal emergency, Jonas wants him to "Come by the loft—"

"What?" rolling away from the insistent window light, the sheets smell like stale sperm, what time is it? "When?"

"Now, right now. And bring food, tacos, something, I haven't eaten since yesterday—"

—so he arrives with a takeaway bag of Blue Moon breakfast churros that Jonas snatches at once, pointing backhand toward the granite counter, the steel appliances and pyramid of black mugs like an interrupted product shoot—"There's coffee over there, somewhere"—while simultaneously speed searching, on a screen the size of the wall, a Factory feed that runs continuously—

—and "Look," gripping his arm, hand grainy with sugar. "That little fuck monkey with the purple hair, Ari, *look!*" at some goateed grapehead grinding with, ah, Darcy, who seems to be having a better time than she usually does, though this could be a performance for the cameras that Darcy surely knows are there. "You ever see that guy on the floor before?"

"I don't know. I know he's not a power user—"

"I know that too, I had Lee check," of course he would send Lee after all available data, including if possible how long the grapehead's cock might be; but the real issue here is Darcy's motive, what does she want from Jonas that this performance might give her? thinking as Jonas taught him, always find the trigger . . . This room was his real uni, this showy loft with its intentionally-pitted concrete floors and new tapestries made to look ruined, blue velvet sofa as long as a limo, this screen an endless scroll of tech artists' links and performers' loops and DJ blasts; and Jonas always schooling him, piling on study after study, reality maps and pivot tables, ESM and duration bias, Lortz arrowing, predictive coding—*The brain's just a big processor, it takes whatever comes in and stacks it up against past experience to drive behavior. The second time you smell saber-tooth tiger piss, you run, that's predictive coding*—and the behaviorists, Fogg, Bandura, Paisley, Daley and Latané, Loftus who showed how easy it was to implant false memories, Jonas shaking his head in satisfaction, *They do ninety percent of the work themselves!*

And the proof of that theory sits here chewing churros and wired on jealousy, who knows what cheating scenarios Jonas has already convinced himself must be true? so "Why don't you take the night off," Ari says, "and take Darcy out somewhere? Let her pick the place. Maybe she's pissed at the Factory."

"She said that? No?" as Ari shakes his head. "So you're an instant relationship expert, is that it? And anyway you're gay, what do you know about women—"

—as Ari shrugs and says nothing, only waits, until "All right, expert," Jonas says. "You're in charge tonight, message me if—No, fuck it. Don't message me unless the place burns down. Tonight is for Darcy," clicking the feed from recorded to live, a silent tango of floor buffers and prop stagers, is that Lee and her glowing clipboard passing by like a ghost? while sidebar scrolling restaurants, which means Ari is dismissed. But as he heads for the door, "That *ForwardFast* interview," Jonas says, without turning, "it got a ton of hits. Nice work."

And Ari smiles, at Jonas but for himself: because whatever he had said to the journo or to Lee, the truth is that the Factory needs him, why else had Jonas searched him out, when everything was already in place? the concept, the site, the potential funders—a parade of suits, of handshakes and smiles, that parade ending with two shady VC bros, bearded Goran and Marko, Jonas had introduced him as *Ari, my secret weapon,* then shooed him away—Ari who understood what the guests would want because some part of him is a guest still, dreaming that Dark Factory will give him everything he wants without having to name it, because he can put no name to it, and neither can they.

Now, in the gold elevator, the operator asks, "Lobby?" in a tone so flat that Ari almost laughs, not in mockery but disbelief, what kind of person takes a job in a cage? and keeps it? so "Here," he says, when the scrollwork gates reopen, offering one of his blunts. "For your break."

"I don't have breaks," the operator says. "Have a nice day."

Bonus Content: Jonas Siegler

The Factory is always more than what you see

Everybody has to have a fantasy

Phenomenal consciousness vs access consciousness

Gibson & Walk visual cliff

Elsa Beech's sanity equation

Available immersive landscape variety of RL > Y despite RL physical parameters?

Dopamine affects vision, higher eyeblink rates indicate higher dopamine levels. Dopamine produces heightened euphoria and improved concentration and memory

The white LEDs made every day an endless day, Jonas there below those constant lights, harvesting more confidential files from his supervisor's workstation: DR. LISA on the desk nameplate, an Infinite filtration bottle and a stuffed white rat in a labcoat, her password was RATDOC1, it was almost too easy.

Dr. Lisa sometimes stayed late, but never as late as he did; if he stayed late enough he saw the maintenance crew roll through, two women and one man, blue and brown uniforms, DNA FACILITY SERVICE, had the lab hired them for that name alone? The maintenance people sometimes nodded to him—*Working hard?*—and *Got to,* he always said. *It's how the job gets done.*

The job, his job: thirty years old and drilling data since college, a BS in applied behavior analysis that led to the internship that became this job, *students will acquire direct research experience and review relevant scientific literature,* though he was already old for an internship, had spent his twenties hanging out at clubs, drinking too much to keep from going back to his place, because it was no place, a beige one bedroom with a kitchenette like every other unit in that anonymous building. And *It's a secure profession,* his student advisor had advised him, *you can have a successful career if you go on for an MS.*

continued on page 024

continued from page 023

But after a year in this lab, under these lights, he had developed his own idea of what a successful career should be.

So he went back into the clubs, but this time for sober research: what entertainment modules were they using, how did they deploy DJs, how did they use video, or Y, or both? site after site, night after night, in the real world and online. But no one anywhere seemed to be doing what he was studying to do: cross the lab with the dancefloor, use the rules of behavior to make a club—his club—into a one-of-a-kind destination, where patrons would always get what they wanted, because he would know what they wanted, and when their wants changed he would know that too, not because of someone else's market research or any wonky onsite click-and-stick, but through the changeless chemical hungers of the body and its brain.

And the more he saw, the more he wanted to include, his plans grew more complex: not just a dancefloor but multiple floors, and professional performers, and bartenders with rock star aspirations. And Y was nonpareil at creating a personalized environment, and all the best clubs had it, so there would have to be Y too, and techs to run it.

But the tab for all this was far steeper than he could hope to swing even with multiple business loans and buy-in from friends and friends of friends, he had to have serious investors. So he did that research too, not banks or institutions but individuals, some maybe not the most ethical, the shady side of legal, a few of them far into that shade, but the money was definitely there. He hustled and pressed for introductions, set up the meets, made his pitch—an objectively excellent pitch, he had skimmed the cream from Dr. Lisa's work, bolstered it with convincing industry metrics, tailored it to flatter and excite—but somehow it did not excite any of those money men enough to involve them, something vital was still missing. What?

The cleaning crew arrived on his floor, busy vacuum drone in the white lights, so he logged out of Dr. Lisa's desk, and headed out for an exploratory drink at a new place people were posting about, or an old place made new, the Skidmore Revue. It turned out to be more scrappy than he had expected, the building badly needed a mechanicals upgrade and the tech was half-functional, but there was energy on the dancefloor, crammed with excited people chanting *Laser dance, laser dance!* And at the very edge of the floor, toasting them with a neon pink cocktail and a nuclear-grade smile, was a young man in a tight pink t-shirt who seemed to know everyone, and everyone knew him, they all wanted him to come and dance, *Laser dance, laser dance, Ari Ari Ari!*

And when that dance was over and the cheap projections flashed back on, he made his way to the bar to ask the bartender, *Who's the guy in the pink?*

That's Ari.

I got that part, as the young man crossed the floor, swift and still smiling, set his emptied glass in a bus tub, had his cheek kissed by a sweaty patron, disappeared backstage. *He's, what? the owner here? Manager?*

He's in charge of the fantasy.

That's a hell of a job description.

The bartender gave him a sideways look. *Everybody has to have a fantasy.*

That's right. You're right—

I didn't make that up, it's from Warhol.

The art guy?

Andy Warhol, the bartender's nod. *He made parties like they were art, and people loved it, they called it the Factory. Ari's the one who told me about him.*

Yeah? How long has Ari been working here?

Since before me. You want another drink, sir?

"Sir," god, did he look that old? but not too old to make a fantasy come true, make it his reality, get him out of that fucking dead-end lab so *Double it,* he said, and tapped in the notes ARI SKIDMORE LASER DANCE, as the bartender bent toward the speed rail, and the beat picked up again, the dancefloor lights changing from neon green to flashing white, before they flashed out entirely and the whole club groaned.

04

The rain rides in lines down the garage windows, gray on gray, Max works on the palm-sized trail cam as Teresa glances at the door—"Last week it still felt like summer. I can't blame that teacher for canceling. I told her we're open until November," glancing at the door again—

—and a knock, a man in an expensive-looking black waxed raincoat: "Good afternoon, thanks for taking the time," to do what, book a day? is this another teacher? Not in that raincoat.

As Teresa pulls on a poncho, Max wraps the trail cam's cracked casing in strips of electrical tape, will it stick in this damp? it will not, he tries again. Then Teresa is back, offering him a rain-spotted business card and "I didn't," she says, "give him an answer, yet."

"Answer to what?" The card is thick paper stock, blue embossed with white lettering, HECHMAN PROPERTIES. "You mean this guy wants to buy—"

"He made a preliminary offer, yes. Because—Max, listen. Next spring the bus line's route will be changing, it's expanding. So this property will be—"

"Be what, valuable?" It comes out as scorn but it is truly shock, that Teresa would even talk to a developer without telling him, asking him. "I thought you already valued Bitter Lake."

"I do, you know I do! And I want to make it work—"

"By selling out to a, a land rapist?"

"—Max, listen! If we were to find another site, closer to the city, he has properties we could tour—"

Properties? buildings like Dark Factory? nothing like this room, the piled props, the tarp, this world he made with his vision and his sweat, not his after all because "It's not plug and play, Teresa, it's a world. A whole world."

"Max, please, Bitter Lake could really work—"

"I can't work like that."

"Max," Teresa wiping her eyes, is it the rain, is she crying—

—and the muddy access road feels very long, even longer the rainy wait for the bus, unbearably slow traffic through the clogged late afternoon streets, someone's baby on that bus wailing the whole way like a newly damned soul. And TanzStudio when he arrives is bustling, eager after-work students warming up past the floor-to-ceiling windows, he is jostled through the doors by two men in suits who could have been colleagues of the real estate developer, maybe they are. At the front desk he asks for Mila, but the receptionist shrugs: "Mila's gone," gone where?

But just outside he spots a tulip umbrella, like a fresh blossom sprung from the rain, Mila surprised beneath it: "Max, you're here? Good, come have a drink with—Something is wrong?" but "Nothing," he says, leaning in for a kiss, tasting hibiscus lipstick, taking her hand, his other hand to his pocket to find like goblins' treasure the cracked camera, he must have kept it when he left, another thing that does not belong to him. He keeps pace with her long-legged stride past 25 HOUR FASHION and HALLO SCHÖNE and some new pop-up selling, what, sunglasses, its storefront windows two enormous unsynced blinking eyes, half-listening as she goes on about her day and her students, this drinks date to celebrate Katya's good fortune, Katya's new gig—

—but "Here?" as they turn the corner onto Neuberg Street, "Katya works *here*?" halting in the shelter of a metal awning, the performers' entrance, while Mila's tone turns corrective, a teacher's tone: "People need jobs, Max. Artists need jobs! And Katya is a wonderful dancer, she deserves a big audience," while he stares up at the new and even more elaborate signage, the dark bully flash of Dark Factory, black-on-black and undeniably, unendurably cool—

—as that performers' door opens, Katya throwing her arms around Mila, and "Hey," a man's voice behind her, a looming, growing smile, Ari Regon's smile. "Hey Max! You finally made it to the party."

###

Fresh drink in hand, Ari enters the box as the techs settle in beneath their headphones, speaking their coded poetry, like tagging is poetry, like poetry is poetry, understood only by those who already understand. A few techs have offered to school him on Y and its workings, just last week Clara had tried again, Clara the lead tech with her coal black flattop and tattoo, her dry Kiwi twang: *Come on, Ari, don't you want to know how all this stuff really works? It's only our species' finest moment.*

You think?

No lie. We're the eater species, but Y is endless, no way to use it up. In a way it's our natural habitat! You should hear Davide on the topic—

Davide, he's your renegade, right? Where's he working?

Nowhere. He's a bit in the bunker just now . . . What if I made something just for you?

How about just for yourself?

From here he can survey the floor—the runners and barbacks' silent movie horseplay, the first floor DJ's early visit to the first floor bar, Annelise's bar—and click through the feeds, DJ stations, graffiti room, candle room, second floor performers' gate, third floor gate, performers' main entrance. He scans more slowly through playback, looking for intel on Darcy's boy toy, but finds instead a surprise: a man with a cheeky little beard just outside the performers' entrance, huddling with, is it Lee? it is. Less than twenty onscreen seconds but more than enough time to make a plan together; he watches that exchange again, shakes his head, bookmarks the timestamp for later use.

And a second sip of the new drink is more than enough, a too-sweet slurry of gin and brandy and some creamy third liqueur, fat Luxardo cherry sodden on the bottom, the mixologists want to call it the Red Eye . . . He had offered one to Max, *This round's on me,* Max hunkered silent beside the bar, furtively scanning the landscape, was Max comparing and contrasting that polished bar and the gleaming curve of the ramps, the three-story ceiling of projectors and Q-cams and pin spots and scent drops, to his own cheap handmade environments? Max with the beginnings of permanent eye bags, musky t-shirt and unintentional beard, as if he might be sleeping rough in his outdoor show or whatever it is. Compare and contrast *that* with his realer-than-thou trailer interview, and though Jonas had shrugged it all off, *Not sure what you see in him, the guy's a walking trigger,* Ari had been justifiably pissed: not just because that interview had been his idea, but because Max, though a humorless dick, clearly has vision: that doomed and wild garage show, with its flamethrower olive oil tins and howling sirens, the coughing, puking, stumbling patrons, Max always points, orients, to the real thing.

So while the fresh hire, Katya, and Max's pretty girlfriend traded dancers' gossip over lilac spritzers, he asked Max how things were going, working hard? but *Bitter Lake is closed,* Max declared—the girlfriend clearly startled by this news—so *All right*, the idea alive as he spoke it, he had to hide his smile, he knew immediately it was genius. *Why don't you come here? Door's still open.*

What?

Why not? I know you hate the Factory, but—

I don't "hate" Dark Factory, in the sourest tone imaginable, as the girlfriend continued to stare. *My objections are totally on philosophical grounds. Any place that sells itself as a real experience—*

But you've never even been on the floor. Come on, you're a professional, you can't call a show without seeing it.

And Max's look then was so peculiar, half-challenge and half-despair—"*Come here" and do what?*—all he could do was meet it with a look of his own, no challenge, pure invitation, he knew he had won when Max finally looked away. And *Quality control*, he had said, as if there had been no pause at all. *You can show me what you see, everything you see, everything you think is wrong with the Factory—*

I could do that now.

—and get paid for it as a consulting subcontractor, a doubly, no, triply, useful idea: Max's critique will be as honest as a punch in the face, the Factory can only benefit from that. And Lee wants to play games, have her own plants? so will he, and tweak Max back, a little, for that supremely shitty interview. *And you can always walk away whenever you want*—which Max did, towing the girlfriend, and he had let him go, they both knew Max would be back. And he had commenced his own nightly reconnaissance stroll, bottom to top to end at the box, to scroll and sip and wait for Jonas—

—who enters finishing a call, Lee behind him, Lee with a fresh haircut like the sleekest guard in the prison yard, and "We've got a new guy in Quality," Ari announces. "I hired him today."

"Without any vetting?" Lee up in arms at once. "Or an HR interview? How do you imagine you have that authority—"

"Jonas already interviewed him. It's Max Caspar."

The name clearly means nothing to Lee, but Jonas smiles, half-glancing up from his phone—"You finally landed him, huh? Lee, this is a guy we've been looking at for a while. Stay on him, Ari, let me know what you get—"

—as he stares at Lee, not a spider this time but whatever eats spiders, and "I'll hire whoever I want," he says, so quietly that only she can hear. "And I can manage my social life for myself, thanks—Jonas," raising his voice, still staring at her, at the liar's blush rising at her cheeks and chin, he lets the threat hang until "Jonas, this Red Eye's fucking awful. I'll go tell the guys in Mix."

###

Sunlight sparks the tins hung in the rowan trees, they shine as if they burn, and Max sweats as he climbs and stoops, gathering the props for disposal: those tins, and the soft disintegrating paper hive, and a stray mask tucked into a tree's hollow mouth, like the classical mask of tragedy; those old masks have names, Sock and Buskin, Teresa once told him that . . . He had believed Teresa was the solution, his solution, to those almost-possible worlds, his degree trajectory; Teresa had understood why academia was a dead end, understood too his hostility toward Dark Factory, the whole endeavor as brazenly artificial as Jonas Siegler's attempt to recruit him, right after Perfect Circle.

Perfect Circle had been worse than a disaster: not a tragedy, no one was hurt, but the rented garage burned to its foundations in that hungry uncontrolled fire, the city classed it as a second-degree misdemeanor, he had had to borrow from his parents to pay off the punitive fines. So when he was invited out of the blue to consult about an ambitious new performance project, he was more than normally broke, he was warily, irresistibly curious, he went: to a warehouse already deep in transformation, stacked crates and light bars and a tricked-out office trailer where Jonas Siegler was waiting, surrounded by mounds of logo t-shirts, boxes of fobs and shiny badges, DARK FACTORY COMING SOON, they must have spent a fortune just on swag, they must have had a fortune to spend. Jonas Siegler was wearing a stagey hardhat and one of those shirts, and sucking at an energy drink: *Need a jolt? There's the cooler.*

No thanks, civil if not friendly, *"Dark Factory," that name's supposed to be ironic? That's what they call a robot workplace.*

Jonas Siegler had ignored that. *You were pointed out to me, Max, you must be good at this.*

Good at what? I'm a reality artist.

Dark Factory's all about engagement. The minute, the nanosecond, you buy your pass, whether you're at the door or streaming, you touch the Factory and it touches you back, it reacts to your expectations—

—but he had not bothered to hide his disdain, born of a strange disappointment he had not expected to feel, what had he thought would happen here? what else could have happened? Finally he had interrupted Jonas's promo reel, like throwing a spike strip under a speeding truck: *This place was supposed to be something totally new, but what you're saying, all you're saying, all of that's already been done. A lot.*

That's right, anybody can put together a decent nightlife experience, the tech's already there. But a masterpiece? as the trailer door swung open, no knock or pardon me from Ari Regon rolling in in some eyewreck get-up, mirrored sunglasses and a fat blue cigarette, and *Max,* Jonas Siegler had said, *you know Ari, Ari's my number one guy on the floor*: and Ari Regon had smiled, the same smile he flashes in every post and interview, as if he might be the most self-satisfied person ever to exist on the planet.

And himself so visibly aghast, *You're the lead designer?* that Ari's smile dimmed, then reignited as Jonas explained that Max would be hired not for Dark Factory's making but only its staffing, as if he would subordinate his philosophy to that empty vision? to Ari fucking Regon? recalling the last time he had seen that toothy smile, at Perfect Circle on the night of the fire: people coughing and fleeing, people throwing up, his own stumbling panic, and Ari Regon standing just outside the fume zone, watching and smiling, so *No way,* he had said, no longer civil. *It's not for me.*

Jonas Siegler had not seemed displeased, or even very much surprised: *No? Thought you were a reality artist* and *I am,* he had shot back, *it's what I do, what I went to school for—*

Then what's your issue?

The issue is, none of this is real.

Jonas Siegler's expression had not changed. *Dark Factory will be real to everybody who experiences it.*

And really successful, Ari's shrug, that blithe shrug was the last straw, so *Toilet paper is successful, if you wipe shit for a living*—though he should not have said that, shouted it, or slammed the door either, as he fled that trailer and that site, the huge banner flapping after him in the wind like dragon's wings—

—and at the garage now he sees a car, quick and as black, who the fuck is that? Teresa's developer? his hurried jog down the path, prop sack in hand, just as the passenger emerges: Ari Regon, in a perfectly faded red t-shirt and red wraparound shades, hot spot shades, Y-compatible, and "I've been trying," Ari calls, "to get hold of you, don't you even have a MePage? Mila said to come out here—"

"Mila said? You talked to—"

"Why aren't there any signs? Where's the lake?" which makes Max laugh, not much of a laugh but his first for days and "No imagination," Max says, "no surprise there. You want the tour? Come on," turning again for the paths as Ari catches up, that quick magpie gaze, he never stops talking—

"So the set-up's like, what, Hansel and Gretel? They follow this path and they get breadcrumbs? Dirt crumbs?"

"They don't have to follow any path, they can go wherever they want, or go nowhere, or leave. I don't tell anyone how to experience Bitter Lake."

"Why not?"

"If you have to ask—"

"It's an experience, you must have some parameters, how else do you manage the flow? Or enforce the door, if you don't use geofencing? Or—Fuck!" and "Look out," Max's smile as Ari stumbles, "that's a tree root, there are lots of them out here. And holes, and rocks. It's the real world, it's not engineered for safety."

"Oh," shrugging off the barb, "you grew those coffee tins from coffee beans? But it is fucking pretty—"

—as Max follows his gaze to the rowan trees, their changing leaves as red as Ari's shades, as the berries that the birds will eat, the siskins, Mila told him that . . . Mila said nothing when they left Dark Factory, her umbrella furled to a tight baton, but when he tried to take her other hand she stopped dead, just outside a busy teahouse, and *Why did you tell him that Bitter Lake is closed?* her small deep frown. *When did that happen?*

He had tried to explain, to lead her away from those sidewalk tables of tea drinkers watching them like impromptu street theater, but *"Ask Teresa," what does that mean? Bitter Lake is yours, Max!* though his ownership ends where Teresa's property deed begins, he had tried to explain that too, but Mila had gone off on tangents as twisty as the paths, her schedule at TanzStudio, *I traded off most of my classes next month!* and his own constant condemnation of Dark Factory, yet *Now your mind is open, to work there? Why?* while a part of him wanted to snap back *Artists need jobs* but instead he had said, *To fight an enemy you need to go behind enemy lines.*

Why do you need to fight at all? Why are you always so angry? then with a sad embrace *I can't talk to you,* she had said, which was the worst of all, did she mean then, or ever? or never? But apparently she can talk to Ari, what else did she say to him, what else did he ask her? And why does Ari being here somehow disrupt the entire feel of Bitter Lake? with those showy glasses flecked with iridescence, and the red t-shirt printed in streamlined Cyrillic—"What does that say?"

—that question startling Ari from his absorption, his contemplation of the leaves in the breeze, the way the light strikes them is a magical effect, maybe the Factory should add a nature room? with a pool of bubbling water, no, bubbling champagne, a champagne fountain and a haptic moss carpet, light through the trees but not sunlight, no, moonlight, starlight, they could use reactive spots, they could install it on the roof and call it Dark Park—"What, my shirt? It says 'Emperor.' It's from the Holy Roman Empire, ever hear of that?"

"Not the way you probably mean. So you're an emperor?"

"I used to be."

"Quit or deposed?" which makes Ari laugh, he shakes out a blunt and "Want one? Or are you too pure for this, too?" as Max shrugs and takes the light, takes a hit, coughs in sudden unaccustomed pleasure, hits again and "You smoke these all the time?" he asks, throat tight. "You must be constantly junked."

"I have a tolerance . . . Who's she?" as Teresa heads toward them in purposeful haste, denim jacket tied at her waist so the sleeve ends flop with her momentum, Max feeling somehow cornered between the blunt and Ari, does Teresa recognize Ari? her obvious wince says she does—

—and "I see," Teresa says, "everything's changing, now. Will you excuse us? Max, Mila said—"

"Where is Mila?"

"I just talked to Mila—"

"Will you excuse us, *please*—"

—so Ari shrugs and ambles off smoking, over the hill and into the woods: "woods" is stretching it, this place even more minimalist than that fiery garage, a sparse little no-man's-land, this is what Max prefers to the Factory? exalts over? What a meat snob! And if he were a ticketholder, what would he do here? watch Mila the dancer, how long can that last, a live woman has to stop for breath sometime. So then what? pick up sticks, sit under the trees? he could do that for free in any city park, why come all this way and pay to do it? And the refusal to enforce experience boundaries means that the MR factor here is completely uncontrollable, anything can and probably does fuck up whatever surface tension Max can conjure: sudden rain, or passing trucks and planes, or really any loud ambient disturbance—

—like the scene playing out between Max and the denim jacket woman, he hears the shouts as he winds back toward the garage, hers entreating, Max's final—"Teresa, this is done—" the woman folding in on herself, those hanging extra arms at her waist like a heartless visual joke, doubly empty handed as she retreats, while Max stands static, biting his lower lip. And "My mouth's numb," he says as Ari approaches, "what's in this shit," but it is not an actual question so Ari provides no answer, just waits in that breeze cut with a faraway stink, acrid and industrial, through his red lenses everything looks hot.

Finally "It's her site," Ari says, not an actual question either and "Her site," Max says, "but my piece. All my pieces are site dependent, situational, and, you know, durational. They all end."

"Right, the end of the world. And after that is heaven?"

"You believe in that?"

"You make your own heaven, I believe *that*."

"And yours"—Max shifting from foot to foot because he needs to move, to go, leave Bitter Lake, another world not his, never his—"yours is Dark Factory. 'Make your night,' isn't that your line?"

"Actually it's Jonas's line. But you won't have a lot to do with Jonas, you won't need to talk to anybody there but me."

"Because you're my boss."

"I don't think of it that way," knowing that Max does think of it that way, and what will that mean on the floor? will Max be useful, will this turn out to be a mistake? but still that utter certainty, this is no mistake, this is one of his genius moves so "I'm due back. Want a ride?" watching Max consider the plod to the bus stop, the slow stop-and-go, against the ease and speed of a car that someone else will pay for, Dark Factory will pay for. Finally Max nods, sits silent on the drive as Ari checks his phone—

"Why don't you have a phone, Max?"

"I do have a phone."

"I mean a real one."

"It's real enough."

—until they reach the city's outskirts, no shops or bars or flats here, just a commercial cleaning company, a tired-looking bus yard, a warehouse the last outpost before a nowhere zone, grubby and hazardous and only good for speeding through, but "Stop," Max says, one hand on the door, as if he is about to leap into a tuck and roll. "I'll get out here—"

—and he does, striding off while Ari glances up and down that wasteland avenue—"What the fuck, does he live here or what?"—and "No one lives here," the driver says, his pinkish bug-eye sunglasses a bodega knock-off of Ari's own shades. "Only baggers. Sleep in bags, shit in bags," scornfully accelerating away from that warehouse building, WEIR PAPER on a faded painted sign, crumbled brick and old trash and bright scrambled tags, a clump of weeds waving in the backwash breeze like an audience calling for more.

Bonus Content: Max

Art is a virtue of the practical intellect

— Jacques Maritain

Meat Man! a shout, an echo, *Meat Man, where are you?* and *Down here!* Max's shout back from the truck well, its festering motor oil like tar mixed with quicksand. *I'm down here!*

No one answered, no one heard him, he sighed between his teeth, his breath tasted like that oil. This night had already been a struggle—the chain escape ladder half-retracted, jammed and too far to reach, the truck well's engine hoist rusted out and unusable, the noise DJ still AWOL, a rising tide of rumors that a pack of disgruntled Kunstfarmers were coming out to shut him down—but he had not expected it to go smoothly, what he had expected it to do was work.

Hey! Down here!

The things he made never did go smoothly, were never easy or meant to be, is the world easy? Is creation? His first Kunstfarm effort, untitled and nearly derailed before it even began, was a raggedly coordinated flashlight raid through the uni grounds, light forced into dark places, broken windows in the dorms and the Admin building; campus security had been up in arms but he was able to argue his way out of that. The next one, the mad underground séance that was "Buttercup," with its dead vegetable carcasses and eerie booming trashcan soundscape, had unintentionally disrupted the department's high gloss Y showcase—a happy accident as far as he was concerned, the whole showcase was just a fawning thank you to Kuntsfarm's tech benefactors—but that time it was the students who were pissed at him, most of them had had work on display in that showcase, it was how he got his scornful nickname, and the smell had lingered for weeks. This time, he was off campus, this abandoned illegal warehouse his temporary world, a lightless cavern for "Faustus Dance Party" with its death-cold mocking humor, meant, like its namesake, to raise hell; RAISE

HELL was the actual poster slogan, big red ransom note graphics over a grinning brutalist face.

And this was like everything he made, maximum intensity on minimal funding, scrounging for spaces, for transport, for power tools and polysilk and solar batteries and chem resistant gloves, borrowing what he knew he could never return, burning bridges while he raced across them, sacrificing friendship to art. Sometimes he was so tired he could not open his eyes all the way, last week he fell asleep in the middle of an argument with Jenny, his ostensible girlfriend, Jenny the fiber artist who had jabbed him in the chest with a push broom handle: *Are you actually sleeping? While I'm standing here telling you—You're impossible, Max! You're actually humanly impossible!* Then Jenny had flung down the broom and stormed away, had not come back to the site, apparently they were finished as a couple, and those fiber webs were unfinished too.

Down here! HEY!

He had thought Jenny believed in what he was doing, what he was making and why it needed to be made: it was why he had to go to art school, despite his parents' mystified dismay, *You were going to be a professional gamer, a game designer, now you want to be an artist?* Long before he was Meat Man he was Spacecase, known and teased for his furious focus on *Vee-3,* his last and favorite game, runaway pastronaut in an alien real time cityscape, always lost, always on the lookout for clues. The game itself was finally modded to death, but by then he had stopped playing it, stopped playing games at all once he admitted to himself—an irrevocable admission, like two plus two will always make four—that everything he had invested in *Vee-3,* not just the countless hours but all the thought, the fierce imagination and months of heartfelt strategy, would always be at the mercy of its tech, could always be twisted into something that might exist only because of that tech, and there would be no end to that process, never any end with any game. So he had made an end, had deleted himself from *Vee-3* and enrolled at Kunstfarm to do battle with tech—with games and Y and the slick and malleable, hyperreal specificity, all-pervasive,

continued on page 040

continued from page 039

all-consuming, commercially unstoppable—Kunstfarm where he was a consummate outsider, except to other outliers like Jenny, and Dr. Kaiser, the only professor willing to debate with him: *Max, physical life is the bedrock to our discipline, any discipline, to life itself. We can agree on that at least—*

And a reality artist needs to work in the real world to make real worlds. "Art's action consists in imprinting an idea in some matter"—In matter, *real physical matter—*

You're reading Maritain? I don't think that's actually what he's positing there.

As a professor here, you wouldn't.

And his own unchanging reality was to make more worlds, even if he made them in a vacuum, a quixote tilting at windmills, even if he was always broke and mostly alone, stuck in this pit where his boots squelched in that motor oil, where the ladder hung just out of his reach and *Hey!* he shouted again, as loud as he could into the uncaring silence. *Down here!*

Then a tac light beam found the pit, and two faces, his two onsite assistants, peered down—Jake the video artist and the other one, a freshman with green hair, he could never seem to remember the freshman's name—and *There you are!* Jake called, *what are you doing down there? The DJ's here, she wants to set up—*

I'm stuck! The ladder's jammed—

Hang on, as one of them braced the aluminum armature and the other banged and jockeyed the release, banged again, until *Look out!* and the rungs rattled down like incoming ordnance, he ducked, then climbed—

—and was back on solid ground, striding off in his gummed and sticky boots, Jake and the other trailing after with the tac light, to find the DJ, make the noise, fling open the gates of hell, it was too bad there was no way to have fire involved, next time he should definitely make something with fire.

05

“Here,” the brusque blonde handing Max a sealed bag with a t-shirt and generic tag, hardly registering his presence beyond the necessary tablet click. “You’re in, what, QC? You’ll get your real nametag by end of shift.”

“I’ll take him now,” from the doorway, the blonde’s nod in sudden full attention—“Oh sure, Ari”—as Ari in silver buccaneer’s earring and full Factory black leads Max away from the HR intake room. And “Gulag much?” Max says, because he has to say something, he feels unaccountably unnerved, why? “ID and a facial match, just to get a t-shirt?”

“And thumbsign the NDA, right?”

“I wasn’t planning on disclosing any of your trade secrets, but yeah, I signed,” noting that everyone they pass, the performers, the grunts and support staff, all offer Ari that same quick deference, he cannot keep from asking “Why are you asking me to do this? paying me to do it? A lot of people must want a gig like this.”

“And you don’t. How about a NooJuice?” plucking a can from one of the bar carts, joking then clearly not joking, “I want to see what you see, I told you that already . . . You can change in there, and leave your bag,” nodding to the performers’ lounge and lockers, then leading a highlights tour of the floor, all the floors, the full bars and drink stations, explaining the DJs’ and dancers’ set deployments—“We do it in threes, a hype number before and a transition after”—and usage of the tiara—“Set it however, just make sure to bookmark your settings"—as all around them the feeling escalates of clockwork chaos ticking toward performance; Max knows that feeling but never at this scale, like diving from a pond into the ocean, he swallows the questions he cannot ask, he is supposed to be here to give answers—

—and "After your shift, " Ari says, "come find me in the box," what the fuck is the box? but Ari is already leaving, joined by a pair of floor runners, while a tone like an enormous plastic bell makes the whole building echo, as if something vast has been struck into life. Then the lights change, the patrons start to enter, the night begins: and despite his best or worst intentions, despite that nervousness now bordering on weirdly actual fear, Max launches himself into the midst of that crowd, determined to keep his eyes open, stay on top of whatever will happen here tonight, *you're a professional*—

—but almost immediately finds himself enmeshed, fly on the wall, fly in honey caught and caught off-guard by the constant shift and self-perpetuating level of detail, the sheer strength of the peripherals: the haze of it, the maze of it, the see-through ramp that spirals up in a fog of scents like floating flowers, the sudden mirrored sheen of a wall, so the self seems to walk into itself, the room filled with hundreds and hundreds of wax candles with flickering flames indistinguishable from true fire except they burn nothing, exist as nothing but light that itself does not truly exist, their curling smoke never touching his lungs—

—as he struggles to find his mental footing, or at least map the spatial layout: how big is this building anyway, what floor is he on? the one with those candles, or the one with the roomful of graffiti, has he seen all the specialty rooms? Did he already pass this upside-down bar, or are there two? or more? And is this bewilderment just a symptom of his self-imposed refusal of Y, the tech expanding since his gaming days, even since his Kunstfarm days, such a long time since he played a game, someone else's game, someone else's world; or is it something else? "Presence" is the term of art for all Y interactions, and he has always been high presence, what some people call susceptible, but he never expected to feel so agitated here, so very unhappily good.

As he makes his way through the crowd—these human moving parts all part of that greater whole, most of them loud, some of them laughing, some obviously junked or drunk, some who seem as bewildered as he, wandering up and down the ramp from dancefloor to splashed booze to flashed ass to fake fuck to who knows what—he wonders what menus they have chosen from the tailored sidebar cornucopia, where do they intersect with his reality, do they see him as a blur or an effect or as himself or as nothing at all?

And sometime during the evening—who knows what time, time too is managed here, everything is one long now—he sees Katya, but a Katya he has never seen before: swift and burnished and wearing a headdress and mask that cycles through a stream of stylized faces, human and not, how would Mila look in a costume like that, a costume as beautiful as she is? *She deserves a big audience* . . . If Katya sees or recognizes him, she gives no sign.

Then the first floor DJ blasts a manic fusillade, he feels it in his feet, his chest, like the whole world might be breaking apart: and the three dancefloors go simultaneously, blindingly silver as the crowd cheers, for the light, for the beats, for itself. And the silver dissolves like ice in sunlight, the Y dials down and down and disappears as the house lights rise, rosy and resistless, while a thumping machine, a true factory noise, sounds on all the floors, and the crowd leaves, a noisy moving mass, then pairs and trios, then stragglers on the ramps, then gone.

And Max tugs off his tiara, feeling all his senses disengage at once, feeling how leaden his body actually is, how pummeled and sweaty; meat reality. A helpful runner points his way to the box, a crow's nest control room where through the long windows he can see Ari talking, arguing? with a narrow-faced woman in a pale blue jacket; where was Ari all night, up there? or down on the floor, had Max passed him without knowing, had he been watching, hidden by Y? What does Ari see, when he walks through the Factory?

Now Ari sees him, emerges to lead him not to the performers' entrance but through a different set of doors marked NOT AN EXIT, into chilly air that smells like lager drums and dumpster reek, in the whirr of vent blowers and departing voices echoing down the street. And "So," Ari says, lighting up. "First impressions?"

"It's—not what I expected."

"That's not what I expected to hear. You didn't find anything to hate?"

"Wait," Max shaking his head as if to clear it, "give me a minute," to bring Ari's measuring smile: "I'm hungry. Get your bag, come on—"

—two long blocks east, blocks that feel like escape tunnels after the Factory's nonstop throb and flow, the visible world like, what is it like? a dark glass, a glass darkly? to end at a scruffy all-night diner, CHEAP BREAKFAST filled not with revelers but regulars, the hospitality crew. Max sees a few people he knows from his own shows, none of them seem to recognize him, but everyone here apparently knows Ari—

—and "Don't overthink it," Ari swallowing black coffee as if it were water. "Just say if the Factory's real or not."

Max lifts his water glass; it feels oddly heavy, he sets it down again. "I'll say this, no made environment can be seamless, but you come fucking close."

"'Close' how? Where are the seams?"

"Jesus, you want a full-on critique? I've been there exactly once—"

"You had plenty of opinions before you even saw it. Before it was even open," Ari's gaze relentless, waiting, waiting, and when Max still does not answer "Here," sliding out of the booth, tossing him a black and silver square, a string of numbers mixed with symbols, CASPAR MAX QC. "Sleep on it. I'll see you on the floor tomorrow."

"It's tomorrow now," Max's mutter after Ari's departing back; rubbing his eyes, enormously tired but far too wired to think of sleep. He checks the staggered overnight bus schedules, not staggered enough, he just missed the next one back to the squat and the last one is an hour from now. But Mila's flat is within fair walking distance, so he walks, step by step to regain some equilibrium, count those steps, count blocks, breathe in and out—

—but Mila's flatmate is the one who finally opens to his knocks, wide awake and smelling faintly of wine: "Mila's not home yet, Max."

"Can I wait for her?"

—in Mila's room, old flowered cotton sheets, the scent of chamomile and peppermint SportsRub, a rack of costumes like shed and sparkling skins, a tray of tiny seedlings at the window, and atop the bookcase a duck sculpture made from an old wooden ninepin, its painted, lashy, blue-white stare staring down as he waits, and waits, and finally turns off the light. In that dark, his shirt's Dark Factory logo appears to show different words entirely, what does it say? does he even want to know? and "No use hiding in a duck costume," he says, turning over to hide that glow. "The ball will find you wherever you are."

###

Blinking in the sun, three hours' sleep, but now Ari walks toward the abandoned paper mill: a larger building and a smaller, the walls tagged with glyphs and boasts, BIG BOYZ TOPZ!! and WALID #1, the gaudy acid pink of PINKEYE BABY, the horned grinning face of GOATSBOY IS HERE, a scatter of yellow FUKs. The air is still, he can hear his own footsteps through the crunchy glass and asphalt chunks and prickling weeds gone to seed, pink nettle and rye grass, a lone white butterfly drifting by over clumps of trash, grey and waterlogged blue, the color of the sky between long rains. A faraway dog barks and is answered by a cheery human voice, both dog and human invisible, playing fetch in one of these dead buildings? fetching what? but no other walkers or explorers, *no one lives here,* he sees no one—

—until he does, a woman and a man hunkered between one of the doorless doorways and a hip-high mound of plastic bags; they look wary and ageless, they stare at him until "Hey," he calls. "All right to go in there?"

They say nothing; he does not advance, respecting the etiquette.

Finally "You looking for Meyer?" the man says, his voice unexpectedly mild, an accent hard to place, maybe Swedish. "You looking to buy some shit?"

"No. Just to walk around."

"You a journalist? Tourist?"

"No."

The woman murmurs to the man who shrugs, she nods to Ari—

—and his phone tings, an alien chime in this otherworldly hush: Jonas. He thumbs ***UNAVAILABLE***, and "It's my day off," he says, to the phone and to Jonas, to himself, to the buildings, what is he doing here anyway, why has he come? Is he looking for Max, could Max actually be skint enough to live here? And will Max do any better tonight, was last night's disappointment a kind of backhand compliment to the Factory? *No made environment can be seamless, you come fucking close* . . . Seams, where are the seams.

It takes time to walk around the ground floor—the mezzanine is inaccessible, no way up besides a rusted ladder missing multiple rungs, no thanks—and step by step, by habit and instinct, he evaluates what he sees, everything he sees, everything around him: that ladder, the Everest pile of splintered shipping pallets, an abandoned van with an imploded windshield, metal drums marked with faded hazmat logos, all the walls filled with repeating tags—more GOATSBOY, TROJAN99, UP YERS with long squiggling black arrows—and thick clumps of greenish wire like plastic moss, half-grown saplings working to be trees, the irregular drip of water, the smell of old mold and fresh animal piss and his own smoke . . . What if you infused this place somehow with Y? and brought in a few hundred people and a DJ? what would you get, besides a line at the clinic for tetanus shots? For some reason he remembers Paperhangers Night, a monthly party he started at the Blue Balloon, everyone handed a colored paper hat on entry, he would call *Pink hats! Yellow hats!* and those people would dance, why is he thinking of that now? because this building was once a paper mill?

"Keep it real," he says to the building.

Outside again, the sun is in retreat, and there is shit, with luck not human, ground into the tread of his shoe. Scanning for a Hopper but none are available, so he walks, tramping back through the trash, almost out of the nowhere zone as he sights a structure definitely inhabited, grinding music inside, bicycle skeletons outside, EASTFIELD painted on a piece of plywood over the door, where a car zips to the curb and "I don't pick up here," the driver calls, the same driver with the bodega shades, "but I recognized it was you." Ari nods his thanks, scuffs his shoe before he climbs inside, his phone tings again, Jonas again, ***UNAVAILABLE***—

—as Max sits at the kitchen table watching Mila make a smoothie, bluish protein powder, slow steel spoon, framed by the plants at the window, the stacked yellow plates, the stick-on calendar, *Birds of the Seasons*. And "Why didn't you come back," he asks, "last night?" but she does not answer, silently offers him a glass, he shakes his head. "Mila. Why—"

"I was at Katya's."

"Katya was at Dark Factory."

"She said she saw you. Why did you come here?"

"I wanted—" to think, process, he had not meant to sleep but had slept, his dreams so bloated with mad detail that he woke sweating, overcome by the smell of SportsRub so he had to open the window, knocking sideways another little tray of plants, cursing and setting them as right as he could in the dark, then sleeping again to even worse dreams, nightmares of trying to hide from Dark Factory, or hide in it. "I wanted to talk to you. Why didn't you come back?"

"Max," turning her gaze toward the window. "I have an opportunity. In Rotterdam."

"What opportunity?" but he barely hears what she says next—an invitation to be part of some performers' teaching collective, one of her students knows the head of the cultural bureau—because the way she says it says everything, and "Mila," loud, louder than he means to be, "what's this really about? It's not about dancing—"

"It's a very highly regarded collective! And Frau Ansler recommended me personally—"

"You're going to go dance in Rotterdam, OK. When are you coming back?"

She looks at him, saying nothing, saying nothing until he says, "You're not. Is that it? Is that—"

"Yes."

"Because of me?"

"Not only you. But I spoke to Teresa," and it all unravels from there, his unkind and high-handed treatment of Teresa, his bizarre decision to close down Bitter Lake and take a job at Dark Factory—even though Katya dances there, she had celebrated Katya dancing there!—and work for Ari Regon—

"What did Ari say to you?"

"He asked, where could he find you? And all I could think to say was Bitter Lake. And I thought, how do I know Max, really, if I can't even answer that?"

"You did answer! You do know—"

"Bitter Lake was wonderful, I loved it. I'll never forget—"

"Mila—Mila, I love you, I—"

"Oh Max," with such patience, no grief in it at all or even anger, it is that patience that drives him out of the kitchen, into the bedroom to scrabble for his shoes, where are his fucking shoes, and the Factory nametag that he hangs around his neck like a noose—

—and "Max, wait," Mila in the doorway with one hand out, he stops, he almost reaches for that hand but "Deborah will need a new flatmate. And you need to move from that squat—"

—but what he needs immediately is to go, leave this room, this flat, for the stoop, the street, the bus to another street not far from where Ari's Hopper had left him, none of Ari's business where he lives because where he lives is just a square with a chair and a table and cot, living there because he can live nowhere else, not at Bitter Lake or in a lover's bedroom, former lover, Rotterdam, God damn everything—

—shoving open his unlocked door, nothing there to steal, nothing there but him, on that little bed, hands pressed to his head, the clinging scent of Mila's bedroom overwhelming him like tears.

###

The Factory reeks of citrus, a strange and irritating orange, and "What's that stink?" Ari asks a runner pushing a cart of cocktail add-ons, white coconut straws and blinking drink flags, she shrugs and points vaguely to the walls: "The ductwork got cleaned out today, they said?"

"With what?" clearing his throat, now his mouth tastes like orange too. "Sex clinic spray? Lee," because there she is, dressed in sparkly gray pants and jacket like someone's suburban aunt out on the town. "What's the issue with—"

"Maintenance is running another soda cleansing, they said it would clear before doors tonight," which sounds, smells, improbable, but even more improbable is Lee's tone, almost pleasant, why? Now he sees that the runner's cart is also loaded with jars of cherries, blood red and bobbing like little science experiments, because "We're taking the Red Eye live tonight," Lee says, noting his look. "It tested very well."

"How could it test well? It tastes like fruit puke."

"You're welcome to check the eval with Mix," still pleasant, noncombative, and to seal his suspicions she nearly smiles, it might even be her real smile: "Can I ask what you've learned from your friend Max Caspar?"

"Nothing I want to share, yet. And he's not my 'friend'—"

"Why so pissy? And it's your day off, why are you even here?" Jonas in a plaid Gloriosa jacket as red as the cherries, clapping his shoulder like a fond father. "Listen, the date was great," while Lee disengages, another anomaly, usually she fights to stay in any talk between him and Jonas, what is going on? "I took Darcy to the Onion Room—skyline view, private booth with a fully stocked love cabinet, fucking magical, no pun. We should definitely do something with our roof space, there's no view, but—"

"I have some ideas for the roof." Ari clears his throat, clears it again, the citrus smell seems even worse. "When I was out at Bitter Lake—"

"Is that where you were when I called?" Jonas almost smiling, not overtly fake or unfriendly but something is definitely off, Ari tests it with a shrug—"No, but I was working. I'm always working"—with his own smile, so many smiles at the Factory tonight—

—which makes Max's arrival almost a relief, that stunned and frozen-looking frown, as if recently struck from behind by a two by four, though mostly groomed and correct in his t-shirt and new nametag. But as Max walks up, Jonas walks away, echoing Lee's retreat, why? and "Tonight," Ari clearing his throat again, leading Max to the ramp, "tonight we're going to hang out together, Max. We'll start at the top, and work our way down to—Hey," nodding back to the passing dancers who nod and smile at him, one of them is Katya, Katya who looks at Max just a little too long, so "Your girlfriend," Ari says, why? another test, is it a reflex, a behavior instilled by Jonas? will he start drinking NooJuice next? "You can get her a pass, you know, staff gets a free one every month."

Max stares straight down through the ramp's transparency, as if he marches into the void and is glad to go. "Not needed."

"She's a dancer, right? She'd enjoy it—"

"She's moving," which explains both Max's heightened gloom and Katya's speculative stare, so "Sorry," Ari says. "Been there."

"Girlfriend left you?" harsh. "I doubt that."

"Boyfriend left me," startled to hear himself say it, he never talks about Karl, ever, to anyone: he can feel Max look at him, then after a climbing moment, "Mila's going to Rotterdam."

"Fuck Rotterdam, then. Mine went to Basel."

"Fuck Basel then."

As they reach the top of the ramp, Max looks up, to the black enclosed sky of the ceiling, sniffing—"What's that smell?"—as Ari looks to the floor, the moving silver dot of Lee, the red line of Jonas, watching them converge, and "Probably the next cocktail," he says. "It's almost door, let's go."

After the tone sounds—past Ari's nudge, adjusting his own, "Set your tiara to default, so we see the same things"—Max emerges from the mesh-shrouded performers' catwalk into the brighter, blue-lit darkness of the public hallway, to peer into the graffiti room, its walls ghostly with last night's writing, mostly drunk spelling spiraling in lust or love—*Suk me Kevvin! Julio mi Amor, Britta + Susan endlessly*—mixed with the occasional cryptic or funny or pithy notation, *All vision is relative, dance till U can't!! Reality is a Verb*. Anyone logged in can read them, anyone present or with a streaming pass can add their own, as Max does now, one-finger writing in stark neon white, *Dum vivimus vivamus* and "'While we live,'" he translates to Ari, "'let us live.' It's from Epicurus."

"What?"

"It's Latin."

"You speak Latin?"

"No one speaks Latin," as beyond Max's shoulder a new tag flares into life, *Do the Hokey Pokey*, as green as phosphorescence in some underwater cave, what the fuck is the hokey pokey? and "Want a drink to start?" Ari steering him to the nearest bar station, a half-circle of steel stools inside a curved skyline panorama that morphs from Berlin to New York to Nairobi to Montréal to the Factory logo, then back to Berlin, and "Champagne," Ari says to the gangly bartender. "But not that fake Clicquot. Gold label," and the bartender nods, the bubbles changing in the pour to minute golden fireworks, the effect so silly and charming that even Max

has to smile. The first floor DJ starts his set with a massive industrial thump, a skitter of static, a cawing cry, "Dark Factory, let's *worrrrrk!*" and "Let's go," Ari says, tossing back his champagne. "Let's find those seams."

Of all his nights at the Factory, this one feels to Ari the way a patron's always seems, like a dream, pure presence as he leaves behind his own accustomed role to follow Max's tack from floor to floor, Max who, with Ari beside him, feels somehow both safely invisible and like a soldier walking point, up and down the ramps with the rest of the human stream, like a stairway between heaven and earth, as the Factory's endless details open onto more details, like a nest of matryoshka dolls: the synchronized Y kickline bracketing its human dancers with multiple insectile arms and legs, the DJs changing out in a smooth shared alphabet of beats, while the walls pulse and run with a waterfall of lyrics in English, German, Farsi, and above it all white glitter explodes and races through the air like swirls of self-aware snow.

And the champagne leads into a series of Factory screwdrivers, black vodka gleaming as if cut with fresh metal shavings, another bartender at another bar offering them a Red Eye—"It's brand-new tonight!"—to Ari's politely withering smile and "Anna Achor," Max says, drinking, blinking, Max feels half-drunk, maybe more than half. "You know her unstallations? She calls them unstallations because—"

"Who's Anna Acorn?"

"Never mind. Corollary discharge theory, you know what that is?"

"Like that restaurant where everybody went blind?" Ari half-recalling one of Jonas's tutorials, Jonas passing by now in his gaudy plaid jacket, he had passed them on the ramps too, is Jonas following them? so "Come on," pivoting Max through the buoyant crush as a topless woman in a red crown dances between them, her body bent like a boomerang, while a man with golden ram's horns winks at Ari, curling hair as dark as dark chocolate, his skintight t-shirt reads LOVE ME TENDER MOTHERFUCKER, Max is still talking—

"—because identity, human identity is intrinsically fragile, it's—Ari, *listen*—"

"I am listening!"

"—identity's just narrative plus hallucination! The real difference between zöe and bios—"

"Who?"

"Are you just fucking with me now? Think of it like a K-hole—"

"The Factory's the opposite of a K-hole—"

"—or performed psychosis turning into actual psychosis—"

"You're saying, oh come on you're not saying that Y is a gateway drug to losing your shit? That's been disproven a million times—"

"What I'm saying," the liquor overlaid with the unreality making him louder, as if he must shout to be heard above the beautiful lie, so beautiful here, he would like to disappear here, how the fuck can he want that? "What I'm *saying* is that we're always on the verge of losing our shit, we always have been! So we made up stories in the, the caves, around the campfires, to keep from falling apart—"

And Ari laughs rudely, as the chocolate man dips those horns and licks those lips in his direction, more gorgeous than any real man could ever be, while other bodies lurch and angle past them, are they all becoming happily psychotic? would they care if they were? Would he care? *Ari Regon is the face of Dark Factory, some would say the heart of it* and he laughs even louder, the vodka and champagne and blunts and lack of sleep all hitting him at once, he laughs so hard that Max grabs his arm in alarm and "Jesus," his gasp, "you're the worst date ever! Just. Show me. The seams—"

"Show you how, why do you keep saying that? *We're* the seams—"

—and Ari stops, stares, his phone tings, high priority, Jonas, ***BOX NOW***, too much coincidence to be coincidence because what Max just said, oh what Max said—"Come on," almost dragging Max through the humid scrum of the crowd, up to the box where "Wait here," stationing him just outside the door, "don't move—Lee!" half-shouting, inside the box feels calm and airy, like a place of pure thought, like a lab. "Where's Jonas?"

"Aren't you going to bring in your coconspirator?"

"Max?" too heady to be goaded, impatiently messaging Jonas, *here im here*. "Max is none of your business—"

"It is my business. It's Factory business," and Lee smiles, is that a smile? Lee armored in her sensible silver, clipboard held up like a shield. "Max Caspar is a commercial rival, and—"

"Rival? 'Commercial'?"

"Oh laugh, Jonas doesn't think it's funny. Jonas was very disturbed to hear you spoke to Max Caspar offsite—"

"Are you still spying on me? Jonas won't think that's too funny either—"

—as the door slams open, Jonas with a face so ferocious that both Ari and Lee go silent, the techs glance at one another then adjust their headphones, shoulders protectively hunched as "Darcy," Jonas says, flat, "just left for Brussels. With her fuck monkey. She said the Onion Room made her feel like a down-market porn star—Goddammit, Ari, that was a serious error in judgment!" and seeming then to see Lee for the first time, "What the fuck are you doing here? Not now!" as "It's happening now," Lee stepping between then, her back to Ari an instant wall. "Ari's made another serious error in judgment. With Max Caspar—"

"Jonas, listen, we've been doing it wrong. The seams—"

"What seams? You smell like a barback's rinse tub, are you drunk?"

"No, no no. I was with Max, and—"

"And what?" Jonas looming over him like a building about to fall. "What's the real story with Max Caspar, what kind of hustle are you running here?"

"What?"

"You bring him in, you hire him, you push me to take time off, and then you're 'unavailable, unavailable,' looks like a hustle to me! And I don't need this shit tonight, on top of Darcy—"

"Fuck Darcy—"

"Ari, watch your mouth!"

"—I know what I'm doing, I know the Factory better than you do—"

"*Ari!*" a roar so loud that the techs jump even beneath their headphones, Lee covers her mouth with one hand. "Who the *fuck* do you think you are!"

And as Ari pushes out the door, Max stumbles back—"What happened?"—confused and unsteady in Ari's wake, across the floor and into the clutter and hush of the performers' lounge, where "I'm out of here," Ari says, tiara thrown down, bag grabbed up, blunt clenched between his teeth. "Go back if you want to, finish out the night," while Max struggles to parse out that furious silent play—Jonas Siegler's eruption, Ari's glow like a fire doused with piss, and the woman, the one Max had seen before, her stare as calm as quicksand—but as if he can say nothing else until the question is answered, he asks again, "What happened?"

But Ari is already moving, out of the lounge and swift to the street, bag swinging, smoke trailing, Max tries to catch up but within two blocks Ari has disappeared—

—and up ahead, like a sudden mirage, the CHEAP BREAKFAST sign, maybe Ari is in there? he is not, but Max drops into a seat anyway, to stare at the overhead lights' reflection on the countertop, the laminated menu cards, the drops of condensation rolling down his water glass, the toast granular and wet with butter: so much intricate detail, as if the Factory has somehow followed him, swallowed him, as if a game has just leveled up—

—and "Dark Factory," says one of the other diners, red smile and green hair, one green-and-blue lacquered nail tapping the dangling nametag. "You work there, Caspar Max?" and "Yes," Max says, staring at that hand, then at his own hand, his strange and empty fingers. "Yes and no."

###

The brass elevator gate rattles back, an inch of the visible shaft, as Ari thumbs Jonas's number again: up all night for another night, but the inspiration is still alive, even on this dry-mouth morning after. In the empty hall with its empty mirrors he applies knuckles to the slab of the door, applies his fist until "Ari, for fuck's sake," Jonas irritable and glum in creased white dojo pajamas, the late morning light shows every line on his face. "Why are you here?"

"To talk to you."

"Aren't you done running your mouth?"

"Just let me in—"

—to stand between the tapestries' threadbare knights and the screen, its constant ripple from floor to floor to floor, and "Lee," Jonas says, "is nonstop begging me to fire you. And your buddy Max, the industrial spy."

"Lee's been spying on me," leaning to that screen, searching backwards for the Carlos meet, searching again, but "It's missing. That whole timestamp is missing—"

"That door cam's shit, we all know that. Forget about Lee. Max Caspar is the issue here."

"That's right. Last night—"

"I don't want to hear about last night," Jonas arms crossed and glaring on the sofa like a king on a throne, a king confronting treachery. "Where were you all day yesterday?"

The no man's land of the paper mill, its gestating silence, the shit ground deep into his shoe, he will have to throw those shoes away. "I was alone."

"Alone doing what?"

"Thinking."

"Thinking?" and Jonas suddenly calm, the anger dropped like a discarded tool. "It was no problem poaching you from that Skidmore guy, was it? You know what he told me? he said 'Ari's a maker, give him anything, anything at all, and he'll make something out of it.'"

"Jan said that?"

"I know Lee's been watching you, she doesn't know I know but I do. And I was OK with it. Because I've been watching you too."

"I came here," louder, as if he stands on one side of a chasm and Jonas on the other, "to tell you what Max told me, and show you how we can make the Factory—"

"I already made the Factory, that's why you work for me. Do you want to keep working for me?"

"Am I in trouble now? Am I fired?"

"You're on hiatus."

"What does that mean? Go stand in the corner till my brain shuts down?"

"It can be unpaid hiatus. Last chance to tell me what's really going on—"

You can always walk away whenever you want, who said that? he said it, to Max, so "All right," his nod. "I'll show you. I'll invite you—"

"Don't," Jonas's footsteps one step behind his own, "don't you walk out of here, Ari, *don't*—" then the door slams so hard the nearest mirror trembles. In the elevator he feels the operator's glance on him, impassive, "Have a nice day—"

—and outside it is a nice day, a gusting breeze to lift the saffron yellow leaves, the sun muted from scorch to sparkle. He stops at the first Kaffee Kart he sees, the tall barista nodding gently to earbead music; the caffeine rush swamps his thirst for sleep, he feels again that strange persistent elation as his phone tings, Jonas, ***Fired as of now—***

—and at the Factory, the performers' door gives no entrance beep for his tag, that was fast, that was Lee. But "Hey," his wave to a pair of approaching dancers, Alix with black racer shades and shiny bicep wraps, and Katya in striped leggings and stocking hat, like an elegant human spinning top. "Can you key me in? My tag's dead—"

—and inside the first person he sees is Max, of course it would be Max: haggard in his wrinkled Factory t-shirt, satchel in hand and "I forgot my stuff," Max says, "last night. Ari, what *happened* last—"

"I just got fired. Come on—"

"You *what?*" Alix's half-shout as Ari keeps walking, while Max stops dead, how can Ari Regon be fired from the Factory? Ari Regon *is* the Factory—

—and Katya blocks his path, her hand up like a cappie's: "Wait. Mila asked me to ask you something."

He feels his face stiffen, like a wooden mask. "Why can't Mila ask me herself? Why won't she answer—"

"You ask yourself that! Do you want to hear or what?" and when he nods, lips tight, "Mila says that Deborah's all right with the sublet. So are you going to take the flat?"

Take the flat? go and live in Mila's room without Mila? He never wants to see that place again. "No. No way."

"Good. I hoped you wouldn't—"

—and as Katya stalks off Max stays where he stands, a short pause that feels very long, feels like a precipice or a sudden reprieve: if Ari is fired, he could walk out of here right now, could leave Dark Factory and never come back—

—then jogging to catch up, just a step behind as Ari pushes into a glassed-in office that looks like a working demonstration of disorder: every visible surface covered with mix sticks and light cards and empty juice cans, kidney-shaped pouches stuffed with fat matte tubing, samples of swag, a long glass table piled with even more piles, files and papers that Ari quickly sifts through as "I know it's here," Ari says, to the table, to Max, to himself. "Jonas never throws anything away—"

—as "Ari," from the doorway, the quicksand clipboard woman from the box, her smile showing small square teeth. "Do I need to call security?"

"Call whoever you want, Lee," his shrug, this must be Lee's happiest workday ever, the vindictive validating thrill of seeing him *and* Darcy gone in less than twenty-four hours. "Call Jonas if you—*Here* it is," tugging from a deeper strata of the mess a brown and brittle dog-eared folder, sliding it into his bag as "What are you doing?" Lee's voice sharp with sudden alarm. "Put that back. You're fired now, you can't just—"

"Fired without cause. The optics," with another shrug, as if placing a knotty problem solely in her charge. "You know they won't be great on that."

"You'll be escorted out! Your bags will be searched—"

—but no security appears, no one accosts them, though Ari is stopped over and over for questions and hugs and sad handshakes, and "Holy shit," doleful from a maintenance worker at NOT AN EXIT, stained Factory sweatshirt and red hoop earrings, a heavy yellow brace belt, "this doesn't even seem real! What are you going to do, Ari?"

"Right now? Get some breakfast. And then," lighting up, "get busy. Right, Max?" turning that smile Max's way: the smoke smells dryly delicious, breakfast sounds even better, but as they leave "What happened last night?" Max asks, the sudden sun a white sear in his eyes from a truck's side mirror. "Are you ever going to tell me?"

With mild surprise, "You're the one who told me," side by side down the sidewalk, in the block's growing flow of noontime backpack toters and rushed delivery trikes, around a pair of traffic workers setting construction cones in some meticulous arrangement, a bus stop with an arrival display showing useless green in all directions, and into a noodle bar, SEAWEED PALACE, where a buff and buzzcut server in a Neue Welt t-shirt smiles at Ari—"Soba, right? Your fave, babe, cold and spicy"—setting to the counter cups filled with what to Max look unpleasantly like green graveside worms. And "What's the matter?" Ari says, reaching into his bag. "You don't like noodles?"

"The matter?" plucking at his shirt, last night's shirt, as if that night has still not ended, his own seams feel as if they are fraying and his dreams were even worse, were actively atrocious: wandering some world where everything was porous, to touch was to be swallowed, he woke not sweating but ice cold. And why does Ari look so fucking *happy?* "The matter is, you dragged me into this, this petri dish—"

"I didn't 'drag' you anywhere—"

"—and now you're out? No," as Ari offers the brown folder, "I don't want to see that. I don't want to see anything—"

"You'll like this. It's all theory, and you're big on theory—"

"I'm not a theorist, I'm a realist!"

"A realist?" Ari's laugh not amusement but a kind of delight. "After all your lectures? And I saw Bitter Lake, remember?"

"You saw the site, not the show. You can't call a show without—"

"I saw your garage show, didn't I? The only thing that wasn't theory was the flamethrowers, those flamethrowers were straight out of BurnOut—"

"Whatever you're doing, whatever you think you're doing, I'm—"

"—I bet you played a *lot* of BurnOut—"

"—I'm done!" launching himself off the stool then out the door, Ari after in two steps, too late, leaning to call from the doorway, "Max, come on, we have shit to do!" as at his shoulder the server says, "Never chase a man, babe, it only makes them run faster . . . What do you want with your soba?"

Next to the noodle bar is a florist, its window's display of voluptuous white flowers, splayed gardenias and thick-petaled dahlias pressed almost to the glass: and Ari breathes in the sudden scent of lilies, lilies cut with leather like the cologne Karl used to wear, bought from the airport duty free, he claimed it was an aphrodisiac, *rub some between my shoulders, Ari*—that smell rich and half-decayed and potent, so potent it feels as if Karl is actually there in the flesh, as "What do you want?" the server asks again and "You," Ari reaching backhand to touch him, cup him, the server makes a little laugh—

—and in minutes they are wedged together beside the employees' lockers, the server, Tommy? Timmy? muting his grunts as Ari leans in hard, eyes closed and working to catch that scent again, of Karl naked beside the bed, then "You OK?" the server asks, Ari in near-collapse, struggling to catch his breath, and "I'm good," Ari whispers. "It's good."

"You need to eat more, babe. I'm going to get you some nice carbs."

With the takeaway bag and a grateful two-finger wave—the server's name, he now remembers, is Timothy—he heads home, a trip that seems to take forever, why are the trains so slow in the middle of the day? to sit and eat and fall asleep, wake with a headache and seaweed flecks on his shirt, confused by the long shadows at the windows, how is it nighttime already?

By habit he starts to log in at the Factory, then stops with a pang, and checks instead the flood of messages and posts, the rumor mill in high astonished spin: shocked friends and loyal partisans and a few mocking haters, journos' requests for comment, including Jake from *ForwardFast*, and two exploratory messages, one from someone at Caprice and one from Skelly at Junket, ***Feel like talking?*** And now a deeper pang, feeling the loss of it, the Factory his reality for so long: all those nights on the floor, indelible and fleeting, all the friends like Annelise and Clara and Alix and Eli, the DJs and performers who passed through, the patrons whose names he never knew, who were only gorgeous glimpses, moving smiles in the dark—

—and Jonas, jesus, how many hours had he spent in that office? and the box, and the loft, talking and smoking and wrangling over details, the hiring tiers and power user rewards, hot tags versus clickables, aroma pores versus scent drops, Jonas's first choice for the name—SatisFactory, *that* was a weeklong fight—and the choice of Chockablock for the final brand design, Jonas mulish, *Why them? When they cost at least twice what everybody else does?*

Everybody else looks like everybody else. Chockablock doesn't.

You sure you're not getting a kickback? a joke, he had treated it like a joke, but now everything Jonas has ever said, every pushback, every compliment, especially the compliments, is tainted; not just because Jonas is being unjust, he is, but because Jonas is so willfully blind: the Factory could take this idea, this truth—he knew it was true as soon as Max said it, beautiful, obvious, of course—and become ten times what it is, a hundred, why has no one else made this jump? not to close the seams but open them up, all the way up—

—so "All right," fingers to his forehead, pressing that ache, "all right," talking to who, this empty room? or Jonas? or runaway Max, what the fuck is wrong with Max? or the ghost of Karl, and where had all *that* come from? so mindlessly hungry, his dumb cock still in love . . . He rises again, to drink ice water and watch the wired windows become a mosaic of green arc lights, white headlights, purple sunset clouds, the red LEDs of the corner café's CAFÉ, how long will he keep this view? the rent here is crazy expensive, and blunts cost money too. His father always used to preach *Save half your pay for a rainy day,* was that why his mother had gone? sick of the dull infrequent treats, of waiting for the rain to finally fall? *While we live let us live,* Max had said that too—and through the growing dark his growing half-smile, at least now he knows why hiring Max was such a genius move.

Bonus Content: Ari

dum vivimus vivamus

Trying to be as quiet as the quiet hallway around him, its smell of dust and fabric softener, digging around in the pot of fake red geraniums for the spare key, no way was he going to knock—but somehow she already knew he was there, she opened the door: "You're home," just after six, just rolled in from dancing, he was high, not falling down high but when he blinked he knew he looked sleepy and sweaty and completely trashed; he smiled.

"Sorry, Mama. Lost my key again."

"You want coffee? I'm making Turkish," her favorite and his, the beans ground to powder, the thin porcelain cups, gold-rimmed and old and expensive; his father always said if she used them too often they would break, she always shrugged. He knew his mother thought his father was afraid of life, of using things up, worried there would never be more: she was not afraid. Neither was he.

He slid into a chair at the square oak table, beneath the bland landscape photo of beach dunes, beige sand and a line of calm blue sea, beside the window's view of low-rise apartments and prim trimmed trees, as she boiled the water and coffee to a careful foam, some people added sugar but she never did. She poured her cup, she poured his, he yawned and belched and tasted lager, said "Excuse," and "Thank you," wondered if she could smell that lager on him; he had been drinking shooter cans of Barrel Roll with Antoine and some boy at Blank Frank's, he had already forgotten the boy's name. The boy kept saying *You're so hot, you're so fucking hot,* and when Antoine went for more Barrel Roll, the second boy had pressed against him, tried to kiss him but he had turned his face away, buzzing from the lager and the smoke and the beats and the heat of the dancefloor and the feel of the boy's hard cock rubbing against his hip, he wanted to hold onto that feeling, like a wave rolling higher and higher, hold it till the crest then let it all go at once—

—school today? They called yesterday, the attendance officer said—Ari? Ari—

What, blinking, and she shook her head, not angry: *Drink,* she said, *you must need it.* And he smiled again, an apology, trying to be awake for her, to listen; the coffee was perfect, he told her that, *You always make it perfect, Mama.*

Your father's very worried about you.

He's worried that you're not worried.

He meant to make her laugh or at least smile, but she did neither, she sipped her coffee and gazed at him with eyes that people said were just like his own, family resemblance, only hers had pretty little lines at the corners, like the lines a kid draws when he draws the sun, radiating lines; even as a kid he had known his mother was very beautiful. She sipped her water, always serve water with Turkish coffee, and serve it in a crystal glass, that was her rule.

She had very few rules: she never asked what he did at night, she seemed to understand that he was safe, was fine. And he was fine, was dancing, hanging out with friends he met online or at Blank Frank's, shirtless boys and shouting girls, out searching for the party, for the place where he could ride that cresting feeling every night, he knew it was there and he knew he could find it, *I want to make things happen,* he told Antoine. *Big things. I want them to happen to me.*

continued on page 064

continued from page 063

School had nothing to do with that, any of that, though his father lectured him endlessly: he was sixteen years old and school was his way forward, the path, he must stay on the path—The path to what? did his father think he would go to uni, get some job, live his whole life in an apartment just like this one? Sometimes he heard his parents arguing about him, they never got loud the way his friends' parents sometimes did, no screaming or name-calling but he could feel the anger between them, thick and cold, like a wall made of old dead lead.

And the click of the bedroom door opening, closing, the sound of water in the lav, and *Your father,* his mother said, so he drank the rest of his coffee in a hurry, the dark residue on his upper lip, bitter, he licked it away—and saw suddenly that she was upset, sad, why? He put his hand on top of hers, she put her other hand on top of his, looked at his fingers and said *You're biting your nails again,* not to scold but to show that she saw he was feeling restless, it was something he did when he felt that way, restless or upset. What did she do, when she was upset? *Are you going to go to school today, Ari?*

Mama. What do you want me to do?

I want you to have everything, she said; she pressed his hand. *Everything that's yours.*

Then she took her hands away, took their cups to the sink, took up her purse and her olive green work bag and *See you tonight,* he said, and she smiled at him, he would always remember that, her beautiful, beautiful smile.

And then his father was there, in the baggy blue checked robe that matched his blue checked slippers, they made a shuffling sound on the kitchen floor and *You're up early,* his father said, filling the enamel tea kettle. *Ready for school? Where's your mother?*

The sun was in the windows now, the Turkish coffee cut the lager crash. He stood up, drank down his crystal glass of water, and *She left already,* he said—

—and in twenty minutes he was gone too, hair still dripping from the shower, backpack on, unlit cigarette in his mouth as he climbed onto the SR train, to ride past the apartment blocks and parking lots and the fenced-off water treatment plant, the sloping concrete banks of the cold brown river, into the city for the day, the night, to search for the party, and end up at midnight in a warehouse squat with a line of blacked-out windows and a bitchcore DJ from Cologne, and a boy who called himself Racer, who tasted like canned vodka and smelled like Club cigarettes and FastPharm body spray. His father messaged him again and again, but he did not see or answer those messages until much later; his mother did not message him, or come back to him, that day or that night or at all.

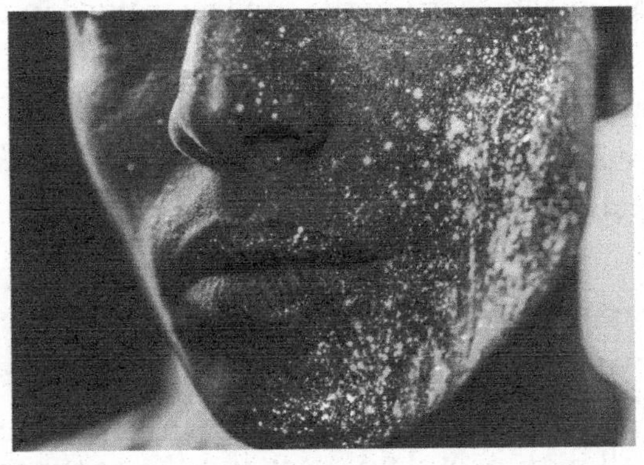

06

Max waits on a bench in the glassy TanzStudio lobby, clearly out of place in his shabby black jacket and stained work vest, eyed by the receptionist at the check-in desk as two dancers loiter and gossip: "I heard Ari Regon was trying to own Dark Factory, like straight up buy out that other guy, Jones—"

"No, no. Hector's boyfriend is a tech there, and he said—"

"—own it and run it—"

"—it was all about some girl. Marcy somebody—"

—and what if he corrected them, what if he told them he had seen that famous fight, was there that famous night? almost three weeks ago, but it could have been an hour or a year, it all feels like one lurid timeless whole, from the time he walked into the Factory until he walked, ran, out of that noodle shop. And his equilibrium, his perceptual balance, is still skewed, his vision too . . . Which is why he is here, to find Katya, Katya who knows how to reach Mila: Mila is the most grounded person he knows, he needs to talk to Mila now.

The doors open on three older women, dance bags and expensive Balboa workout wear, is one of them the one who got Mila the Rotterdam gig? and right behind them is, yes, Katya, arm in arm with a tall man in a plaid scarf and Dragonistas ball cap, so "Katya, hey Katya!" Max up from the bench like a spring-loaded tool. "I have to get in touch with Mila, it's important—"

"'Important,'" Katya's echo, her visible disgust. "Max, why

would I help you? You treated Mila like a servant," and as Max's mouth opens in angry disbelief "Shut up," snapping her fingers right under his nose, stacked silver rings, a strange disdainful gesture. "A servant, an employee, in your great art production, Bitter Lake, big deal! I told her a hundred times what you are! And you talk shit on Dark Factory then you work there, are you trying to get Ari's job or what? At least they're both shut of you now—Come on, Ed," as the man in the scarf looks back in refracted contempt at Max standing with his mouth still open, what hateful bullshit is this? Mila a servant! And Ari—

—as the receptionist stares at him, the two dancers stare, the three glossy women stare: so out the door, walking fast past the papierie with the oversized origami face, are those wide blank eyes staring at him too? past the back-to-back sneaker shops with their booming sidewalk speakers, *If you knew! if you knew! what the fuck would you do!* and a freelancers' work share café where industrious people work on their handheld realities. He feels the hole in his vest pocket grow larger as his fingers find it, feels as if he walks beneath the weight of the world, not his world, *shut of you, shut up,* shut out . . . Mila is gone, Bitter Lake is gone, he has not seen Ari since the noodle shop, *shit to do,* what possible shit could Ari have meant? and what if he had stayed to see that folder opened? But leaving was the right thing to do, because onsite or not, fired or not, Ari Regon *is* the Factory, is everything he needs to flee if he ever wants to get back to normal, get his vision back, his life—

—and stopped at the curb between an empty old-style metal newspaper box, and a man in a reflective tracksuit holding a squirming white dog—"Wait, we have to wait"—as a recycling truck lumbers in beeping reverse, while across the street a chubby young woman with a red cross backpack gestures to a man on the stoop one step below her, shopping bags in his hands and tight pink jacket, red sunglasses, jesus christ is it—

—Ari, yes, and Deborah, Mila's flatmate: because this is Mila's old corner, Mila's old flat, he walked all the way over here without even realizing, how the fuck did he—But before he can pivot and escape, Ari spots him, Ari waves, and "Max," Ari calls with that sunny smile, "hey Max! Looks like I'm moving in."

###

Deborah is no nonsense and exact: this much for rent, this much shared space in the kitchen pantry, this bedroom that comes with a bed indelibly scented with haylike ointments—Deborah was apologetic about that, but to Ari the smell is like a summertime field, and this flat is the opposite of an expensively remade industrial showplace, is exactly what he needs, openly old, shabby, solid, the sky here feels closer to the ground. Deborah had offered to empty the room of the stray items it still contains, bookcase and globe lamp, but he has brought so little with him, clothes and toiletries, his insomnia pillow, a Sexxy Boy coffee mug he had once bought for Karl, because it was so easy to leave everything else behind.

The guests at his moving-out party had been impressed by the loft's sumptuous built-ins, the black marble walk-in shower, the giant platform bed like an altar to fucking and sleep, everyone had loved the bed, the guy who took the sublet said he took it because of that bed, and the sound system. The DJ from Dusseldorf had said the system was amazing, *It's almost got a Klipsch vibe*, and *Well,* his own shrug and smile, trying not to stare at that extremely hot DJ, slim taut body and black unruly hair, deep brown eyes, *it's not as tight as the Factory's.*

I've never played the Factory, the DJ shrugging back with his own smile, an especially sweet smile, who had brought that DJ to the party? He had not stayed, by the next song he was gone . . . So many people invited and all of them came, bringing blunts and bottles and friends, all his Factory friends with overlapping tales of what the place is like without him: no one does his job because no one can, but Jonas is far more visible on the floor, and Lee is flailing, making enemies instead of allies: *Poor Lee,* he had said, meaning it, but also meanly laughing. *Be careful what you wish for.*

Then Annelise had tugged him aside, to offer her gunmetal flask of throat-scorching plum brandy, homemade and illegal, Annelise the queen of the circuit parties, he had insisted Jonas hire her first of all. And *Everybody's wondering,* Annelise's nod at the crowded room, the windows cranked to vent the slow clouds of smoke, *where you're going to end up.*

I am too.

Somebody said Caprice wants to hire you?

Somebody is right.

But he had already said no to Caprice, and to Skelly, though Skelly's offer had been particularly solid, and even to Meghan at Your Eyeballs, the smallest and his favorite of the houses, Meghan who thinks like an artist and raises endangered orchids—her profile is always an orchid, those fringed alien blooms—though every refusal ups the unknown ante, they all think he is holding out for something, and he is. But what it is is a mystery to him too.

Even Dodi had asked, Dodi the last survivor of the Holy Roman Empire, inviting him for drinks at Shout Bar: massive Dodi even more massive, still snapping his caffeine gum and sporting a new face tattoo, purple and blue, like an elegant permanent contusion, *I heard you got fired from your job,* a situation Dodi had seemed to find hilariously apt. *"Job"? I always said you were a magician in the making! The Empire, that was never meant to be anyone's job. All we had were t-shirts—*

I still have mine.

—and psychic wounds. Is there growth without pain? Ask the caterpillar. Ask the corpse!

The server had paused beside their table, long blond braids and greening nose ring, a speculative smile—*You're Ari, from Dark Factory?*—prompting Dodi's prideful shrug: *Ari was an emperor first, the Grand Marshal of our Grand Prix. Remember, Ari?*

I remember.

A hundred naked people racing through cardboard tunnels in a warehouse, the prize was a pack of Gitanes. And they stood outside in the snow to smoke them, still naked! And Dogpile, people painted themselves with melted chocolate, they licked and sniffed and rolled around like puppy dogs, remember, Ari?

I remember, remembering best that feeling of shared making, everyone driving toward the same end in different ways, a self-taught orchestra of pleasure and chaos, as *Kiss Your Mother,* Dodi had said, *I'm running the blackout nights there now. Michael likes them, don't you, Michael? Why don't you come some night and play with us?*

So tonight he will, in a flash new jacket from Shake Up, gold and white, no more Factory black and "Are you going to a party?" Deborah asks, at the kitchen table with her tablet and a bottle of Medoc.

"Just out clubbing, have some fun. What are you reading?"

"Seneca," tilting the tablet to display a white marble face. "He's a Stoic. A philosopher."

"Does he speak Latin? I learned some from Max," to bring Deborah's smile; Deborah had been unsurprised by Max's stoopside arrival and departure, and when Ari had asked with more than a little irritation *What the fuck is Max's problem?* she had offered a diagnostic shrug: *From what I've seen, Max is mostly his own problem.*

Now "Seneca," she says, "says that a wise person doesn't care about ownership, or wealth, or," reading aloud, "'his body, his eyes, his hands, even his very self, but lives as though he had borrowed them.'"

"Pretty hardcore."

"He was also Nero's tutor," refilling her glass. "Have fun."

And he tries: at Barbells, convex mirrored ceilings and blue neon poles, the muscle boys and girls and their preening Y avatars, in the smell of Rum Kings and posing oil; then at Astro, helium booths and a bouncing spacewalk dance floor beneath black artificial skies. And in both clubs he sees people he knows, people who know him, who sell smoke machines and beat wax and Percodan smoothies, who dance at the sex parties, run the LARPs, play the weeklong AI war games, they all ask how he is and he shrugs, smiles, restless, why? when this is his world and always has been, since his teenage days of basement raves and Barrel Roll and Blank Frank in a mylar thong and red plastic bowler hat, ringmaster of the party snake, forever hungry, forever eating its own tail.

Still restless, still time to kill before Kiss Your Mother, so he roams the fishy dark along the riverbank, the shining row of aluminum bar booths like upended flashlights, and "One hundred thirteen proof," boasts the bartender at Urban Bourbon, activating the bottle's pop-out label, four shrill fiddle notes and a tinny drawl, "Kentucky Hollow, the world's first authentic bluegrass whiskey!" He takes the tasting shot, makes a face at its sour heat, then is off to the Playpen for another shot, iced pepper vodka, too early there for any real action though he sees a few posers, a few eager loungers, he is taken in hand and he lets himself go, buoyed by the thrust and heat, thinking of nothing—

—then out again, smoothing back his hair, popping a spearmint chew, checking his phone as he slides into a Hopper, the driver wearing tight plastic gloves made to look like lock-up tattoos, BAD on one hand, GURL on the other, and "Kiss Your Mother?" the driver says. "I know where that is. It vibes OK, but the smell, ugh."

"Scat play?"

"Gross lavs," accelerating, turning east: Dodi's venue map must have changed, the Empire's old catchment area was up by the farmers' greenmarket, that long lovely dead end of the Park, where after a marathon weekend he would exit, yawning and tingling and damp, to smoke and watch the manmade lake grow sunrise pink, while the farmers unloaded their stepvans, cartons of cabbages and peaches, sacks of figs as big as he was. But this car's lights light up dull metal shutters with sprayed-over tags, a gated-in bodega, a patrolling cappie van, and the shadowed shapes of people who might, or might not, be there for the club. At the door he gets a blast of one bouncer's cologne, like a clove marinated in sweat, as the other bouncer stamps him through, a smeary glow-in-the-dark imprint of lipstick lips on the back of his hand—

—and inside the apricot vodka is as sickly sweet as a Red Eye, Dodi snaps his gum at the end of the bar, and Michael the

blond catches his eye and dances harder, whipping those braids for whatever he thinks Ari Regon can do for him, as the DJ segues into speeded-up slutcore in a crude confetti of hot spots, thermal mapping lights that dim, dim, dim—"Blackout! Blackout!"—until the room becomes a lightless field of questing, groping, fingering hands—

—and the Hopper driver was right about the lavs, so foul that even he, veteran, is driven outside to piss into the weeds. As he zips, he stares into the sky, another blackout, all clouds no stars, the music's bawl beating at the walls, as if the whole place is shouting to be freed, shouting at him, *shit to do*—But theorist Max, stonewalling Max, scared Max clearly on the run from him, why? and impossible to get hold of, no MePage, no workable phone. Yet *Ari's a maker, give him anything, anything at all* so why does he even need Max? why not just "Go," he says aloud, and starts walking, his stamped hand still faintly glowing, his gold jacket a beacon as he heads alone into the dark.

###

The angel on the peeling Raphael label is lifting off, or landing, with golden wings: all angels are messengers, Max remembers that from Sunday school, so "What's the message," his mutter, setting that bottle next to the other empties as he rises to go piss. The lager buzz has long gone sour, empty bottles, empty room, will he see that angel on the bottle fly away next? is he permanently losing his shit? He has not spoken to Mila, has not spoken to anyone, has spent so many hours, days, in this empty room that even being drunk is doing something—

—but his vision has not changed back, has not improved, has maybe gotten worse: in the shadowed hallway, as the service elevator's terminal groans mesh with Zelly's bike shop kill metal, he sees that the bulb above the lav door has gone out again, or is just gone, and a man-sized shape looms there, reaching for him—

"Whoa, hey! Don't hit me!"

—and embarrassed then to see it is only his neighbor, the bearded coder in another obscure science t-shirt, this one marked with a big silver *Sr*, the chemical element of what? surprise? And "What's the story with this?" the coder asks, proffering a paper, a flyer, TENANTS MEETING BLDG SALE.

"I don't know," not taking the flyer. "How would I know?"

"I heard some producer bought it, for 'Swan Lake'—No, not Swan Lake, but something with a lake in it, some entertainment thing. And you make shows, don't you?"

"Not anymore—"

—stepping into the age-stained lav, piss echo and the stink of pink industrial soap, the square speckled mirror that his glance carefully avoids, is he going to spend the rest of his life *not* looking at things? mirrors, lager bottles, that flyer, *some entertainment thing, something with a lake in it,* maybe Teresa really has gone commercial, maybe Bitter Lake is the new Dark Factory, maybe the whole world is the fucking Factory—

—and back in his room again, he roots roughly through a mulchy pile of socks and sweatshirts and notebooks, drags out his wrinkled Factory t-shirt, slings on the CASPAR MAX nametag: because what he needs to do now is not look away, run away, but exorcise this miasma, this sly perceptual sabotage, go back to the Factory and see whatever the fuck there is to see, whatever implacable reality, stare it down and make his vision whole again. And with Ari gone everything will be easier there, and safer—

—and from the performers' entrance he can already hear it, the dancefloors' meshing beats like one massive arrhythmic heart, his own heart beating faster as he keys the tag, the door opens for him, he is inside. Tiara on, its settings set recklessly wide, he hits the floor, climbs the ramps, scans the addled palimpsests of the graffiti room and the constant flicker of the candle room, the meaningless bombast of those dancefloors, watches the patrons shriek and dance and perform for an audience of one, of their own eyes, nothing here for him to see—

"Max Caspar?" a woman's voice, "Max!" Lee's voice from right behind him, but he does not jump, he is proud of that, only stops and turns and waits for Lee to confiscate his tag, call security, have him thrown out or arrested for trespass. But instead Lee says, "Come with me—"

—to the relative quiet of the nearest pocket bar, this one with a spinning interlocking wall of metal gears, half clockwise and half counter-, like teeth in a hundred mouths, or a machine made for inducing nausea; Lee wears a gearlike metal hair band below her tiara, her face looks tired but her eyes are very bright. "I can't say I'm surprised to see you here. Ari's onsite too, I expect?"

"I have no idea where Ari is."

"Really? Then why are you here?"

"Because I'm an artist—"

—an answer that seems to surprise Lee, saying it surprises him too. Something red lights up on her clipboard, she mutes it with a tap and "It's interesting you should say that," she says. "We're interviewing for Ari's position, for someone on the floor. We haven't met with any artists, though, that's a very interesting thought—"

"What do you mean?" as the gears around them click and mesh. "You mean me?"

"I think that could be workable," showing her teeth, is that meant to be a smile? With Ari Lee had always seemed ill at ease, at some unknown disadvantage, she is not at a disadvantage now. "You came back here for a reason, didn't you?"

You talk shit on Dark Factory then you work there, are you trying to get Ari's job? not Ari's job but maybe truly his own, to find that visual schism, *to fight an enemy you need to go behind enemy lines* so "I'd be willing to talk about it," he says, cautiously. "Talk to Jonas Siegler again—"

"Jonas fully trusts my recommendations, I can hire whoever I want. And you could start," consulting that clipboard, "as soon as this weekend, HR could draw up a 30-day renewable contract, say. If you're ready."

Raising his voice over a sudden dancefloor roar, as if the Factory itself is cheering for this turn of events: "I'm ready right now. But don't expect the second coming of Ari Regon, because I'm not like him at all."

"I believe that's very true," she says, while behind them the gears gnash on. "Welcome to Dark Factory, Max."

The grasshopper drinks the champagne, the ant carries the cork

I was at Angler-Forman for almost four years.

That's in your resume?

Yes, leaning over the desk, no other chair in this office, trying to look at ease in her brown silk jacket and blue pinstripe slacks—she had worked very hard putting that outfit together, to appear creative but not too creative—*I was head assistant to the corporate events manager, but most of the day-to-day responsibilities were mine. My duties—I can show you*—the bullet points already prepared, she was ready for a grilling on that resume, questions on her lack of industry experience, she had all her answers in the cheap little Tab-It; the much more efficient, much more expensive Sensa tablet was corporate property, she had to leave it behind when she left Angler/Forman, her sole regret.

Head assistant to the corporate events manager: at first that position had seemed like success, like a career, something big and engrossing and equal to her talents. But in three years and seven months, day in and out, nothing had changed, her superior ideas and plans always blocked by that manager, vague and dithering Althea: Althea who always asked the same questions, maddeningly simple questions about vendor matching and chain deployment, who had never even formally introduced her to the partners, Ms. Angler and Mr. Forman, forced her to trail behind at the boring and poorly-conceived events that she herself could easily have upgraded and run with a decent staff, even without a staff, she could have done it alone. But three years and seven months with no hope of promotion meant nothing would ever change for her there.

So she had no choice but to promote herself, to look far across the corporate fence, past insurance and into entertainment, experience events, she did her due diligence then applied for a position at a company called Tenth Wall, they were nearly as corporate as

Angler-Forman. But the Tenth Wall hiring manager had pointed out, correctly, that event experience or not, she had no experience at all in the actual field. Which meant she needed a company as new as she was, a risk-taking, start-up company—

—like Dark Factory, that seemed to consist of a built-up warehouse with a great deal of hardware, this horrifically chaotic office, and Jonas Siegler, the owner and founder, who was openly disinterested in her bullet points, who offered her an energy drink from a cooler instead: *You like NooJuice?*

She had never had it before, she took a sip; the taste was horrid, like ground-up vitamins, even worse than Boostie. She said, *Refreshing.*

He seemed to approve of that answer, approve of her too for reasons she did not immediately understand. And the rest of the interview was Jonas Siegler's monologue, his origin story of how he had created Dark Factory: but she knew how to listen, and what she heard was that there was real potential here, she could run this whole company with a tablet and sleepless work, because Jonas Siegler was brimful of plans and theories but plans and theories would always be less useful than policies and procedures. And the more he talked, the more excited she became, though nothing showed on her face, nothing but a small, engaged, encouraging smile.

And when he finally stopped talking, to guzzle his own can of juice, *I believe,* she said, *Dark Factory will be a premier entertainment experience, a destination experience. And I can be uniquely helpful, I have an extensive risk assessment background along with my organizational—*

You need to meet Ari, and what did that mean? more hoops to jump through, or was she hired? *Ari Regon, he's my number one guy on the floor,* and what did *that* mean, number one on the floor? Was it some performance term? another item to add to the internal learn list she was already compiling—

—as a young man entered the office, skintight black jeans and a wide white smile, that smile not meant for her or for Jonas Siegler either, it appeared to exist purely for itself, to demonstrate a level

continued on page 078

continued from page 077

of self-confidence that she had never encountered and could not imagine possessing, she hated Ari Regon on sight. And *This is Lee Davies,* Jonas Siegler said to that smile, smiling too. *Lee's leaving the insurance industry, she wants to be part of the magic here.*

Ari Regon put out his hand, so she shook it, smiling, her lips felt stretched and thin but she kept on smiling, refused to stop until he did, until he dropped her hand and stuck a cigarette into the corner of his mouth, was it a cigarette? and handed one to Jonas Siegler, did not offer one to her. And *Insurance?* Ari Regon said, snapping his lighter, that smile reappearing in the smoke. *That means you know how everything can go wrong. Now we'll show you how everything goes right. Welcome to Dark Factory, Lee.*

Number one on the floor? Not again, not another Althea, this was going to be her floor, her factory, her advancement so *I'm looking forward to working with you, Ari,* she said, and made another smile before he could do it first. *Very much.*

07

The counter is a pleasant mess of dinner prep, chopped mushroom stems and onionskin, warm oily splashes of broth and "This is good," Deborah says, dipping her crust in the shallow yellow bowl. "Thanks for cooking."

"My mom taught me how to make it . . . What did you do today?" nodding at her canvas backpack on the chair, marked with a stern red cross, ASCENSION SERVICES. "Save lives? You're a doctor, right?"

"Not even. I'm a radiology tech, I looked inside people all day."

"What did you see? Secrets?"

"Physiology. Mortality. What did you do today?"

"Bought bread. Chopped onions. Slept," because once he left Kiss Your Mother he had kept on going, like his teenage walkabout forays, sure he could find what he was looking for, or that it would find him: passing rowdy loiterers and tired shift workers and drunken flocks of boys and girls, locked shops and all-night takeaway bars, the slow blue overnight buses, the vibration of the trains under cracked asphalt then smooth concrete then square-trimmed pocket lawns; his legs aching, mouth dry from too much smoke, breathing in the half-decayed scent of a faded flowering hedge, was it hawthorn? as he turned up the bakery street with the rhythmic slap of feet rising behind him, a runner with sneakers flashing red and white, red and white, a pink and white wrapper tossed back in the runner's wake; he had stuffed that wrapper into his back pocket, Raspberry Kisses, a smiling mouth to match the faint inky mouth still stamped on his hand—

—and "Raspberry Kisses?" Deborah surprised as he leans to throw it away, "I didn't think they still made those. My great-grandpa called them sky candy—the war pilots," to Ari's quizzical look. "They dropped candy to the kids. He never forgot."

"Would you?" a treat come from nowhere but real enough to roll in your mouth, you would never stop looking up—as his gaze is drawn across the alley to another kitchen's light, someone busy in that window, not the usual stocky tenant but a slim dark-haired man at the sink. "I'm going to smoke, want to come out? Maybe someone will drop something nice on us—"

—as they stand side by side, his blunt and her wine, at the weathered rail of the little porch, a colder breeze as night comes on again, the twilight sun erased line by line by clouds, cobalt and ivory. And the man in the window looks even more attractive from this vantage point, that graceful body, he is about to ask Deborah if she knows that man—

—but she tells him about her friend Peggi, Peggi the former café manager who is working to create some sort of immersive club: "Peggi's been to Dark Factory, she's the one who told me about it."

"What's her club like?"

"Nothing yet. She has ideas but I don't think she knows what to do, except spend all her savings."

"Want me to talk to her?"

"If you did, she would be thrilled. And I'd be thankful."

"Sure," as the kitchen light goes dark, ending that little show, that immersive imagining. "Why not?"

Blunt pinched and glass empty, they step back into the kitchen's warmth, Deborah clearing the table as he scans his phone, to learn that he has been invited to a two-day cattle call network party, a drink and think, in Bonn, that he has a ten percent discount waiting at Beatriz's salon, that a friend from the suburbs, Antoine, is getting married, ***Erik and I really hope you can make it!*** that Dodi is annoyed that he left Kiss Your Mother so abruptly, ***how long you stay, 10***

fucking mins? and, from a range of sources, inside the Factory and out, that Max Caspar has just been hired to do his job.

###

The t-shirt has been replaced by a black dress shirt, and Max's new nametag has no department designation, for this job that seems to require nothing beyond that shirt and a nightly debrief in the performers' lounge, Lee asking complicated, jargon-heavy questions he not only cannot answer but does not even understand: about LBEs and recency bias, floor-to-pour ratio, drag-back and ubiquity stake, clicking away at that clipboard that never seems to leave her hands, until she says *Thank you, Max,* and his shift is over. Being an artist seems to have no bearing at all on his hiring; Lee did it for a reason, he can smell that, the way he would smell bad wiring on a site, but he has no idea what it is.

Jonas Siegler he has seen twice, first in a supremely awkward meeting in Jonas's office, Lee hovering, smiling, Jonas did not smile and *You're on board for real this time,* Jonas had said, an odd choice of words, was Jonas recalling that old trailer interview? or did he mean Ari's truncated two-night stand? Then a few nights ago Jonas had cornered him in a third floor alcove, Jonas in a fuzzy yellow coat with a stand-up collar like a vampire's cape, to ask *You see Ari much?* though seeming to disbelieve his answer—*I don't see Ari at all*—and *The Factory,* Jonas had said, *is always more than what you see.*

Right now he tries not to see a white-suited creature in a wire mask, a headdress of intricate white lights and reflective white paint, human eyes in a machine head: Katya in tonight's costume, her white-lipped smile a sneer—"You know there's a pool going? How long it takes you to get fired?"—Katya merging back into the moving herd of dancers as Lee appears beside him, as sudden and quiet as a spy, to ask, "Are you friends with her, that performer? Outside of Dark Factory?"

He could lie, but why? "She's friends with—a friend of mine. What does that have to do with anything?"

"You're not here to socialize."

And that is true, at least for him: trying to gather information, and the ones onsite every night, the dancers and bartenders and techs, the techs especially, may or must have seen things that they cannot explain away by Y or booze, but if he asked, who would answer? No one here engages with him beyond necessary questions or directions, as if he is a chore inflicted on them by Jonas and Lee, and the ones who were closest to Ari treat him like a traitor, a deliberate usurper, *there's a pool going.* Theoretically he *is* doing Ari's job—and for so much money, he suspects he is not getting paid anything like Ari was, but god all the money—while Ari lives in Mila's old flat, and how surpassingly strange is that? as if they have somehow swapped realities. . . . Yet Ari is the reason he is here at the Factory at all, Ari is responsible, in some chaotic way, for everything that happened, Ari like a human distortion field, strange attractor—But he could never explain that, all that, any of that, to any of the people here; only Ari would understand.

And through this night, as he roams the floor, watching, making notes, he finds himself wishing—surprised by the wish and the truth behind it, startled by its force—that Ari *was* here, that he could turn to Ari and say *Did you see that?* even if the answer was a laugh.

Finally the machine noise that signals closing rattles through the building, and he heads to the performers' lounge, hunching on a wire chair to collate this night's dogged tally of realities on the back of a flyer he found behind one of the bars, XCITEMENT wsg LOST IN THE STARS; these notes he titled on his first furious night, *Fuck the Factory.* He writes as fast as he can before Lee arrives with her clipboard, his pen making tiny exclamatory holes in the flyer's back, while the lounge begins to fill with moving bodies, with chatter and laughter and complaint, the ting of phones, the cooler lid banging open and closed, life happening all around him as he sits bent over the paper, a lone determined island of concentration, as if no one can see him, as if he might not really be there at all.

###

"I heard you were working here," the skinny guy looking Ari up and down, one elbow on the narrow wooden bar, as Ari readjusts yet again the white bar towel tucked at his waistband, no matter what he does it drags or bunches, how do real servers manage it? and "I am," he says, "but Dreamtime's not actually open yet. So—"

"You don't remember me at all, do you?"

"I have a terrible memory for faces," a pleasant lie, who is this guy? no one he worked with, definitely no one he fucked—then noting the oversized and over-stickered bag, recalling the bench outside Jonas's office, and "Come to the Bomb tonight," the DJ says with an unfriendly smile, tossing swag on the bar, a cheap red lighter, red and black ace of clubs stickers, DJ AMAZIN ACE. "Maybe I'll put you on the door."

And as the DJ struts out, "Who's that?" says Floria, the younger sister of Beatriz, just as striking as Beatriz though with a smooth-shaven head, and "Just a guy," Ari dropping the towel in annoyed defeat. "A guy I didn't hire, once."

"Those stickers are gross. Listen, Peggi wants us, staff meeting," the staff being Floria the server, storklike bartender John, and Ari the hands-on helper; though Ari, everyone understands, has a greater role here, Ari is the guru to Peggi's dream.

Peggi had been stunned by his unannounced arrival—*Hi, I'm Ari Regon, Deborah sent me*—Peggi with her headful of ringlets and wrists full of bracelets, Peggi who had earnestly shared her philosophy, her urge to nurture the frantic world and feed it dreams. And he had surveyed this odd little spot, this storefront so far afield of his usual arena that it is, had to be, what he was looking for: like the Blue Balloon, Skidmore and the Factory, now Dreamtime and his own seeking have met, meshed, and this launch will somehow be his testing ground for those human seams. And *You coming here this way, out of the blue,* Peggi had said, as if she had heard his thoughts, *this is why I believe in miracles.*

That gloating DJ is just a blip in the stream of reactions, of dismay and confusion over his new gig, of questions he never answered beyond a smile until ***It must be about something***, the message from Meghan at Your Eyeballs, ***maybe you can tell me what that is?*** But his own message in return—***looking 4 it***—had been so truthful he nearly hit delete, then amended a big-eyed wink, then smiled himself at Meghan's answer, ***When you find it we'll all know.***

And this time Skelly had not messaged but called, peering out from some black-walled meeting room like a wary cave explorer, a beard and a Rocks Off ball cap: *Ari, brother, what is up with you?* so *Beta,* he had said, taking a can of white wine and a seat at that toylike bar, angling his phone to give the best view possible of the space. *I'm in beta.*

In what, a café? What do you call that, artistic license?

You could call it that.

Reason I called, you know the industry's hitting some walls, molecular experience, that buzzword for user-shaped content, everyone is going molecular now. *So Junket's thinking small.*

How small?

That's proprietary. But, leaning closer to the screen, that chinline beard so precise it might have been trimmed with a laser, *I could tell you everything if you'd just sign on. We could even talk about preglobal, that's unofficial but you totally deserve it—*

—as Peggi bustled by with her arms full of drapes, those night-dark silks dragging on the floor, nighttime, dream time, he has been having trouble sleeping again, even in the flat's quiet bedroom, why? And *I'm here now,* he had shrugged to Skelly, who had shrugged back: *If you change your mind—Remember, the world moves fast.*

And that is truth, the world moves faster all the time, and Junket is much bigger than the Factory, thinking small, they would want him for that—They. He. Which world is his? Skelly's results-based gaze-at ratio, or Peggi's yards of silk? Or is it all the same? because Peggi too is chasing the molecules, thinking small . . . And his own headshake, something here he is not yet understanding, the problem not of scale or even skill, what is it? is it him? Even the Blue Balloon Ari could have strolled in and had ten good ideas in ten minutes, but now—

—as he follows Floria into the cluttered backroom, to perch on some unopened cases of Cool Cups amid piles of off-white batting and rolls of shining paper, across from a large and incongruous horned mask. John hands around tasting cups of "Cloud Soda. At first I was going for cloudberries and osmanthus tea, completely ethereal. But to make it more universal, I tried club soda and lime, and rubbed the rim with a jalapeño. Jalapeños are hollow, clouds are hollow," everyone sipping, Floria gives it a thumbs up, and "Ari," Peggi watching him over her cup, "what do you think? And have you thought any more about the soft open date, is it too soon, or—Ari?"

"Sorry, I was checking out that guy," pointing to the mask. "Who's he supposed to be?"

"Pan. Or Cernunnos, or Dionysus. The figure represents ecstasy, fertility, male potency—"

"Horny," Floria's rolling eyes. "Figures."

"An artist friend made it for a decoration, but I didn't think it really suited the idea of Dreamtime. What does it say to you, Ari?"

—but he does not answer, memory's spark of the false and gorgeous horned man, LOVE ME TENDER MOTHERFUCKER, then "I'm going to smoke for a second," feeling them all watching as he hops down from the boxes, props open the delivery door—

—and into the alley with its clammy bricks and soaked piles of recycled cardboard, an exhaust fan blowing from the nail salon next door, faint benzene reek so he keeps walking, down to where the alley meets the street's concrete tributary: if he looks left, that street joins the larger, more bustling avenue, if he looks right he sees the red timer lights of the tracks, and further up the swollen black rags of clouds massing and scudding in the unstable sky. Where is Skelly now, in those clouds, on a plane? Where is Jonas? does Jonas know that process file is missing? those notes and ideas and conclusions that now seem so much beside the point, any point, as to make him wonder why he took it in the first place.

And where—back to the wall, lighting up, feeling the smoke fill him—where is Karl? recalling a time near the end of their time together, a chilly, rainy afternoon just like this one, trying to persuade Karl to go see some dance performance, *They're from Miami, they're sexy, you'll like them,* as Karl paused to adjust his coat, collar turned just so, then *Why are you looking at me that way?* Karl had asked. And at Ari's truthful answer—*Because you look amazing*—Karl had smiled, a rare smile of such weary sympathy that Ari had smiled back at once, and *You,* Karl's arm around his neck, an open embrace, another rarity. *You are such a dreamer, Ari. You need to wake up.*

You can dream while you're awake.

It's still just a dream.

—as a fresh raw breeze hits his face, and he closes his eyes, presses his forehead into the bricks' rough reality, because no matter where Karl is or ever will be, they will never see each other again even if they do: that dream is over, has been over, Karl knew it first but now he knows it too. And pushing off from the wall, eyes open again, his murmur to no one, "Love me tender, motherfucker—"

—and "Ari?" someone calling from the far sidewalk, a man's voice: shorter hair now, the wild curls half-sheared, but the same slim grace, the same deep brown eyes, the DJ from Dusseldorf under an ocean blue umbrella. "Ari, is that you?"

"Hey—Hey, hi! I don't know your name—"

"Felix."

"Felix, hey," feeling himself flush, warmth in his face, his chest. "You're in town? You're playing?"

"I'm taking a break, staying with my friend Mikel, he's got a place on Elisabeth Street. Nothing fancy, but it's nice, right next to a bakery—"

"Elisabeth Street? off the K line? It's got an alley kitchen?"

"Yeah. You know the area?" as the rain starts to fall again, and Ari starts to smile, for Felix, for the alley, for sheer coincidence, he points back to the doorway's framing light and "I do," he says. "Want to get a drink?"

Bonus Content: Felix

we don't know what it's doing and we don't know what it wants

The competing smells of Zilla gin and hair product and faint hopeful sweat, and *Got to love these fireball martinis!* Bobo too loud and right in his ear, almost a year and Bobo was still hoping to date him, fuck him, something, Bobo glommed onto him as soon as he walked into the club for Didi's set; Bobo was Didi's brother, she called him Bobby. *You want a martini, Fefe?*

"Fefe," jesus. *No, no thanks.*

Want to dance?

Maybe later.

As Bobo wandered off, momentarily defeated, he rubbed lightly at his shoulder, his new tattoo: black-spotted foxglove flowers with a twist of barbed wire, from a print he had seen in a restaurant uptown; the flowers' beauty had struck him, stayed with him until he finally looked it up, the photographer was called Edward Steichen, he had looked up Edward Steichen too. And right after his very first gig here, without even a shower or sleep, he had gone straight to Mystic Ink with that foxglove image, and said *I want this:* as a marker, a celebration of the milestone, an indelible symbol of growth.

continued on page 088

continued from page 087

Though Mrs. Gutiérrez had tried hard to argue him out of it, not the ink but the decks, she had insisted that *You belong at the piano and nowhere else. Not playing at people's parties, or in some bar—*

It's still music, Mrs. G.

I don't say it isn't! But would Glenn Gould have been a DJ? Would Mendelssohn?

Some people say God is a DJ, which had riled Mrs. G. even more, she was a hardcore Catholic, she had a tabletop shrine to St. Cecelia in the practice room, the red votive candles always lit, a time-curled little notecard taped beside it, *We bring our small gifts to the tall altar.* And *You have a gift,* she had said, with the frown that brought lines to her forehead, the frown that meant she meant business. *We don't choose our gifts, Felix, they choose us.*

Yet if that were really true, then all his daily practice, his lessons with Mrs. G., the high school competitions, would finally have been rewarded, he would have been at the conservatory now; he had even played the Poulenc, his Poulenc, for the audition, so certain that he would win. But instead of the full ride scholarship, he had earned only an honorable mention—there were seven other honorable mentions—more than a disappointment, it was a judgment, he had failed. He told Mrs. G he would always respect her and the work they had done together, bought her a giant new blessings candle, and that was the last lesson of all.

But his downtime playtime with a bedroom set-up, with Ableton and Mixta—and it was playtime, those beats, that discovery and easy flow—got him gigs right away, at parties, yes, then at the Zipper, where it was all bag check sex and poppers and dirt cheap coke, and Franky Lee's where the line for the lavs got so bad people would piss into empty glasses, and afterhours at Kinky's and members-only Metropolitan, and rough underground Stardust where every night saw at least one tussle and half the people were strapped; and then onto the bill at BeatsFest, just a neighborhood festival but it was a very big neighborhood and his set had filled the street.

Then Didi brought him in with her at House of Hello, where

the booker and the patrons were notoriously picky, but they had danced for him, almost all of them had danced, even the rich girl; Didi told him that that girl was super stinking rich but she seemed like a regular girl, a fun girl, she had come right up to him after his set and said her name was *Genie, like the lamp. And you are fucking magical.*

So Mrs. G. was right at least about the gift of it, both the gifts: the piano gave him subtlety and precision, the beats gave him thunder and velocity, and both showed him that he was a musician, he was meant to play, he had a real place in the world . . . Over his bed he hung a lamp that looked like a globe, and sometimes he would lie back and consider its glow, and promise himself that he would leave that bedroom and that block, would go everywhere, play everywhere; and in that world, someday, one day, he would fall in love.

He knew that he would know love when it came: not only would it be more than pickups and blowjobs and guys circling him the way they always had, of course it would be more than that, infinitely better, deeper, enough to pledge himself to, to say *This man is mine*. But when that man arrived, however he finally arrived, he would *know*, the way he knew that the beats were for him, and the piano, and the foxglove flowers—though the piano had cast him out, and foxglove could be dangerous, foxglove could stop your heart or rev it till it faltered, yet that was love too, he was ready for that; he was so ready.

But no love tonight at House of Hello, so instead of a fireball martini he ordered a green apple shooter, stood alone to sip it and wait for Didi's set, until *Hey, looking tasty,* a different voice in his ear, a glossy, stocky guy in a QuikFix t-shirt and pinstriped Grigori vest, definitely Grigori, and a gleaming steel K-Sex watch. *What you drinking? I'm Rai,* Raimundo Silva, who was a big deal at Culture Bodega, who knew all the agents and bookers, who said *Felix Perez, yeah, heard you're really up and coming!* then bought shooters for them both.

And as Didi's set began, Raimundo Silva grabbed his hand with

continued on page 090

continued from page 089

a sure and greedy grip, towing him out to the floor to dance a little, then shout in his ear, *Come on out to the smoking patio!* for what, a smoke? an interview? a DJ job? a blowjob? But it would not be that way for him, never that way, he would get whatever he got with his beats, not his ass or who he knew or who knew him, his gift would take him wherever there was to go. So he only smiled at Raimundo Silva, and kept on dancing, gazing up at the club's gridded ceiling as if he could see right through it to the stars.

08

Haphazardly browsing the aisles of a FastPharm, where are the toothpaste tabs? Ari is distracted, looking mainly at his phone, another video of Felix Perez: Felix in yellow aviator shades working loping beats for a woozy crowd, black barricades and hard blue skies; then another in some nearly lightless bunker club, the audio distorted, a sudden close-up of those eyes, that smile . . . After their sodas were done, he and Felix had lingered alone in that cramped back room, while he explained that *I wanted to try out some new things, new ideas,* though Felix had not asked, Felix the only one who had not asked. *That's how I got here, to Peggi.*

That Peggi's got sharp eyes, I watched her watching you. And that mask, how wild is that mask! as for Ari the sudden mental flash of Felix masked, horned head tipped to the sky, where is that from? while Felix talked about his own last gig, a private birthday bash at some high-end wurst joint, for *Wulf from Wafflesauce, you know him, right?* And Ari's nod in return had a certain longing, not for Wulf the producer or his pedestrian Wafflesauce events, but for that knowing, that ceaseless and energized circuit, the way things happen among masses of people, the strange human magic of crowd dynamics. *Not my normal venue either, but there are lots of places to do the work—a wursthaus, a café . . . But you won't be working here long,* not at all a question and *No,* he had agreed, surprised. *I don't think I will.*

Then I'd better come back when you're open, with that smile, and a quick social hug, was that all it was? and Felix out the door then, his umbrella left wet behind.

Now Ari thumbs up yet another video, watching until a random message disrupts his concentration, an interview ask that he half-reads, then deletes—then sees a man at the end of the aisle, and "Hey," he calls, holding up a garish purple box with an even more garish hypermasculine silhouette. "Super Pleasure Pak, want to split it? You can have all the Shegasms."

And Max's startled blink—"No thanks—" Max who looks less haggard but more driven, a Big Market grocery sack hung from one arm, his Factory tag hanging from one of the ratty denim jacket snaps, motorcycle boots that look stiff and new. "I don't really have a sex life right now, I'm here to buy band-aids."

"Do you still eat?"

Crossing the block through veering, hurrying bodies and umbrellas, over the flooded curb's litter armada, they enter together the busy, steamy Not Dog: vegan coney dogs and onion rings and fries, clear bulbs of bubble tea, coffee in blue tin cups and "I'll buy," Max says, as they slide their cafeteria trays onto a crayon yellow table, beside three chattering teenagers in blue and gold school uniforms, St. Anselm's Academy. "It's Factory money anyway."

"Factory money, right." Friends on the floor keep sending him pictures, rude and mocking, the tag is Moon Man: Max standing stranded at the edge of the ramp, or hunkered behind a laddered rack of shot glasses, or goggling at a group of groping patrons, Max in his tiara and rumpled buttondown like a boy abandoned at the circus, Max in the belly of the beast. And as something buzzes in Max's sack, "You have a real phone too? Wow, you're really buying into this, it's amazing what you'll do not to work with me."

"It's not mine, they made me take it. And you're right—I mean, to work with you," seeing that Ari has changed, as if some slickness has been roughened, some smoothness breached, like a carapace, or a seedpod. "Listen. Hypocognition, you know what that is?"

Taking one of Max's fries, crunchy with salt and dusted with fennel, delicious. "You know I don't."

"Hypocognition is the inability to recognize something that we can't understand, if we can't see it we can't say it. But I'm starting to see what's going on with the Factory, it's not a commercial construct, it's—"

"Save it for someone who works there," taking another fry, seeing that Max's nametag has no department specified, so what does he do every night, besides wander around looking lost? "I'm at Dreamtime now."

"Dream time," the words repeated as if they are foreign to him, to anyone. "That's your new job? Doing what?"

"Here," pointedly ignoring the question, reaching backhand into his bag to pull out the stained brown folder, Jonas's folder, "take this. Read it, don't read it, whatever, just stick it back on Jonas's desk when you're done—Hey," as Max takes the folder, one shirtsleeve riding up to show a stylized black cat, mouth squared in a roar. "I'm thinking of getting a tattoo, where'd you get that done?"

"Erik the Red. He's got a studio in the squat, Eastfield squat—Look, I was coming to bring you this," extracting from that grocery sack a creased sheaf of, what is it, band flyers? LOST IN THE STARS but on the back Ari sees a sloping torrent of text, underlined and circled, *Fuck the Factory* and when Ari raises an eyebrow, unmoving: "It's notes. Notes I wrote for—"

"Notes? Is *that* why—Jesus, Max, you hate the Factory, you love the Factory, you're at the Factory, just enjoy it! Maybe it'll cure you of your hypochondria—"

"—Hypocognition!" so loud that the teenagers glance their way and snicker, Ari goes on: "And just so you know, Lee thinks you're a spy. My spy."

"A spy?"

"Jonas does too. Does Jonas ever talk to you?"

"He asked me once if I saw you much—How can Jonas think I'm a spy? He's the one who wanted to hire me—"

"*I'm* the one who wanted to hire you," for insight, an eye to see things like the seams, but his instinct must have malfunctioned, nothing here but fluky, flaky Max wandering his own head the way he wanders the Factory floor, moon man lost in the stars, so "I'm not reading this," pushing the papers back across the table, pushing the tray away, "it's your job to fuck the Factory now. Thanks for lunch," taking one last fry, up and out while Max watches through the steam-smeared windows, face half-hidden by the yellow Not Dog sign, a winking dog in a chef's hat—

—as Ari wades his way onto the dripping platform and the already stifling train, a train that almost immediately after departing slows and stops for what feels like a small eternity, some unidentified electrical outage or disruption, nothing to do but sit and sweat until finally it starts again, a stop-and-go crawl all the way to the next station—

—where he escapes to the street, the wind fluttering the puddles and the last clinging leaves, walking fast through the slowing rain, still annoyed by Max, more than annoyed, who does Max think he is? running off, then reappearing with an armful of notes, as if Ari would even read them, even gives a flying fuck about the Factory now . . . Turning down Elisabeth Street, passing Peter's Pita, he thinks again of Felix, when will Felix play again, why is Felix not playing here? and realizing as he turns the corner that what he bought at the pharma was the Pleasure Pak, not the toothpaste tabs—

—and spotting at his stoop a wink of mustard yellow, the winking Not Dog dog, a takeaway bag tied prominent and tight to the railing against the wet. He stares at that bag, at the recycling bin just beside the steps, at the bag again, then with a hard sigh through his teeth—"Oh fuck you, Moon Man"—bends and frees and carries the bag inside.

###

Two maintenance workers cruise by in a rubber-wheeled cart, one singing a spoofing song, the other laughing at the lyrics—"You want, what I got! But I'm not! Jodie at the door, no no no—" both ignoring Max as he heads the opposite way, keeping one eye open for Jonas, though it is hard to imagine Jonas being in the building this early, and another for Lee, who might sleep here for all he knows, in some fully-equipped surveillance sarcophagus, *Lee thinks you're a spy, you came back here for a reason, didn't you?*

In his satchel is Jonas's folder: the meticulous behavioral studies and highlighted conclusions that went on to create Dark Factory, *this petri dish* for sure but what is cultured here, and meant to grow? All these process notes note only that: process, never intent, nothing to even indicate that Jonas has any greater purpose beyond "pulling the triggers," for what? to make enough money so the doors stay open, the research pool stays full? And in those pages' margins—he has read them all—are sketches, of a cube, a trail of stars, two eyes open and closed, so are those symbolic comments, or a right-brain drawing exercise, or random doodles, or what?

And where in these notes is Ari, *my number one guy on the floor?* Why had Ari wanted them, taken them, tried to show him? and now has lost all interest? Ari who seems to have lost all interest in him, too. But when Ari reads *his* notes—He had wanted to explain that those notes are rough and barely organized, but what if Ari is reading them as a finished piece? or as satire, making fun? *You hate the Factory, you love the Factory*—And *I'm the one who wanted to hire you,* what does *that* mean? does Ari think he is a traitor now, too? Yet no matter what, Ari has to read those notes, Ari has to see—

—and stopping now before Jonas's office, its dark glass walls like closed eyes, a new poster posted, silver words and silver clouds, OVERTIME, what is that about? Inside is only silence and the same fossilized mess, so he drops the folder, pivots to go—But should he put it back where Ari had found it? under one of those avalanche piles? any one, just lift and cram and—

—footsteps, measured and coming closer, he freezes like a felon but the footsteps pass and a machine starts up, a low vacuum drone. Reaching again, his elbow rattles some unseen metal tchotchke, a flat box of t-shirts starts to slant, he grabs to right it—

—as the lights go on, bluish-white, inescapable and "You?" Jonas says, Jonas in a tailored black shirt and old-fashioned tie, patterned with skulls, rows and rows of skulls, doom's happy chorus. "What are you doing? Give me that," snatching then examining the folder, to gently clap it shut, and "Max," with a smile, the happiest smile Max has ever seen from Jonas, happier even than the skulls, "it's time to talk about what you're really doing here. Sit down."

"I—"

"And don't lie."

"I'm not going to lie," sinking slowly to the edge of the room's only chair, a leather recliner, its upholstery sagging like a strong body gone to seed. "I'm here to make notes—"

"Take notes, you mean. You know it's unbelievably juvenile, Ari using you this way. Not to mention inefficient, I mean, look at you."

"I'm not a—"

"Shut up," still smiling. "Here's what's going to happen: you're going to keep this file, and you're going to tell Ari that whatever else he needs to do whatever it is he thinks he's doing, he has to ask me for himself. All right? Think you can do that?" holding out the folder, that long insistent arm, what else is there to do but take it—

—as Lee appears at the doorway, Lee also in black like a shadow without its tethering body: "Jonas, Dolores just—What's all this?" in sudden alarm. "Max, what are you—"

"Remember," Jonas ignoring her, "tell Ari," hooking a white jacket from the back of that recliner, out the door again as "He thinks I'm a spy," Max says, "you think so, too," Lee who stares at him, what does she see? Lee who has been at the Factory for how long, how many nights up in the box and down on the floor? so "Don't you wonder," in sudden strange entreaty, "don't you ever wonder what this place is really *for?*"

"You're not a spy," her stare freezing, "you're a Trojan horse. A Trojan pony! Tell Ari I said well done," and in one swift and seething motion she slaps off the overheads and slams the door.

###

The back room is freezing, is the heat in here glitching, another fail? Ari shivers as he strips off the costume pajamas, black silk tuxedo pajamas, a blunt in his teeth, hearing Peggi's weary knock—"Ari?

You're still here?"—one last task before he can call this trainwreck over, he bites down on the blunt so hard it breaks—

—but "Ari, hey," from, oh god, not Peggi but Felix, Felix in a slim blue jacket thready with something silver, even in this light he shines. "I just heard this was on, I got here quick as I could," but "It's over," Ari says, shirt hastily dragged on. "We're closed."

"You—All right," that smile dimmed but not defeated, running one hand through the curls growing back. "Want to get a drink?"

"Maybe," past a pause so long it becomes actively painful, "maybe I should just go home."

"One drink. Mikel told me about this swanky place uptown, it's supposed to have an amazing view," the city as seen from the scratched and bulbous plastic windows of a dome, because the swanky uptown place turns out to be the Onion Room, and "Mikel needs to up his game," Felix says, as they stand at a brass-railed side bar, white wine and Bushmills. "The view is nice, but this is a lot more crushed velvet than I expected."

"Down-market porn star," Ari says, the wine cold on his lips, a cold pain behind his eye, a headache, a brain ache. "Darcy was right."

"Who's Darcy?"

"Jonas Siegler's ex."

And Jonas will, should, piss himself laughing at the stream of Dreamtime posts, the ones Ari has seen so far are not even cruel, just confused, or reeking of the kindness of pity: pretty shots of the twinkling storefront lights and paper stars and cotton clouds, his own close-up determined damage control smile, a crowd of bodies milling before the doors that never even opened, Dreamtime apparently in violation of some arcane zoning code, how had he not verified that first with Peggi? what a basic fucking thing to miss! So the temporary permit was voided on the spot, John in his tasseled nightcap forced to pour away the wine, Floria still trying to serve the Cloud Sodas as the silent white-wigged DJ packed up her gear, Peggi bewildered in her ruffled sky blue nightgown while Ari in the ridiculous pajamas darted between the implacable Hospitality officer and the stranded guests—industry friends come to support his new venture, curious Factory power users, even Deborah was there—still trying, struggling to make everything work, nothing had worked . . . Now he bites back a yawn—almost no sleep, even Peggi had finally gone home but he had stayed onsite, rehanging the stars and rearranging the barstools, how many ways can ten stools be arranged? molecular experience, what a joke! and "At least," his glass set down empty, "this place is functional. That puts it one up on Dreamtime."

"So what happened tonight? Who was your DJ?"

"Suzie IQ," generic hushcore, not his first choice even with his budget, Felix's eyebrows go up, stay up, and "Next time," Felix says, "call me."

"If there is a next time."

"Shows go south. It happens."

"This is different."

"Different how?" and when Ari does not answer, "Ari, come on. Was that place really your dream?" another question that surprises, not a question at all, he looks at Felix and Felix looks at him, until "Do you," Felix asks, his smile returning, "still have my umbrella?"

Leaving the Onion Room for the train, packed with revelers making the noisy nighttime rounds so they stand and sway, their bodies in motion together, then walk side by side, not talking, somehow not needing to, to the flat where "This is a nice view, too," Felix jokes, peering out that kitchen window at his own darkened window across the way. "I see a woman in here, sometimes, your flatmate I guess . . . Do you ever see me?"

Ari does not answer, turning instead for his room, the umbrella unearthed from a rumpled pile of clean laundry and "Wow," Felix following, pointing to the old globe lamp. "I have that exact same lamp at my place in Queens."

"New York, you mean?" The room feels different with Felix in it, smaller, more intimate; Ari's gaze stays on the globe. "I thought you were in Dusseldorf."

"I was, I was booked there for a little," bending to browse at the bookcase, the photo books that Deborah has stacked up to take away. "But I was ready to move on . . . Oh, hey, Steichen! You like him? I love his moon on the pond picture, this one," leaning close to show the photo, doubled trees reflected in still water; Ari feels his breath and Felix's in tandem, a strange and somehow beautiful thing, Ari's heart feels foreign in his chest, a feeling he cannot name, does not want to name, cannot stop feeling and "I was looking," Ari staring down at the photograph, "for tattoo ideas—"

And Felix shrugs off the silvery jacket, slides his shirt from one shoulder—"More Steichen"—flowers inked there in subtle blacks, their cupped curves and spots and "Foxglove, from another one of his pictures. But somebody said I should have gotten lilies."

"Lilies?"

"Lilies are nocturnal, they release their deepest scents after midnight. The ultimate club flowers," smiling, inviting Ari's smile, Ari's hand rising to touch the foxglove tattoo, to slowly rub his thumb against that warm bare skin, to turn his face to Felix who turns to him, their kiss as natural as breathing, as flowers blooming, they are kissing still as Ari pushes one-handed at the door, creating a world of two—

—that is enough and more than enough, more sweetness even than pleasure though the pleasure is acute, long hard thighs and arching back, perfect ass and that soft greedy mouth, the taste of Bushmills and clean sweat, the subtle scent of vetiver; then Felix drowsing, hair mussed and damp, one arm warm across his chest—

—and waking on the gray cusp of dawn, blinking and thirsty, a second tumbler of water carried back from the silent kitchen as in a rustle of sheets Felix rouses, eyes half-open and "Thanks," his smile, taking the offered glass as Ari slips back into bed, into a sleep so deep that the window's spreading uncurtained sun, the sidewalk traffic and slow-braking delivery trucks, Deborah's morning movements through the hallway, cannot disturb or even reach him, they are only foam on the seas of his dreams.

###

Deborah grinds beans for coffee, a dark sharp aroma—"Want some?"—and Ari at the table yawns and smiles and nods: Up most of the night again last night with Felix, this time in Felix's room much like his own, small and square and already furnished, Felix is even more transient than he is but Felix's space feels more settled, as if a real person actually lives there: Striker headphones and olive green DJ bag, striped scarves hung from a flea market mirror, a little traveling apothecary of vitamins and cold sprays and helpful lotions, a pair of vintage jewel-toned juice glasses beside the bottle of Bushmills; and Felix in the bed with its lumpy hummocked mattress, the lamplight throwing shadows from his body onto the blue-striped sheets. They had talked for hours, warm together in those sheets, the moon bright and gone at the window, Mikel coming home, opening doors, running water, leaving again, and *I came here,* Felix said, *when I stopped playing—*

You're done playing?

No, I'm not done, if I'm done I'm dead. But at that birthday party—I told you, Wulf's party—it was like I was looking at my life from the outside, like it was a room, this lit-up little room. And inside people were dancing and partying, but then they'd quit, they'd go and new people would come, then they'd go and I'd still be there, playing.

Like an elevator operator.

Right, exactly. So I left—left the box, the circuit, the clubs, word-of-mouth Überlauf and manic D-Lux/D-Lite, deliberately grotty Thanx 4 Nothing, the ugly and impressive Temple Club where the bouncers all wear Grigori suits—although *I've never played Paris, Marseille but not Paris. And I've never been to LA. Want to go to LA?*

And do what? It's too hot there—

What about Iceland? joking, half-joking, setting the bottle aside and *Are you still stressed about Dreamtime?* then when Ari had not answered *The first time I saw you,* Felix said, *at Dark Factory—*

You were at the Factory? When?

With Mikel and his ex once, I wanted to check out the DJs. And

I saw you—I thought you looked like, like a forest king, what's the one with the horns? a stag, right. Like this creature in its element, the way you moved, you owned it, all I could think was I have to play for him someday . . . Ari, there's so much we could do together, I want to do things with you—

We just did.

Yeah, we did, with a kiss, that mouth so soft and so demanding. *But I want to make you dance.*

Now Deborah pours full a travel mug, bags a raisin brioche, and "I'm seeing Peggi after work," she says, "for a drink. It's too bad about what happened, can't she use that place at all anymore?"

"Last I heard it's on hiatus," an unhappy echo of Jonas, *unpaid hiatus*, and *That Hospitality goon,* he had said to Peggi, the two of them at Dreamtime in the sad late afternoon light, still-filled Cool Cups and slowly spinning stars, one Floria feather stuck to the bar. *Did he say who called it in, who made the complaint? I know some people at Hospitality, I could try to find out* but *That doesn't matter,* Peggi had said, without accusation or blame, arms crossed tight as if to hold herself together. *If Dreamtime isn't working even with you, it's not going to work.*

Don't say that. I thought you believed in miracles—

Oh, I do. If you could help me now—to take down and bag the curtains, box up the wine and mixes, John knew a gray-market bartender who could take them off her hands. *And you take this,* offering the mask, that horned backroom deity potent and strong: he deserved no god, had done nothing for Peggi or for Dreamtime, but *He belongs to you,* she had insisted, so to please her he took the mask, balanced now on the bookcase in his room, wise blind eyes staring at the door—

—and as Deborah leaves "Tell Peggi I said hi," Ari says, then fills the sink, squirts the lemony soap, stacks and rinses and glances across the alley, what could he and Felix do together, if they could? What is he going to do? Pump bottle in hand, he swabs the counters next, his mind not elsewhere but so intensely present that the vinegar fall of the droplets, the plump blue sponge, the varied green of the window plants all seem to be parts of a puzzle that displays itself patiently, frustratingly, waiting for him to put its pieces together, like assembling a show, an event, a party; maybe all life is a party, is it a dance party, a surprise party—

—and lifting one of the plant pots to brush away some minuscule dead leaves, he finds behind an even tinier spider's web, its inhabitant busy with those white intricacies, one strand to another to another, like Max at the Factory, *if we can't see it we can't say it* . . . He plucks the leaves but leaves the web, then searches out the untouched Not Dog bag, to sit again at the table with the last of the coffee and a pencil, and page through, and page through, and begin to read.

###

Already the squat's drafty communal kitchen is full: the guerrilla coders, the hair braiders, the people who deal in mostly stolen racing bikes, the indeterminate squatters, Max's coder neighbor with the other coders beside the hasty, tacked-up poster, TENANTS MEETING BLDG SALE, as Max stands near the door, only half-listening, brooding about his notes: Ari has never answered him, has Ari read them? has Ari even looked at them—

—as Oskar the landlord stands beside the peeling laminate counter, its empty bottles and crushed-up takeaway bags like the remnants of some retreating army, and "You still have plenty of time," Oskar says, tugging one strap of his baggy denim coveralls. "To make arrangements."

"'Make arrangements' means move out," calls one of the braiders. "What if we want to stay?"

"There's a buyout. Decent money," from another voice, a young woman's voice from the midst of the crowd: thick glossy brown hair chopped to her chin, a mint green hoodie with a laughing cartoon face, KACTUS KWEEN, and "You from that Lady thing?" calls Zelly the biker. "Gentrifying bitch—"

"He's the one who sold your building," the young woman unfazed, pointing at Oskar who says, "Everybody just, let's just calm down? And maybe you step out," pointedly to the young woman, who shrugs and cuts straight through the crowd, tossing a brash look back as the voices rise again, a look directly, invitingly at Max—

—and in the quiet hallway, "Where's a good place," she asks him, "to get coffee?"

"There's coffee in there."

"I can't go back in there, nobody likes me in there," and Max almost smiles, at the sheer jaunty confidence of her tone, so "The Dregs," he says. "It's right down the street, red door, you can't miss it."

"Show me. My treat," one hand out, a small warm hand, a thick gold ring circling one thumb. "Marfa Carpenter."

Out into a burst of sunlight, the sky a cold and endless blue, they pass the windowless liquor store, the wurst shop blasting Roadkillers, the bare defiant sidewalk tree tinseled ironically for the holidays, to the Dregs, its walls spackled with tear-off ads and defunct band flyers and dozens of overlapping tags, the booth scarred with old cigarette burns, their knees almost touching beneath the table. And "I write culture profiles," she says, muting her buzzing phone in the hoodie's kangaroo pocket. "For *Blog Out*, mostly. I'm covering what Glenda Vitale's doing here—Glenda Vitale," to his mystified shrug. "The Lady of the Lake lady? the one who bought your building? Are you one of those arty types who don't plug into the real world?"

"No, but—What exactly is Lady of the Lake?" so she gives him a working précis: swimmable tanks with relatable Y mermaids, one-on-one lily pad encounters, an entertainment reality experience meant to soothe and enrich and "I know about those," he says, "I used to make them. Not to soothe," shrugging, "but."

"What do you do now?"

"I work at Dark Factory."

"Yeah? I've heard a lot about that place," checking her phone, thumbing a message, then "Let's go," tugging up the drooping hood, it makes her look younger, like a teenager out for a lark, or to burn something down. "We can talk on the way."

"On the way to where?"

"Dark Factory."

Bemused, as if he has inadvertently stepped onto an invisible moving walkway, her walkway: "You don't need to get back to the meeting?"

"I got what I needed," and as if quoting "'The tenants' meeting was well-attended, if combative, with gentrification being their main concern.' I always get stuff."

In the droning warmth of the bus, between a dozing old hipster in a scrolling ballcap and two sullen, squabbling girls—"You lie all the time, you liar!"—Marfa Carpenter starts up a rapid string of questions, how does interactive art happen in this city, what are the pitfalls, who runs the cliques? that Max answers by using his own shows as examples, the techniques and disasters he knows best, until they leave the bus at the stop just outside CHEAP BREAKFAST, the sidewalk smokers, the lingering smell of burned toast and "I really appreciate this," Marfa says, "all this backstory. You're super knowledgeable, Max."

"I'm glad. I mean I'm glad to help. Left here, on Neuberg—"

—where a knot of tourists in wrap hats and parkas surround a City Ramblers guide, all pointing their phones at the Factory façade and signage, the black doors and interlocking gear-shaped handles, and "Big budget," Marfa says, taking her own photos, not the way a tourist would, swift and professional. "So what do you do here?"

"I'm—a paid observer," but because that sounds too much like nothing, and because Ari still has not answered him, he tells Marfa about his notes: not why he is making them, but everything he sees, talking to Marfa is somehow very easy, she makes it easy, she listens closely, she is a writer after all. And "They sound intense," she says. "Can I read them?"

"Right now Ari's got them."

"You mean Ari Regon? You're friends with him?"

"'Friends,' not really."

"He was king baller here, wasn't he? What happened?" but let someone else tell her that story, everyone at the Factory has heard about Dreamtime's failure, Lee had made a point of pointing it out:

Poor Ari couldn't even pull the right permit, his little show closed on opening night. It's a shame to see someone fall so very far, so very fast, though to him it had all made a kind of sideways sense, Ari had never belonged there, could not have belonged there, it was only dream time—

—as Marfa's phone goes, the thumping drum intro to "Shorty's Here," *Shorty breaks the peace peace peace!* and "Gotta jump," she says, "but we definitely need to talk more. Hit me on MePage—No? OK, hit me here," phone pointed at him, waving as she goes and he watches, the way he might watch a skyrocket rise and arc and disappear in a shower of flammable sparks—

—as Ari and Felix head into the Eastfield squat, its streetside doors flanked by two men in shapeless sheepskin jackets, stiff new-looking respirators hung around their necks, are they security? Inside, the walls are gaff taped with overlapping and contradictory posters, some half-ripped or angrily defaced, LADY OF THE LAKE with big blue eyes in bluer water, TENANTS MEETING BLDG SALE, SAVE THE SQUAT!!! The service elevator does not respond beyond a series of distant groans, so they find the stairs, more posters posted in the cold concrete stairwell, the wet odor of fresh wheatpaste, and "What are you going to get?" Felix asks as they climb. "The eyes?"

"I don't know." Making sketches on Max's notes as he read, he used to do that during Jonas's lectures, he has that drawing with him now: one eye open and one closed, but put it where? between his shoulders? on his forearm? neither as elegant a placement as Felix's own, those tattoos so organic to that perfect skin. "I'm not even sure I want one. Where'd you get yours done?"

"One in Brooklyn and one in D-dorf," holding the stairwell door, a sign beside it crusted with decades of rust, a faded white cartoon finger pointing at a menacing yellow HAZARD. "The foxglove was for my first real booking. The dandelions were for the first time I was booked out of the States. Milestones," with a certain smile. "I've been thinking about getting another one."

But at the tattoo studio Erik the Red is not inside or expected, because "Erik just moved to Detroit," says a young woman in a white djellaba, gold wire-rimmed glasses and a dark forest of braids. "I worked with him, I'm Lily."

"Lilies," Felix says, nudging Ari.

"Which one of you wants the ink? Or is it both? I do couples' work, too," Felix smiling again as Ari does not, Ari pulling from his pocket that folded flyer: "I had an idea. Can you work with just ideas?"

As Lily examines his sketch, Ari watches Felix examine the clipped cluster of old school flash art, his head tilted in a way that casts his face in deepening shadow, the glass block window shows the day is already half-gone. They had meant to get an earlier start, but the quick playful sex turned into an hour in bed, then two, Felix up on one elbow, Ari lying beside to touch that second tattoo, exploratory fingers just above Felix's heart, his heartbeat quick and strong and *Flowers,* Ari's half-questioning smile, *more flowers?* and *Dandelions,* Felix said, *you look at them and think, if I was going to make this plant, design it, this isn't the way I would do it, little random parachute things on the wind. But dandelions always come back.*

Then "Did you write this?" Lily asks, "is it poetry?" one pink-nailed finger underlining the words, "Curiosa felicitas," but Ari shakes his head: those lines, those notes, Max's notes had startled him, not the abrasive term paper he expected, instead an intricate list of all the things Max sees at the Factory, night after night after night, things that he himself has seen a thousand times a thousand, but the way Max sees them—What Max seems to be asking, or saying, is that all these things are somehow part of some other reality, and what the fuck can that mean? besides being proof that Max is extremely high presence, Max should not be working at a place like the Factory, should not even go to places like the Factory, how did Max manage to make his shows? or play games? How does Max manage to walk down the street—

"What language is it? Italian?"

"I don't know. Felix, do you—"

“Listen,” Felix says, voice flat, one hand up, and when they listen they hear: voices, not on this floor but from somewhere inside the building, growing louder as a door slams, another door, something heavy falls, someone in passing bellows “Save the squat!” and “Oh shit,” Lily rising in alarm. “They said this might happen today. You guys need to go,” at the door now, an anxious hallway peek. “Stay away from the freight elevator, there’s back stairs down by the weed people—Seriously you need to *go*—”

—Ari sliding off the stool, Felix winding his scarf and tucking the ends tight, Lily audibly locking that door behind them, one lock, two, and “Jesus,” Ari turning toward the commotion, more shouting, an irregular metal thumping, the unmistakable sound of breaking glass. “What the fuck’s—”

“This way,” Felix towing him down the hall, past a rusted door marked WHEELS & DEALS, a slowly spinning bike rim mounted above, the next room with no door at all, just mounds of shrouded shadowed junk like disassembled monsters, then LEAFY GREENS and a skunky smell, Felix balked by the dogleg turn, “Stairs, where’s the fucking—Here,” a metal door painted the same sour shade as the wall, no signage, no handrail, no one in that stairwell until there is, a boy with a boom mic and balaclava charging past them, hitting the crashbar on the ground floor door as “Whatever happens,” Felix’s arm locking through Ari’s, protective and firm, “don’t let go—”

—and they exit into a maelstrom, the stench and smoke of burning rubber, excited curses and chants, “Save the squat! Save the squat!” a window smashing in a blast of glass as the sheepskin guards, respirators on, block the front doors, and a woman in a cherry red moto helmet, face shielded, swings her bat again, at them? but Felix dodges, not away but somehow under the arc of her swing so she misses, staggers, falls back into the surging crowd—

—while Felix keeps angling Ari toward the building, getting the bricks to their backs, then into a cautious crabwise walk, a faster walk, a sprint down the block past a rubbled lot, a coffeehouse, a shiny silver tree, a wurst joint where Felix swerves them inside, pushing Ari gently onto the one stool open at the counter, below plastic holly and green cardboard reindeer and "You're really good," Ari says, breathing hard, "in a riot."

"I used to play some pretty fucked up clubs," Felix shaking his head, tugging free his scarf. "Once at Stardust a guy pulled a gun on me in the middle of my set."

A cable worker in an egg-yellow vest hurriedly orders, "Würstchen special," glancing down the counter at them, "make it a takeaway," as a cappie van speeds toward the squat, its sirens painfully loud. A server with gold hoop earrings the size of dinner plates skips the music from Melted Elves to Rookie Bitch, turns it up to rival the siren, and "What did you do?" Ari asks, his hand finding Felix's, squeezing it tight. "When the guy pulled the gun on you?"

"Saw God, I guess," Felix says, squeezing back. "Kept on playing."

###

Report to me now, Lee's message an hour before shift call, Max arriving with gloveless fingers aching, still light outside but suddenly very cold, the temperature has been plunging all day. A line of dancers, techs, and staff stand restless outside the performers' lounge, where Lee taps rapid on her clipboard, Lee in a stiff-looking gray jacket like a military uniform, informing the tech sitting opposite that "HR will have your separation packet. Effective tomorrow—"

"Tomorrow?" the tech up from his chair so fast it tips backward and falls. "Boom, just like that? Who's going to work for you people? Techs talk, you know—"

"Max," Lee not looking at him, one pointing finger, "the box. Jonas wants you," igniting a groundswell anger from that waiting line—

"So he's safe, but we get the shaft? Yeah, that's fair—"

"If Ari was still here—"

"Nice work, Moon Man!"

—and Max feels himself flush, is that what they call him here? Moon Man, Meat Man, Mad Max, Spacecase—

—and in the box a determinedly jovial Jonas is holding forth in yet another new shirt design, OVERTIME above the silver cloud, COMING SOON its shadow below: "Dark Factory's not capital-C corporate, but our trains run pretty much on time—Right, Max? Deirdre, Dolores, this is Max," as two women rise from the consoles' litter of empty coffee cans and licorice wrappers and discarded cable twists: dishwater blonde and black ruby lipstick, vintage leather jacket and tailored linen shirt, identical calm smiles, are they new techs? and "We're looking forward to working with you," the tailored one, Dolores, says, as blonde Deirdre agrees with a nod.

And "HR will have some stuff for you," Jonas says, "in my office, wait for me there. Max, you stay," but Jonas stands staring out the long window for a long minute, that view so panoramic yet so contained, Jonas a literal overseer, but over what? a world, a toy, a trophy? What does Jonas want to see, a self-replacing legion of customers? Ari, walking up those stairs? The silver cloud on the t-shirt reflects a flashing console light, a splash of green, a splash of green, like a dying pond, like old cold algae, *overtime* backwards is *time over.*

And finally "Those two," Jonas turning, bending to the cooler, scooping out a can, "the D Team, you've heard of them? No? Doesn't matter, Ari has," and then a rattling cascade of jargon, all Max can really grasp is that somehow the D Team will compress, or weaponize, the Factory's features into an exclusive and expensive pleasure box to be installed on the roof, where "The view will be totally internal, the D Team has that covered, do they ever. Overtime is going to change everything here," then Jonas pauses, waiting, for what? applause?

Instead Max points to the window, the unseen line below: "Is that why you're letting all those people go? Who's going to do their jobs?"

"Are you trying to do mine?" crushing the can to flip it dripping to the bin, it hits the lip then tips inside. "Did you tell Ari what I told you?" and when Max shakes his head, "I knew you wouldn't," with the air of a general prepared for every move on the battlefield. "But you'll tell him about this. Go on, go—"

—back down to the shadowed floor, the main bar with its jittering lights like jarred and struggling fireflies, as the Factory devolves into some empty gold key penthouse, another world modded to death before his eyes. And suddenly Max is so immensely tired of everything, of this place, of waiting for Ari, Ari gone now from Dreamtime into what, no time? is it time to give up on Ari? why make more notes that Ari will not read?

And a slam, deliberate from behind the bar, the bartender in her black bandanna aims a hard unfriendly stare his way, and "What?" he says, staring back, tired of the hostility too. "What do you want."

"Nothing from you, Moon Man."

"That's not my name," pulling out his phone, *a real phone now, you're really buying into this,* but not anymore: Let Jonas carry his own inciting intel, he will talk to Ari, will do it right now, will demand to have back those unread, unwanted, unusable, irreplaceable notes, will let Ari go, and let the Factory go fuck itself.

###

Snow falls like glitter in the dying white sunlight, as Ari walks he sees no one, not baggers, not taggers, alone in the cold at the paper mill, no one knows where he is and he is trying to be nowhere, phone off and thinking nothing, letting his mind float—

—but his thoughts keep circling back to Felix: yesterday he and Felix had wandered through the crowded riverwalk market, its bankside trees lit and ribboned for the holidays, stopping at Urban Bourbon where Felix downed a shot, then frowned at an incoming call: *Just a second,* pacing away, shoulders up, distressed? pissed off? until finally, loud, *I said I'd think about it!* then immediately ending the call. And *I'll tell you later,* Felix said to him, but said nothing more, not on the rest of their walk, not in bed, not when he said goodnight and headed back across the alley alone . . . News important enough to withhold, what was it, who could agitate Felix that way? *I was ready to move on,* so is Felix leaving, heading back to New York, to someone who demands him back? Or is it a new gig, Ibiza, LA, Basel, *if I'm done playing I'm dead*—But why should Felix tell him everything, or anything? what are they to each other? *There's so much we could do together, was that really your dream?* How does Felix understand him so well?

Because Felix is right about Dreamtime: though he is sorry for the way it ended he is not sorry to be gone, the Factory is on his mind now, Max's strange notes have brought it all back. He has even considered asking Felix to go there with him, imagine Felix on that dancefloor—

—but what is he going to do about that, or about anything? Keep hanging out in Deborah's flat? keep hanging onto Max's hazardous notes? keep making nothing? Why is he even here, wandering this empty place? and "*Fuck,*" aloud and lighting up a blunt, his eyes slitted against a sudden rush of wind across that emptiness, a blast of grit—

—and "Hey," someone calls, a very young man, a teenager, approaching with a friend, two friends, middle class bangers in puffy red Heyday jackets and thick-soled trainers. "Got another one of those? Got some to sell?"

"No. Sorry."

"We're not narcs," the leader smiling, stepping closer as the other two snicker. "Far from it! We just want some shit, we know people here sell—"

"Not me." There is no one else around, nothing but the silence and the snow. "You want Meyer, he hangs out in there," pointing to the larger building, it seems for a moment that might work—the two sidekicks turn, but the first keeps staring and smiling, the first wants more than just smoke: making a grab for the blunt, then the empty canvas bag at Ari's shoulder and "Fuck off," Ari snaps, stepping back. "I don't have anything."

"Then why are you here?" asks the smiler, making another grab, now Ari sees the wide eyes are all pupil, this kid is already junked so "Walk away," Ari says to him, stepping back again, stepping on a fist-sized chunk of concrete, hoping this will not come to anything like that, when was the last time he got in any kind of fight? beyond scuffles in a club, the bouncers always there before shit can get too real and "I said," harder, "walk away—"

—and the smiler is on him, slapping open-handed at his chest, aiming for his face, Ari shoving back, older, taller, stronger—"Fuck *off!*"—but now all three are on him, mauling at his bag, his jacket, now the smiler has something in his hand, something that strikes Ari in the back, a blow that somehow weirdly calms him, something bad has happened but things will not get worse as "Oh shit," cries the smallest of the trio, "oh shit, Benny!" and as Benny the smiler turns on his lieutenant Ari punches him in the side of the head, hard enough to hurt his knuckles, hard enough for Benny to sag and let go—

—then he is moving, the second of the three still hanging onto his arm, tearing off his jacket as Ari elbows back, half-running, really running, not cold but warm all over, sweating, his body feels wet—

—and inside that larger building, crouching beside a pile of pallets and split cabling, shivering now, shivering hard, listening hard but hearing nothing until "Hey," from behind, he scrambles to his feet, "hey, you OK?" a man and a woman in bundled layers of coats, it takes a second to recognize the bagger couple from before, and "Need help?" the man says in his mild voice. "You got jumped, shitheads jumped you?"

"Some kids," he says; his voice sounds odd.

"You're bleeding," the woman pulling out a taped-up phone. "Sit down, I'll call for a wagon—"

"A what? Is it bad?"

"Just sit down," she says.

And in the long minutes between her call and the arrival of the ambulance—"They always drive slow, to get here"—the man hunts out his jacket lying in the snow, ripped through the back but otherwise intact, even his phone is intact, even the blunts are intact so he gives them to the man and woman, and when they hear the sirens approaching "Come on," the woman says. "We'll walk you—"

—out into the light again, the fading light and the cold, unbearably cold, he is shaking so violently he can barely stand upright, his knees are buckling but the snow is still falling, silvery white, incredibly beautiful in the unseen sun, and "It's beautiful," he says to the paramedics, as they pull at his shirt, pull out the long blue padded stretcher—"All right, sir. Up here now, all right—" and he lies sideways, head turned and blinking into the sky, he can feel the snow falling onto his face, his open eyes, the pain is coming on now, the world is rushing by and he is rushing with it, so fast and so cold, so beautiful.

###

"Patients' exit," says the discharge nurse, "is that way," pointing where the arrow points, down the mint green hospital hallway. Max says nothing, only stares at Ari, his forehead in hard furrows, and "I'm Marfa Carpenter," says the woman beside Max, small and formidable in hoodie and boots, a quick measuring gaze. "I'll be your chauffeur today—"

—as Ari leads them down that hall and through the lobby's milling knot of anxious visitors and med techs and waiting wheelchairs, out to the car park where the air on his face, in his lungs, is cold and fresh after the night's antiseptic reek, the smell of blood and bleach and latex; it hurts to breathe, he breathes deeply, coughs, winces, breathes in again, climbs into a sea green sport sedan that looks nothing like anything Max would be involved with, neither does Marfa Carpenter, so who is she to Max?

But right now he has other things to consider, he has a zip pouch of pain pills and antibiotics and skin compresses, and a belongings bag with his silent phone and mutilated jacket, ruined in the fray with those little shits, little junked-out Benny who had shanked him with a screwdriver, according to the ER doctor: *They carry tools, not knives, in case they're stopped and searched. Your coat took the brunt of it, Mr. Regon, you're very lucky,* just pain and sutures, a slash not a puncture, no organ damage, nothing that will last beyond a scar. *Do you remember much of what happened?* and he had nodded, did they think he had bricked his head along with his phone? He remembers everything.

Now the car's windows show him the moving world, nothing so fast as yesterday, he shivers in his shirt until "Here," Max leaning back with a hoodie, brand-new and branded Lady of the Lake, big blue eyes on either side of the zipper; he can see in Max's eyes that Max wants to say more, wants to talk, wants it a lot but will not, why? Because of Marfa Carpenter? who drives like a wannabe racer, braking too hard, cutting off a bus that blares its displeasure, barking "Which way, left or right?" and "Left," he and Max answer in tandem: she gives them a look, makes a quick and queasy swerve around a slowing Hopper, another hard brake at the curb, then "You look a little pale," she says to Ari, "you have somebody to give you a hand? Or we can stay a minute, no problem."

"I'm all right alone," feeling suddenly awful as he says it, he shivers again, he climbs the stoop as the car zooms off. Inside the silent flat, he sheds the hoodie, checks his useless phone, then finds a bottle of Gerolsteiner to swallow two of the antibiotics, one of the pain pills, he hates pain pills, what he really needs is a blunt, what he needs—

—and knocking, Felix knocking, Felix looking startled to see Ari move so slowly to the door, and "I waited for you till ten thirty, why didn't you—Oh jesus," seeing in one stunned glance the bloodstained shirt, the pills, the cloudy hospital bag. "Ari, what *happened?*"

Trying to joke, "I saw God," but at the look in Felix's eyes his own eyes fill, a hot and sudden moisture and "It's all right, I'm all right," arms open to hold and be held, to feel Felix's breath against his skin, and "It's OK," Felix says, he can feel Felix's heart hammer. "Baby it's OK, I'm here."

###

The Factory phone beeps Max's shift reminder, a sound almost lost in the rumble of a hi-lo, this cold old squat busy with new noises: this morning he woke to the high whine of a winch, as the last of a trio of deep oblong tanks was tugged and maneuvered into place on the main floor; next will be the fluid fill, Marfa has informed him, its manufactured buoyancy somewhere between salt water and zero G, then the Y mermaids, the "mers," the real unreal ladies of the lake. The tenant floors are all but empty, his coder neighbor is gone, Zelly is selling off his stock of bikes, the squat has not been saved, though the Lady of the Lake repurposing looks less like a Factory-level makeover, or takeover, and more like an industrial spa; another spa. Mila was right, he should have moved.

Now "Hey Max," Marfa calling from the kitchen, still a kitchen but already morphing into a meeting room, a workspace, "want a dinner bagelwich? If I can open this stupid thing?" so he steps in to brace the sandwich box that she saws with a blue plastic knife. Marfa barely comes up to his shoulder, she is almost tiny compared to Mila, yet Marfa never seems small . . . But why should he think of Mila in connection with Marfa? there is no connection. And as the box finally yields, "Hummus and peppers," she asks, "or hummus and garlic?"

"Peppers. Thanks," taking the freighted bagel, its wrapping spotty with grease. "And thanks for all the hospital stuff, too."

"De nada."

"No, I owe you one." In the gust of shock after the cappies called—Did he have any information about the assault on Ari Regon? his number was on the victim's phone just beforehand, was he certain he did not have any information?—he had messaged Ari, called, called again, no response, no response, but Marfa had seen his alarm, and *I'll find him,* Marfa had said, and she had: located the correct hospital, offered Glenda's car, offered to drive, *You can see for yourself what's going on.*

And now she shrugs, though he sees she is pleased. "How's Ari doing, now?"

"I don't know."

"That paper mill place is bad news. Why was he out there all alone?"

"I don't know that either."

"Here's an easy one," with half a smile. "Are you ever going to let me read your notes? I really need your perspective, that insider's perspective, for my piece—"

And because he does owe her one, because he cannot show her notes he still does not have, "You want some real insider's intel?" he says, reaching to extract from his satchel the battered brown folder, Jonas has never asked him for it, Jonas thinks Ari has it anyway. "Take a look at this."

She flips swift through the pages, back to front, then more slowly, eyes narrowed in a look he has not seen from her before, a look he cannot parse. "Whose are these?"

"Jonas Siegler's."

"Jonas Siegler? The guy who—Seriously? Max, how did—*Seriously?*"

"Oh, that garlic smells good," from a woman entering, very tall and blonde in a leaf green loden jacket and incongruous glitter earmuffs, nodding to the sandwich box, offering her hand to Max. "I'm Glenda Vitale. From Lady of the Lake."

"I'm Max. I live here."

"Yes, I know. Marfa's told me all about you," about him? what is there to tell? He looks to Marfa but she is avid over the folder, seems not even to notice that Glenda Vitale is in the room, Glenda Vitale who says, "I hope we can talk shop sometime, Max, I understand you've made some very intriguing environments. Bitter Lake, isn't that the name?" and what would Teresa say if she saw this build-out and this budget? Teresa who had tried her best, *Bitter Lake could really work,* he was the one who had shut it down, *her site but my piece.* So by way of apology, though Teresa will never know, "I had help," he says. "Teresa Capua, she's the one you should talk to."

In his room again, he readies for tonight—his last shift at the Factory, his contract unrenewed by absent Lee—thinking again of Ari in that mortal green hospital corridor, Ari bewildered, no not bewildered, abstracted, in his ruined shirt like some hardcore *vérité* costume, the word made bloody flesh. He has messaged Ari three times since that day, but Ari has not responded, Ari is still done with him, Ari will never read his notes, he takes up his phone again—

You still have my notes?

yeh & ur hoodie

Startled by the instant answer, he takes a long breath. ***When can I get them?***

@ flat now if u want

So out and hurrying for the bus, to stare sightless from the window, the gleaming holiday decorations hung red and gold on more prosperous buildings as the bus rolls through more prosperous streets, while freezing rain scatters like flung glass across the glazing pavement. Trying not to slip in that slick, he strides up the block, apprehensive, excited, telling himself not to be, telling himself to expect nothing more than a handoff on the stoop, at that flat where his heart had been, was it broken? broken open? a place he never wanted to see again—

—but once inside, he can feel that the flat is now another place entirely, the undertone scents of coffee and smoke, the kitchen table crowded with water bottles and red bakery boxes and paperwork folders, though the window plants are still there, and so is the bird calendar, *Birds of the Seasons,* the last bird of the year is a siskin. And Ari is there, wrapped in a gray cable sweater to his fingertips: "I was going to smoke a minute. Come on out."

The freezing rain has abruptly changed to snow, thick flakes in a hurry to cover the roofs, the streetlights, the alley's bins and draped scooters, and "White Christmas," Ari says, leaning on the porch rail, just past the snow's reach; his back hurts, though the hurt bothers much less than the nearly constant itching, and the incipient scar, a very ugly scar, he sees that every time he uses the compresses. But Felix says it can someday be made part of a magnificent tattoo, *Like a winding vine, or even barbed wire*—Felix so much more distressed by this close call than he is, he has told Felix it was an experience, an experience he never would have chosen but is glad he had, no not glad, what would be the word for it? Max would know. "I hope Santa brings me some weed, I've been extra good this year and I'm extra broke. And it works better than those fucking pills."

Max takes the blunt, its taste like burnt leaves, feeling the lift begin, the infrequent inner ease. "Why does Y always edit out the pain?"

"You want the pain?"

"How can you believe anything that doesn't have it?"

"No edits," hitting the blunt deeply, voluptuously, the purl and seep of the smoke, the soft susurrating exhale. "At that paper mill."

"What happened out there? The cappies said you were assaulted."

"Some kids jumped me with a screwdriver."

"Christ. They stabbed you?"

"Not legally, I guess, but yeah. But I wasn't really scared. I felt—" like an opened seam, lying open on that stretcher, staring all the way into the depths of the sky, all the way into life, not as if that were a special thing, some rare transcendence, but exactly that it was not. "I felt like I didn't need anything. That everything is already here."

Silence between them, a siskin lights on the porch rail, gray and yellow, a small life undaunted by the storm. Finally "Dum vivimus," Max says, "vivamus."

"Curiosa felicitas . . . What does that mean, am I saying it right?"

"No. 'Curiosa felicitas' means 'careful felicity,' like something that seems spontaneous but was really a shit ton of work."

Now the snow falls harder, the siskin is gone, the blunt is done, the smoke dissolved, and as they step back inside "Here," Ari says, "here's your hoodie," hung shapeless and blue on a hook by the door. "The design's not that bad, actually, it's kind of—"

"Fuck the hoodie. My notes—You read them?" and when Ari nods, "Then why didn't you answer me? What did you think?"

"I didn't answer you because I didn't know what to say." *I want to see what you see,* he had thought he had seen that already, thought it twice and thought it wrong, it took the paper mill to open his own eyes all the way: high presence Max not just seeing things but seeing *into* things, is that hypocognition? does it even have a name?

Clara had told him once that no one really knows the way Y works on the brain, the way no one really knows what snow looks like on a stretcher, spiraling down, he could have watched that snow forever. "What I think now is, you're seeing real life like it's Y. So what are you going to do about it?"

"Do?" taking by reflex the folder Ari hands him, ASCENSION in square blue letters below a stylized flying figure, an angel, a messenger, and a jolt to see inside his own handwriting, like seeing his face in a mirror he had not known was there, reading out loud the first line he sees: "'Trust the empire of the senses'—"

—as Ari's face goes blank, a blink, then "Max," his smile, that eureka smile. "Jesus, you did it again."

"Did what?"

"What you just said! Like Dodi's old shows, but with no experience boundaries. The same way you did yours! *That's* how we could do it—"

"Do what," but not a question, knowing that this is what he ran from, what he ran to, *shit to do*—

—as the back door opens on a gust of cold, on Felix in a new white parka, and for Ari the deep inner flash like stars colliding, his whole life falling into place at once, he is falling in love with Felix, has already fallen, and he and Max, oh, *shit to do* as "You ready?" Felix asks, looking from Ari to Max, trying to decipher the context, a testing smile. "Hi, I'm Felix."

"Hey, I'm—Fuck!" as a phone beeps, his Factory phone, a fast stern series of beeps, "that's door, I'm late—Ari, we have to talk," coat and hoodie bundled in one arm, folder jammed under the other, does Max know he is smiling? And "Happy holidays," Felix calls after him, then when the street door slams, "What was that all about?"

"Everything. Will you play for me?"

"Sure," a quizzical smile, then seeing Ari is serious, his smile changing, blooming, "Absolutely! Baby, what's going on?"

"Everything," again, urgent, radiant, his hands on either side of Felix's face, that mouth, those lips that taste of spearmint balm and bergamot tea and Felix's own secret taste, the feel of the cold radiating off the parka, the deep itching pain in his back, he has never been so happy, life has never been so good.

###

Ari wakes alone in a world of white—white light on the ceiling of Felix's room, the window toothed with ice—and rolls over with an enormous yawn, a long delicious stretch, every muscle in his body feels renewed. Last night *It's a lot,* he had said, *I'll tell you everything later,* as he and Felix went off to a champagne tasting at a friend's pop-up jewelry shop, gold trays of bubbling flutes, solar candles and green tinsel moss; then a holiday party upstairs at the bakery, honey stollen and cardamom biscuits and black rum punch, white roses bunched in a Mestemacher tin, and Felix playing the old-fashioned upright piano, Felix a little drunk, caroling in a mash-up of three languages, *Noche de paz, noche de amor,* hanging on his shoulder as they floundered back through the drift and blow of the snow. Felix had slept then, but he lay awake, thinking of this new thing that could be everything, Max's vision mated with what the Empire had always tried to achieve, novelty, community, and all deployed with, amplified by, the Factory's resources, the performers and the techs. And Felix to play, oh Felix to play, *I want to make you dance:* this is what the Factory was made for, what he is made for, this is everything.

Now from the hallway, Felix's quiet voice, "Mikel, hey, don't apologize, you've been great."

"It's just that Andrea is coming," Mikel's anxious rumble. "She's in from Lyon next Tuesday, and she—"

"Not a problem, we're good," and the bedroom door opens, Felix in black track pants and bedhead thatch and "You're awake," Felix says, "finally. You were sleeping so hard," and "Who," Ari yawns again, climbing out of bed, "who's Andrea?"

"Mikel's ex. She's coming to town, she needs a place to stay. But it's perfect timing, really," half-smiling, closely watching Ari's face, is Felix nervous? "Because Blaze called again. My booker—"

"Your booker?"

"—he's really been after me to get back to work. I said I'd think about it," *I told you I'd think about it!* which solves that riverbank call, but why is Felix nervous? "So Mikel saying this now—Everything happens for a reason, right? Because now it's time for your new thing."

"Right. You can put your stuff at my place, I'll talk to Deborah. And we'll get with Max—"

"No, I mean your new thing. In New York."

"New York?" as a whuffing drone starts up outside, a snow thrower, Ari raises his voice above the noise. "No, this will be at the Factory—"

"Why are you yelling? And how can anything be at the Factory, the Factory fired you, remember? And hired Max Caspar—"

"Jonas fired me. And I'm not yelling—"

"—and this place, this fucking place almost killed you—"

"Stop that," feeling the sudden chill of his nakedness, the crawling itch of the scar. "Felix, you said you would play for me. Last night you said—"

"I will. I am! Ari, be for real—the Factory, Dreamtime, you're done with all that, you're bigger than that," as the snow thrower falters and chokes into silence, the room feels smaller, as if it is constricting, as if it will not contain what is about to happen, what is happening here to them? "And you say you want to do everything, OK, good, great! In New York I know a lot of people, a lot of spaces, we could really make things happen—"

"Happen for who?" *You're Ari Regon you're famous, now give us a kiss, want to go to LA* and he says it again, throat tight, his voice a stranger's, he sounds strange even to himself. "Happen for who? Did your booker ask you that, too?"

"What's that supposed to mean?"

But he does not answer, will not answer, standing distant, frozen, heart pounding like a creature trapped under ice, the silence between them hardening until finally Felix turns away, shoulders stiff, facing the blank white window—

—and Ari drags on jeans and a hoodie, a new black hoodie, his holiday gift from Felix, flowering vines stitched in weaving lines, grabs up his blunts and bag, and goes.

###

Max's back is cramping, the space heater barely working, he chews an energy bar chased with cold tea from the Dregs, a second glad and focused day spent in this chilly room: the tablet notebook is nearly full, a student notebook just like the ones he used to buy for Kuntsfarm, those first determined steps down a new path that was, is, this same path, has he been walking in a circle all this time? A perfect circle?

Half the notes are rapid research about *Dodi's old shows,* Dodi Malor and the party world of the Holy Roman Empire, slapstick DIY surrealism and anarchic carnival sex, Ari's name surfacing again and again in those word-of-mouth accounts, as cheerleader, ringleader, emperor. And the other half is his attempt at a theory of vision, *you're big on theory*, in a way Ari was right . . . And if these things he sees—and not only at the Factory, things like bare tree branches that scan like concrete poetry, so close he had to squint to miss the words, or the strange rebus arrangements of urban detritus, cigarette butts and lost single sneakers and crushed-up takeaway bags; or even this cheap smart pen, its blister package promising MAX WRITABILITY—If all these things are somehow not *what* he sees but *how* he sees, how he is, now, then *what are you going to do about it?* And oddly, nearly eerily, as if Ari can hear his thoughts, his phone tings—

meet @ factory in 20

It's closed tonight

i know meet

My contract expired, I don't think I can get us in

meet

—so out into the slippery crunch of snow cleared just enough to make a sidewalk path, half-melted then refrozen into pits and jags, his breath a clean cloud suspended in the cold twilight. And at the performers' entrance, Ari is waiting, shivering in a black hoodie, but looking so wretched, his wattage so dimmed, that Max stares, what the fuck happened between their kitchen moment and this?

Yet expired contract or not, no one has deactivated his tag, the door opens for them: and inside everything is still, like an empty church, or a mind caught between thoughts. And "Someone should be here," Ari says, "there's a funders' event tonight. What's that fucked up smell?"

"It's from the clouds, cloud dispensers for Overtime, they're incompatible with the HVAC. Everybody's coughing," as he coughs. "Wait, what funders' event? How do you—"

"Look," halting below the high cliffs of the storage racks, just before Jonas's office, pointing out in the dimness ahead a quick fugitive figure, long gray coat and flat beige bag, a woman who sees them too but does not slow or stop until "He's brought *you* back?" Lee's scowl at the office door. "Just in time for the Titanic launch? Lucky you."

"No, I'm still fired," considering her, Lee looking smaller somehow, and angrier, and sad, in all the time he has known her he has never seen Lee look sad. "I heard you got fired too. Sorry."

"Heard from who? Your spy?" though Max looks clearly aback that Lee is fired. "And you're not sorry."

"Not really. Are you sorry you drank all that NooJuice?"

"I hope he chokes on it. But you fucked him properly, didn't you."

"I didn't do anything to Jonas."

"Yes you did," insistent, the bag clutched tight. "He's got financial issues, *acute* financial issues—I've seen those numbers, he's losing money, he keeps borrowing, his investors own him. And he has no idea what he's doing with Overtime! But none of that bothers him half so much as losing you."

A silence between them, Max somehow excluded, then "He shouldn't have fired you," Ari says. "You were a shit to everybody here, especially me, but you did your job . . . Is he here right now?"

"Why don't you ask his concierge?" her scowl returning. "Or his overpriced Overtime cows?" past them into the office, her phone's light a searchlight over the piles, stuffing a folder into that duffel, a handful of old Factory swag, one of the desktop burner phones, and as she leaves "Don't try to say I took that," Ari calls after her, while Max reaches to click on the office overheads: "What's going on, she's fired? And what happened to you, you look like shit—"

"Turn those off, there are cameras," in that office, that empty room that held so much of his own life. "What's going on is, I did some brand research. I talked to Jonas—"

—but first he had fled, fled Felix—why he said what he said to Felix is a lunatic mystery, he loves Felix but what can Felix really feel for him? want from him? be for him?—fled the flat and the city on a sluggish SR train all the way to the far suburbs, streets he used to know, to buy a bad espresso at a café that once was a doughnut shop: when he was fifteen, he had met a dark-haired boy there, an ecstatically beautiful boy, they had flirted then kissed then fumbled in the alley behind the bins, the sun throwing their joined shadow against the wall. He recalled his pure astonishment at being touched by, chosen by, someone so beautiful, afterward he had looked everywhere for that boy, asked everyone, but never saw him again . . . And walking then to his family's old apartment building, how many times had he escaped through those doors, relieved to be leaving for the real world? yet nowhere to go except back, his aching head against the scratched train window, phone in hand in case Felix messaged, but Felix never did.

Instead it was Jonas—***Come talk, loft, now***—in the reek of artificial pine, an enormous gilded tree, a picked-over party plate of red and green treats, and Jonas in an Overtime t-shirt with a new silver streak bleached into his hair, Jonas looked the way he looks when things are going wrong. But the same annoyed familiar tone, *Sit down, you look like hammered shit,* so familiar that he had felt a spasm of hope, if he could only make Jonas understand—And as if in confirmation, *Isn't it time*, Jonas had said, *for you to get over whatever your problem is?* as though his leaving had been entirely his own fault. *You belong at the Factory and you know it.*

I do know it. Listen—

But Jonas had not listened, again he had not listened: *Overtime's in overdrive, the build-out's a week ahead of schedule, and there's going to be a private party on New Year's Eve. Remember I told you we needed to do something with the roof?*

I remember.

Overtime's a prototype, it's going to change everything, that's why I got rid of Lee. This needs a totally new mindset, and Lane Durand—

You fired Lee? Who's Lane Durand?

—he's a hotel guy, I need that, that whole hospitality angle. But Lane's all work and no brain, not a brain like yours, anyway. And then the real reason for Jonas's summons, that private party, a funders' come-on event—*No one works a crowd like you*—as his hope flattened to a hard weariness, and when he shook his head Jonas's face changed, not the angry glare but something else, something bleak and worse: *I was ready to give you another chance! Well fuck that. Stay away from the Factory, if I see you on the floor again, it's trespass.*

Then out into the cold, back to the flat, to stand and smoke and chew his thumbnail already chewed to bleeding, checking the unlit kitchen window through one endless day and into another, until he could bear no more darkness. But only Mikel answered his shaky knock, Mikel who told him that Felix is leaving, Felix has a new gig, he should talk to Felix about that trajectory, but *Felix won't answer me*, he had said, and that was that.

And now he stares from the depths of that exile and heartache, as Max stares back in confusion: "Why the fuck would you talk to Jonas? What did he say?"

"He said to stay away the Factory or he'll call the cappies."

And Max's laugh makes Ari finally smile, his first smile in days, and "Listen," Max says, "I made some notes. For you—"

"Can I read them later? We should go."

"Go where?"

"Upstairs."

"And do what?"

"I don't know. Let's go."

Side by side, still no one in sight as they climb the ramp below the enormous new Overtime banner—its logo so dull, like a couples' night wine brand, that even in his misery Ari rolls his eyes—as unseen vents emit one fat puff, then another and another, an acrid half-soapy smell even worse than the Orange episode, and "You think Jonas is on the roof?" Max asks, coughing again. "With the D Team?"

"What the fuck's the D Team?" so Max explains about Deirdre and Dolores, Ari has heard of them, Ari is not impressed: "Deirdre and Dolores are hired guns, they don't develop, they implement. So who's really making this? And who's that—"

—a man heading up the ramp, sandy razor cut and a clipboard, Lee's clipboard, calling up "Are you here for the walk-through?" as the clouds intensify, rolling plumes of smelly white, then "You," the man nearing them, slowing, staring, staring at Ari. "Wait, aren't you—"

—and they simply disappear—

—past an oversized frameless mirror, the access door to a small storage room, Max smothering a laugh at this sleight of hand, Ari leaning against that door to survey the room's contents: a cache of cocktail napkins, *100 Serviettes,* a portable soundbox rig, some warped and discarded tiaras, a box marked *Chapeau de fête de paillettes* and "You think," Ari says, opening that box, "Jonas is really up on the roof?"

"I can go look. What are you going to do?" as Ari extracts a party hat, steeply pointed and glittery pink, to pop it sideways on his head like a renegade unicorn as Max laughs again, coughs again, then "All right," Max turning for the door. "I'll keep you posted—"

—then out, everything still quiet and he is quiet too, cautious and quick as a character in a platformer, up and up to the third floor, past the public areas to end at a line of doors, which one is the roof access? The first is card-locked maintenance storage, the next one is marked ACHTUNG PELIGRO DANGER ELECTRICAL, the next one—

—and every light in sight leaps to full disorienting power, floor lights and bar lights and a warning light directly in his face, its orange strobe like automatic fire—then the lights drop out again, blinded he blinks, blinks, feels a draft of cold air drifting from another, unmarked door—

—that door propped open on a half-built landscape, roughed-in squares with tarped-out walls and a pile of construction detritus, like an abandoned stage set at the end of some unloved world. A loose knot of people stand beside those structures: Dolores in an oversized fur coat with Deirdre in leather, the building manager, another man in a red breakaway vest stenciled CONSTANT POWER, the sandy-haired man from the ramp—and Jonas, coatless and loud and manifestly pissed: "Say that again? I just sent you the second payout, a huge payout by the way, so say that again. Say the panel's fucked—"

"There's nothing wrong with the panel, Mr. Siegler," says the red vest man, measured and annoyed, "it tested out fine three times. The problem is somewhere in the interface. Your building manager says—"

"My building manager can't keep the fucking clouds from falsing!"

And the roof's fresher air is at instant war with those clouds' residue, Max's throat feels full of dryer lint, irresistibly he coughs again—and the sandy-haired man hears, sees, points: "You, who are you? You were down there with Ari Regon—" and Jonas hearing the name turns on Max like a tank turret fixing on its target—

—while below, Ari races down the ramp and across the silent floor, out the door, because on his phone is finally Felix—

Say goodbye

wait where r u

Kitchen window, say goodbye

WAIT WAIT

—slamming out and desperate for a Hopper, there are no Hoppers, he hurls himself onto a train just leaving but that train is balky, after two stops he has to ditch, dashing through curbside puddles ringed sharp with ice, he skids and sprints around a slow-turning pedal truck, past a line of bare black sidewalk trees and a blazing pink phone store, TALK@ME, his phone tings again—Felix? no, Max, ***Shit's going sidewise up here***—a stitch burning in his side, his vision speckled with sparks so he must stop, sagging against a storefront where the windows show a massed arrangement of white flowers, leaves nearly black in the grow lights: and the florist inside pointing to the *Open* sign, her t-shirt reads FELIX—

—and the air of the shop is impossibly lush, moist as an open mouth, as Ari sees that her shirt says FLORA HELIX: he almost laughs, he must look completely crazy, breathless and wet with sweat. And "Those," he says, pointing, "two of those," tangerine orange and wild tropical blue, two long stalks of birds of paradise wrapped in clear crackling paper that he carries like a torch the last of the way—

—to see Felix framed by that window, and "Mikel said you came looking for me," Felix says, angry and arms folded, the beginnings of a patchy beard, wearing a long gray sweater, Ari's left-behind sweater. "Well, here I am. Say goodbye."

"Felix, don't." Ari's hands are shaking so hard the flowers tremble. "Don't go."

"Why shouldn't I? I told you, the first time I saw you I saw a king. But you think I only want to ride you, you think—"

"I don't think that," Felix so true, too good to be true, *people always do what they want to do, I want to do things with you* because Felix is not Karl, not the boy in the alley, never was or could be, so "I'm sorry," Ari's voice trembling too, "and I'll go wherever you want, if you still want me to, if you still want me. But you said you would play for me. So come with me. Right now."

"Now?" startled, more than startled. "I have a gig, my flight's at 8 a.m.," as Ari sees the piled bags, battered black and zippered, the olive green DJ bag, the horned mask from Dreamtime atop it all, and "I lied to your flatmate," Felix flushing, seeing his gaze. "I told her you said I could take it."

And Ari reaches, the flowers an extension of his hand, to Felix's shoulder, the foxglove shoulder, touching Felix like a lover, a consort, everything he feels is in his eyes. "Bring it. Just come with me—"

—carrying the mask and the flowers, the DJ bag, a liter of mineral water from Mikel's fridge, Felix handing that water to Ari as the Hopper arrives, the mask between them on the back seat like some benign and temporary beheading. And Felix half-angry, half-laughing, "What even is this thing?" plucking at Ari's neck, the pink party hat still dangling on its elastic cord.

The Factory as they reach it is lit only by orange emergency lights, the only open entrance the loading dock doors manned by towering Eli the security stalwart, Eli who offers Ari a high five, and "Is this all the light we have?" Ari asks him. "What happened to the power?"

"Whatever they did on the roof blew us dark. Maintenance is still trying to access the aux generators."

"They tried to dry run their funhouse, and kaboom!" Marfa Carpenter popping up like a jack-in-the box, how is Marfa Carpenter here? "That's quite an accessory you have, Ari. Last time I saw you it was a bagful of drugs."

"Where's Max?"

"Inside. Are you—"

"Ready?" he says to Felix, who looks past all puzzlement—"How am I playing anything without power?"—as together they enter that welcoming darkness, Ari leading up to the little storage room where "Here," pointing with Eli's extra flashlight, offering Felix the soundbox rig. "This is battery, right?"

"Jesus, that's, what, a Kaori? I haven't used one of those in forever . . . Battery, yeah, but there's no way to get the volume," to Ari but mainly to himself, gingerly investigating the soundbox as Ari props the light for him, the mask on the floor a watching silhouette, the flowers set beside it like an offering. Then as Felix zips open his DJ bag, Ari says, "I'll go get us a drink—"

—descending in the last of the clouds floating ghost white in the ghost lights, to the first floor bar where hasty candles flicker like fireflies as he roots in the wet backbar funk, until "Hey asshole," a peeved female voice, "get away from my bar," Annelise in her chic black bandanna and ugly Overtime shirt, Annelise who laughs out loud when she sees who it is: "Oh my god! You're back?"

Kissing her cheek: "Got some champagne for me?"

She reaches for a gold label bottle, pours herself a shot of Herradura. "*Salut!* So Jonas finally got smart again, he knows this place is spiraling—What," as Ari shakes his head, "you're not here for Overtime? Then why are you here?"

"To dance," as his phone tings, an answer from Max to his ***where r u***—But no, this is Clara, ***Eli says ur onsite?*** so he detours with the bottle to the box, remembering his last time on these stairs, those first few moments of spiking and certain joy, the same joy rising now—

—and "You picked a funny night to visit," Clara says, running a hand through her already-rumpled flattop; beside her is another tech, a new one, eating veins of red licorice, Cherry Spoolies, from a bag ripped open on the console. "Unless maybe you know what the fuck's going on? Power's still out, the D Team isn't answering, Jonas isn't answering—"

"I don't know where Jonas is. Lee was here, though."

"Lee? I thought Lee was fired?"

"She is."

"Jesus Christ on a cracker—"

"Are we still doing an Overtime run?" the new tech asks, a half-panicky wave toward the windows, a novice swimmer in the murky end of the pool. "What are we supposed to be *doing*?"

"Power's coming back," Ari says to Clara. "Why don't you make something? For yourself?"

And on the ramp again, he can hear it, a commanding heartbeat thump, he sees his own glee as he hurries toward the mirrored door: and Felix with the soundbox, headphones half-on, eyes half-closed and "Hey," Felix says, rapt, "I lost myself a minute . . . I got it working," and "Keep playing," popping the cork, passing Felix the bottle, a kiss of cold bubbles. "Just keep playing—"

—while Max watches Marfa heel-kick a doorstop chunk of gray

detritus—"This should hold—" how did Marfa know he was up here? stranded in the sudden exodus as the power went out, the electrician stoic, the building manager defensive, Dolores questioning Jonas who shouted back, then roared at Max, then deliberately slammed the self-locking door . . . He was not at all sorry to be left alone, to wait for Ari, and gaze at the neighboring buildings, their windows shutting down for the night, lights and no lights and the streets' own lights, palest green on the snow below to turn it temporarily to spring, as far above that manmade cloudscape, the night's true clouds began to clear, the stars arrived. And beyond those stars lies a wider, purer void, past his vision or any vision, let there be light—

—but Marfa is saying something, something about Ari, "—palace revolution, or what? People are super hyped down there, people are really—Max? Max! Be careful—"

—Marfa's small, gloved fingers closing tightly on his arm as he leans over the roof's edge, far over, pointing not up but down, into the street and "Look," he says, to the void, to her, to himself. "People are coming—"

—solo or in pairs or groups, little moving shapes forming a line like a chain linking itself into life, like proteins linking, or is it protons? or both? a chain that grows and converges at the emergency entrance, as he and Marfa stand watching—until he sees a snow-dusted box of tiaras, brand-new tiaras, and breaks open that box to toss them down, one then another and another—

—as the people below miss or catch those gifts from above, enter the darkness curious or bemused or excited—

at Dark Factory its free tonight!?!?!

hey whats @darkfact 21 & over? 17 get in?

Rico said sh*t is poppin

—messaging friends who message other friends, who enter through NOT AN EXIT to roam the floors and explore, Annelise pouring for anyone who steps up because everything is chaos and nothing is working and Jonas is gone and "Ari's here," nodding to another bartender who nods back, sharing cherries from a rolling supply cart, while Alix the dancer arrives with half her troupe, Katya among them—

Ed u got 2 get over here

Davide come to the box, ur going to love this

DF stream's working FINALLY!!!!

look at this stream Genie, look

—cheers rising as the power flares partway on, some lights light and some do not, the graffiti room glows as new tags immediately appear, *be the beauty, ALICE HURRY, dreaming I am dreaming you now.* Y is intermittent but functional, as a third tech, Davide, arrives to frolic in the freedom of that emptiness, long scribbles of purest light that bunch, release, reform, grow again and larger, beside galloping stilt-legged creatures and planets that carom and collide in soundless bright explosions—

Y is bananas, never seen it like this, never seen anything like this

im wearin a top hat drinkin free grey goose lol

Ramp races!!!! GO SABRINA GO

Bring the flowers in the van, all the flowers, park by the load-in

—and a man in a GREENERY 2 GO jacket arrives with wrapped bouquets of asters, purple and gold, fresh and fading, their arrowed petals sticking like skin to the lexan of the ramps, while other people carry other offerings, heart-shaped cookies and fat cupcakes dusted with drugs, dripping snowballs and black feathers that float and spiral in the dark—

—as Alix and her troupe caper on the ramps, stretching, leaping, pursuing the Y creations, inviting the patrons who laugh or freeze or try to dance along, starting a game of ragged tag as the beat rises, crests, rises again—

—and Felix emerges from behind the mirrored door, Felix masked now in silver, the horned man, with Ari beside him, dancing, pink hat dangling, sweat springing, Felix making him dance—

—while that pied piper beat climbs and echoes through the building, to gather other dancers until they finally reach the roof, the door wedged wide and now everyone is dancing, dancing, standing still and dancing in the caterwaul and shout, someone

is singing, someone else joins in, a chorus watched by Max with Marfa at his side, led by Felix in soundbox ecstasy, Felix whose beats are immaculate, calling out, calling to Ari and the dancers and the stars "Again, again, again, again—"

###

Fraktur is quiet, a bubble of dust and old alcohol, fresh cedar cleansant and faint unkillable human grime, light filtering in as the clouds finally lift, this last hour before the dark. Ari sits beneath those skylight windows, black flowered hoodie on against the chill, coffee balanced against his knee, thumbing a message to Meghan at Your Eyeballs; he has not answered any of the other messages, so many—and three in three days from Skelly, ***Saw your beta! Want to talk? Let's talk soon***—but Meghan is different, Meghan is thoughtful, Meghan has waited until today to ask him—

Stuff everywhere about your thing

ikr

Your Flower Man's a top avatar on Beat Buzzer

krazy

What really happened there?

its a lot

—because it *is* a lot, more than a lot, he sees that in image after image after video after post—that weird and priestly Flower Man, the happy writhing writing of the graffiti room, a disembodied head with blinking pink teeth, a woman's face distorted by a scream that might be joy, a swarming confusion of cappie tac lights, bodies slumped in the snow on the street, black flying forms against dawn windows and wet sky, a tumult of dancers, himself among them, and Felix, Felix wild and beautiful in the mask—and in message after message from Factory friends, industry friends, random friends, frenemies, another one just an hour ago from Dodi, ***Alarms keep triggering, roof's a fucking rookery, where does it end DOES it end? A rough beast slouched out of the Factory, no wonder they want to put you in jail hahaha!*** Dodi also shared a newsblog link about some woman's injury lawsuit, a badly broken pelvis and shattered sensibility from falling off a streetlight pole, the news story said she was lucky to be alive. And this morning, just before they slept, Felix showed him a new video of those streetlights, somebody called Bricklayer had recorded them to Saki Usomoto, then "Kid A," then a piano piece Ari did not recognize but Felix did, the lights always seeming to sync to the music no matter what that music was, Bricklayer swearing ***Didn't edit this at all, this is how it is?!?***

The Factory itself is closed, at least officially, the techs and dancers and support staff furloughed or quit, Deirdre and Dolores are rumored to be negotiating out of their contracts, Overtime is over. And Jonas is rabid, is everywhere, on Kickchat and ZPO and Nightlifer and Tickets Please, insisting that the Factory will reopen, that he is suing Ari for noncom and lost revenue and brand infringement, none of those lawsuits seem to be happening yet; but there are definitely cappie charges, trespassing, theft and vandalism, the worst is evading arrest. He asked an old Empire friend, Gershon the lawyer, what to do about that, and Gershon suggested *My partner Margareta, she specializes in entertainment law*—but pay her how? He has no job, and the last-minute plane ticket was steep . . . Jonas had watched it all unspool on the loft's screen, no way he had not, it was everything he ever wanted to see, the Factory making everybody's night; if Jonas had wanted the cappies there sooner he would have called them sooner.

Though Jonas is not at all the reason he had boarded that 8 a.m. flight—*I asked Blaze to get me out of town, this was just the first thing he found*—and as Felix slept across the aisle, exhausted, he had cried into a crumpled beverage napkin, in a kind of confirmation shock: that same paper mill feeling, only exponentially larger, as if the Factory, the building, everything had shifted into a whole new rotation, like the carnival ride when the floor drops out and all that holds a spinning body to the wall is that invincible spin, and he and Felix and Max and everyone on that roof were spinning too.

The last he saw of Max was in that spin, Max staring blind into the sunrise sky, Marfa Carpenter latched like ballast onto his arm. He had messaged Max from the little airport terminal, then the bumpy transit bus, then the sunny brick courtyard at Fraktur as Felix met inside with April, the club's owner, until finally Max responded: a lurching, lagging call from the depths of his squat, background clangs and bangs and Max's eyes wide in some stunned state of post-traumatic pleasure, or alarm, as if Max had had his own screwdriver moment, maybe not as sharp but just as deep: *Ari? Ari! Do you know Krishna?*

No. Max—

The universe in Krishna's mouth—

—that was it, we made it happen—You look junked, are you junked? Are you OK?

No. I mean I'm fine, I just, I haven't slept. Jonas asked me where you were—

Don't talk to Jonas, don't tell him anything—

I told him you were gone. Are you gone? Where are you?

I'm gone. But I'm coming back. And you need to get with Clara.

Who? I don't—I saw—

—but Max abruptly gone then, and Felix back beside him: *We're good here, let's go,* onto another, newer bus, its route winding over and beside greenish canals jammed with commuter boats and pedal skiffs, through streets scuffed and shabby, then polished and touristy, then back to scuff, tagged-up alleys and a bakery tiled in black and white, its logo a hare leaping over a black and white world, for a black espresso and a fat white doughnut. And on the bakery steps, Felix's arm warm around his shoulders, Felix joking, not joking that *Your Kaori, baby, it totally changed my flow! And you were right, you didn't need New York to make things happen.*

I didn't know that was going to happen.

Yes you did . . . I've seen some wild shit at clubs, people just letting go, getting out of themselves, you have too. But never anything like that. And I heard, as Felix's arm tightened in unconscious tension, like a body about to leap, *I heard this—hum. Not noise, not feedback, a hum, I heard it. I played to it! And the dancing, everything, everything that happened, happened inside that hum.*

Knowing the answer before he asked: *Did it stop, after?*

No. If I listen for it, softly, closely watching Ari's face, *it's still there. Does that sound crazy?*

No.

Felix plays at night below these skylights, and Ari dances, and shares hotgrass shots with April, agreeing with April that Felix is amazing, that Felix draws crowds; waiting after each set with a double shot of Bushmill's, to kiss his flushed face, stop on the way home for morning frites and doughnuts and coffee, lie in his arms in their little furnished flat, spooning, sleeping, waking, fucking, talking, watched in calm approval by the horned mask hung above their bed.

And in the borrowed comfort of that bed, at the scratched-up kitchenette table, at the windows, Felix is listening: from his headphones Ari can hear snippets of Sino thrash and Berlin beats, koto and teencore and skronk, solo piano and full orchestral classical, human voices chanting in a stadium, a temple, a church. Sometimes Felix shares what he hears—*This professor, he hears the hum too, he's got this whole aural map*—and sometimes he records: Ari's breathing and Ari's voice, or the streetside laughter and shouted arguments from the bar that everyone calls Corner Bar, or the beep of boats and stutter of scooters, splashing water and glass wind chimes; or sources sounds from other places, wilder places, ocean waves and blizzard snowfall, wind rush, birdsong—*Hear that?* Felix enchanted, *that's a kingfisher, mating!*—and even from space, the moving rustle of satellites, the deep bell of Venus, the cold whistle of Pluto. Last week, as Ari climbed beside him into bed, Felix put one hand to Ari's chest, the other hand to his own, and *It's in us too,* Felix said, *like a vibration, can you hear it?* And yesterday on the bus, leaning back against the seat's worn plastic, Felix asked, *What do you think really happened, that night?*

I don't know what happened.

But what do you think?

I don't think like that.

You brought me there.

I just—I wanted you to play.

And now Meghan is messaging back, a row of question marks, ***Did you find it???*** and his answer a spinning top, endless spiraling black: ***ITS A LOT***

—as footsteps cross the dancefloor, percussive and quick up the steps, Felix in his white parka carrying a Jinki's Kitchen bag, sharing out cartons and napkins and paper packets of sauce: "I got soba, and seaweed salad, a double order, and those chickpea slider things . . . April said she wants to talk. I think she's going to offer me a residency."

"You want to do it?"

"What I want is to figure out the hum. Not 'figure it out,'" his shrug baffled, graceful, intent, "but I know I need to listen more, a lot more. And play. And," leaning over for a kiss, "be with you. But if I do this, what are you going to do, here?"

"Here's as good as anywhere," his own and sharper shrug, rubbing the chopsticks together as if kindling a fire. "I can't go back to all that cappie shit, and Jonas. At least Max is doing all right there—"

"Doing all right doing what?"

"Working with Clara," Clara who was his second post-plane

message—***sending u max he knows what 2 do***—because Clara had her own peak moment, with renegade Davide beside her in the box; Clara has just started her own shop, Fantastic Fantoms, *I had the name picked out already, I've wanted to do this for a long time.* And Max is with her, working with Davide like *Peas in a pod, how did you know? I've never seen Davide click with anyone like this before*. "Clara likes Max. She says he's quirky."

"'Quirky,'" spearing a long green stalk, neatly catching the sauce drip. "Isn't that a synonym for batshit . . . Did I tell you Genie messaged me again? She keeps asking what happened."

"What do you tell her?"

"I tell her to ask you," showing him that newest message, ***u have 2 clue me, u always do!!!*** with a picture of the two of them in some janky DJ booth, Felix with shaggier curls then, black vest over a bare chest, and Genie with electric blue hair and a fishnet bra, her skinny white arms wound around his neck, she looks feral, comic, utterly devoted, they wear the same shades, sleek baby blue with bright red hotspots—

"Are those Persephone? Wow. Not cheap."

"Yeah, she wanted us to match. And money's not a thing for her, her family's huge, big evil real estate gobblers. But Genie's not like them," with real affection, Genie the rebel met on the loose in the clubs, hurling herself into his beats, Genie a friend for years . . . So much of Felix's life he does not know, only pictures and snippets of stories, a high-end friend, a map of clubs, a globe lamp in Queens, will there be time to know it all? why would he think that? And "Genie's fun," Felix says. "Even if she does have issues."

"What issues?"

"Drugs. Rehab. She just got out again, she—" pausing as a door slams below, more footsteps, bootheels, and "That's April," setting aside his chopsticks and carton, leaning over the railing to call, "We're up here—"

—as Ari slurps the last of his soba—good, but not as good as Seaweed Palace—then heads further up, to the very old and iron-latched roofside door. Outside, careful onto the clay-colored tiles, the quaint and dangerous step gables, he leans back to take in the view: the shadowed brick courtyard and unlit FRAKTUR sign, the loitering bikers on the rusted and rickety pedestrian bridge, the empty street with its yellow and black roundabout sign, endlessly circling, like his own brand-new tattoo. Closing his eyes as the sun shifts, its sinking dazzle on his lids, the tiny lines of veins like some internal roadmap, the Blue Balloon Skidmore the Factory Dreamtime Fraktur—

—and "Hey," April's voice, April with those butch brown boots and long girlish curls, April taking the light he offers for her roll-up cigarette. "It's nice out here, the sun really heats up these tiles. Maybe I should put in a smoking balcony?"

He lights a blunt for himself, it tastes like dust. "There's lots you can do on a roof."

"This whole space could be updated. Get some subs in the floor, fix up the courtyard—I worked hard to get it where it is, but things can always get better. Like now, with Felix! He's going to be our first resident—"

"Congratulations," with a smile; he likes April, her crocodile's tenacity and workaholic's joie de vivre, he used to be April, happy in the scramble, what is he now? his mind still dancing, in beta, in exile, a rough beast, *a hustler, you don't really believe,* Karl's old cruel taunt but Karl was wrong because he does believe: in the chaos and the breakage, the soundtrack streetlights and the Flower Man, Felix's hum and Max's vision, he does not understand but he does believe and "It's going to be great," he says. "Everybody is going to love him."

people need a way to be lost

The lobby was blue, glass and light, no clouds at all in the circle of visible sky. Ines's phone trilled, trilled, stopped, trilled, as the elevator opened with a faint atonal tone and *Ms. Hechman-Weir,* from a serious young man in a Hechman blue suit, one of the assistants, she could not immediately recall his name. *Your, uh, visitor is here—*

She can see that for herself. Do you chew her food for her, too?

Genevieve, please. And thank you, you're from HR, aren't you, you're—

Martin Burkowski, with a serious smile. *Did you need anything else, Ms. Hechman-Weir?*

I want a drink, Marty. A Club-Mate—

A what? I can get—

No, she's fine. Genevieve, there's ice water in the meeting lounge. This way—

—Genevieve following, surly and startling in another one of her outfits, rhinestone headphones and artificially torn jeans, a howling clownface t-shirt in screaming orange and ugly blue; Genevieve's hair was blue too, her mouth browned with scabs. Ines felt her own lips turn down, righted her expression, poured from a white dispenser on the credenza, tall glasses for them both, while Genevieve slumped in the blue armchair nearest the door.

I've read your outpatient report.

Oh Jesus, can you ever just cut the shit? I thought I was coming here to sign bank paperwork. Was that a lie?

No. She sipped her water, then opened the folder, the discreet Branwell logo, the reassuring thinness of that report, as if what was wrong was manageable in a minimum of steps. *But first we need to discuss your treatment plan—Genevieve, you have to listen to this whether you want to or not.*

I can hear you fine. Music helps me focus.

Your case manager had encouraging things to say, she believes you're an excellent candidate for total recovery. But the bottom line is—

"The bottom line—"

—you can participate in your recovery and get better, or continue to fight it and get worse. Much worse. A loose thread hung from her jacket sleeve, she nipped it with her nails. *Because your body won't tolerate these repeated detox episodes, and your cardiac function is already impaired—*

You're the one who doesn't tolerate things! Like me. Like my name. Like my life! Up from the chair, arms flung out as if the conference room was too small for her, as if the world was too small; she had always been this way, all those family trips to family properties, New York and Denver and Santiago and Bonn, no matter where they went Genevieve was always restless, sniping, moping, always trying to escape. *Clubbing keeps me alive! All my friends are there, Felix is there—*

A DJ is paid to be there. And the drugs are there too.

Poppers aren't addictive—

Your case manager—

—and Remblex is a drug too! Does that say, pointing to the Branwell folder, *how bad the diarrhea gets? People call it the Remblex runs, the Remblex race—All you see are the nice nurses and the pretty reflection pool, does it say how they make you stand around that pool and chant like a fucking robot, "Let me flow like water, let reality be reality," then hurry up, back to your room before you relapse!*

As Genevieve ranted, Ines stared at the slatted ventilation duct; her temples hurt, her throat was sore, her allergies were very bad this year. She had considered going in person to tour Branwell, but the grounds were full of acacia trees, and there was a serious site emergency in Ottawa that week; instead she had given the case manager her private number, *You can reach me anytime, day or night . . .* Her father had said once in an interview that she was the best property manager in the industry, *There's nothing Ines*

continued on page 142

continued from page 141
can't fix. The week before he died, lean and wasted in the medical recliner, he had said, *Your sister is your call, now.*

And *Your sister,* Cal said, *will drag down anyone who'll let her, remember how she acted at our wedding?* She and Cal had met in Zurich, a cocktail fundraiser at the Dolder Grand, he had never heard of Hechman Properties but *I couldn't stop looking at you,* he told her later. *I thought you looked like Jeanne d'Arc.*

Like someone about to be burned?

Like you could lead an army.

But still she cannot lead Genevieve, ragged, rageful, ungrateful, offered everything she needs to be well but Genevieve would rather take drugs with a grinning party DJ, so many pictures of "Genie" and Felix, Felix, Felix—

So you want me to stop clubbing and do what, start hustling for Hechman? Like you do? I'd rather die.

That's not helpful. Your treatment plan—

Fuck this. I'm out of here—

Sign the treatment plan, Genevieve, or I won't unlock your account.

It's not your money!

It's mine to administer—

You can't—

—but it's your choice.

She drank the rest of her water, flat and cool, as Genevieve swore, threw the pen, slammed out of the lounge and *Ms. Hechman-Weir?* the serious young man cautiously reopening the door. *Are you, uh, do you need anything?*

I need to be an only child, she thought, but that was not true, not what she really wanted; she had tears in her eyes, she blinked, blinked, pinched the bridge of her nose very hard and *My allergies,* she said. *They're out of control today.*

Mine too, the pollen count's terrible right now. Have you tried Ginger Sniff? It's kind of a silly name, but it really works, reaching into his suit coat for an unopened inhaler, sympathetic, energetic Martin Burkowski, he looked to be the same age as Genevieve. *No, take it, please. I want to help.*

09

The Not Dog line inches forward, Max checks his list again—two fennel fries, three dogs, three onion rings, no, four onion rings, Davide just messaged, that message amended with a video of the moon, like a blue plum revolving in the bowl of the sky—

"—your order? Sir? Can you input—"

"What? Oh sorry," tapping the order pad, he feels as if he says that a lot now, not in distraction but its opposite, absorption: because that video moon is the same shade of blue as the nametag the counter clerk wears, and her hair is wound in a complicated crown of braids whose braided pattern is almost exactly repeated in the ad blinking on the counter, the Not Dog dog, whose tail-end waggle uses the same beat pattern as the "Trash Panda" anime theme that Davide likes to blast, *Ho-ly trash, ho-ly panda—*

"—order's ready. Your order—"

"Sorry," again, hurrying to gather then load the bags into his bike's roll-top panniers—that bike bought rehabbed and cheap at Zelly's move-out sale, not a titanium racer or commuter special, just a sturdy black three-speed—and refasten his cycling jacket, skid padding and reflective strips, to merge into the lurch and idle of early afternoon traffic, Hoppers and buses and trucks, beside other and speedier bikes, their riders helmeted or with hair flying, weaving past him as he pedals across town toward what urban purists call the demiburbs, that sparse light industrial area past all but the SR line, still within the city limits but several worlds away from Not Dog, and Dark Factory—

—and the Pegasus Grille, where last week Adam Kaiser had grilled him at a quiet table in the corner, beside painted golden statues of anonymous Greek gods, ice cold retsina and mushroom souvlaki, and Adam's troubled frown, *I heard that you were at Dark Factory the night of the incident. Tell me exactly what you saw.*

At first he had not answered: what he saw? What he sees . . . The day after that rooftop night, after a few hours' ragged sleep, he had started a research journey through the list of things that could cause the brain to trick the mind behind the eyes, psychobiological, psychophysiological—like pareidolia, the insistence on finding patterns where none exist, or apophenia, the assignment of personal meaning to random data—but that research only proved that this sight, insight, came from the outside in, was fed by the Factory's tech, not by the way he used it but by the way it used him: like a self-aware kaleidoscope, *the Factory is always more than what you see,* showing him this vast and intricate map of reality, like hints in a maze, or levels in a game, as real as the sight he uses to guide his bike.

But none of that was any answer he could give to Adam Kaiser, so "*Homo ludens,*" he had said instead. *Your lectures, remember?*

Huizinga, yes. And "Was ist Schön?" But this sounds more like Arnheim's entropy! Do you remember Brecht's Verfremdungeffekt, the play as representation of reality, not reality itself? as Adam folded and refolded his napkin, his gaze like a guide's lost on a familiar path. *Half my students, more than half, believe that what happened at Dark Factory is going to change the whole field, the whole discipline. And they're quitting—*

Quitting your class?

Quitting Kunstfarm! They say they've been misled, they're agitating for tuition refunds, the department admin is blaming me—I need you to come and talk to them.

And he had stared into his piney wine, that tiny wine dark sea on the white linen square—recalling another talk with Adam over another table, *What they're really after subsumes reality,* and his own scornful reply, those students should be schooling him—that stare so prolonged that Adam finally raised his voice, his teacher's voice: *Max? I need you to—*

I heard you. When Quixote fought the windmill, who won?

This isn't a joke! It's potentially very harmful—

Harmful to who?

To the department! And to the students, it's a shared delusion, the longer they hold it the more pernicious it gets—

Adam, listen. If everything partakes, is that the word, partakes of reality, whether it's a created effect or not, literally everything? and if you can see that? Things are going to change for you.

Adam had looked away then, deliberately away from him, with the headshake he used to use in class when badly disappointed, then *You've changed, Max. Changed a great deal in a very short time. Is that Ari Regon's doing, too?*

Marfa too has noticed a change—*You're doing it again, Max, that looking-at-nothing thing*—though Marfa is also different since that night, her warm hand clasping his in the rooftop tumult: now they sleep together, never planned and always at her instigation, always in his dilapidated bed. The first time, he had been startled, then caught up in her confident hunger, their shared heat, but almost immediately, embarrassingly, fell asleep still inside her, to wake to full disconnection and a fresh ache for Mila, her long strong body, her grace, her wide dreamy smile. And whenever he and Marfa are together—more than just rote sex, there is warmth between them, but how much?—he feels that ache, though he tries to ignore it or cover it with talk, asking Marfa questions about her writing, questions that she sometimes answers with an anecdote, or shrugs off, or swats away with a joke: *I don't have "process," Max, I'm not a real writer like you.*

Last night she had stayed all night, also a change to have a body next to his in the bed, the grumbling space heater had failed again but the cold did not seem to bother her, none of his squalor seems to bother her except that bed, *Even a blow-up mattress would be better, even a bagger would toss this thing!* In this early morning's too-bright overhead light—someone, not him, has repaired the fixture, the light makes the room look worse—she pulled on balloon cargo pants and a ferociously orange ModoMaman hoodie, ModoMaman grinning and driving a bulldozer off a cliff, and *I'm trying to get an interview with Jonas Siegler,* she said. *Have you talked to him at all?*

Not since he talked to me—

—in the stunned hush of Ari's morning after, like the hours just after a natural disaster, the cappies heading floor by floor to herd people out: a cappie found him on the roof with Marfa, his arms locked around his knees, the cappie forced her to leave but delivered him to Jonas, why? because he was wearing his Factory tag? And Jonas was dry-eyed and beyond rage, shoulders crucifixion-stiff, nearly vibrating in his vision like a wonky Y effect: *Where's Ari, Max? Tell me, or your ass goes to jail too!*

Ari? as if the answer must be evident, it was evident: Ari last seen dancing, fully on fire and throwing sparks, Ari gone from the roof with Felix as the music spiraled out and the stars disappeared in the sun's sudden rise. He had watched it all, immobile from the cold, not feeling the cold, just eyes in that light, he had had to remind himself to breathe. *Ari's gone.*

You fucking moron, I know that! Wait there, Jonas's one-handed shove to propel him toward the steel bench outside the office, where he had instantly slept, or passed out, to be wakened again by a medical attendant who was also somehow a cappie, who took his vitals, *Your pressure's pretty low, do you feel dizzy?* then took his statement. Marfa urged him to download that statement, so he had—an unfocused repeating ramble, as if he was trying to reach earth with some coded dispatch, a moon man—then shook his head and hit DELETE.

And *Did I tell you I changed the byline?* Marfa watching as he gathered his jeans and yesterday's soiled socks, an antique but clean henley, its BurnOut logo so faded as to be nearly invisible; it always feels odd somehow to be naked with Marfa outside of bed, why is that? *It's MCSq2, for Marfa Carpenter and Max Caspar. Let's grab some breakfast and talk about that.* But he had busied himself dressing, his back to her—*I can't, I have to work*—because he has work to do, writing to do, every day now, with Clara Dix and Davide.

Clara had invited him to meet in a gamers' nameless password-only pub, a place he had not even known existed, hidden beneath a mixed-use retail building, a nutrition shop and a dog groomer. At first he had felt strange there, in that makeshift basement bar with screens looping retro speedruns, then abruptly, supremely at home, as Clara bought a round of chewy black lagers, Clara said *Ari says we need to work together on this new thing you two are dreaming up. I'm down for it.*

Work how?

With Davide, we'll go see him in a bit. He can be intense, but Davide's a bulldog angel. If a thing can be made in Y, Davide will find the way.

And she was right, is right, Davide is intense. At that very first meet, Davide in a baggy band t-shirt splotched with grinning little faces, Böse Kinder, a band Max had never heard of, Davide had leaped from one thought to another like a creature on melting ice floes, from AI philosophy to intercorporaiety to the combat superiority of Sumerian warriors to the history of reality design, Davide was even more knowledgeable on that topic than Adam Kaiser, though Davide's shrug was scornful when Max mentioned Kunstfarm, *I went to Central Saint Martins, whatever, it's all shite. So school me, what's the rubric here? Clara says you and Ari got this party started.*

And he had explained, haltingly, trying to keep that explanation purely conceptual, theoretical—if everything in a landscape was alive and connected, literally everything, what would that look like? feel like? operate like?—until finally Davide interrupted: *Sure, I got it, it's like all the constituent components at once. Like if "Nude Descending a Staircase" was actual, I got it* but *You lost me,* Clara had said, *about five klicks back. Want to write that stuff down?*

So he did, he does; and if Davide can be offensively pedantic about his writing too—*Max, if it's a story, you need rails, like a movie script. Interactive, it's game design. Anything else is a dissertation, you got it?*—still Davide's investment in this work is paramount: whenever he arrives, day or night, whether Clara is there or not, Davide is in the cockpit, that circle of monitors and multiple tablets, tiara and earbeads, fully connected to every reality he inhabits, in this work, their work, their game.

Clara was the one who decided it had to be a game—*Any onsite footprint might activate my noncom, you see the shit Jonas is doing to Ari! With a game, we're in the clear*—and the premise is hers too, an apocalypse scenario on a tropical island, the player exploring that island for supplies to build a craft and escape on the empty seas, or make a livable structure to stay and restart the process of civilization, while meeting other island dwellers, other players, along with a small cast of NPCs. Her proposed avatars are simple, but of such a complex and layered simplicity that they make the games he used to love look like arcade cutouts, Clara is operating at the top of her game, too.

And all of this, the game, Clara and Davide, all comes to him from Ari, Ari who is gone but *I'm coming back,* though Ari seems to be in no hurry, checking in from that club where he roosts, or hides, what is it called? Rupture? Rapture? talking to Clara, consulting and directing and advising. But Ari needs to be here, the way it was in the room with the mirrored door, and on the roof, those flying sparks—

—like the speckling mud that flies past his face as he fantails through the mirroring puddles, bike wheel spinning into bike wheel, pushing the bike and his body as hard as he can, as if he no longer exists as anything but velocity and sight—until a clumsy bump over a pothole, he almost hits a litterbot at the curb, has to brake hard before the building's doors, breathing hard—then catching the faint salty scent from the panniers, recalling there is food to bring inside.

The elevator functions, but he always takes the stairs here, up three flights to FANTASTIC FANTOMS, neat white letters on the off-white door, Clara buzzing him in—"Thanks for the chow run—" to shuck his boots on the black rubber doormat; Davide has a rule about shoes inside, Davide has rules about a lot of things. And "Did you get the extra onion rings?" Davide's hopeful call. "How'd you like that onion moon, it's from a cult in Zagreb where everyone believed the moon was a giant onion. Also a bar called Moon Club. Not the same people, though."

As Max unpacks, noting with a certain cyclist's pride that none of the bags have spilled, Clara makes space in the kitchenette, and Davide sets out green tea and Action sodas on a folding table covered with old stickers for prototype games, a cautionary mosaic of the unfunded and the never-played, Davide calls it the cemetery. It is a quiet meal, three heads bent over three devices, until Davide crows over some news, "Alastair's in dev now at Caprice?" one finger twirling an onion ring, his malice so innocent that Max and Clara share a smile. "He said he was going to make the new *Rector Rising*, but he went all corpy. Big game energy!"

"Not everyone's as dedicated as you are, Davy," Clara says.

"Not everyone's as crazy as I am."

"I didn't say that."

"I did . . . *You're* not like Alastair," pointing that onion-ringed finger at Max, who half-smiles, and shakes his head in agreement, feeling a certain benediction in Davide's judgment. Then "Cool shirt," Davide peering closer. "But that logo's not Y. How'd you get it to do that?"

"Do what?"

"Be there and not there."

"*Trompe l'oeil*," Clara says. "Like everything."

"Everything but us," Davide says, and Clara nods, and after a brief shy hesitation, Max nods, too.

###

"Sto Lat," April says, shouts, into her phone, "Sto *Lat*, Jackie's picking them—Sorry? Can you—Ah lovely," through her teeth, tugging out her earpiece, "signal's gone again. Want a shot?" stepping behind the bar to the giant chrome juicer, its jet engine roar for two hotgrass shots, turgid green vodka cut with lemongrass and eye-watering pink peppercorns: Ari downs his in a shuddering gulp, April swallows, coughs, croaks a laugh, "Keep you alive forever! Keep me going through this weekend at least," leaning on the bar to roll a smoke with her crunchy Chinese tobacco. "Felix is ready, right? He's happy?"

Happy? Yesterday, awake before him, drinking tea and recording beside the half-open window, when Ari rose on an elbow to ask *What do you hear?* Felix had lifted his cup, and *Wind chimes,* with a smile. *The wind. Everything. Wish there was a balcony . . .* To April he says, "He's ready to play," though Felix was surprised almost to insult that April had not consulted Ari on the event's mechanics, *She's got you right here and she didn't even ask?* But April showcasing Felix is another perk, like the residency, that she offers to bind Felix to her club, and if Felix stays, so will he, April knows that; April has never brought up Dark Factory, what happened there, but he knows she knows that too.

Which might be one reason why Silver Landings is so ambitious, a one-day festival with a local DJ pair to open, then the second-tier but still tight Crispie Atoms, then Felix as star and headliner, along with an erotic mentalist, whatever that is, and a dance troupe from Warsaw, and Sto Lat the famous street art duo, Sto Lat in town already to consult on some commission so April had piggybacked onto that, a frugal move to save on travel costs, one he might have made himself. In a producer's reflex he had checked out their portfolio of murals at clubs and mixed-use venues, paintings that filled three-story walls or peered around blind corners, some were fully visible only in the dark or from a drone, but all of them shared the same striking visual confidence, Derek Ferris's confident eye.

Now "Jackie ought to be here any minute," April consulting her phone, so Ari follows her out to smoke below the jagged silken lines of clouds, while a flock of pigeons, white and gray and greenly iridescent, settle to the pavement, then rise again as a scooter growls by, its driver hidden under a red balloon helmet. A muddied white van rounds the corner, April snuffs her smoke—"Here they are—"

Sto Lat, two men, one tall and self-possessed in blue and white digital camo and paint crusted boots, the other red-cheeked and squat as a wrestler in a long-billed logo cap, toting a sagging canvas backpack. April offers her hand to the tall man, as "Greetings," the squat partner says to Ari. "Robbie."

"Hi, I'm Ari Regon."

"The Dark Factory guy?" Derek Ferris turning, hand out, a large and mobile hand, mint green paint faint around the dark knuckles, a rumbling bassline of a voice. "People are talking so much craziness about that place, is it true? Or just craziness?"

"Things can be crazy and true."

Derek Ferris's gaze sharpens, a focus Ari can feel. "You a philosopher?"

"He's the DJ's boyfriend," Jackie says, Jackie the dour house manager in her sad pastel rain slicker, jingling her lanyard keys, that visible badge of authority, Jackie does not like him any better than Lee had, maybe for the same reason. April gives Jackie a quelling look, then "Come on," holding open the door. "Let's go see the courtyard—"

—but Robbie lingers on the dancefloor, peering at the skylights and "Changed a lot in here," he says confidentially to Ari. "Used to be the Pearly Gates, fungus everywhere, you felt like taking a Z-pack just walking through the door! Not that that would have stopped us."

"You guys go everywhere, looks like."

"'Sto lat, sto lat," Robbie trying for the melody, "'may you live a hundred years,' Derek named us that 'cause he wants our stuff to last. Like Herculaneum, heard of that? Oldest tagging in the world, geezers writing 'I got blown here' on some coliseum wall . . . Guess I should go see what we're doing here," with a friendly nod, art's nomad off about his business—

—as Ari returns more slowly to the door and the street, Felix asked as he left *Where are you headed?* and *Get some shit,* he said, which was true, though the shit he bought from Bubbles at the wine shop is overpriced and harsh as wood shavings, but he could have done that later, the truth is he is restless. Ravenous to work, all he can do is direct from a distance, and watch as this new thing begins to grow: last week Clara told him *Davide says "In its shape is its reason," and things are starting to shape up*—Clara industrious and nimble, mining her industry contacts for seed money, finding a workspace, reporting that Max is working hard, although *Not everything he writes is something we can actually use, it's more like, uh, poetry.*

Just let him write.

But from Max himself only silence since their one and only talk, until yesterday morning, very early, who gets up as early as Max besides Max? there in his Lady squat monk's cell, grocery sack on the cot beside him, harsh overhead light and no smile—

Hey, Ari—Wait, are you asleep?

No, I'm up. We just, I just got to bed.

You said before that you were coming back.

I am.

What happens if we finish before you can get onsite? The project's going fast, and it needs you. Clara needs you—

I'm talking to Clara, we talk all the time. But I'm still on the cappie shitlist, remember? And Jonas can pull his noncom anytime—

That stern Max stare: *You need to be here.*

—but he is not there, is here in this aimless afternoon, his phone showing his world's news—rumors of internal turmoil at Junket, Caprice hiring techs for a full rebrand of Anamorphosis, Tenth Wall touting a members-only AI club called Charli Paris—plus a few new articles about him that read as if they were written about a stranger, some far-seeing renegade guru, *Ari Regon Remakes Your Night* and *Panic at the Disco?* as if he had been intentionally deployed, by who? himself? *secret weapon* to shut the Factory down?

Then a new and cryptic message, from Max—***Talk to Marfa***—Marfa Carpenter, why is she always around? at the hospital, on the roof, she had even set up an interview with Felix: that alert and leading tone, he has heard that tone before when a journo has a definite get in mind, so what is Marfa's get? She ended that interview by suggesting Felix and Ari do another one together, as just out of screen range, he shook his head at Felix, firm and final. But here she is again with her own message, video attached, ***hey it's Marfa Carpenter, we really do need to talk***, he deletes it without even looking; what he should do is talk to Max about Marfa, and tell him to watch his back.

The avenue turns and he turns with it, away from the tourist-bait hotels, zinc bars and cozy overpriced cafés, the streetside granite flowerbeds full of greenery rotting in the wet, down to their temporary neighborhood with its chip shop and 24 hour pharma, the queer bar Eluki's where the fashion students all hang out, shaved heads and bubble pipes and long dangling scarves, the wine shop where loitering Bubbles shoots him a wave, Hare Bakery where he stops for a takeaway coffee—

—and "Special today," says the frisky barista with the sculpted blond scruff, tucking into his hand a warm sample of something dark with chocolate and starred with salt. "I made it just for you."

"It looks good."

"So do you," that hand still on his. "If you like it, I can make it a *lot* bigger."

And Ari smiles, acknowledging the flirtation, but his smile is so clearly no thanks that "Your man," the barista sighs, turning to cap the takeaway cup. "He is lucky-lucky."

"I'm lucky," with a different smile, a new kind of pride, *your man* . . . He and Felix have healed from the brief awful grief of their disunion, a long quiet talk in the little flat, hands clasped across the kitchenette table and *We belong together,* Felix said. *We need to trust each other.*

I trust you.

Then trust yourself. I do!

He looked at Felix's hands then, so strong and warm around his own. *You're the one who played.*

Oh you're the one, I keep telling you. And we're meant to make things together, things that last. Trust that, too.

So new tattoos, to mark that bond: for Felix a small stylized

minotaur head just at the base of his spine, *The sacrum,* said the tattoo artist, a bald Parisian who looked like a warrior monk, *this is sacred. And the triskelion,* tapping Ari's wrist, three equals whorls of purest black, *life and death and the afterlife, it's all one dance, hey? This and Mister Minos, here, you fellows must be mystics!* and Felix had laughed then, as if surprised.

Now he carries the bakery bag outside, the clouds parting for a burst of sun, its fleeting heat on his neck and cheek, an impersonal caress that disappears again as he crosses the pedestrian bridge over the canal's steady current, a delivery boat, a bob of businesslike ducks, a floating clump of pink anonymous trash, then down an alley unruly with rainbows and monsters, full moons, penises, eyes, tags in endless conversation, HALT DIE FRESSE and BOUCHE SUCRÉE and $KING$ and IN 2 SIN, to a rusting access door that opens on his second tug. Up to the fourth floor, key in hand, an old-fashioned key for an old-fashioned lock, he hears Felix—

"You know, the mural guys. The artists—"

"No," a high hoarse voice in answer, a woman, "I mean 'sto lat.' What's that?"

And stepping inside, "It's a wish," he says, "a wish to live a hundred years," handing the little wrapped treat to Felix, who takes it with a sweet and claiming smile: "Hey, there you are. Genie, this is Ari—"

—as a young woman rises from the fusty needlepoint loveseat, half-draped in a puffy red blanket, her hair no longer deep blueberry blue but short slick plastic-looking white, whiter even than her skin, her hand moist and very cold even though the flat is warm. And "Too long," Genie says, shaking his hand, shaking her head, rolling big haunted hazel eyes. "A hundred years, that's just too long."

###

The old desktop clock displays a blue 12:00, noon or midnight? has it stopped working, has time stopped? as Max shifts against the chair's bowed arms and spongy headrest, while Davide rocks his own chair back and forth with jaunty cricketlike creaks: "PCI," Davide says, "perturbational complexity index. It's a way to measure consciousness if the subject can't interact with an external environment. Kind of diametric to what Ari was doing, with that whole corpy rat lab thing."

"Jonas Siegler was the one in the lab, Ari never—"

"Put your ears down, Ari's cool. Now! See this?" creaking again, scooting back so Max can lean in, and watch a fantastical aggregate of time lapse growth, fat speckled caps and squiggling stems and ballooning lacy skirts, tendrils snaking and boiling fast as thought across all the screens at once, a subtitle celebrating *The Multicellular Revolution!* as Davide grins, delighted, why? until finally, mystified, "It's mushrooms," Max says.

"It's mycelium! Not plants, not animals, network-based, self-teaching, knowledge-sharing organisms that also remove and transform toxins, and ding ding ding, bonus round, they live pretty much forever. So! If we make Birds of Paradise like mycelium—"

"Make what?"

"The game. What, that's your name," clicking onto another screen to highlight a scan line of Max's narrative, *sky's the limit for the birds of paradise*. "Clara needed something to plug into her prospectus, and this fits, it fits molecularly. So Birds of Paradise is—Ugh, 'New Bitch'?" as Max's phone plays the silly rat-a-tat beat, *new bitch new bitch gotta let me thru bitch,* Marfa had added that tone for herself—

—and her message is flagged ***URGENT big news, meet me asap***, with a destination marker for some new café, Milagros, so "I have to go out for a minute," Max says. "You want anything?" But Davide does not answer, Davide is already back with the mushrooms, mycelium, *not plants, not animals,* not human, inhuman . . . Birds of Paradise, he does not even remember making that note, but Davide is right, it fits.

The café is equidistant between Fantastic Fantoms and Marfa's own squat, a dormlike journalists' hive, its hallways one loud continuous babel. He had met her there once and she introduced him to the people they passed as *My friend Max Caspar, he's the writer from Dark Factory,* did she imagine that made him sound interesting? Marfa is opaque to him much of the time, her motives and the workings of her mind: last week she had asked if Max Caspar was his real name, then if it was short for Maxwell, then smiled when he told her, reluctantly, it was short for Maximilian, *Max-a-million! Of the Holy Roman Empire?*

What?

That's a super cool name. And byline.

Not for a kid.

Trust me, it's better than Marfa. "Barfa" wasn't even the worst one.

A polished tin sign marks the café storefront, a quote lettered on its windows, TO BE A REALIST YOU MUST BELIEVE IN MIRACLES. Inside, Marfa is nowhere, but under a hung scatter of cotton batting clouds he sees Deborah, she sees him too, lifts her teacup in greeting: "Hello, Max. My friend just opened this place, it used to be called Dreamtime."

"Dreamtime?" in surprise. "Where Ari was?"

"Yes, for a little. Do you hear from Ari, since he left?"

"Sometimes," fighting the sudden sad urge to ask the same about Mila, does Deborah ever hear from her? but "Mila," Deborah says, and his shoulders jump, his heart, "she'll be staying with me again. But Ari left so fast that some of his things are still in the—"

"Mila's moving back? When?"

"In April. She has a residency at TanzStudio."

"A residency? for how long? Is she—"

"Hi," Marfa's voice from right beside him, Marfa looking Deborah up and down as if assessing an opponent. "I'm Marfa Carpenter. Max's girlfriend."

He feels his face go wooden—"Nice to meet you," Deborah's civil nod, whatever else Deborah might have said about Mila she will not say now—then Marfa steers him to a two-top table below a shining mobile of cut-out stars and "'Girlfriend,'" he says, not sure how to say it, but it has to be said. "Marfa, listen—"

"Girlfriend, whatever," her pointed shrug, "it's just a way to talk about us being together. You like being together, don't you?" and of course he enjoys the sex, as he enjoys her zest and fearlessness, her brash quick mind. "But I'm not in love with you, Max, if that's what you're asking," and his own headshake so instant and so firm that she makes a burlesque clown frown: "Oh no, Romeo!" Yet something seems off, has he somehow hurt her feelings? when she has no feelings for him? His own feelings remain with Mila, Mila is coming back—

"So hang onto your shit, here's my big news. Dark Factory's being sold—Uh huh," enjoying his startlement. "It's not a hundred percent final, nothing like this ever is until the thumbprint clears. But look," displaying footage of a nearly empty restaurant or bar, oak shelves and backlit bottles, a stand of toothed ferns, a man in a Rocks Off ballcap and a very pale blonde woman in a black business suit, speaking but without audio, as a third person appears momentarily, a nondescript man in a garnet red pullover. "The story is, Jonas Siegler has big money problems," as he recalls Lee in that Factory dark, *I've seen those numbers, his investors own him*. "So Ines Hechman-Weir, that's her, she's buying it for Hechman Properties—"

—that name somehow familiar, what is Hechman Properties? watching the video to its end, the ball cap man's vigorous hand motions, the woman's calm decisive nods, the pullover man appearing and disappearing like a clumsy effect. "Who's the guy in the hat?"

"That's Darrin Skellman, he's a VP at some big experience company."

"Who's the other—"

"Welcome to Milagros," the server at their table, smooth-shaven head and neat black apron, a flamingo-pink feather tucked like a pen behind one ear. "I'm Floria. Golden milk is our special beverage today."

“One large,” Marfa sliding her chipcard onto the table, and as the server leaves, “It’s still confidential, but Ari needs to see this. I’d contact him myself, but when I tried he blew me off.”

“You talked to Ari?”

“I interviewed Felix Perez. Ari wouldn’t talk to me. But he needs to know about this,” and she is right, because if someone else owns the Factory, then Ari should be free from Jonas, Ari could come back. He pulls out his phone, ***Talk to Marfa***, sends it, shows her, she smiles.

Then “I have to jump,” she says, “I’m interviewing this weapons-grade bird watcher, her handle is Crow Chick. Thank you, boyfriend,” her arm a quick warm circle around his neck, then she is off, threading purposefully through the tables and out the door.

And Floria is setting down his drink, “Can I get you anything else?” so “Uh, a Cloud Wrap?” the first thing he sees on the menu, everything here sounds like magic, this drink like a fairytale elixir, yet the taste is a tonic mix of almond and pepper and, what, turmeric, a strengthening, earthy brew; is that what the window sign means, miracles are realism with a fairytale name? And what will Ari do with this news, the Factory being sold, will it bring him back? wondering as he drinks, then eats, the handmade stars revolving above him like a brand-new constellation, his thoughts shifting irresistibly from Ari to Mila, to April, to *a residency, she’ll be staying with me again.*

Bonus Content: Marfa

We put our slight gifts on the tall altar and hope for the best

Marfa?

Her mother's fluting voice, her mother calling as if she were a kid, in the upstairs bedroom that was not really a bedroom, it was her room: white plastic blinds, white walls without posters or pictures, a twin bed, the same crappy twin bed she had used since she was a kid, a pile of empty Boostie cans, and her narrow metal desk.

Marfa, your father's here!

She checked her phone again, checked in at her DocNotes scribes' dock, to see two new and contradictory reviews posted for Scribe Marfa C.: *Marfa C. is very fast and efficient; Marfa C. is unfriendly and difficult, do not hire!* but no new jobs waiting in her queue. She never told anyone she worked for DocNotes—worked, not wrote, writing for a transcription service app was not in any way writing—except for Dickie, Dickie who was trying to hook her up with BlogOut, *They need somebody reliable for culture profiles, can you write culture profiles?* and *I can write anything,* she had told Dickie, because it was true: she was fast and she was accurate and she could produce any content on demand. Dickie had other demands, or requests, that were not going to be met, she knew Dickie had a crush on her, more than a crush, but that was totally Dickie's problem; she did not have that kind of time, emotional time, for Dickie or for anybody else.

So far this week she had had two offers, one from a freelancers' catchall site, one from a junior journalists' collective—most of those journalists were younger than she was, some were just out of high school, and all of them had more credits to their bylines than she did—but neither of those were paying gigs. And she needed a paying gig, a steady gig, she needed money to get herself out of this room, away from this place and its constant

continued on page 160

continued from page 159

threat of going nowhere, she needed to *go* and her writing was what would get her there; even though her writing was nothing like it should be, she had tried so long and worked so hard but everything she wrote still seemed so basic, all skill no spark. But it was all she had.

Her parents had told her again and again that she could live in their house as long as she liked—as long as they could still pay the rent, they had never owned a house, never owned anything, always iffy—her parents in the middle of their "best friends' divorce," what a stupid thing to call it! If they were best friends they would have stayed married. But her mother was really married to her painting, and her father was best friends with a lot of people, most of them men; and one of the men was Leland Cardenal.

Leland and her father had been best friends since CalArts, she had always assumed they were fucking, though her father was relatively hot for a father and Leland was dopey-looking, big weird earlobes and a little pot gut; but that fucking never seemed to bother her mother, when Leland was in town they all went to gallery openings together. And afterward Leland would sit and talk art world gossip over bourbons on their back patio—"patio," just a squared-off space of black plastic paver stones, mismatched lawn chairs and Christmas lights strung on the privacy fence, everything cheap because they never had any money, her arty parents; it never seemed to trouble them, they thought they had life figured out, life was for art . . . Which was why they had named her what they named her: falling in love at some stupid installation in the desert meant she had to be Marfa. If she had had a normal middle name she could have pivoted to that, but they were big Frieda Kahlo fans too, and "Kahlo" was even worse than "Marfa." People at school had called her "Barfa" and "Arfa," barked at her in the halls, that had trained her to hit first whenever she could, and keep her footing no matter what.

But if her parents had had any sense, they would have stopped fawning over Leland and started asking him for introductions, because Leland had contacts all over, in Houston, in New York,

London, Leland was a very big deal in a much bigger world. On his last visit, a stopover from São Paulo, he had brought presents for them, a black furry hat-type thing for her father, and a gold ring for her mother, a scaled snake ring, the snake gripping its own tail: ouroboros, the ultimate symbol of self-power. Her mother had not liked the ring, called it "sublime" but never wore it. She thought it was gorgeous, although it was too big for her own smaller fingers, she would have had to wear it on her thumb—

—and *Marfa!* louder, her mother on the stairs now as if she were an actual kid so *OK!* her shout back as she logged out of DocNotes, slapped her tablet closed, *I'm coming*—to do what? spend an hour drinking pointless coffee with her father while he cried about how much he valued their family life?

But downstairs her father was beaming, her mother too, and Leland stood between them, why was Leland there? and *Leland's got a surprise for you,* her father said. *He wants you to—*

Let him tell her, Bry!

And then they all looked at her, and she felt an odd heat rise up her back, her spine, the opposite of a chill, the feeling that something very good was about to happen, as *We'll get a little lunch,* Leland said to her, *and have a chat. Do you like chile rellenos, Marfa? They do a nice plate at Augustina's.*

Sure, that's great. Augustina's was expensive and reservations only, which meant Leland had thought about this beforehand, whatever it was; Leland in a tailored shirt, smooth gray linen, and she had on a raveled Strap-Ons hoodie, so *Excuse me a second,* she said, and hurried back up to rip through her closet, nothing there that would work for this, so into her mother's room, her mother's wonky oak wardrobe, to grab a white shirt, also linen, the sleeves were too long but if she rolled them up she would look reasonably professional. And on the wardrobe shelf, beside the ruffled scarves and the chipped enamel earring box, was the little blue jewelry bag, the ouroboros ring—

—that she did not put on, not then, slipped it into her pocket, she felt it there like a bone or a bullet, digging into her hip when

continued on page 162

continued from page 161
she climbed into Leland's rental car, a deep midnight blue car with a driver. And as the car pulled away from the house, from her parents and their world, *Bryce and Ami,* Leland said, *they tell me that you write.*

I do. She made her voice calm, engaged, she took out her tablet, her hands were steady. *I'm writing some culture profiles right now, actually. I specialize in writing about art.*

10

April is silver, from hair band to high-top sneakers, toting a silver bottle of antiox water; already she has put out some fires, telling Ari that the security wristbands were falsing, "Had to nip that in the butt! Or bud, is it bud? And Crispie's a no-fly, goddamned windstorms, but I've got somebody else already on the way. And what a dead gorgeous day!"

And it is, bright and dry in the courtyard where Sto Lat is already hard at work on the wall's unfolding fantasia, hot garish pinks and vivid golds surrounding a curious trinity, lean skullhead and slick grinning salaryman with oversized ears, and in the space between them a growing body, a man's bare-chested white body. Derek works, ignoring everything, as intent as if drawing the world into first being, while Robbie in a paisley bandanna crows "I love this shit!" brandishing a Sure Shot can, its odor so strong Ari can almost taste it. "Allyl hexanoate! It smells so *yellow*—"

"I'd huff it," Genie calls, Genie in matte wraparound shades and dusty rose faux fur parka too warm for the day; the Genie he expected from the louche 4 a.m. pictures and rehab boomerang is not this frail joking down-to-earth girl, only her eyes are lost, is that why she wears shades most of the time? "It looks like a dandelion on steroids. I went to a rave once in this huge dandelion garden, I love gardens—"

"If you like flowers," April offers, too eager, Genie seems somehow to make April nervous, "there's a greenhouse right here in town—"

"Just up the Whatever-strasse," Ari nods, "by that fish place we went to," knowing because he sometimes goes to that greenhouse, to walk the damp solitary warmth of its gravel paths, through hundreds of blooms and spangled bushes and small fantastic trees, all grouped according to some system, he never reads the little white name cards, if he stands still enough long enough he knows he feels them grow. "They have gardenias there, birds of paradise, they have everything—"

"I want to see! Let's go right now."

"Oh," April's anxious laugh, "maybe not just now? Doors are just about to open—"

"Come on," Ari says to Genie's rebellious frown, "I'll show you something cool right here—"

—the steep clay gables of the roof, a precarious perch for Genie to sit and uncurl from the parka, like a cold flower finding the sun, and "Will this bother you?" he asks, wedging himself nearer the safety of the balcony door, lighting a blunt, head half-turned to blow the smoke. "Since you're clean?"

"'Clean,'" with quote marks, "unless you count these," a half-mashed packet of herbal RoseBud cigarettes, "or the Remblex, I take fucking Remblex like it's my job." Finding a sharp scrap of loose tile, a pebble of glass, tossing both into the air, leaning precariously far to watch them fall onto the Silver Landings queue, the unkind opposite of sky candy, and "'We learn from our falls,'" she quotes again, leaning back, "'when we survive them.' That's from refusal class."

"What's refusal class?"

"Rehab. You ever do drugs?"

Tapping ash: "Not really my thing."

"I used to get flat as a board on K bombs. But poppers—Superpop, sugarpop," her half-mournful smile, as if sharing the names of dear departed friends. "Overuse can stop your heart, blah blah blah. But I love them. Poppers are for dancing! I've been dancing, clubbing, since I was fourteen."

"Same."

"Wish I'd met you then. You, me, and Felix, we would have *ruled*."

She puffs a faultless smoke ring, another; Ari tries and fails, she laughs and "Weren't you paying attention," she says, "last night?" during dinner at the fish place, Genie's treat on a corporate card, *Ines can pay for some fun*. She and Felix had shared an enormous briny seaweed salad, she and Ari had had an intensive smoke ring tutorial on the patio, *Make a fish mouth*, demonstrating, *like this. Now kiss the fish!* and Felix had laughed, they all laughed, they finished two bottles of Pol Roger champagne while Genie drank club soda, and "This morning," she says, "I taught the barista how to do it," she and Felix brunching on lattes and lavender doughnuts at Hare Bakery, while he slept in.

Felix said that she had popped up at the flat like a gleeful refugee—*Surprise! You're playing, I'm here!*—dragging that shiny stolen red hotel blanket, a suite already booked but *I hate hotels, I grew up in hotels, I didn't have a "home" till I was twenty,* Genie careful to explain to Ari, to include Ari in everything, to the point where he had murmured to Felix while she was briefly in the lav *You two can hang on your own if you want*. But Felix had shrugged and smiled: *Genie's a lot, I know. But she likes you. A lot.*

And "I read some stuff," she says, slipping off those armoring shades, squinting in the unclouded light. "About you."

"I read some stuff about me, too. Keep in mind it's mostly bullshit."

"There was a profile in *ForwardFast*," the one by Jake the journo, it seems like a thousand years ago. "It said that you were the one who made Dark Factory really work. And Felix said I should ask you."

"Ask me what?"

"I heard what happened, party people always hear, even in rehab. Look," phone in hand and leaning closer, he can smell her, smoky rose and ghost sweat and creamy makeup, cover-up, something bitter and medicinal beneath, "look at this," a journaling site of Factory memories and stories and dreams, a new post popping up as they watch, ***can u hear the future? cuz mine sounds like crying*** and "'Auditory,'" Genie quotes from the categories, "'olfactory, somesthetic'—I had to look that one up, it means sense of touch. These people all got a taste of something special there. So what did you give them?"

A sound check beat begins below, a DJ's testing stop-and-go, not Felix; this morning, fast asleep beside him, Felix had been making little sounds, little glottal growls, as he did it he started to get hard. "What did Felix say about it?"

"He said I'd have to hear it for myself. And that you guys are in sort of a holding pattern, here," taking a last long drag, crushing the filterless end to paper and hot shreds with an expert snap of finger and thumb. "I'd been here a couple times, when it was the Gates, it was super scummy but I liked it. So I got in touch with what's her name, the new owner, and said I would sponsor."

"Sponsor—You mean Silver Landings? You're paying for this?"

"Not all of it."

"What for?" staring at her as if she has changed into something else, a new Genie, the real Genie? "For Felix? Felix never said—"

"Felix doesn't know," closing her eyes again, he can see their roving motion behind the tissue-thin shivering lids, see that the skin around her mouth looks abraded, permanently parched or burned beneath the soothing makeup. "You want to know why I quit using? Because I promised Felix I wouldn't die high. The last time, they found me in a urinal, the EMTs shocked me up and my sister stuck me back into Branwell. She likes Branwell because it has 24-hour concierge shrink service, just like a hotel—What?" her eyes open again, staring at him, still lost, very cold. "Don't *you* ever want to leave this fuck-forsaken planet?"

"No," and without knowing he will, he tells her about the paper mill, the way the sun had looked, and the snow, the wet warmth of his blood in the cold and "I have a scar now," he says. "It's healed, but I'll always have it."

A third Genie is visible now, older somehow, very serious. "Can I see?"

Pulling off his jacket, untucking, lifting his shirt, feeling the air on his skin, feeling her careful fingers finger the scar, and "I never felt better," he says, tugging his shirt back down, "than I did right then."

"'Better' how?"

"More—here."

"More alive?"

"Better than alive."

"Felix said you got hurt, but he didn't say how. Felix was *freaked*."

"Felix worries too much."

"Felix loves you," her sideways smile not yearning so much as, what? confirmation, proof that love exists, that she has seen it. "And he's my very best friend. So if you don't mind, I'll love you too—"

—and the beat steadies below, so "We should go," he says, and they do, her hand clutching his shoulder, for balance? safety? friendship? The floor is already filling up, rising chatter and blinking wristbands, the shiny Silver Landings banner stretched high behind the bar, above the old sign that advises *EVERYTHING WILL BE OK JK!*

And "The man himself," Genie pointing to Felix. "He looks like a prince," all in black, his hair brushed back, chatting with a jaunty quartet who must be the Warsaw troupe, they have that alert and muscular, utterly casual dancers' grace. Genie steps to the bar—"A Club and club. Club-Mate and club soda—" as Jackie marches toward those dancers, her hands full of paperwork, and Ari puts an arm around Felix, who turns to kiss his cheek, and "I brought you a treat," Felix says, handing him a little black and white bag. "April said you were on the roof with Genie?"

"I was. She has something to tell you."

"Yeah?" with mild interest. "Did you hear Crispie's not coming? So I'm up sooner, after the local boys—"

"Kid Yello," Jackie corrects, just like Lee she seems to hear everything. "Kid Yello is in for Crispie Atoms, I'm picking him up in twenty—"

"Tonight," Ari says, "everybody is going to dance for you," leaning to kiss again, not a peck, not his cheek, with a sudden heat that surprises them both: cupping his face, sucking his tongue, sacred, yes, that mouth and that body, that passionate listening mind, Felix at last leans breathless back and "No Kaori," his murmur in Felix's ear. "But why don't you go get your horns—"

—then stepping into the courtyard to unwrap the little treat, thick purple icing on airy white cake, as the first DJ is joined by a second, identical gold skullcaps and gold-striped soccer jerseys, April calling "Give it up for the Victory Brothers!" while Derek draws and Robbie sprays, and the body in the mural's center receives its crown of yellow flowers, its handsome face, its large and liquid, staring gray-blue eyes.

###

The holiday lights still patiently twinkle in the windows of HALLO SCHÖNE, though 25 HOUR FASHION has gone, and the blinking eyeball pop-up is papered over. TanzStudio's dancers are heading off with their gym bags and cigarettes and phones, none of them notice Max on his bike as he rolls slowly by . . . He had come to this place before to seek Mila, but has not checked the TanzStudio site for her actual residency dates, has not contacted Deborah, has not looked—has never looked—at Mila's MePage, has made up his mind then unmade it over and over, as if floating on a tumbling tide, like heart-shaped human flotsam: he will message Mila to say hello, will invite her for tea or a drink, will avoid her at all costs. *A servant, an employee, in your great art production,* what if Mila thinks that too, could Mila possibly think that? would he somehow deserve it if she did? *Mila I love you. Oh Max.*

He puts Mila not out of his mind but deeper inside it, and rides away, down that block then another and another, dark streets then brighter, the stream of headlights and traffic lights and blue-lit directional signs like one of Davide's console lectures, from the avatars in Birds of Paradise to actual birds to actual paradise, to

John Milton, Borges, Bloy, Giordano Bruno, Hermes Trismegistus, floral agriculture, habitat destruction, the role of choice and consciousness in human society, the limbic effects of gaming, the three billion gamers playing online at any given moment, the enormous potential playability of B of P in any Y-compatible spot on earth, to end where it always ends, at Davide's favorite destination, MIW theory, many intersecting worlds, and all of them intersecting with the godhead, every myth originating in that same quantum neighborhood though only a god can see every light, every street, every face on the face of the earth—

—as he slows, coasts, pulls up blinking, wheeling from the dark into the lobby's lights to see Clara stepping out of the elevator, Clara who looks almost corporate, neat charcoal suit jacket and square envelope bag, her rampant flattop tamed. When she sees him she calls, "Fingers crossed! I've got a drinks meeting with a guy from Zeus Cap, a friend set me up."

"For a golden shower?" he says, then wishes immediately he had not, but Clara recognizes the phrase's mythological meaning, Clara smiles: "Oh, all the gold. If this guy likes our pitch and bumps it up, they could feather our birdhouse all the way to launch. And we need it, my burn account can only go so far. But," twitching at her sleeve, a nervous motion, he has never seen Clara look nervous before, "this isn't my turf—I'm good at making things, not talking about making things. God, I wish Ari was here! He's catnip to people like this, Jonas used to bring him in for funder walkthroughs just for the mojo."

"I bet," Jonas whose supposed sale of the Factory has still not been announced, has that stopped happening, has the deal fallen apart? Whenever he asks Marfa she frowns, *I told you nothing's final till the thumbprint clears,* so is Ari waiting for his own reasons, before he answers Marfa? or does Ari have other knowledge of whatever the fuck might be going on? but none of that is his turf either, and the only thing that really matters is that Ari is still not here. He has asked Clara a few times when she thinks Ari might be back, but her answer is always a headshake, *He is where he is until he isn't, I guess. At least we can all still work together.*

It's not the same.

Funny, you of all people to say that! Don't let Davide hear you.

Now "Isn't that your motto?" he asks, as she twitches her sleeve again, is she trying to cover her tattoo? "The Fantastic Fantoms motto?"

"Money people don't care about mottoes, all they care about is ROI—There's my Hopper," as headlights trundle up the street, she sucks a breath like an athlete in the chute. "With my shield or on it . . . See you later."

Upstairs, the workspace is too warm and almost fully dark: he snaps on the white tensor light, the tiny desk fan, and "You know what this is?" Davide calls in lieu of greeting, one finger highlighting the neon orange image of a walnut-shaped blob. "It's the adult human brain on hallucinogens. When it's dosed, that brain exhibits *way* more plasticity and malleability. Just like a baby's brain."

"'Trailing clouds of glory.'"

"Right, right! 'Heaven lies about us in our infancy,' people thought Willy Wordsworth was just being religious, but," making the onscreen brain pulse now, a merry rhythm, "neurological infancy is the human state that's actually closest to the godhead. How old were you when you started playing games?"

"I don't know. Six? Five?" the memory of hunching in the dimness of the bottom bunk while his cousin Tomi slept atop, playing Corcoran's Cork until his aunt made him stop and go to sleep. But the urge to play, Adam Kaiser used to say, is inborn: *All games are a bedrock recapitulation of existence, even babies' games of peek-a-boo, I see you, you're there, I don't see you, you disappear. Why else do babies laugh when they see the face again?* the laughter of confirmation and relief, proof that the universe does exist—

"—Griffiths and Barnett, their stuff on mushrooms and mysticism, too bad it's not ethical for babies to be in those trials. Want to do some acid?"

"No thanks."

"Want a pretzel?" offering the crackling chairside bag of Wheaty Bites, beside the bottle filled with alarmingly pink vitamin water, or whatever is actually in there, brought over in liter jugs by Lukas, one of Davide's guerrilla coder friends, *Don't ever refrigerate that, dude. Ever.*

He settles in below the tensor light, to amend a growing list of interactive objects to be deployed throughout the game: flowers and squashed Solo cups, scraps of paper, melancholy frogs, the skull of a dead bird, a snarl of fishing line, a red and almost too perfect apple. On his screen, the narrative map is beginning to resemble a fractal, or a virus slowly spreading; Davide has already provided a cheerful sidebar lecture on viral fatality, linked somehow to its cell fractal geometry, *the more complex the faster it kills you!*

And how will this play, to its players? Twice last week he was contacted by former Kunstfarm students, Adam's ex-students who were there that Factory night, who heard that this game is being made and that Ari is involved—heard how? Davide's coder friends have been signed to silence, but who else knows?—the students asking if they could work on it, could beta, could play. Clara had refused, but Davide was more sanguine: *They're going to get in anyway, it might as well be through us.*

You want to ride herd on those kids, Davide? Never mind, don't answer that. The answer's no.

And as the hours edge toward morning, Davide begins to talk, not the usual lecture but a musing and personal murmur, like a mind thrumming to itself in the middle of the night: "What's your favorite game, do you have a favorite? For a long time mine was Catastrophia, remember Catastrophia? the dragon women? Winged Victory with that ice axe, twenty-seven foot wingspan, she was a fucking queen!" as that game's theme rumbles from his speakers, like Wagner cut with vintage house. "When I was fourteen, I played Catastrophia every minute I wasn't sleeping or wanking, so my mother put me on Clorhiderol, now they call it Remblex. I think she was afraid of what could happen, afraid it *would* happen—"

"What would?"

"I told her I wanted to live in the game, prayed to be able to live in a game—"

—and the stylus stills in his own hand, thinking of those eager students, of Adam Kaiser's objections, *potentially very harmful,* and Jonas's notes, *humans are just a walking set of triggers.* And Ari has found the deep ones, the ones that change a life: in visible ways like his own, maybe more still unseen, like landmines waiting to be tripped, maybe everyone there that night has some version of that change? And people did get hurt, accidentally but they were still hurt, so is there a moral aspect to all of this? *Too bad it's not ethical—*

"—answer that prayer, people are going to love B of P like I loved those dragon women. And if—"

—as Max's phone goes, he ignores it, it goes again, he sees it is Ari, how is it Ari? Ari messages, he never calls. But that is Ari, half-closed eyes and sweating, glowing, a man's arms wrapped around him, a skinny man with a shock of yellow hair, not Felix. And Ari's gasp through the background beats, "Watch, Max *watch—*" turning the phone to show a half-stripped couple on top of a bar, are they fucking? they are, lifted legs and bouncing hair, blurring, jarring, orgasmic, then a crazily framed sign, BE OK JK! then a horned body made of shadows and pink light—

—and "Ari," he says, shouts, "Ari, what's going on? What's—Davide, look at this—"

—and Davide turns, looks, looks, then pulls off his headphones and pulls up a Kickchat livestream on his main screen, the phone in Max's hand like a little puzzle piece of that pulsing whole, as they stare together at the flow of flesh and silver excess, everyone in the place seems to be fucking or just about to, and "Whoa," Davide's crow, "look at that backbend! And the DJ, hey, that's Felix Perez," Felix in the mask, that silver animal growing closer and closer until it fills the screen in Max's hand and "Listen to that," Davide's shout, turning it up, beats pounding through the speakers like a giant's joyful heart, "Max, we *need* that! *That* is a soundtrack!"

###

The erotic mentalist, a jolly older woman in a thigh-slit coral cheongsam, bows again to friendly hoots—"Thank you, Ricky and Adele, for sharing your pleasure with us!"—hand in hand in hand with two giggling volunteers, as Ari stands with an undrunk vodka, waiting for Felix whose set comes next. Further down the bar, Genie elbows in for yet another refill, Genie who now wears a glittery silver top hat, sponsor Genie, *her family's huge, you guys are in a holding pattern here,* has she talked to Felix yet—

—as at his elbow, Robbie appears, flustered and anxious: "Hey, you seen Derek anywhere?" Derek Ferris who had weirdly bolted just as Kid Yello arrived to start his set—not much of a set, repetitive booming beats and bawling shouts of *Yello everybody!* and *Welcome to YelloLand!*—Kid Yello painted at the center of that courtyard mural, the same eyes, insanely yellow flowers just like his yellow hair, even the cockshot stance and the sexy one-sided droop of his mouth is dead on. Though how did they know to paint Kid Yello when he was a last-minute add? so "He's got an issue?" he asks Robbie. "With the DJ?"

"Dunno, I didn't even know they knew each other! But I can't find him, and he's not answering. And he didn't sign the piece, he always signs the piece—"

"I can take a look outside—"

—angling past the doorway pack of smokers, by habit he starts to shake out a blunt, then slides it back, no urge to smoke or drink tonight, he feels oddly good but somehow tense, no not tense, eager, why? He scans the street, the parked and staggered scooters, the empty warehouse space next door, its two yellowed security lights staring down at their own shadows—

—as a figure, a man, a tall man, Derek Ferris detaches from those shadows, strides to stop just a jarring step away and "You," Derek says to him, with an odd and furious grin. "*You're* good with this type of shit, right, Mr. Dark Factory?"

"What type of what shit?"

"This!" as if they have already been talking, arguing. "It's not paint-by-numbers, you have to leave room for the energy, the muse, whatever you want to call it, and I do! I always do—"

"Slow down," taking a prudent half-step back. "Listen, Robbie's looking for—"

"Robbie! Fucking Robbie thinks it's cool!" even louder, the shout that comes before the punch, is Derek about to go off on him? a good three inches taller and with a practiced artist's reach, Ari takes another step back as "*This* is the piece," Derek brandishing his phone so Ari must lean forward to see: an image of the courtyard, silver figures in a vortex of blue lightning, abstract patterns, nothing like what is actually on that wall, so "What are you saying?" Ari staring at that image. "You didn't mean to paint Kid Yello, or what?"

"No I didn't 'mean to,' I didn't even know the guy existed! And those other assholes—"

"What other—"

"If I painted Jesus Christ, would it be the Second Coming in there now?" one long furious finger pointing to the club, then shouldering past, not back inside but down the empty street, in the smells of paint and propellant and rank adrenaline—

—as from inside a muffled feedback whoop, "Are you ready?" so Ari slips back into that heat, the crowd massed below the black skylights, April on the mic, up by the decks: "I said are you *ready!* For Fraktur's resident superstar, the idol of Silver Landings, are you ready to give it all up for *Felix Perez!*" to raucous cheers, wolf whistles, upturned faces sparkling with glitter and silver paint, expectant eyes—

—but no Felix, only silence, the crowd's applause confused then faltering, still no Felix, only April, her tense and amplified, indrawn human breath—

—and Ari feels a physical chill, thrill, feels his cock abruptly stir—

—as the god appears, horned and silver, arms raised—

—and applause, even louder as the spots shine hard and pink, drenching Felix as the beat drops, and people start to move: and Ari moves too, that beat like a second heart, hyperaware of his body, of the stretch and glow of his muscles, the sweat at the back of his neck, a bead down his spine, another, a tickle like teasing fingertips as that beat swells and peaks, bottoms out, swells again—

—while voices start to rise in the mix, human and not, *Je t'aime baby, je t'aime!* lovers' throaty murmurs, the kingfisher's mating cry, deep animal croons and the rhythmic splash of water like the rush of blood through the body, like the rush building in this building, the voice of everything alive seeming to say the same thing, *je t'aime baby, je t'aime*—

—as on the floor, people, couples, strangers, bodies start to touch, hug, rub, kiss, mouths open, in twos and threes and more—a tall woman skins off her shirt as another woman in a silver suit coat cups her from behind, the erotic mentalist sways with her volunteer couple, another couple climbs atop the bar, a man in red jeans grinds against the stacks, a boy in a shiny crop top clambers up to the decks to be wrestled gently back by April, her silver makeup streaked like robot sweat, as another boy immediately takes his place, on his knees in sexual prayer, while Genie dances by, top hat gone, shades gone, white face feverish and slack—masked Felix moving all these bodies as if they are literally in his hands, the warm palms of his hands—

—and Ari's gaze stays on him, the mask not a mask anymore but part of Felix now, like that tattoo is part of him, there at the base of his spine, the memory in his own mouth of how the skin tastes there, right there, just above the cleft curve of his ass, that body a part of his own body, part of him, their love a living thing, ecstatic, immortal—

—and someone's hands are on him now, Kid Yello, jacket unzipped over a bare white chest, those blue-gray eyes wide, mouthing something about jewels? juice? vanilla breath hot against his cheek, Kid Yellow tipping shaky to his lips a jumbo can of Van Vodka, sweet as a first teenage drunk: and he drinks, he lets himself go, because everybody, every body, is a particle, a drop, in this wave of humming heat, of sex and play and delirium, everybody is hot—

—as from far away he feels himself groping for his phone, because his mind knows what this is, knows that Max has to see it, Max has to "Watch," his gasp, "Max *watch*," the dancing, the fucking, a couple on the bar is fucking as the Warsaw dancers, bare breasts, bare chests, surround the decks—

—and phone up but forgotten, cock aching, he wades through breath and flesh, irresistibly toward Felix who seems to see him though the mask is nearly eyeless, who turns that silver face his way through the spurting smoke, the beat throbbing and beautiful and meant for Ari alone, calling him, touching him, fucking him, *je t'aime, his body his eyes his hands his very self, love me tender motherfucker*—

Bonus Content

"Dancefloor"

by Julian Zero, Endlessly Musik

When we dance
When we dance
You move like everything to me

On the dancefloor
On the dancefloor

I watch you sleep
I watch you sleep
You look like everything to me

On our dancefloor
On our dancefloor

When you smile
When you smile
You are everything to me

You're the dancefloor
You're the dancefloor

11

"Shit, what time is it?" Marfa rolling over and up in one motion, like a rumpled angry gymnast, Max hunched on the opposite edge of the morning bed. "I should have been gone an hour ago . . . Are you watching Ari's Happy Endings porn again?"

"It's called Silver Landings."

"I know what it's called—"

—as he clicks replay to watch it again, seeing what Ari wanted him to see, that what happened on the roof has happened again. But this time he has distance enough to see the sheer strangeness of it, the whole thing less carnival and more ceremony, is that the word? or sacrament? all those bodies stripped and moving together, all wanting one thing, as if they were already Davide's mycelium . . . Since that night, Davide has campaigned for Felix to do the B of P soundtrack, but Clara is not convinced; Clara is at odds with Davide over his coders' army, too, as they struggle in a sudden stew of new problems, mainly build issues that Max cannot help with, does not even fully understand. And he is not a fan of that army either, especially the one who likes to roost in his chair, Lukas the jug-bringer, grinning white and skinny, with round brown-socketed eyes.

And Fantastic Fantoms' cash flow is drying up—despite Clara's colleagues' support and donations, his own funds kicked in too, why else does he have it, *it's Factory money anyway*—because the meeting with Zeus Cap had not gone well at all: *Some of that's on me,* Clara said, *I was way too nervous. But the guy definitely needed something more to engage with, so that means faster dev. Max, you have to finish first so we know how this thing ends.*

But *No,* he said, knew he had to say. *I can't.*

What do you mean you can't? as Clara and Davide both stared, united then in their dismay. *You can't write? You're blocked?*

No, I could do it. But I can't.

Because before he writes another line he and Ari have to talk, not just trade quick elliptic messages, they need to sit down face to face in the same physical space, the actual fucking world, and come to some understanding of what is happening, what might happen if this, whatever this is, continues to mutate and to grow; Ari is the only one he can ask, the only one who can answer. But Ari and Felix have left Fraktur, to go where and do what? Ari's answer to his own direct and troubled ***Where are you?*** tells him nothing, Ari offhand and mysterious, wrapped in some outrageously fluffy black robe, looking like a king on vacation, ***lap of lux pretty krazy***—

—as "Freddie," Marfa exasperated, staring at her phone, its light washing across her tired face, "Freddie, again?" Marfa also tense and frazzled, arriving very late last night, wearing a new jacket—a gray tac jacket, security-lined and technically invisible, *Sometimes you need to go dark*—and carrying a bottle of sour red wine and a bag of roasted walnuts, to chew and drink and sleep, blanket dragged over her head, she did not want to talk or touch. And neither did he, he almost asked her to leave, why is she even there? *girlfriend, boyfriend,* what kind of friends are they to each other anyway?

But suddenly, eyes bright, all annoyance swept away, "Freddie says," Marfa announces, "Hechman Properties is doing an acquisitions reveal. Live presser, right now."

"Is it about Dark—"

"No one knows what it's about, that's what makes it a reveal. But knowledge is power. Let's go—"

—and because knowledge is power, because he has finally remembered the blue and white card from Bitter Lake, did Teresa ever sell that lonely little forest? because he is not going into Fantastic Fantoms, he goes along with her—

—to the Hechman headquarters, a leafy and echoing blue glass atrium, steel benches and slim birch trees bedded in white pebblelike stones, no real stones could ever be so uniform or so pristine. He hangs back as Marfa joins the journos already clustering before a wheeled lectern, where a young functionary in a blue suit launches into a statement that Max ignores, watching instead a small curtained-off square beyond that lectern, like a holding area or a temporary backstage—where three women emerge, dishwater blonde and scarlet lipstick, black leather and gray pinstripes, Deirdre and Dolores following the pale blonde woman from Marfa's video, who in person is even paler, black suit and a martial walk, as "Our COO," the functionary says, smiling with sober but visible pleasure. "Please welcome Ines Hechman-Weir."

"Thank you, Burk," says Ines Hechman-Weir, taking that lectern to announce in economical sentences that Hechman Properties has just entered the entertainment market, has purchased the successful experience creation company Your Eyeballs, to be immediately renamed and rebranded "Your Own Eyes, because we plan to engage consumers with a new and exclusive reality experience. With artists like these involved," one hand to indicate Deirdre and Dolores, who smile at her the same way they smiled at Jonas in the box, "we're very confident that you'll like what you see with Your Own Eyes—"

—and that cues a series of projections all across the atrium walls, eyes blinking and winking and cycling through colors, one pair three stories tall, a thousand swarming like flies, while up and beyond the lobby trees, in the circular central skylight, sun parts the slow-floating clouds, round and tranquil and indifferent, a god's eye view—

—and "Come on," Marfa quick and furious at his side, "let's go. I need to get with Freddie—"

"I have to get back—"

"I do too, I left my fucking tablet under the bed. But this won't take long," the Hopper speeding on premium run back to the journo dorm, where her strident shout—"Hey *Freddie!*"—cuts through the noise of the ground floor hallway, turning heads and summoning a shambling colleague who looks to Max like his old coder neighbor, minus the erudite t-shirt and with a shorter, shittier beard. And "Carp," says Freddie, giving a smile to Marfa, a nod to acknowledge Max so minute as to be deliberately rude. "Get what you went for?"

"Ha fucking ha. We need to talk—"

"Remember," Freddie tapping the FULL PRIVACY sign next to a meeting room door, a timed steel locker mounted below, "it's blackout in here," inserting his phone into one of the security slots. "For you too, Carp. I know how you roll—"

"Shut up. Here, watch this," Marfa flipping her phone to Max, his sideways grab, he almost drops it. "Five minutes, Freddie. Four," Freddie still smiling as he closes that door behind them, the sealing click of blackout—

—as Max looks around for a chair, finds no chair, leans into a U-shaped window well to wait, and recall the last time he saw Deirdre and Dolores: on that cold and endless roof, just before but unpresent to the real experience, are they sorry they had not been there, or glad? *hired guns, they don't develop, they implement, who's really making this thing*? But if Hechman Properties has bought this other company, does that mean that the Factory sale is off for sure, should he tell Ari about that? in his lap of lux, wherever and whatever the fuck that might be? Frowning, thoughts churning, his thumb taps absent and nervous on Marfa's unlocked phone—

—and the screen comes suddenly alive with two side-by-side videos: one a woman in a striped burglar costume pointing comically to a whiteboard, *10 NEW SECURITY FIXES YOU NEED NOW!* and the other the video of Ines Hechman-Weir and the Rocks Off ball cap man. But now the man in the garnet sweater is at that table, his face not smooth so much as unused, like a mask kept in a box, and the audio is working: the ballcap man speaking, *Ari Regon found an entire level of presence, available user presence, that no one even knew was there. And not only did he find it, he demonstrated incredible vitality even in the MVP—that's minimum viable product, Leland. All over Neuberg Street.*

And it's reliably recreatable? Ines Hechman-Weir's tone sharper and more daunting than at the press conference, no public charm filter engaged. *Without the volatility? Because—*

—but her voice, the sound, is drowned by a pair of journos stopping right beside him to snap at each other in rapid French, so he must hunch deeper into the window well to block them out, like listening down a tunnel or a bottomless well, straining to hear—*Not a defect, it's a feature! And Ari already has a great relationship with Junket, and with me*—the phone so close to his face that he cannot see the arguing journos, does not see Marfa approaching until her hand lands on his arm.

###

"What airport is this?" Felix asks, and Ari shrugs: side by side beside a check-in kiosk, their bags already trundled off by a red robocart, Genie by the cloudy curbside windows with some functionary in a blue suit, is he a Hechman employee? because Hechman is suddenly everywhere, suddenly a sponsor of more than just Silver Landings: Felix and Genie had argued over that on the plane, before the plane, in the car—

Genie, what the fuck! You told me you stopped taking things from your family, taking money, you told me—

It's not their money, I have my own money, Ines unlocked access as soon as I got out! And you said Ari had legal trouble, and they have all those lawyers—Felix, don't be this way, I never thought you would be this way!

Just like you never thought of asking first?

You've always been so good to me! I wanted Silver Landings to be good for you—

—Silver Landings that is all over his feed, ***Totally Bacchanalian beats, u cum just listening, Now its Fuck Factory! Mister Minos is so hottttt***, people calling it a dance orgy, a sex riot, Ari Regon making more disruptive magic with his hot DJ, what had Peggy said in that Dreamtime back room? ecstasy, potency? Bare asses and torn shirts and blissful people coupled, tripled, on the bar, in the courtyard, on the sidewalk, right in front of the cappies, the stolid Korps with their latex gloves and face shields called in to shut it all down, who had called them? the nonexistent neighbors? Would Jackie be the one to ask? And live sex in a club apparently requires a string of permits that Fraktur does not have, so the health department got involved, the club's license is under review, the residency was definitely over.

And while Felix cashed out with April, unhappy with her too—*She could have been upfront with me, even if Genie told her not to*—he had stepped into the late morning quiet of that courtyard, half-expecting to see that the mural had also changed, to what? a threesome? a circle jerk? But instead he saw Kid Yello, though not in yellow this time, a baggy white Coupé sweatshirt and slouchy violet pants, peering at his painted self—until Kid Yello saw him, and blushed a boyish pink: *This painting, it's cool, but my mouth don't really look like that. And I'm usually taller.*

"Usually"?

I mean I'm like—tall . . . Those Sto Lat dudes must be big fans of my shit? but he had not answered, not his mystery to explain, had Derek and Robbie ever found each other again? The mural was still unsigned. Then *Hey,* Kid Yello said, *you and me—It was great, right?*

Wild night, yeah, his own hazy memory like the aftertaste of too-sweet vodka, dancing with Kid Yello in the pulse and sweat—but Kid Yello's hand was suddenly on his, warm and smitten and *Ari,* Kid Yello said. *We had like a connection—*

A connection?

—we were together, we were dancing! *I even told you my real name—*

What's your real name?

Julian! And I'm really feeling that, I have like feelings. For you—

—and his smile half for Kid Yello, Julian, and half in tribute to Felix, would this have happened any other way except on that floor, in that heat borrowed from Mister Minos? so *It was a great night,* with a purely social hug. *See you later—*

—then into the businesslike luxury of the private car to the private plane, the flight attendants handing them flowers as they boarded, glossy ivory gardenias in gold-edged tissue; Felix had taken one look and set his pointedly aside, as Genie watched with a tense and gloomy stare. And *Gardenias are special flowers,* the senior flight attendant said, her lilting tone an attempt to soothe that tension, *they symbolize lasting friendship,* while the junior attendant, his tone just as soothing, asked, *Can I offer you gentlemen a beverage? Coffee, Kava Lite, sparkling water?*

White wine?

Certainly. Chenin blanc? Or we have a fairly amazing Gewürztraminer.

Amaze me, but *Water's fine,* flat from Felix, before they had reached cruising altitude he and Genie were arguing again—

—and now "Do you need in-town transportation," an airport worker in red to match the robocarts, "where are you headed?" but "Ask her," Felix pointing to Genie, and as that worker walks away, "Where *are* we headed?" Ari says. "I know I'm supposed to meet with lawyers, but did anybody say where?"

"Who knows. Someplace they own. Here comes the ride," as a blue town car glides to a stop, the deferential driver nodding to Genie who finishes her call—"We're leaving right now. Call the kennel, make sure Ranger's at the house"—then climbs into the plush interior, sparkling water and coffee at every seat, as Felix pops in earbeads and closes his eyes, lacing fingers with Ari who sips a coffee, gritty and thick as needed medicine, and watches the landscape through the tinted windows, another small corporate jet descending as the town car turns up an access road, away from the bland regional airport and onto the highway, a median forest of stout bluish evergreens, the silvery afternoon sun playing hide and seek all the way to their destination—

—that turns out to be The Birches, a deluxe residence hotel, brutalist white concrete and stark black doors, and as the car smoothly bypasses the long valet queue, "You guys," Genie asks, her voice small and dry, "do you maybe want to grab a bite?" but "I'm tired," Felix says coolly. "It's been a long week."

Bags offloaded while Genie stays in the car, to be ferried to some other, presumably nonhotel destination, the porter staring as Felix hoists the knobby, shrouded mask—"I'll carry this—" though the concierge in her trim suit offers only a hospitable, seen-it-all smile. In the elevator, Ari shows Felix Genie's anguished message, ***talk 2 him Air PLZ talk 2 him!!!*** and "'Air'?" Felix says, unmoved.

"Autocorrect," his shrug. "She's upset."

"Well so am I. I thought we were friends, you don't use your friends—"

—as the porter keys open the doors to their room, suite, double suite, its cold deliberate opulence presenting as high-end zen, with the baroque contradiction of a white grand piano by the window wall. The room lights rise, an opalescent glow responding to human presence, while the porter departs—"No gratuity, sir. That's all been taken care of—" as Felix sets the mask to a black marble console table, beside a vase of jade green roses—

—and Ari falls slow and theatrical backward onto the enormous bed, its linen spread the granulated white of beach sand, with a subtle scent of, what? verbena? synthetic hayfield? some new curated molecule? and "Hey," his laugh, holding out his arms from the depths of that bed, in sudden glee, in joy, "hey Mister Minos," still laughing, as Felix turns to him, as Felix finally smiles. "Come on over here, amaze me."

And the heat between them has a raw new need, the way it was backstage at Fraktur: door left open, jeans ripped down, mask flung, and afterward Ari, dizzy, thought to raise that mask to his own eyes, look into those endless placid sockets, then thought better and set it down again, as Felix muttered *I could feel them, all of them, like all of them were you . . .* Now the mask is hidden but that need is the same, as Felix, fierce, strips and holds and enfolds him, skin electric with sweat, tongue and fingers and panting into his open mouth, "Je t'aime, baby, je t'aime," then flushed and spent, falling into a doze as Ari kisses the pulse still beating visibly in his throat—

—then Ari is out of bed to investigate the suite, its dull and manicured courtyard view, a minibar already custom stocked with rosemary water and iced espresso, an emperor-sized marble bathroom with a shower calibrated to needle or soothe, raw silk towels and a foolish magnificent spa robe, like being hugged by a giant black marshmallow: all part of the package for an experience consultant with Hechman Properties. That news, his news, is still proprietary, only Felix knows, but Max has been messaging all week, ***Where are you?*** so now he answers ***lap of lux pretty krazy***, though who knows what Max will think when he explains? According to Clara, Max is having some issues of his own.

And Felix has resisted all this as stiffly as he resisted that plane ride, while Genie waited weeping in the car: *Ari, why would you say yes to all this mess!* but *Their lawyers,* his own quiet insistence. *They can get Jonas off me for good, get me right with the cappies—*

So what Genie did, we'll just pretend that's OK?

I didn't say that. But no Genie, no Silver Landings. And Silver Landings means this can happen anywhere—

You said you would go anywhere with me.

We are going somewhere.

Now in the main suite the lights have changed again, gold as a hovering sun, as Felix fiddles with the hotel tablet: "I'm getting us food. You want espresso? Wine?"

"There's espresso in the minibar. Can I get soba?"

"I'm sure you can get anything you want here."

"Felix, how long do you plan to be pissed off about this?"

"Until it stops. This kind of money, they buy you—"

"They try to. But—"

"But what?" tossing down the tablet. "This gets you away from Jonas Siegler, good. Now what?"

"Now the game needs to launch."

"And what's that going to do?"

"I don't know—"

"You don't know? You always know, you always—"

"—until it's done! And we're almost there," taking Felix by the hand, those warm and restless fingers. "You said you wanted out of that room, the little room where nothing ever changes, well, here we are. And look," with a coaxing smile, "we have a piano—"

—and Felix gives him a look, apprehension and trust and something else, something indefinable, then crosses to that white behemoth to sit and play: a classical piece, calm and fluid and lucid, almost sad, his touch very sure, his face remote. And afterward, in the hush the music has created, Ari says in wonder, "That's amazing. I didn't know you could play like that."

"That," hands still on the keys, "was Poulenc. Nocturne number one, in C, my good luck piece, my audition piece—I was on a shortlist for a conservatory scholarship, full ride. But," with a swift and complicated run, nearly flawless, "they gave it to somebody else . . . So OK," slipping off the bench, slipping on the discarded robe. "Everything happens for a reason, so OK. Wine, and soba, and a fucking frosted doughnut, two doughnuts, why not."

While Felix orders, Ari perches in the squared circle of black comfortless armchairs, who could relax in chairs like these? thumbing through messages, nothing here he needs to care about, nothing back from Max, or from Clara who keeps messaging about Max, ***He's heading off the rails, can you talk to him?*** Clara who has invested everything she is and has in the game's success—until a message from Meghan, flagged ***URGENT, Ari seriously?***

srsly what

You didn't see? Check your feed

m wtf???? W T F

No clue no notice, they just told us. This is about you?

1st i heard

—about the death of Your Eyeballs and the birth of Your Own Eyes, a newly trending topic, a repeating clip of a woman in a black suit, Genie's sister Ines who looks just like Genie though older and colder. And his feed is a sudden yammer of rumors and speculation, Deirdre and Dolores will definitely be running it, Deirdre and Dolores will definitely not be running it, Deirdre and Dolores are just placeholders until a real experience manager can be brought in, who? names floated, promoted, upvoted, dismissed, his own name surfacing again and again—

—and ***URGENT*** again and all caps, from Max, ***WATCH THIS NOW***: a video of Skelly, clandestine in some dark-paneled steakhouse bar, with a jug-eared man in a red sweater, that man is distantly familiar, why? And Ines Hechman again, Skelly pitching to her, about what? about him, *Ari already has a great relationship with Junket, with me*—and "Fuck," he says, to himself, to the phone, to the air. "How much money do these people *have*—"

"What?" from Felix at the door, as the food arrives on a lacquered trolley, a glistening bulb of soba, a black platter of honey-colored pastries, and "Here," Ari says, not smiling, handing him the phone. "Listen to this."

###

The walk to Big Market co-op is cold—somehow Max has lost his black knit cap, he has had that cap since Kunstfarm—but bracing and cloudless, the street trees' shadows crisp against the remnant snow, the opposite of those stunted lobby trees beside the hectic Hechman eyes . . . He has not seen or spoken to Marfa since that day, left her tablet for retrieval in Glenda Vitale's office, refused to answer any of her messages because *You already knew*, his accusation, as Freddie stood by watching, maybe Freddie was in on it too. *You knew they weren't buying Dark Factory.*

That presser—I'm as shocked as you are, believe me—

Believe you? You asked me to lie to Ari. You told me—

Max, listen. You don't understand—

You're right, I don't. But Ari has to see this. Send it to him.

I can't do that! I—Max, wait, all right! I'll send it to you—

—and she had, and he had sent it immediately to Ari, ***WATCH THIS NOW*** though Ari's eventual answer made no immediate sense—

write

Did you watch it?! It's about you

just write

Not until we talk. Face to face

im there in a little

—and what did that mean, *there*, here, how? And if Ari is part of this other company, will it make things better, or worse? What happens to the game if—

"Max?" a woman's voice, it stops him on the co-op steps, "Max!" and he turns back—

—to see Mila at the curb on a blue City Cycle, her hair braided back, pale fringed scarf and mud-spotted skirt and "You looked so purposeful," Mila calls, "I thought, oh, Max must be on a mission!"

"You're here?" gripping the railing, for a moment it feels like he might fall. "Deborah said you were coming in April—"

"The workshop is in April, but TanzStudio brought me in early for some staff work. Max, how are you?"

"Can we—Can I buy you a coffee?" in REDDY ROASTERS, the stand-up coffee bar just inside the co-op, stamped tin ceiling and plump zucchini muffins, cherry red bags of coffee lined up on the scratched steel counter, *Today's Roast is Reddy!* And as they take their cups "How are you?" Mila asks again: but before he speaks he looks, only that, has he ever seen Mila this clearly before? seen her at all? Not just her endlessly remembered beauty, soft braid and strong shoulders, the line of her dancer's body, but the warmth of her, the depths of her calm, like a well, a wellspring; she is complete, Mila, nothing missing, nothing lost.

So "Good," he says, he clears his throat, he says it again. "I'm good. How's your new place?"

"Oh, it's wonderful. Look," leaning closer in the scent of chamomile, to show him a pocket garden of winter fig and ivy, a little room with deep blue walls, a long mirrored studio blurred with bodies in motion, and "My students," she says. "Yusuf, Katy,

Leo—they're more demanding than at TanzStudio. And much more serious, sometimes they say, why should we even be learning to dance, with the way things are in the world." And he sees by the way she shows those pictures, the way she smiles then frowns, *the way things are* is that she belongs, now, to these students, to the blue flat and the pocket garden; in no way will she ever come back here, back to him, *Mila I love you, oh Max . . .* Something tightens in his heart, something loosens, he takes an aching, silent breath. Then "What do you tell them?" he asks.

"About my nana. You've heard that story before."

"Tell me again."

"After Nana took me to dance class, we would sometimes go have a treat in the park, an ice cream, and watch the ninepin players. And she would say, See how when one pin is hit, all the others fall? So the reason we dance, it's to learn to hold each other up."

"That painted duck, on the bookcase—"

"To remind me. But Max," with more than curiosity, kindness there and a certain concern, "what are you doing now, are you making a new show? I still think of Bitter Lake, the birds, that little stream, it was a real world. You gave it everything."

Everything, including her, and whatever they might have been together; and though he had wanted, before, more than anything, to tell her what he sees now, *that* he sees, what he says is "Look at this," thumbing up Ari's Silver Landings video, watching her as she watches, and "The silver show!" she says. "I heard about this from Elin Nowak, she was there with Polonez. See, there's Elin, right by the DJ—"

"That's Felix. He's Ari's boyfriend."

"Ari Regon?"

"We're friends now. For real. We're—making something."

"Katya told me about what happened at Dark Factory," Katya who had danced on that roof, he remembers Katya's bare feet in the snow, her laughter, he had never heard Katya laugh before. "I'm sorry for what I said to you, I should have trusted you were following your work. And now you have people like yourself to work with!

Gifted, and focused—Oh Max, I am *glad*," so emphatic and so true that in simple gratitude he reaches for her, a one-armed embrace that she returns, the way old friends will embrace, the past present in their touch. And "I'll let you know," he says, leaning back first, a half-step back, an infinite step. "When it's done."

"I'll come and see it."

"This one will come to you . . . Good luck with your workshop. Break a leg."

Smiling: "Dancers say *merde*."

From the tin-framed window he watches as she climbs back onto the bike, waves once, then rides away, her long scarf lifting, its white fringe like rootlets on the breeze: and he knows that whatever the game might show him, whatever paradise life gives him to see, nothing will ever be more beautiful to him than this, than her, that wave, right now.

###

Struggling to work the lock pad for the outer door, then manually operate the inner door, and "Sorry," Ari says to the woman at that door, Ines Hechman-Weir in tortoiseshell sunglasses and a trim jacket that reminds him of the porter's at The Birches. "It doesn't trust my thumbprint yet."

"That shouldn't be happening. I'll have maintenance look into it." Setting down her Gunther bag, sunglasses politely removed—old school glasses, Chanel, no hotspots—as polite to take the mineral water he offers, but refuse the espresso: "Thank you, but I'm very allergic to caffeine."

He dumps a peppercorn shot into his own cup—"Hope this doesn't bother you"—a doubled and cleansing rush as he drinks and watches Ines glance around the loft, as if she is taking inventory: the disorder of delivery bags and boxes, a half-opened set of new glassware next to a spiky blue and white flower arrangement, *Welcome Home from your friends at Your Own Eyes!* and the silent mask on its wooden ottoman throne, Felix's battered duffel like a glam-slumming, toughened world traveler, his own wet boots by the door . . . Genie had sent them link after real estate link, grotty brick flats and quirky pieds-à-terre in party neighborhoods full of clubs and coffee bars, all with two bedrooms, one for them, one for their permanent houseguest? But their "personal relocation specialist" had presented this loft via walk-through in The Birches suite: a Hechman property on an upscale street between a Japanese tapas bar and a wine store, with a rooftop forest of sculpted dwarf evergreens, trees and not trees, and an onsite spa, a chef's grade communal kitchen, a 24-hour "innovation lab" that had made Felix pause in unwilling interest: *A studio? There's a studio there?*

The whole building's been redesigned with our tenants' creativity in mind. Would you like a tour of the lab?

I don't care about a studio, Felix had muttered to Ari, leaning back from the screen. *We don't have to take that place—*

—this place that was their next stop after Ari's meet with the Hechman lawyers, an efficient two-person team with a shared desk and dutiful assistants, one taking clipboard notes, one video. The first lawyer had assured him that the criminal charges were being dropped on procedural grounds, the second had dismissed Jonas's non-compete: *You were already hired when you signed it, Siegler gave you no additional consideration—*

Consideration?

You didn't obtain anything of value in exchange. Higher salary, more extensive benefits, a new title—

I never had any title.

—nothing you weren't already entitled to receive.

So I could have just told him to fuck off?

What Mr. Siegler's got here is basically toilet paper.

Toilet paper is successful if you wipe shit for a living.

Excuse me, what?

Nothing, sorry.

Then freed of Jonas and the cappies, but bearing a whole new burden—both those lawyers had explained his actual terms of service, the golden handcuffs, though he has not yet told Felix, there has to be a way out of that too—he and Felix had departed on yet another private plane, a quick hop night flight with cold sauvignon blanc and hot chocolate chip cookies, and the moon for a fellow traveler; in this Hechman world things happen when they are called for, everything is available and obedient, and what a strange enabling, disabling, way to live.

Now "I'm glad to see you're settling in," Ines says. "Moving can be stressful."

"Stress," his nod to that Gunther bag, where a phone inside keeps tinging, discreet, inexorable, "I bet you're a fuck of a lot more stressed than I am. With your new company."

"It's true, we would normally plan for more reactive space after an acquisition. But this industry seems to move very quickly—"

"The world moves fast."

"—so we needed to keep abreast of the learning curve. And now that your legal issues have been resolved, you can—"

"Your Eyeballs," interrupting politely but deliberately, a power move Jonas taught him: Ines reminds him a little of Jonas, that same sense of an inner drive, though Jonas's is a sports car and Ines's is a bullet train. "They had a team in place already, a really good team, that would have saved you some time. What do you want me for?"

She takes a sip of her water, strategic and slow, a different kind of power move. "Our core business is property. Property is physical space. Physical space needs to be activated to compete effectively with digital experience. And your events are definitively real world based, and uniquely impactful," did she mean the Factory, or the Silver Landings fucking? or both? He imagines Ines watching those videos, making notes. "For Your Own Eyes to take full advantage of that commercial potential, we needed—we wanted—you."

"You could have just contracted me in, as a consultant. You didn't have to hire—"

"I don't buy a building floor by floor. And Your Own Eyes will require all of your assets."

"Assets? You mean skills, or—"

—the door buzzing twice, impatient, twice again, this time he gets it open on the first try, and "Isn't this crazy!" Genie's crow, checkered newsboy cap and black denim jacket prestressed and pretorn, the couture version of Max's old jacket, Genie lugging in a rust-flaked bird cage half as tall as she is, a cracked plastic bird hanging inside. "I got it at the Jumble Flea, Felix will *flip* when—"

"Hello, Genevieve."

"*Shit*," stopping dead as she sees Ines, abandoning the birdcage in the middle of the floor as if it suddenly no longer exists. "Why are you here?" pulling out her RoseBud packet, her face hard. "Ari, why did you let her in?"

"Her name's on the building."

"Genevieve, please. And if you have to smoke—"

"I don't. I could just take drugs."

Ari sees that missile land, no need to search for triggers, everything between the sisters is on full display: hellion versus caretaker, party urchin versus corporate operative, *I didn't have a "home" till I was twenty, our core business is property*. And "Ari," Ines says, taking up her tinging bag, setting her glass neatly to the kitchen island, "we'll finish our chat at the office. Genevieve—"

"Stop *calling* me that, just go—"

—and before that door has fully closed, Felix is there, with the key fob and a bulging canvas sack, wine bottle under his other arm: "I got your coffee, there's a fancy bodega right around the corner. Ines was here?" looking from Ari to Genie and back, Genie still sallow with anger but mustering a smile, and "Go have your smoke," Ari says, and she nods, tugging at the iron door to the balcony, closing it almost all the way, a gap left, just wide enough to listen? as Felix asks, flat, "So what was that about?"

"Just a chat," Ari turning so only Felix can see him, putting a cautionary finger to his lips. "Then Genie came. Genie brought you that," pointing to the crusty tilt of the birdcage, Felix giving it barely a glance before he turns to unpack the groceries, coffee beans and oat milk, corn chips and Earl Grey tea, half a dozen blood oranges, the wine, dry white, its label a spiral of gold, a trio of falling stars. And "That A&R guy," Felix says, "Ilias, from Indigo. He called again."

An orange rolls toward the counter's edge like a runaway planet, Ari catches it before it drops. "What did you tell him?"

"I told him no thanks. Again . . . I might check out that studio today, Alaine just sent more stuff—the trance thing she did in Lisbon, Majiic Mountain, remember I showed you? It's hum, just infinite hum, you can just disappear in it—"

"Alaine who?" anxious from the balcony, a question Felix does not answer; though Ari asked his silence about the video, *We can't say we saw this, Ines can't know,* that video has frayed to breaking the friendship between Felix and Genie, Felix distant and Genie bereft, her attempts at reconnection more and more frenzied: endless check-ins and useless gifts like that birdcage, bringing her dog for an equally frenzied visit, a yipping bundle of curly brown and white, Ranger the sherpapoo who ignored Genie's commands as if she were a stranger, sprayed piss all over the lobby, tried to bite the concierge.

So "Genie," he calls, "want to take a walk?" half-smiling as Felix mouths *Thank you* and hands him an orange that he tucks to his pocket, leading Genie out and to the elevator, where her descending rant—"Ines has always been a vampire! We shouldn't even be in this vampire place!"—continues till they part on the corner, Genie flinging herself into a Hopper to go who knows where, what does Genie do when she is not with them? Try to wrangle Ranger? practice her refusals? scream at Ines everything she hears?

And somehow he has also pocketed Ines's left-behind shades, as he walks he slips them on, the world goes sepia: his world, his streets, the phone stores and shisha parlors and brick alleys spongy with old moss and fresh trash, the corner charging station glowing, a handful of boys in Kash Money puff coats hanging out beneath its brim like the boy he used to be, they call out as he passes—"Hey sexy, hey!"—and he smiles back, stops to trade a smoke with the boldest boy, a blunt for a Club cigarette. At Seaweed Palace the soba is still the best, Timothy wraps him in a hug, and at the salon—the new spa fragrant and bubbling below, everything painted a swoony peach—Beatriz in her new high-collared smock rakes his hair with scandalized fingers: "Where have you been, don't they have shears there? Sit in that chair right now."

And then calling a Hechman car for a quiet ride out to the paper mill, where the snow has receded, ice melted in the sun's belated brilliance, everything shines: hard-cratered mud and winter brown weeds and faint green hopeful growth below a new universe of tags, blaring tangerine and fervid pink, every *i* dotted with a flower, ICKI LOVES U ICKI SEES U GOD IS ICKI. His body tightens, the wary flesh remembering attack, but this time he is not alone: a bald man in excavator's boots with an exuberant wolfish dog, a trio of serious young women shooting video, white headscarves and camera and shotgun mic, and the woman and man who had helped him, his old tote now hung among their many bags, they tell him their names this time, Cassie and Wilhelm, they ask him how he is.

Then he takes the car all the way up to the Park—"I'm good here, thanks—" to walk the central path to its end, old gravel gray and guttered from snowmelt, the lawns empty except for a lapping pair of runners and a teenage girl sternly working out with a complicated set of colored hoops. Between the farmers' weathered greenmarket stands and a lonely steaming yakitori van, he stops to eat the orange, split the purple segments, suck the juice, gazing at Dodi's closed-down building and its faded FOR LEASE sign, what does it look like, now, inside? smell like? moldy drapes, the dancing ghosts of sweat and smoke? Nothing survives of that empire but memories and t-shirts, where is his own shirt, left at Deborah's, left at the Fraktur flat? Gone?

And his phone tings, a hidden number, ***Chat in 3 2 1***, because that number is Skelly: beardless now and wearing a brand-new ball cap, ink black with a streamlined gold J, a new logo for Junket? and "Hey," Skelly says, "great to see you, finally, you look great. New look for a new gig? So what would you call that, Your Own Eyes?"

The breeze is cold on his face, cold through his shorn hair. "Using me to try to get with Hechman, what would you call that?"

"I'd call it business. They wanted an experience partner, of course Junket's going to take a swing. And I've been clocking you for how long, now? I think it's fair to say we have a relationship. But," leaning in with a smile as wide as that little screen, "let's talk about your love shack. The engagement, you don't need me to tell you it's outstanding. The music, it's great that you have the exclusive on that DJ. The public meat sex, that might have been a little much, but we could disney that, tidy it up with some Y—"

"I'm not really the guy for tidy."

"Does Your Own Eyes know that?"

"What do you want me for?"

"You see what Tenth Wall is trying to do with Charli Paris? Your veridical metrics could crush that without even breaking a sweat. And when you factor in first mover advantage, sky's the limit! So between you and me, whatever she gave you, I can match it. Was it global?"

"Global *and* molecular."

"What?" that smile even wider, like a song still playing on an empty dancefloor. "Don't sell yourself short, brother—"

"I'm not selling myself at all," to Skelly who had tried to sell Junket as the house that could deliver Ari Regon, or to Ines, how long did it take Ines to understand that she already had the backdoor hook-up? Felix, her sister's best friend, is that why Ines let Genie pay for Silver Landings? *I have my own money, Ines unlocked access.* "I'm off the market now. See you."

Back on the train and glad for its stuffy warmth, his cold fingertips still sticky from the orange, he taps through his latest pictures of Felix—a passionate pillowside gaze, barefoot and focused with earbeads, arms folded on the boxy sofa with Genie at its other end, Genie staring hangdog as if she might cry—then scans the pinging flood of messages, everybody knows he is in town again, everybody wants to see him—

Mikey Trouble, ready to play

Aha the magician is back!

Hi, it's Alain redhead bedhead remember, ha ha!! can't wait to get together again!!

This is Jake from ForwardFast, I'm authorized to offer compensation on a first-look profile

I'm an erotic psychologist and I'm very intrigued by your sex dance

Is it true you're reopening Dark Factory?

im supertight w Felix Ferez heres my loops

Still dancing I see

—that last from someone called BodyMan339, who is BodyMan339? rising as the train slows to check that profile, and see with a tiny jolt that it is Karl: a nearly-bare MePage with paid ads for yoga pants and vaguely porny-sounding muscle supplements, Karl not in an upscale spa in Basel or anywhere else, standing unsmiling between two women in matching t-shirts, discount aspirational, LIVE THE BLUELEAF LIFE! Karl's hair the same, still hot, Karl has not changed. But he has, seeing that face he feels nothing but a final relief, does not respond or even bother to block BodyMan339, only tucks his phone and climbs to the street—

—where now it is even colder, a thin scar of gold glowing behind the clouds, night coming on like house lights going down. Walking faster, weaving through the arm-in-arm couples clustered outside a retro piano bar, passing the glossy façade of a makeup shop, NEWLY YOU, a sample basket of little mauve packets and a pop of acid green, a plastic daisy dropped among them, so defiantly fake that he has to smile, and stop, and take it—

—and read another message, ***makin new beats, u want 2 hear?*** from Kid Yello: Kid Yello who proudly proclaims his friendship with Ari on Kickchat and Beat Buzzer and everywhere else, who sends sound clips and silly jokes and the occasional cock shot; he had shown the latest one to Felix, who made a pointed shrug, *Well, he's got the right handle anyway. KY, cheap and sticky.*

Guys also call him Tri. For tripod—

Yeah, I get it, unsmiling, and Ari had laughed in surprise, to see that Felix was, what, jealous? and kissed him, a nibbling kiss that started at his lips and moved down and down, chin chest belly cock, until they lay together on the floor by the balcony door, Felix smiling again, stroking Ari's back, fingers warm against the scar and

It's getting better, Felix had said, *a lot better, we can start thinking about a tattoo pretty soon* but *I don't want to cover over it,* his murmur, lips against Felix's throat. *I don't ever want to forget.*

As he enters the lobby, the concierge makes an instant, anxious beeline: "Your lock pad should be fine now, sir. And your delivery is already upstairs," sir? what did Ines say to that poor concierge? By their door sits a massive florist's package, gold foil paper and roses, three dozen, four? red velvet petals and thornless stems as long as his arm, with a note, ***♥♥ Luv U Both!!! from your Genie.*** He drops the green daisy into that thicket, lugs the flowers inside—

—to find the loft silent, no Felix, he messages but no answer. So he waits, and waits, steps still waiting onto the balcony, not with a blunt but the bottle, not needing the wine either but wanting it because Felix chose it for him, Felix chilled it for him, the taste of citrus and faint astringent flowers, of long-distilled sweetness finally ripe. And finally a reply, ***busy rn baby, listen!*** to the start of a session in that top floor studio: Alaine Majiic's subtle binaural beats and Felix's response, intense and dense as a net weaving itself, or, what is it called, a fractal? Fractals inside fractals . . . His pulse drops, then rises as he listens, the music at work like the wine inside him, when that music ends he sends a message to Max—

im here

I know. We need to talk

2mrw

When?

early early

—and fishing out the half-bent Club, its taste harsh and instantly familiar, to smoke, and finish the glass, his elbows on the bone-cold iron rail in the float of the smoke, thinking of Ines and Skelly, his question to them both, *what do you want me for?* Whatever they want he could never give them anyway, he knows less than everyone thinks he does but more than maybe anyone else, not what this is but what it could mean, to pull this trigger, *an entire level of presence, available user presence, that no one even knew was there, I'll show you, I'll invite you,* he takes one last drag, sends one last message—

hey im back

—to Jonas, then flicks away the cigarette and steps inside.

###

Pink and gray outside, just dawn as Max climbs the stairs to an emptier floor than Fantastic Fantoms', the unmarked door at the end of that hallway: but before he can knock, the door opens on Ari, smiling and unshaven in a black hoodie. A moment's confusion, unsure how to greet each other until Ari pulls Max into a hug, then tugs at the knit cap he wears: "You're an Octo guy? I seriously wouldn't have figured."

"No—I don't know, Davide gave me this. Why, what's Octo?"

And Ari laughs, partly because Max will always be Max—Octo is a gym porn mascot—but mainly because he is happy to see Max again, Max whose face has lit up for Ari, does he know that? Max who sees everything but himself?

And Max feels his own smile, his own, what? relief? to see Ari actually, finally here, they regard one another until "You look," Max says, "different."

"So do you."

"I got a haircut."

"So did I. And a tat," pushing up his sleeve for full display, and "That's Celtic," Max says, inspecting the whorls, "and Toltec. Body mind spirit, land sea sky, creation destruction resurrection—"

"Why is yours a cat? Are you a cat person?"

"It's the nahual, the avatar, of Tezcatlipoca. He's an Aztec god, his name means 'smoking mirrors.'"

"Sounds like a gamer. Come on in," into this workspace that is still half storage space, though between the cardboard crates and folded movers' tarps there is a Sleepy Queen air mattress and a pump toilet, a pockmarked old table with a sleek new Raptor screen, an espresso machine, and "Want some?" Ari taking up a black cup—one of a pair that came with the machine, just like the ones in Jonas's loft—to sip, and yawn, when has he ever been awake this early? without having come straight from a club? As he climbed out of bed, Felix was just climbing in, in a kind of pleased trance: *Did you listen, baby? did you hear?* "So, I'm here. And Clara says you're on strike."

"I'm not on strike. I told her—I told you, we need to talk."

"All right," leaning to wake that screen, toss Max a tiara from a box below the table, a Ringer dual mode, top of the gaming line. "Let's talk inside—"

—and Max steps first into that work in progress, an empty beach, flat turquoise sea and bruisy sky with a heatless white sun, no shadows from that sun, the shadows will come later. His own avatar is still just a stock model, but the guest avatar strangely suits Ari, its halo like van de graaf energy, fully charged—

—as Ari looks around, taking everything in, half-archeology, half-cartoon, and "This is what the funders saw? The frame lag seems a little fucked, Clara said there were some issues. And Clara said you were going to fix that sun."

"No, it's part of the narrative. It's sunset here, always sunset."

"I thought it was sunrise. What's the loop track?" the piping background cries, alien and sweet, it sounds like Felix's research, and "Birdcalls," Max says. "Birds indigenous to the hemisphere, Davide wants to integrate them with Felix's soundtrack, or something. Felix is doing the soundtrack, right?"

"Or something . . . What are those?" pointing to the sketched scatter of skulls and what looks like trash, it is trash. "What do they do?"

"They're reactive touchpoints."

"Do they talk?"

"Davide wants the skulls to sing."

"I bet he does. So how far does it go, in here?" walking on, leaving the waves and the sand that looks wet but feels like nothing yet, for the empty undulating slope of the dunes, as the looped birds whistle and cry, cry and whistle. As they climb without resistance, without stumbling or sweat, Ari thinks of the Hechman world, how it always feels this frictionless and free of obstacles, everything subject to override design, as Max looks toward what Davide calls the Forest of Unknowing, or the Forest of No Names, where the paths inland will begin; Davide has a name for that too, quincunx, but Max feels no need to point that out, they have other things to talk about now, so: "You play games?" intent, looking not at Ari but at those placeholder trees. "When you were a kid, or—?"

"Just the ones everybody played. Nice view from up here, if there was anything to see. Clara said—"

"You ever play Catastrophia?" then before Ari can answer, "Do you know what this is, all of this?"

Knowing Max is about to say something extremely Max: "It's a game."

"Not a game. Or not just a game. It's another stage, a further stage, of—of what's happening. It's like mycelium—"

"What's mycelium?"

"—the game, the Factory, Silver Landings, all of it. It's affecting human consciousness, actual human consciousness. Human behavior!" his voice too loud, flat in this echoless place. "And when this game is ready, anybody could play it! Everybody could play it—"

"They should play it, why else are we making it? Why did you make your shows?"

"This is different."

"Different how?"

"This *works*—"

—as from nowhere and everywhere, a voice, immense, *HEY YOU TWO* and they jump, Max staring up, Ari wheeling sideways, till both understanding that voice as Clara's, and "Sorry," she says, "volume, sorry . . . How's the dev walk going?" her tone very carefully cheerful, and "We're coming out," Ari calls back, heel-skating down the dune, a shivering glitch at the bottom, disappearing—

—and Max slower to disengage and follow back into that room, another world that makes worlds, linked to screens that make still more worlds, like self-aware matryoshka dolls, like Krishna opening his mouth to show his stunned mother the void: that void that waits beyond everything, *no experience boundaries* so where does it begin? in the game? at a show? or just past those windows, past the plastic-smelling blackout drapes—

—as "Meg," Ari says, to a new face appearing splitscreen beside Clara's, a young woman with puffs of black hair and earbeads like golden vines, a lime green jacket like something out of a fashion shoot, behind a desk module with a potted spotted orchid, sumptuous purple and cream, and a pink poster of a running man, naked and graceful beside floating letters, A WALK IN THE PARK, Meghan who was more than ready to take her own walk, *This isn't at all the way I imagined it happening, Ari, working with you! But I always knew we would.* "Meg, this is Max. Max, Meghan Sorin."

"Good to meet you, Max," Meghan Sorin says, a poised and friendly Brit voice. "I've been enjoying your world building quite a lot."

But Max does not respond, stays so demonstrably silent that Meghan looks questioningly to Ari, who says, "Our walk-through was kind of—intense. Here's what I saw—"

—as Max turns away, facing those draped windows while Ari offers a series of cogent bullet points to Meghan and to Clara, and their vocabulary shifts from metaphysics to bare knuckle business, making to marketing—

"MVP in another, what, twelve weeks? That's still ultra fast, isn't it, given the level of detail—"

"If I had a dollar for every time someone said, what's that there for? But the detail is where everything *is*—"

"Funders will need the bigger picture. I've set up a timeline that I believe is more realistic, more achievable," Meghan who is engineering those funder meetings now. "Ari, can you be there for the meetings? Some of those meetings?"

"I'll be there. I don't know how yet, but I will."

"Thank god," Clara says, with feeling.

Then "Ari," Max abrupt from the window to the door, one hand on the handle. "Come out and smoke," as Meghan raises one eloquent eyebrow, Clara makes a tense shrug—

—and this time Ari leads, not to the main entrance but down

one floor more and through the utility basement, tool racks and shop vac and battered stand of push brooms, then up again on slat steel stairs to a maintenance entrance half-concealed by a peeling green dumpster, where he carefully tugs up the hoodie's hood as Max props that door, lights up a thick reddish stub: "Here . . . Are you in disguise, or what?"

"Disguised as myself. Jesus," on a coughing exhalation, "where'd you get this shit?"

"From Davide. He gets it from one of the coders."

"Rocket fuel. Anyway," with another, more prudent hit, his head already floating, maybe his tolerance has eroded. "I have news—"

"About your disguise? And those drapes? And you showing up here at the crack of dawn?"

And Ari's triple nod to all of that, all one cul-de-sac, he is mired more thoroughly than before because "If Ines finds out I'm doing this, any of this, she could try to claim the whole game as Hechman IP—I know, I know," at Max's stare. "Felix tried to tell me," and Felix was right, though Felix himself is firewalled, none of this can touch Mister Minos or his music in any way, he learned how that was possible from those lawyers. "But I won't let it stop us. I just have to stay in the background, that's why Meghan leased that space upstairs."

Ari, in the background? how is that even possible? but "No one," Max says, "will hear anything from me."

"Not even your girlfriend? Marfa Carpenter?"

"Marfa's not my girlfriend. I haven't even seen her since that video—"

—as they share what they know about those videos until the blunt is done, though "How'd she access them?" Ari asks, squinting through the smoke. "No way from Hechman. And a leak like that wouldn't help Skelly."

"I don't know how."

"Maybe you should ask."

The sun strikes white on the red and yellow signage just beyond the dumpster, PARKEN VERBOTEN, no parking, no stopping, fully morning now so "I better get back," Ari says, "to the loft," to be seen there by the concierge, and the elevator cameras. "And you," half-smiling, giving a tug to the Octo cap, "better get back to work—"

"On what?" face to face finally, gaze to gaze. "What are we making? It's not a game, it's not a show, what *is* it?"

"Remember," Ari's hand to Max's shoulder, Max so earnest and so troubled, Ari with absolute conviction, "remember how you said we made up stories to keep from falling apart? Well, this is the story," giving that shoulder a firm little shake, another, until Max finally nods. Then "I'll be around," Ari stepping back through the shielding door—

—as slowly Max follows, up to the third floor, to take his seat again beneath the smaller sun of the tensor lamp, and see that someone has left on his table, like an offering, a brand-new and better smart pen, IMPROVED WRITABILITY. And "Hey," Davide calls from the cockpit, Davide with sleep's grit in his eyes, wearing a perky stocking cap that looks like a jester's hat, it even has the little bell at the tip. "Heard you hit the beach today," while Clara half-turns from her own screen, Meghan still visible there: Max can feel them all watching, waiting for his response, so "I did," he says, carefully splitting open the blister pack. "There's a lot to do, and I'm way behind. Thanks for the pen."

###

From the smeared bus window Max sees a waiting figure on the empty access road, Marfa in a drooping black cap, gripping a tote bag, watching him disembark, the day colder than it has been, her breath is visible as "Hey," she calls, sounding nervous. "You're early."

"The bus was early," yet she is already here, in answer to his answer to her last message: because Ari was right, they need to know more about those videos' trajectory, *I get stuff,* how? So late last night, after a long day's catch-up on that beach, ***Meet at Bitter Lake tomorrow***, his message, ***you know where it is?***

And her message at once, ***Check your inbox*** to find a zip link for transcripts, interviews with people about the Factory, people who worked there or had been there, with Jonas, and Felix, even Adam Kaiser, all meticulously dated and annotated, her questions goading and knowing and lively, and "You saw what I sent?" she asks now. "Full disclosure, that's everything I got so far for Leland."

"Who's Leland?"

"The guy in the videos, he's the one who sent them to me. And here," pulling off her cap—she has a new haircut, very short, with stern new bangs as if sheared by a knife—holding it out until he sees it is his own missing Kuntsfarm cap, she offers that and the tote bag too, the brown folder inside it, Jonas's notes. "When you never answered, I came to return this, but Glenda said you moved."

"I did," into a ground floor space in what used to be a sugar warehouse, drafty but sound, and three times the size of his old room, with a plywood bed and high dusty windows; Davide ostensibly lives in that building, Davide the one who told him that the space was open, though he has yet to see Davide there, among the artists, everyone there seems to be an artist of some kind. "It's a lot closer to my job . . . You took my cap?"

"Yeah."

"Why?"

"I wanted something of yours."

"What for?"

Her cheeks go blotchy red, her chin, but she holds his look. "Because I thought I'd never see you, I thought you'd never talk to me again."

He almost says *I thought so too* but then does not, instead pulls on the cap as she starts to walk, her hands deep in the pockets of her tac jacket. The bus has disappeared, nothing here but the road and the trees—all the trees seem to be intact, none cut down, nothing dug up or destroyed—and the quiet of their footsteps, the sudden three-note call of a bird, what kind of bird? birds of the seasons, ready for spring. That Marfa says nothing surprises him, is this another of her opacities, or is she waiting for him to start? so "You want to tell me," he says, "about those videos?"

"It's really pretty out here. I wish I had seen your show," and for a startled moment he thinks she is crying, she stops so he stops too, and "Max," her breathing uneven, she is crying. "Listen, I didn't mean not to tell you stuff, I—*Fuck*. I didn't mean to do this, either—"

"It's OK," not knowing what else to say; the bird calls again, those three notes. Finally "I'll tell you," she says, swiping her eyes with her sleeve, she walks again, he walks beside her. "About Leland—"

—Leland Cardenal, an old family friend, *my parents are very arty,* Leland Cardenal a high-end art investor, enabler, who had offered her a way out of an old dead end, set her on a trail toward what he called experience art, to research and document the genesis of Lady of the Lake, Glenda Vitale was more than glad to host her for a chance at meeting Leland Cardenal. "But you were the one who got me onto Dark Factory, and Leland liked that even better," liked all the backstage intel, liked Jonas's notes, Leland the one who told her that Dark Factory was being sold: "And by 'told' I mean played. That video was supposed to get Ari talking, the first one, and if that didn't work I had the audio one. But the mural really goosed it for him—"

"What mural?"

"At Happy Endings, didn't you see it?" phone out to show a clip of a brick-walled patio, a pink and gold mural of two men and a skeleton and "Jesus," he says, not because one of the men is, yes, Leland Cardenal from the video, same big ears, a wide grin unnervingly glad, but because the skeleton has Lukas the coder's face, a singing skull with brown sockets, how the fuck is Lukas painted on that wall? And "When Leland saw *that*," she says, "he got even more invested: 'Look at me, I'm really part of the art!' I know for a fact he's chasing down those Sto Lat guys . . . If he knew I sent you that second video, he'd fire me. He'd sue me—"

"Then why did you do it?"

"I did it for you—"

—as they reach the production garage, its door stickered with multiple peeling NO TRESPASSING stickers, and an official blue and white Hechman Properties sign. But the door is unlocked, and inside everything looks the same: the kitchen table tumble of burlap and twigs and plastic bags, the curling unused flyers, the tarp, the bolt of fake fur for the masks, even the can of Vino-2-Go and the bag of old seeds. And Max pauses, this threshold itself an antipodal point, himself as he is standing opposite himself as he was, he can almost see that other Max, frowning, furious, dissatisfied, longing to do exactly what he is doing now with B of P—

—as Marfa clicks the dead light switch, "No juice in here," but "There should be candles in the lav," he says, and they light all the ones they can find, Blueberry Therapy, Mandarin Mood, while he thinks of the burned garage at Perfect Circle, is the circle complete now? the ouroboros that eats its tail yet is never really devoured?

And "Did you look," she asks, "at the interviews I sent? I still have a list of people I wanted to talk to. I tried with Ari, but he wouldn't talk to me."

"Ari doesn't trust you."

"Do you," not a question, he does not answer: *insider's perspective, sometimes you need to go dark, I'm as shocked as you are*—but *thank you boyfriend, oh no Romeo, MCSq2,* so "I can never tell," he says, "what's real, with you."

The little candles' light shows the breath she takes, another, until "All right," her voice changing, rising, not loud but firm, "here's something a hundred percent for real. Ever since that night on the roof, I wanted—to be your girlfriend. I knew about that dancer, Mila, I knew it was never going to happen. But I wanted it anyway. I still do—"

—and because he cannot say *Yes it will*, or *I'm sorry*—they never could be together the way he was with Mila, and to say he is sorry would be an insult, even he understands that—he says instead, to meet her truth with his, "I read through all those interviews, your questions were great, you get right to the center of things. You're a really good writer, Marfa."

"Seriously?" her smile then a smile he has never seen from her before, unguarded, gratified. "I thought you never showed me your notes because I wasn't a real writer, like you."

"Is that why you never interviewed me?"

"You would have done it?"

"We could do it right now."

"Max—*Seriously?*" and when he nods, "I have my recorder," sliding it from one of her pockets. "I don't have formal questions, but there are plenty of things I want to ask—"

"Here," pulling out Teresa's old chair, the raveled afghan still hung from its back, ready against the cold, "sit here," at that table, the windows darkening as the sun disappears, the candles' lights reflecting, doubled and redoubled in that squared darkness like stars against the fading outlines of the trees, the sky, the road, the outer world, the real world so immeasurably large. Yet this small place was once his world, is his world still, *this is the story,* so "Go ahead," he says, folding the old blue tarp for a cushion, his legs crossed on the dusty floor. "Ask me whatever you want."

###

The song is new, and everywhere, "Basic Heaven 123," and whenever it comes up in his playlist, Ari has to smile—*Basic heaven 1-2-3, we made our own world you and me/Basic heaven 3-2-1, it's not over it's not done*, a wistful melody and a reedy male voice backed by a mechanical grind, a bot revving until it breaks apart in ecstasy and ruin—listening to it now as he leaves the loft building to step into the wine shop next door, TRÈS DÉLICIEUX: cocktail jazz floating in the air, the clerk looking up from a counterside screen, Ari in club wear clearly not his normal customer.

"May I help you?"

"I want to get rich person drunk. White wine. What have you got?"

The clerk blinks, then rallies, scanning the shelves made to look like marble, maybe they are marble, returning with a golden bottle: "*Château d'Yquem,* 2017, an excellent botrytis year. Precise but voluptuous notes of lemon and yuzu, with—"

"It's OK, it's not my money," paying with the corporate card, keying in their floor number for the delivery, messaging Felix, ***heres a toast 4 l8ter*** . . . Felix had approved of his party look, tight black pants and a new gold jacket, a Borisaki jacket, he has never worn anything so expensive, and *I like it when you don't shave,* Felix said. *It makes you look kind of gangster.*

You going to work with Alaine tonight?

Edit through what we did last night. Did you see that link I sent, about the Minotaur myth? Did you read it?

I did, most of it, a very scholarly article he was not sure he fully understood, a maze of bulls and stars and fate, what had that tattoo artist said to them? You fellows must be mystics . . . And Alaine has invited Felix to come and play, more beats, more fractals, at some festival in Malmö, then *A big gig in Barcelona, in a church, a basilica—not Sagrada Familia, but big. The sound would be unbelievable.*

Make plans with her. Get ready to go.

To Malmö? We're going?

You want to go.

I want to play. I have to play—So can you go, now? the game's finished? What about Ines? but *We'll talk about that when I get back,* as he searched out the half-pack of Club cigarettes on the cluttered kitchen island, plucked from the sofa one of Felix's scarves, striped black and white, to twine around his neck. *I won't be late.*

Now in the street he boards the Hechman car, for sure the strangest way he has ever traveled to a club, and early too, too early but Ines lives on corporate time, maybe this is late for her. In the car's hermetic quiet, he feels the vibration of the Hechman phone in his pocket—kept in scramble mode, though Burk objects to that—and this message is from Burk, ***What's your ETA?*** Burk who uses terms like ETA instead of just asking when he will get there, Burk always trailing Ines like a slave satellite thrilled by its orbit; for some reason Genie hates Burk, Genie calls him "Marty." And ***asap*** his answer, unsealing the chairside coffee as he checks then mutes his real phone, downs that coffee, chews his nails, forces himself to stop: tonight is too important to be nervous, he needs to be calm and fully on his game.

And "Here you are, sir," the driver pulling up to Karbon Klub, its doors appropriately black, and outside a hyped and noisy gauntlet of the dressed-up and uninvited, a visible fail for Your Own Eyes' covert guest list. People call his name and he stops to wave, hipshot and smiling, fodder for pictures and posts, then security wands him in, his first time inside a club since Fraktur—

—and the first thing he sees in the sweeping blue lights is the empty DJ platform—the background track already rolling, nothing of Felix's in that mix—as if that platform is part of the swag display below: blue lash-fringed bags with eyebrow handles, each one adorned with a faux DJ charm in the shape of a winking eye, packed with a pair of mid-priced hotspot shades, a golden tube of Morning After eye cream, and a preloaded mix stick full of Hechman marketing propaganda, he had signed off without bothering to listen through it. The haptic shirts had to be discarded as unusable, those eyes stuck shut or opening oddly, randomly; that design is still confidential, but he had slipped one from the office pile anyway to take back and model for Meghan, who had waited to laugh until he did, then shook her head, *They literally do not see.*

The event doc team approaches him—two dutiful and well-equipped shooters, moving from guest to guest as if this was a corporate mingle—but he waves them off to head instead for a central black banquette, VIP seating with a bouncer below, arms folded like a giant chess piece. Dolores and Deirdre are already there, two heads bent over one tablet, two bland tools dressed as weapons, gray silk suit and rough-edged biker glam, always on brand, their own brand, and "Hello, Ari," Dolores says, as Deirdre nods.

"These are the Glasshouse drinks?" as he takes one to sip, champagne noir to go with the décor, an undertaste of bitters, a twisted golden peel; with brief professional guilt, he recalls the Red Eye, why not at least a blue olive for a blue eye? The effort he put into this night, even as a sham, is worse than subpar, for that alone Ines should fire him.

Dolores takes a glass too, but does not drink. "Did you see yourself on Tickets Please today?"

A breakdown of his current followers' metrics, he had barely glanced at it, he barely glances at her, where is Ines? and "I must have missed that," he says, as "There were some surprising spikes," Deirdre says, "outside of the club and creative demos. Entertainment law was one of them—Hello, Ines—"

—Ines in a meat-red jacket and velvet newsboy cap, a thin pinkish line of lipstick, is that a CEO's idea of club wear? with Burk trotting just behind her, his boxy suit more suitable for a board meeting. And "There's quite a group outside," Ines says, sliding onto the banquette. "Dolores, Deirdre, I reviewed those metrics you sent, they were interesting, weren't they. Ari, you're looking festive," what does that mean, does she mean the jacket? "All we need is the DJ."

"We're just finalizing the tiara," Dolores turning the tablet to display thumbnails of what look like jokey Halloween horns. "It will harvest engagement data while visually referencing the DJ mask," clicking through to another series, a dozen images of a rendered concept mask, slick and hard-edged, a monster not a god. "CadFab will do the physical mod, they'll integrate IEM for comm and for safety, and a cam for better event visuals—"

"No mask," Ari says, drinking down his cocktail, "no DJ. I want a brandtrack feed for the launch."

Dolores and Deirdre turn as one to Ines, Burk looks at Ari, a look that locks into a stare as Ines says, "That's not at all what we've discussed. Or approved. Why are you proposing this now?"

"I'm not 'proposing' anything," head tipped back, arms kept loose, a power posture straight from Jonas's body language lectures. "You hired me to make this, this is how I want to make it."

A trio of eager partygoers climb the banquette steps, Burk gestures sharply to the bouncer who turns them back, as "The entire brand launch," Dolores says, dismayed, "directly involves the DJ and mask imagery. A conceptual swerve at this stage is not optimal. We would advise, we would *strongly* advise—"

"You only wanted him for Genie," Ari says to Ines, conversationally, as if he and she are alone: Ines whose look hardens like water claimed by ice, Ines so self-possessed and armored but *humans are just a walking set of triggers* and he has deliberately triggered hers, right in front of her team, a challenge she cannot dismiss or ignore. And he knows he is right, the only reason Ines ever wanted him was to get Felix, *all of your assets,* Felix meant for Genie, why? as a treat? a reward for keeping clean? "But Genie's my friend, not my business. And the DJ—any DJ—isn't part of my contract."

No one speaks. Burk continues to stare at Ari, Deirdre consults the tablet, Dolores watches Ines whose brittle focus shifts as "Ari!" a shout from the floor, Genie arriving in rubbery black, her hair newly dyed to match. "Ari, come and dance!"

His three quick steps from the banquette feel very long—did that work? it has to work—then Genie nooses arms around his neck in a too-hard hug, tows him toward the backlit crescent of the bar where "Have a drink," Genie says, orders, she sounds like Ines, she looks like a floating white skull, thick brown lipstick and wide eyes sunk in kohl, that black hair, "have one for me. I haven't seen you in fucking forever, or our prince. When's he getting here?"

"He's not."

"He's not playing tonight?"

"Not playing for Your Own Eyes. He's—"

"What do you mean, he's not *playing*? That's what all this shit is *for*, he's—"

"—leaving, he's going on tour—"

"Leaving?" Her face changes, eyes even wider. "With that stupid woo-woo DJ girl—You mean leaving *you?*"

"Genie—"

"If Felix can leave you—" and she pivots, almost crashes into a server carrying a loaded tray, pinballs away—

—as he steadies that wobbling server, then heads for the main entrance to steady himself, take a breath, pull out a cigarette; the people still milling take his picture, a woman in spike heels and a sparkly anorak gives him a light and kisses his cheek. The Hechman phone vibrates, Burk, he thumbs back ***smoke break*** as his real phone tings, tings again, a number he does not know—

I just sold the Factory

"The fuck," aloud and dumbfounded, Jonas? on another one of his burner phones? Jonas sold the Factory?

4 real?

Yes, come talk now

loft?

Factory

15

—because the car that ferried him is still here, parked halfway up the block, he slams inside and "Excuse me," the driver alarmed, then confused. "I thought I was waiting for Miss Hechman?"

"She's going to be a minute. I just need a quick lift—"

—across town and down to Neuberg Street, almost empty in the streetlights' hiccup flicker, only a connector bus wheezing by as the Hechman car halts before those bigger black doors, mag chained and stickered now, NO ENTRANCE NO ENTRAR VERBOTEN, while a stretch sedan, headlights off, rolls up from the opposite corner—

—and "Slick ride," Ari says as he climbs inside: the floor and ceiling carpeted in tiger-striped gold, wraparound back seat with a built-in slalom pour, lights like the champagne room at a strip club. "Yours?"

"You know it's not mine." Jonas looks bleaker than Ari has ever seen him, stark dark tieless suit and big cheap-looking gold ring, a gold streak dyed zigzag into his hair, defiantly bright against the lines of his face. "Jesus, look at you, big celebrity on your opening night. Brass fucking balls, though, I'll give you that. Got a smoke?"

He offers a Club, Jonas frowns in disgust then takes it, takes the light and "Where should we start?" on a hard exhalation, that smoke mingling with Ari's, a little cloud below the recessed ceiling lights. "With your Hechman pals? I accepted their offer today."

Another blow, a harder one, Ines is the one who bought the Factory? *All of your assets, I don't buy a building floor by floor, that's what all this shit is for,* how much shit is there? "Congratulations. How much did you get for your dream?"

"I'm fucking drowning, who are you to judge? They probably bought it for you anyway . . . I sold the loft first, my funders were *pissed*. Pissed at you, too."

"Me?"

"Yes you. The way you shut things down," one thumb aimed at those stickered doors, "all those cops and city inspectors, that freak show moving in to drag down the property values, you're lucky you left town when you did. You're even luckier you ended up with Hechman for a blast wall, otherwise they'd be more than happy to fuck you up. Not even for the money, just for the aggravation."

He remembers those sharky VC bros, Marko and Goran in their own dark tieless suits. "Lee said you had acute financial issues."

"She wasn't wrong. Know what else she said? 'Look out, Ari's going to stab you in the back'—"

"Oh fuck that. Fuck you! How many times—"

"I worked for years, *years*, and you blew it all up in one night! Overtime too—"

"I tried to tell you," but if Jonas had listened, where would they be now? where would he be? inside the Factory, or watching the screen at the loft? would Max be there? And Felix, would he even have met—

"—your techno boyfriend, your silver sex party, Your Own Eyes, you get them to do whatever you want—"

"That's not how it is. That's not—"

"Then how is it!" Jonas's shout, a great and naked, final bafflement. "'Ari's a maker' . . . You and your *fucking* brain."

Silence between them, a battered little car slows, stops, a girl jumps out, notes the limo, jumps back in as the car accelerates away. Then a jangly pop beat from Jonas's phone, and "Nadja," Jonas says, slotting his cigarette out the window, flicking on the vent scrubbers, turning the screen to show a pretty, discontented-looking blonde in headband and hot pink unitard, she could be departed Darcy's younger sister. "My fiancée. Lee's a wedding planner now, think I should hire her?"

"A wedding planner?" That furtive beige bag, whatever Lee had taken from Jonas's office had not helped her after all. "Wait, you're getting mar—"

"Quiet," harsh as the phone goes again, three flat metallic tones, "you're not here—Marko, hey, *zdravo*," Jonas's voice changing, half-turning in the seat, one shoulder up like a warding wall. "Right, Nadja just—Right, can't be tardy for the party! See you there," then "Got to go," to Ari, placing the phone in his inner pocket as if it were a loaded gun. "Drinks at the Onion Room."

"The Onion Room?"

"Shut up."

"I had an idea, before, for the roof. I was going to call it Dark Park."

"Dark Park? which makes you what, Ari Appleseed?" Ari almost smiles, Jonas shakes his head, then "The heart of Dark Factory,'" Jonas says. "Remember that?"

"I remember."

"I did a lot for you, Ari. I taught you a lot."

"I know you did—"

—and he puts out his hand, and Jonas takes it, the same overbearing grip, the strange hard ghost of that old paternal gaze: "Well, use it. But your ass better have an exit strategy—"

—as Ari climbs back to the curb and the sedan speeds off, the Hechman phone vibrating—Burk in escalating rigor, ***URGENT Where are you? Are you onsite? URGENT***—messaging back ***acquisition recon UNAVAILABLE***. He checks the performers' entrance, that door looped with yellow mag chain too; by the littered truck wells the NOT AN EXIT doors are locked, the dumpsters placed in haphazard blockade, but from behind those dumpsters he can hear rustling, moving, human noises, he keeps his hands loose just in case as he calls out, "Hey, anyone here? Anyone going inside?"

A long blue hush beam emerges, two women, one in a pea coat with a dark shaven head, the other in a particle mask toting a professional-looking camera rig, are they journos? The bald woman peers at him, then "You want in?" crouching to aim a straw-tipped can at the door seam to spray, spray again, then "Welcome," she says with a conspirator's smile, and he is inside—

—to wander slowly as a stranger through this place that was his place, and now is what? a graveyard, a museum? a playground? its darkness lit by orange trouble lights and winking blue battery lights, all the EXIT signs have gone out. The dancefloor is scabbed with wax, hundreds of candles burned to puddles, and scattered with glass and flowers, not asters this time but pink roses, nearly fresh roses, their scent still alive in the odor of old alcohol and recent piss. There are a few unbroken two-tops left, and at least a dozen shrines made of scavenged cardboard or detritus, some battered, a few look brand-new: one strung with paper stars, like the ones he and Peggi made for Dreamtime; another is full of shoes, single shoes set up like a shop window, a black stiletto, a fat Balenciaga trainer, a brown cowboy boot; another has a painted picture of a golden woman, a celebrity, a saint? stuck in a clump of what might be bandages, sickly smelly beige and white; the largest is stacked like a bookcase, soft curled paper covers and hard square textbooks, topped with a neat cardboard sign, LEARN SOMETHING HERE! And at the center of the dancefloor is an elaborate grouping of pink rocks and empty bottles, all green bottles, Jinro and Kurzat and Jameson, what is that about? From above he hears a woman's laughing shout, a jarring air horn bleat, faint ragged voices singing a song he does not know, it sounds like a church song—

—and circling up the ramp, he thinks of Max, takes and sends a picture, another picture, another, a message, ***@ factory look*** at that dancefloor, those drifts of feathers and dripped bird shit, tags everywhere, some he recognizes, some not, and writing scrawled all around the graffiti room, as if escaping the walls that once held it. The little storage room with the mirrored door has no door at all anymore, the box of party hats is empty, the floor blobbed with yellow paint, is it paint? or some kind of spray glue? And he feels the building's cold, no heat in here for how long, what is that doing to the pipes? or the people? spotting what could be baggers' nests, and a little presswood lean-to at a second floor pocket bar, someone is inside it, he can hear them, they stop moving and wait for him to go—

—up and up to where the drafty roofside door is looped half-shut with neon green polyrope, a smeared and grinning three-eyed face, OPEN!!! JUST KNOCK!!! But he does not knock, heads instead to that floor's best vantage point, where he used to stand and watch the traffic on the ramp, seeing now that the levels of chaos below show a wild intrinsic order, there are paths down there, and structure, the dancefloor rocks and bottles are arranged in the shape of a flower. And his mind shivers as if on the brink of something vast, yet purely personal, what had Max called it? mycelium? everything growing and twining, like those paths, and the vines across the back of his black hoodie, and the pinkish twists of his scar.

Down again, he finds Jonas's office door is locked, OVERTIME posters still on the dusty windows, his breath makes a tiny cloud as he peers inside, remembering his first time in that office: unopened boxes and the blue desk just delivered, Jonas excited and assured, *Here's where everything's going to happen!* Jonas locked out now with his debts, if the loft has been sold then where is Jonas living? and how? *I'm fucking drowning. My fiancée.*

And all the bars must be long dry, but he walks back anyway to Annelise's station, its smart mirror painted over with solemn antlered aliens and a repeating tag in gold, #FINDUMOND, to root through empty serviette boxes and broken soda guns and a musty nest of still-folded Overtime t-shirts, and find an unopened bottle of heart-red wine. He drinks, the wine makes him warmer, he raises that bottle and "Cheers!" his shout loud enough for the past to hear, and the future—

—and three figures far up the ramp shout back and laugh, "Chug, chug!" as he drinks and coughs, then pours out the dregs in a splashing spiral, as a pair of birds, startled, beat their white wings above the clear curve of the ramp, and rise. Outside again, the dumpsters are deserted, the two explorers gone inside or gone away; the sky has changed, he can see the stars—

—and at the loft, the building's built-in balcony lights could be stars too, their small steady shine against the darkness, dim inside where Felix sits on the sofa, Felix with headphones on and listening, listening to the world *if the world was perfect,* and "Hey," Felix seeing him then, surprised, "you *are* early. How was it?"

"Good," shrugging off the golden jacket, "I think I got fired. Where's that wine?" carefully freeing the bottle's cork to pour two glasses, a small testing swallow, and "Wow," because he has never tasted anything like this, the Factory bottle is like kerosene in comparison. "This really is *très* delicious."

"What are we toasting?" as they settle on the sofa, and he recounts his night, Ines and Genie—Felix rolling his eyes at the mask tiaras, half-smiling over Genie's new look, "She always dyes her hair when she's feeling rowdy"—but lingering longest on what he saw at the Factory, all that mutating growth, all part of what comes next, what they need to do—though still the long shadow of that old fear, what if Felix goes and keeps going, what if he never comes back? but Felix needs to go, and how else to keep him clear of whatever shit might head their way from Ines? And maybe worse than Ines, *they'd be more than happy to fuck you up,* the only detail of this night he does not share, Felix worries too much already.

So "You," he says," need to go to Malmö. Set it up with Alaine and go."

"What about you? The game—"

"The game will be fine. I just have to make sure they can launch—one funder walk-through, maybe two, and I'm gone. But you should leave right now."

"No."

"What?"

"I said no," firm. "We belong together, we'll go together."

"We are together," just as firm, "no matter where we are. I trust you. I love you—"

"Ari," on a caught breath, Felix's arms closing tight around him, "oh *baby*, my baby," as his eyes close in full content, he has never said those words before, not to Karl, not to anyone. Finally Felix murmurs, "I love you, too. And this time we go for good. No more Genie, no more games. Just us."

"Just us."

"So OK. I'll tell Alaine . . . Cheers," sharing out the bottle's last toast, watched by the mask, Mister Minos' true and eyeless face: and between those horns the little green plastic daisy, its bloom outlasting the roses long turned to stalks and scum, only the card is left in the empty vase, its creased and doubled hearts, ***♥♥ Luv U Both!!! from your Genie***

###

"These vibrating yoga pants," skullhead Lukas's drawl, plucking at his pant leg, swiveling in Max's chair, nearly knocking into Max waiting silent beside. "Oops, didn't see you . . . Lois said they opened her kundalini."

"That's just Lois-speak, real kundalini is a clear-your-calendar kind of thing," Davide frowning, distracted, wearing a wrist brace, inflated and black, and a shirt with blinking eyes, it smells like skin and snack food. "Max, you ready?"

Max nods, his folded hands unfolding to reach for the tiara, entering B of P in the fading echo of Lukas's voice, "That guy, someone finally unsprung his spring?" as Davide's voice rises in audio: "'Your young men shall see visions' . . . Just bop around, Max, say what you see—"

—and he starts walking, the sun still without shadows but making glitter of the water where it lies, noting the corrected frame rate, the expanded loops of concertina wire, stopping to note a new pile of building materials and an inviting rudimentary axe—

"Max, what's wrong, you can't advance?"

"I am advancing—"

—deliberately, the same grounded feel ever since his talk with Ari, his interview with Marfa, asking and answering until she finally stopped to upload—*This is kind of a mindfuck, I need to make sure I have it all*—while he walked the dark path beneath the rowan trees, their branches stripped bare of berries, but the siskins will be back, the stream still moving and alive, the whole place still endlessly living, *if the Garden of Eden were real, a real place,* like B of P, all one story, Ari was right again—

—and pausing again, to listen, then "The birdcalls," he calls to Davide. "You changed them?"

"Tweaked them. Voices of the extinct. African greys, laughing owls, passenger pigeons, sisyphus ducks. Would have been fucking nice to have Felix Minos do a—Yeah, no, delta *and* gamma waves! Coupled oscillation, neural synchronization," is that meant for him or for Lukas? "I *know* that guy knows Pascal Fries, Tam Hunt too—Max? Is Upstairs Man ever going to get us some beats? Momentum, momentum—"

"I know. He knows," thinking again of the pictures Ari had sent from the Factory, all those words written everywhere . . . He had asked Davide, in one of their late night sessions, how it might work if someone was actually part of the experience, not just playing but actively creating, *Like you said you wanted to, when you were a kid. You think that's something that can ever happen?*

And Davide had swiveled in his cockpit, head back, as if he were pulling sudden G's: *Mushrooms can talk to each other, anything can happen! And it's definitely been tried. It's even been done, kind of. Ever hear of Maven 2?*

No. Is that a game?

A war game. I'll show you.

When he finally emerges, back into the world of rolling chairs and loud crushcore and the unchanging twelve o'clock clock, the room is full of scorched pizza smell, and argument—"Ludonarrative dissonance, we're *solving* that shit—Max, wow, thought you were getting your Maven on. The pizza's gone, but," Davide offering the jumbo crinkling bag of Wheaty Bites, as if he must need sustenance. "Lukas, when you get with Caterpillar Brain, tell her, but don't *tell*-tell her."

"I'll tell her," Lukas says on a yawn, that unnervingly wide mouth. "Her beats are way better than Horny Guy's anyway, you ask me. Later."

And as he departs, "Marfa's here," Clara calls, Marfa in tac jacket and rubber ankle boots, she looks like a courier in a movie, an operative, she gives a smile to Max then turns, all business, to Clara: "I sent Meghan the contact stuff on Leland's groupie. The other one, on the TECMA board, we'll find out about her today—Max, you ready?" because she has come to collect him, to go together to the journo hive—

—where Freddie is waiting in the busy afternoon hallway, in a suit coat and a lime green cap, his gaze fixes on Marfa after a hostile look at Max. "Carp. You seem well."

"Freddie," pointing to the meeting room door behind him, "I am well, and you still owe me. Let's go—"

"You, possibly. But not him. He's not even a colleague, he's just a decommissioned fuck buddy—"

"I'm fine," Max says, "out here."

"No," Marfa arms folded and adamant, "one hundred percent transparency, that's how I roll now," and "Love," Freddie says, flat, "is a wonderful thing."

Phones inserted one by one into the locker, its timer set, they troop as a trio into that small and stuffy meeting room where Max finds a chair that could have come direct from the Factory lounge, while Marfa and Freddie are immediately busy with a harvested document, an LOI from Jonas Siegler, because Jonas has finally sold the Factory—

"—since he's working for, what's it called, Sunset Entertainment?"

"Could be a front. Marko Vic beat a money laundering charge two years ago, but—"

"If Hechman really wants to cleanse the brand they'd raze that building—"

"You see Whirligig?" Marfa projecting the page onto the whiteboard wall, Max taking in the Your Own Eyes logo, a stock shot of a hospital, and Ari in a gold jacket and scarf and purely professional grin, juxtaposed with someone who must be Genie Hechman, blue hair and scowling: *Genevieve Hechman, back in rehab for her struggle with substance abuse, is closely involved with Ari Regon, the former leader of Dark Factory, a culty and lawless party community. Regon is now helming Your Own Eyes—*

—while Marfa and Freddie debate over someone called Kokie, who "Fits through a keyhole," Freddie says, "if you're willing to pay for it. Who's actually paying you, though, Carp?"

"That's actually none of your business, Freddie. We need intel on that museum woman, can you get it or not?"

"Oh I can. Will I?" with a sour look for Max who looks back, thinking how much Freddie resembles a particular species of frog in B of P, his cap in fact is the exact same shade as that frog. "What's the matter with him? Is he on drugs, too?"

"Nothing's the matter, he's an artist. Hit me when you get it—"

—as the lockbox timer buzzes, Max noting as they go the very old acoustic ceiling tiles, the pattern resembling the waves on the shore at B of P, those waves made to echo the waves of radio transmissions, the ones that pass through space forever, what did Davide call them? FRB, fast radio bursts—

—but Marfa does not notice, Marfa is absorbed in her messages, Marfa is busy putting all her skills to work for Fantastic Fantoms and B of P. Clara and Meghan were dubious at first, but whatever vetting they did seemed to satisfy them, and Marfa has been more than helpful, is working now to hook them up with some rich art world funder, some Leland friend; all part of, what to call it, her apology? amends? After Bitter Lake she had been very quiet for a day, then very determined, telling him *If you want this game to happen, then I want to help. You deserve that. And I owe you one.*

You don't owe me.

Max, I can do this.

And "Wow," she says now as they step out, "what a day," pure sunlight, the breeze still cool but markedly sweeter, the street trees' green grown bolder, the birds are back, the kids on rollerwheels are back, the quick whizzing Spoony bikes and Kaffee Karts are everywhere, spring has taken hold. "Want to grab some food? I could use it, and you probably need it. That Milagros place is right around here—"

—with its shiny tin sign and lettered quote, no Deborah visible this time, but a line waiting patient out the door. So they keep walking, her arm looped through his, the way one friend links arms with another: they have not, will not sleep together again, but they are closer than before, really friends; and colleagues, Marfa is another writer after all—

"—Meghan says that Ari needs to sign off on the walk-through, Meghan says it's good to go, or good enough. But Clara says there are too still many gaps in the play landscape, or playscape, whatever you people call it—How about that?" pointing to an alleyside street vendor, a good greasy scent, smoky steel portagrill with seared pita and hot sauce and some fluffy egglike filling: Max eats two before Marfa finishes her first, he did need it, when has he last eaten anything besides bagged pretzels and pocket-squashed energy bars, and bulbs of cold tea?

And "Davide," he says, chewing, "says that there's no way to synthesize actual nutrients in a Y hybrid environment. So we can't eat in there."

"Among other things," tucking her hair back under her hat—longer now, the jagged bangs hang softer—a new red pompom cap, she calls it her red queen hat. "Even if you wear a cath line, I've seen guys do that in tournaments, ugh, you still have to come out sometimes. Nobody can actually live inside a game."

The cart vendor turns up his music, another customer steps up, a gangly boy with a Black Raiders backpack nodding to that beat, and "The Factory theme song," Marfa aiming her balled-up napkin for the dented cartside bin, a deft overhand toss, making the shot. "Lost in the Stars recorded it, and I recorded them."

"That's not the Factory theme song, though. When Felix played—"

"Felix was supposed to make the B of P theme song, wasn't he? But he's off having his own adventures. Liability nightmare! That Swedish festival's lucky no one got killed. Think Ari would talk to me about that?"

"About Felix? No."

"He's a hard guy to figure, isn't he. It seems like he'd be more fazed that Dark Factory got sold . . . You want another one?"

"Split one?" so they do, Marfa tugging the pita in half, the sauce dripping onto Max's hand as red as blood, as Marfa's hat, and "Why do you call it the red queen hat?" Max asks, wiping.

"Because," patting the giant pompom, "it looks like the Red Queen's head—The Red Queen? from *Alice in Wonderland?* 'It takes all the running you can do to stay in one place'?"

"Like the ouroboros?"

"Yeah," surprised, "I guess so. Always moving," turning the ring around her thumb, around and around until "Here," she says suddenly, "you take it," slipping off the ring to push onto his index finger where it will not fit, onto his pinky where it does. "Every garden needs a serpent."

He examines the golden snake's tiny scales, its endlessly open eye, the snake the only one who understood what Eden was really for. "Maybe I'll find the tree of knowledge."

"Just don't eat any apples. You seriously think Davide can find a way to get food into the game? Synthetic food? Y food?"

"Synthetic food," sniffs the cart vendor, spritzing water on the smoking portagrill, "that's not food at all."

"Y food?" asks the boy with the backpack. "Tight! What game is that?"

Bonus Content

Time to rewire the neuroecologies, kids!

Dance, Trance, and Hardhats: How the Walls Came Down at AltFest9000

by Cati Fredericks for Culture Bodega

reprinted from *Culture Bodega*

Start with Mister Minos—though minus his notorious horny mask—then add trance queen Alaine Majiic. Mix well with Hot Blossom and Club-Mate, then realize that you've been dancing in place for an hour, two hours, four hours, the walls around you are vibrating, they're starting to crack . . .

That was the scene at AltFest9000's closing set. All the festival goers were safely evacuated, but it was a tense and surprising challenge for security services. Walter Bakker, senior event security consultant with Safeworld, called it the "Jericho effect," when sustained vibrational pressures affect a building's structural integrity, also known as mechanical resonance disaster. He described the crowd as "security resistant," noting that, although no one was violent or aggressive, "They didn't seem to be processing that security was there, that anything was there. We finally had to cut the electricity." Asked if he felt this might become an issue for other events, Bakker said, "Definitely, depending on crowd size—this was a large crowd, but not a huge one. I've been working [event security] for thirteen years and I've never seen a reaction like this before. We were glad to have the assistance of the *Polisen*."

Lars Lindberg, the festival's founder and administrator, had a much different take. The first to book Alaine Majiic and Mister Minos together, Lindberg said he was expecting an enthusiastic response from the audience, and added that "Nobody was hurt, and what happened to the walls can most likely be repaired. And the beats they played together, they were everything, everything AltFest always means to be: the next thing, the new! *Fan vad jag* älskar *den här festivalen!*"

Alaine Majiic agrees. "When I heard [Mister Minos] at Silver Landings," she said, "I thought, oh this man has got it, he's miles

continued on page 227

12

The rehab place is not a rehab place, or not the kind Ari expected: on a quiet avenue in a part of the city he never visits, quasicorporate and upscale, residence hotels and exercise bars, SAINT EUSTACE has a hushed carpeted lobby and soothing fabric art hangings, *just like a hotel*. At the nurses' station, the aide who halts him is polite but thorough, his ID is checked against an admit list, but "Ines," Ari says, lies, "asked me to cheer up Ge—Genevieve. I've been trying to message," showing his Hechman phone, Genie's face and number flagged ***delivery failure***, Ines's face and name right below. "And I sent flowers, but I guess they're not allowed here," the little rose bouquet confiscated downstairs. "So can I just go in and say hi?"

"Afternoon care checks have already started," the aide says, consulting a purring countertop device. "And your name's not on—"

With his most winning smile: "Two minutes?"

The patients' rooms are laid out like spokes on a wheel, the nurses' station in the center, and Genie is in C2, *Genevieve H.* on a discreet doorside whiteboard; past the lemony disinfectant, the room has another odor, something human and soiled and infinitely sad. Genie is arranged in a medical recliner, anonymous blue robe and disordered black hair, her skinny arms linked to snaky drips, to several monitors, what do all those numbers mean, green and blue and red . . . Genie had left Karbon not long after he did, to race through a maze of clubs then collapse onto a bouncer at the grimy and crumbling Back Door, her heart slamming at some insane BPM,

continued from page 225

ahead, a quantum jump. So I reached out immediately." She did not offer a definition for their set's unforeseen effects, and downplayed her own fainting spell as a failure to stay properly hydrated. When asked if she would collaborate with Mister Minos again, she said, "Come hear what we're going to do in Barcelona."

Mister Minos is Felix Perez, who with producer Ari Regon makes up one of the club world's most intriguing power couples. Regon is currently leading the creative charge at experience company Your Own Eyes, though that company seems to be foundering, at least temporarily. *[See LaTova Smithson's upcoming feature "Ari Regon's Here. Buckle Up."]* Perez was formerly based in New York City, where Raimundo Silva, senior editor at Culture Bodega, laughed as he recalled good times together: "Green apple shooters at House of Hello, back when it was really banging. *Oi sumido,* you still owe me a dance!" And Silva had nothing but praise for the duo of Minos and Majiic: "Their new stuff that's coming, *mas já sei que é perfeição.* Music is supposed to take over your body."

Not everyone is as sanguine as Silva. Dr. Polly Scofield, an audio psychologist at CIT, warns that the depth of this musical absorption could be hazardous long term, and not only physically. "Mostly with festivals, what you'd worry about is decibel level. This is an entirely different phenomenon. We know music can be used to evoke states of psychological rapture, as in various religious traditions, such as the Sufi dervish dancers. And binaural beats are believed—not universally, but widely—to cause certain changes in the brain's response. But in this case, both of these effects are combined, and seem far more intense because of that combination. And if [this state] persists in people after the event has ended, there really is no gauging what effect that might have in the long term."

Felix Perez did not respond to several requests for comment.

To access Culture Bodgea's coverage of AltFest9000, Alaine Majiic, Mister Minos, Ari Regon, Dark Factory, House of Hello, and others mentioned in this article, log in to our Culture Archive.

gossip says it was bad coke and poppers, gossip says that bouncer saved her life. Felix said nothing when Ari told him, only kept on packing, until *She's punishing me,* Felix said, *by punishing herself. And Ines will make everything worse.*

Now "Genie," his smile, "Genie, hey, I messaged you like twenty times—Genie, it's me," but she does not respond, eyes wide and dull, what is in that drip, dripping into her? Finally she shakes her head, back and forth until he understands that she has no access to her phone, then tugs him down to perch on the recliner's wide arm, tugs at his scarf and "Felix," her mutter. "Felix?"

"He's good, he's playing. Look," showing her the clip he keeps on repeat, from AltFest9000, almost three minutes of Felix in full flow, in flower, Felix back-to-back with Alaine Majiic and without the mask, the concrete stage surrounded by dancers, a swaying human circle, he had watched that stream for hours and the dancers never broke formation once. That he could only watch will always be a loss, but the distance made it easier to see, and seeing had made his heart pound: *it's the real world, it's not engineered for safety* because these beats were not heat, or play, this time it was pure power, the whole place alive and vibrating, frightening, the way swimming in deep water is frightening, or a high-spiking fever, or hard sex, the body controlled by something greater than itself, *everybody is going to dance for you.* Security tried to stop them but no one stopped, Felix never stopped until—this video does not show it, but lots of others do—Alaine collapsed sideways on the platform, Felix grabbed for her and almost fell himself. Then the venue cut the power and called in the local cappies, and someone noticed all the stress cracks in the walls . . . All that night people had pinged him, was he there, what the fuck was going on, what was Felix doing, Meghan asking too, ***have you talked to F?*** and he had tried, messaging over and over, ***u good? U ok?*** But no answer until almost noon the next day, ***baby OK*** then nothing else until well after midnight, Felix on a fold-out bed in the corner of Alaine's apartment, hair a mess, wrung out and beautiful, ***it was so strange, god I wish u were here.***

And as the clip ends, he sees that Genie is crying, soundlessly, tears in little clear lines down her dry cheeks, Genie lost in this room without music, without friends, without life, so "Don't cry," he says, starting the clip again, taking her hand. "Come on. Dance with me—"

—and they do, they dance, in the chair, with each other, with no one, with absent Felix, with pain, *I've been dancing since I was fourteen:* he sways her tubed arms carefully back and forth as she nods to that beat, but off, far off, as if she is far away and can barely hear. As the clip ends again, "Get better," he says, "you promised him, remember?" and slowly, from her distance, she nods.

Then voices at the door, three white coats and stethoscopes, "Digoxin, even if she—Excuse me," the lead doctor surprised, "who are you?" and "Friend of the family," he says, kissing Genie's cheek, giving her a tissue her hand cannot hold, it floats whitely to the floor as the self-closing door sighs shut behind him.

Leaving St. Eustace for the street and the train platform is a sideways shift between worlds: health care workers to office workers with portfolios and backpacks, the man wedged on the train beside him looks his own age or even younger, brown work blazer and hair cropped to show a stylish stud earring, does that man have a job in finance, or communications, does he have the life his father wanted for him? or does he go to places like AltFest, and dance until he falls? As Ari rides, he scrolls, picture after picture of the AltFest dancers, sweating, peaceful, stunned by bliss, the opposite of this commuting crowd . . . Felix can move them from one state to the other, Max can too.

He checks the YOO stream, still discussing the Karbon night's sour stall, a few posts from patrons and the rest from industry; even as it was happening he had had an internal email from a Hechman media person, Carmen something, instructing him to forward all journo inquiries to her; he had, and had not read them, looked only at the ones trying to tie that night to Genie's relapse, making all of it his doing—*An "Eye" for Trouble, Ari Regon's Hard Morning After*—impossible not to see those ugly posts, not to feel the sadness and sting, though Felix had insisted *It has zero to do with you, don't even read that shit, Ari, don't.*

He knows Felix is worried for Genie, is upset, Felix had not said goodbye to her when he left, *It would only make things worse*. Felix is in Barcelona now, Alaine posting an update from some sunshine tourist plaza, her round beatific face and looped braids like a nun's, Felix's eyes hidden behind black plastic shades, black pullover and the new bone bracelet, Ari had fastened it on him before he left; the jeweler said bone is lucky. Thumbing a message, ***saw G we danced***, he considers, then deletes it, he will tell Felix later . . . Her tears in the chair, her hand on his scarf, Felix's scarf.

From the train he walks two quick blocks, picks up a Kaffee Kart espresso that tastes burned and flat, then doubles back to hop onto a mostly empty SR train all the way to A Walk in the Park, hood up and face averted from the hall cam—its hinged bracket jacked by Max to aim the camera at the ceiling, the building manager came by to fix it, Max disabled the bracket again—like the running man on the AWIP poster, leaving no trace, he is the running man. In the silent white room, he fires up the espresso maker to brew a sledgehammer cup, then examines the new poster proofs for B of P, its brutalist font and drenched greens and meticulous flowers and apocalyptic sunrise, or sunset, smiling a little at the tagline, "Paradise Is What You Make it," *make your night*. Dropping into the desk chair, he clicks into a meeting, Meghan and Clara already busy—

"—with Rixia Ogbert's rough track," Clara nodding to a background soundscape of fluttering beats like birds' wings, an ethereal and half-distorted voice chanting *Ah ah ah I know it, ah ah ah*. "Ari, hi—Davide still thinks Felix would have been the better choice, but Rixia's great in a different way—"

"And her handle is brilliant. Caterpillar Brain, 'what does the butterfly remember?'" Meghan's own voice is also mildly distorted, her features blurring like a bad security wipe; he has never seen Meghan in the real world, maybe he and Felix can travel to that office with its orchids and wide windows, invite Meghan out dancing at the end of this world. He knows Meghan knows he will leave as soon as the game is ready, though she has not said so to him, or to Clara who apparently does not know, and Davide, who knows what Davide knows? And none of them have asked him about Felix or AltFest—

—as "Good news," Meghan says, "very good news. Maria Morhosa-Smith is definitely open to a meeting."

"Well score that," Clara's hoot, "for Marfa!"

"She's available for a walk-through late this week or early next. Clara, you're certain we're ready? Ari?"

"I'll be there," he says, "just say when. Right now I have to head uptown," another thing that no one ever asks about, his continued involvement with Your Own Eyes.

Clicking out, he fills his palms with dispenser water, runs it through his hair, he needs a shower and he needs to sleep, somewhere, anywhere, no matter if he spends the night in that enormous loft bed or on the blow-up mattress, the insomnia is creeping back, he can sleep only a few hours at a time. Exiting at the dumpster door, he takes an express bus back, hopping off a block away at a minuscule counter café for another espresso and warm *pain au chocolat,* a quick check then mute of his real phone, swapping the hoodie for a wrinkled black jacket from his bag, Ines's tortoiseshell shades still in its inner pocket.

The building is a refurbished walk-up, deliberately old and quaint, and the YOO floor is all chic mismatched chairs and mottled silver mirrors, a half-dozen work suites and a central meeting room with a door made to mimic weathered white barn wood, maybe it really is wood. And the logo eyes are everywhere, staring back above the ID scanner where he leans to check himself in, sliding the shades down his nose, *ID and a facial match, just to get a t-shirt?* The office space is quiet, though the lights are on in Dolores and Deirdre's suite: planning the new and pivoted, stripped-down launch; they still add him on their team mail though none of it involves him, since Genie's relapse he is throttled back, forced to be doing nothing—

—and "St. Eustace," Burk's bark, Burk just arriving too, in a camel-colored car coat and those hotspot glasses, the red dot glowing, is he recording this? streaming it for Ines? "You were just there. Why?"

"Did you know that Genie doesn't like you?"

"Why were you there? You've caused enough harm to her already. And to Ms. Hechman-Weir—"

"If I'm so harmful, how come I'm still here?"

"You won't be," Burk aiming a phone like a gun in his face, aiming it until he must look: at nine long seconds of Davide shambling up to some streetside kiosk, Davide clearly wearing the prototype YOO t-shirt. "Davide Fabron, he works for Clara Dix at Fantastic Fantoms LLC, and she used to work for you at Dark Factory. So this proves—"

"Proves what?" with a shrug to mask the spiked alarm, how the fuck did this happen, how did Davide get that shirt? loose cannon Davide just like those unsynced eyes, no one is supposed to go into that office but him—All that hiding and doubling back, all for nothing! "That swag always walks?"

"—*clearly* proves that you violated the confidential terms of your contract. And your unauthorized visit to the Dark Factory site—"

"That was authorized."

"By who?"

"By me."

"You'll be hearing from HR. And from legal—"

"Want to take this right now?" offering the Hechman phone, seeing that Burk would actually like to take a swing at him, like it very much, if that was something Burk would ever do. "Or tattle to Ines? Because there she is—"

—Ines looking strained but impeccable in navy blue and black, in the doorway of the central work suite, where "Ari," she calls, as if this is a planned meeting; they have not spoken at all since Karbon, about Karbon or the launch or Genie or Felix but "No, thank you, Burk," she says, as Burk starts to follow, she closes the door herself.

And "Is this about Genie?" he says. "I went—"

"I know," taking a water glass from the homey white wood table, a white ceramic pitcher next to a stack of glossy cards, blue-eyed invitations? to what? "I have a visitor alert in place. Was Genevieve responsive to you?"

"We danced," realizing immediately that this is the wrong thing to say, not because it angers Ines but because it pleases her: "Good, that's good. She can be very difficult to engage."

"Burk seems pretty stressed about it. And whatever he tells you about that video—"

"Your contract," speaking as if he has not, "is in force for four more months. Seventeen weeks."

"That's not why I—"

"Pardon me," politely, clearing her throat, turning her back, slipping from her jacket pocket an inhaler, the faint airborne tang of ginger. "Allergy season is here, unfortunately. I'll be able to avoid it next week, I'll be traveling with my husband—"

Husband? Ines Hechman-Weir. Weir?

"—and whether you spend that week sorting through these," sliding those blue cards his way with two white fingers, "or sit in the loft and drink overpriced wine, or insert yourself into more places where you don't belong, you'll remain an employee of Your Own Eyes. Because I will not fire you, Ari, you can test me all you like but that won't happen. And if you're considering resigning, understand that all your associates—including Felix Perez—will be immediately and adversely—"

"Including Dark Factory? What did you think you were buying? When I said yes to this—"

"It was all you had to do," suddenly utterly glacial, utterly punitive, she does not raise her voice but he has the strange dislocating feeling that Ines is not even speaking to him but at him, as if he is a symbol of everything she hates about her sister, everything she will not hate in her sister; but she can hate him. And Felix. Especially Felix. "I arranged everything else, *everything*, to make everything—possible. All you had to do was what I asked."

He sets the tortoiseshell shades on the table, slides them her way and "These are yours," your own eyes. "Have a nice trip."

Leaving then, not logging out, why bother? when Ines is always watching? Stupid not to have known that, dangerously stupid, how long has she known about AWIP? Though the damage is done he still needs to warn Meghan, and Clara, and someone has to talk to fucking Davide . . . Back on the street, he turns by rote toward the loft, but if Ines already sees how he spends his time, why go there? *vampire place,* Hechman place that is not his and never was, though Felix's scent is still on the sheets, a pair of Felix's boots by the door, bottles of rosemary water lined up neatly next to the undrunk wine.

His real phone tings, a push reminder for 3Beat 3peats, a brand launch party, the VIP invite from some DJ called Julian Zero, who the fuck is Julian Zero. Deleting the invite, he lights a Club, nearly the last in the pack, and starts walking, quick and aimless as dusk comes on like a junior lighting designer's effect, and the street segues to theme restaurants and international chain cafés, beech trees faintly feathered with new leaves, sidewalks of tourists doing touristy things on pedal bike gondolas, the wooden benches of a faux German brewpub full of couples in zip-up denim—

—and "Ari? Ari!" a tall figure unfolding from one of those benches, his guard instantly rises, is it a journo? but then he sees it is Kid Yello, how is Kid Yello here? and totally bald? and "Hey," he says to Kid Yello. "New look."

"Ari, hey," wrapping arms around him as if they are long lost friends, or new lovers: Kid Yello's blue-gray eyes seem wider, his face leaner and even better-looking without the distraction of that clownish hair. "Yeah, I wanted something different, the stylist said he could bleach out the color, but who knows what it would look like underneath? And my head, once he shaved it, it's like, round. And you know my real name—So, Julian Zero," almost shyly. "I was going to surprise you, tonight. You're coming, right?"

Julian Zero, 3Beat 3peats, and "Can't," he says by rote, "I have to work," but work on what? on wondering what Ines will do to all of them now, what game she might play? Catastrophia, *all your associates, Ines will make everything worse.* So as Kid Yello,

Julian, crestfallen but still hopeful, says, "Can I buy you a drink at least?" he shakes his head, not No but Not here, and "How about the hotel," Julian eager again, "where the gig is? It's pretty nice, they got a bar on the top floor—"

—and it is nice, pink terrazzo and tall potted ferns and fern-patterned wallpaper, and that top floor bar suite is decked out for Green Apple Vodka, a trio of young bartenders wearing green leggings and tight black frock coats, handing out shots well-chilled though too sweet, the suite's sofa is too hard, does noticing that make him Goldilocks? Ari Appleseed? and "What do you think?" Julian says, leaning closer on that sofa. "Julian Zero. Do you like it?"

"Do you? It's your handle. And your head."

"I did it for you."

"What?"

"Ari, I, I know I'm not on your level, I can't be. But—" the same smile as in the Fraktur courtyard, the same longing look and tripod cock, there they were and here they are and all he would have to do is nothing, let Julian's hand climb his knee to knead and stroke, feeling his own cock faintly stirring, because being with Julian could never be serious, just the quick sticky end to their dance—

—but "Julian," he says, leaning back, "what are you playing, now?"

"Can I play it for you?"

Downing their vodkas, up to Julian's small anonymous alcove of a room, a picture of a sunflower on the wall, a pale yellow bedspread, bags and jacket pushed aside so Julian can nervously, happily share his tablet and his beats, not amazing beats but much better than his set at Silver Landings. And "These are good," Ari says from his seat on that bed, nowhere else in the room to sit. "You've been busy."

"Yeah, I've been working a lot, I—Ari, listen. I really want to be with you," but as Ari shakes his head, starts to rise, "No, I know you have somebody, but—Can you stay? Just . . . stay. We don't have to do anything, we can just talk, or—"

—or listen as Julian plays him more beats, as he slumps a little against the bed's soft quilted headboard, feeling the day's tension, the week's weariness, the room's warmth, feeling his dry eyes close, he could sleep for a hundred years if he could sleep at all—

—and when he opens his eyes again the room is dark, only the glow of the lav light, what time is it? and Julian is in bed beside him, that warm naked head nestled into his shoulder. Sitting up, so sleep-wrecked and bleary that he feels high, he feels the vibration of the Hechman phone, again and again, a series of messages from Carmen the media person—

URGENT Do NOT post or respond to ANY media inquiry, direct ALL inquires directly to me

URGENT The Hechman family will issue their own statement tomorrow morning

URGENT Your Own Eyes is deeply saddened by the sudden tragic loss of Genevieve Hechman. The YOO statement can be found here

—with a link to graphics of tasteful gold ivy and a few guarded sentences, "We will always remember and celebrate Genevieve Hechman's joie de vivre,'" reading it aloud, "What?" bewildered, "*what?*" rereading the messages—then grabbing for his real phone, he has to be the one to tell Felix, cushion the hurt if he can—

something happened 2 genie

—speed searching to find what might already be out there, *Drugs Doom Real Estate Party Girl* popping up on First Talk, a garbage site, who leaked to them? Burk will think he did it. Then he sees the pictures, of Genie and, oh jesus, Felix, the two of them in their matching shades, laughing, tongues stuck out at the camera—

dont look @ stuff msg me NOW

—and a call incoming, some noisy café, chatter behind and around him as "Genie?" Felix says: he looks exhausted, unshaven, wearing a new pink cap with white writing, a deep frown. "What is it, how bad is—" but the audio drops, surging up again in the clatter of a falling tray, someone gives an ironic cheer, Felix louder: "—*happened?* Ari?"

"I just saw her today, we talked about you. But she—Felix, they said she died."

Silence, their shared silence, the café door opens to jingle and slam, Felix stilled by shock—then his stare changing, why? as forgotten Julian leans in over Ari's shoulder, can Felix see him? so "Listen," Ari raising his voice, as if to drown out Julian's presence. "Don't talk to anybody about her, journos, anybody. Especially don't talk to Ines—"

"Fuck Ines! And what's—You—" but no audio again, Felix still talking, *Ari,* his mouth says, *Ari*—

—as the screen freezes, blanks, so he calls back, back, ***delivery failure delivery failure absent subscriber*** and "Fuck!" through his teeth, Julian hunching sideways on the bed, eyes wide like a puppy frightened by human pain. "I have to go—"

—but he must have grabbed the wrong elevator, this one opens not at the lobby but the mezzanine, a noisy milling crowd, more green and frock coats, three enormous green apples hung in a precarious ceiling display over a long table of boutonnieres and wrist bouquets. He tries again for Felix, ***absent subscriber***, as someone chirps from right behind him "Excuse me, are you a VIP?"

—and turning he sees, past that smiling frock coat, a trio approaching, Jonas with his arm around a young blonde woman, sparkly gold dress and deep cleavage, is that Nadja? and beside her a blocky man in a black suit, Marko. Neither notice him but Jonas does, Jonas's eyes go briefly wide, then "Come on, babe," louder than he needs to, steering Nadja sideways. "Let's get you some flowers—"

—as Ari pivots blindly in the opposite direction, there has to be another elevator, or stairs, or something, hurrying past a closed ballroom, an empty meeting room, around a corner that takes him right back into that crowd—

—and right into Marko about to enter a lav, this time Marko sees and "Look," Marko says, voice flat, "it's party boy. Come and party with us, party boy," as another man just behind Marko, a short man with long arms, reaches to grab for his scarf—"Come here—" but Ari jerks back, the man grabs again, grabs his arm this time, a hard grip, "Bitch, I said come *here*—"

—and a huge hollow boom like a plastic cannon, somebody

shrieks, everyone turns as one of the apples smashes into the bouquet table, flowers flying, the apple rolling like a giant drunken bowling ball into the thick of the crowd—

—as Ari yanks back his arm and darts back around the corner, this time spotting an unmarked service door, he slams in and down to the bottom of a service stairway, empty metal shelves and a hi-lo and another door, an outside door with a red alarm box, NO EXIT DO NOT OPEN but it does open, two hotel employees reentering in the smell of smoke and "Uh, excuse me," one says, as the other drops her cigarette. "Guests aren't allowed down here—"

—then he is out, the security lights blooming like orange moons in a rain so fine it is barely mist, like moving through someone's exhaled breath. To the left, the alley leads back to the hotel avenue entrance, so he turns right, walking fast, breathing hard, hailing a Hechman car with his Hechman phone, climbing into its bland blue carapace with a sigh of cold relief as the driver asks, "Where would you need to go, sir?" He gives the loft address, sits back, tries Felix again, fails again—

—and remembers all at once that ride from the airport with Genie, the three of them in a car just like this one, ***talk 2 him Air PLZ!*** and all those pictures, Genie and Felix, Genie with her arms around his neck, Genie on the Fraktur roof, on the plane with the gardenias, the roses and the silly birdcage gift, *Felix will flip, I promised Felix I wouldn't die high,* she kept that promise, but how did she die? alone, in the sterile recliner, in the sound of machine bleats, no beats, no music? Or did the hum come to meet her at the end, like a friend slipping in to dance with her, *he's my very best friend, if you don't mind I'll love you too.*

###

As Max passes the Fantastic Fantoms door, heading for the stairs, he hears Clara's voice inside, hears his name, "—funny, have you noticed?"

"Funny ha ha," Davide's muffled answer, "or funny oh fuck?"

"I hope he stays off the walk-through radar," and away from the funders, Clara telling him yesterday to *Lie low, Max, if we need to we can always find you,* what is Clara seeing in him that spooks her? And Marfa too, her sharp measuring frown when he offered her the sublet on his warehouse room: *The rent is crazy cheap for that much space. Why would you want to leave Sugar Shack?*

I'm onsite mostly anyway, I'm just going to stay upstairs.

What, in Meghan's quote-unquote office? That place is smaller than your old squat.

I don't need a lot of room. I'll be in the game, and the game is big.

"In it" how? you mean playing? Or has Davide figured out how to feed you? Don't smile, something's going on—

And he had smiled, a little, because something is going on, Davide is busy facilitating the preferred outcome, a bit of business-speak he learned from Meghan: Davide the bulldog angel, *if a thing can be made in Y, Davide will find the way.* Davide has given him Maven 2 to study, Maven 2 a game and not a game, to work inside a game, write inside it, you have to get inside it first . . . But that is nothing he can talk about, so he asked Marfa instead about her project, it has a title now, *Making It Real: The Dark Factory Interviews,* and a live link, yellow and black and businesslike, an open invitation for anyone to submit their stories, or request an interview, and *Think I should send that to Ari?* she had asked, then they both smiled.

Upstairs now, he drops his coat and bag, adjusts the blackout curtains to keep the noon glare from the screen, and pulls up his chair, not the one with the headrest but the one brought over from his old squat, now this room has everything he needs: that chair, the screen, the table and mattress and toilet, his wonky groaning space heater, and a six-liter water filtration jug. The coffee maker and cups are stored in the corner with the rest of Ari's things, and Felix's mask, delivered by a Hechman employee, it reminds him oddly of Mila's old ninepin duck: that one was all eyes and this mask has none, but the gaze is the same, and there is still no use hiding—

—and as he calls, Ari seems to be standing smoking in the middle of sunny thin air, the black balcony railing like a line drawn in the afternoon sky, though "Last call for this view," Ari says. "Terminated for cause, finally, I finally heard from Burk."

"Who's Burk?"

"Ines's little helper. People on Kickchat say YOO's looking to hire in Skelly, good fucking luck with that."

"That's good news, right? You had to get away from Hechman."

"Not like this. This was because of Genie."

"I'm sorry about what happened," to *Genevieve Hechman, her struggle with substance abuse,* Genie Hechman is being buried in Bonn, or interred, whatever is done afterward with ashes, Marfa told him that. "I know she was your friend."

"And Felix's friend," as Ari blows a smoke ring, ragged and white in the blue of the sky, they watch it dissolve. "The funeral's private . . . Did some stuff get dropped off there, for me? Did the mask—"

"It's here. You going to leave it here?"

"I don't know. You ready for the walk-through?"

"How's that going to work, anyway?"

"I'll talk to them, I'll tell them that B of P is going to change their lives, because it will. Then Meghan will start getting the money, and the game will get made," with a tired confidence, Ari the secret weapon to woo the art museum woman and her friend, whoever Marfa has lined up—though to Max they all seem like the same kind of person, no kind of person he knows how to engage, but Ari manifestly does. "Where are you going to be?"

"In there. And in here," Max a kind of fantastic phantom himself, the new Upstairs Man since Ari has gone, is gone, where is Ari going now? *Liability nightmare,* does Ari think whatever happened with Felix, that earthquake crowd, is a nightmare? and what does Ari think will happen now, to the game, to all of them? "I'm making some notes for you, I'll send them when they're done."

"I'll read them." They look at each other, the sun in the sky, the sun past the curtains, until the muted ting of Ari's phone, and "Showtime," Ari says, with a long drag on his cigarette, the smoke a momentary cloud around his head. "See you in there—"

—and Max thumbs off his phone, adjusts the tiara as he turns to that other, larger screen, that other world, where once on the shore he walks and keeps walking, straight into the water, over his head by meters though the sensation of being wet is not yet available, so all he feels is pressure, a kindly pressure, and all he sees is an infinite and gently moving darkness, hears his own quickened simulated breath, in this unreal sea no one can die. And in the depth of that darkness something sparkles, very far off, is it meant to be jellyfish, an enormous massing swarm, or something else? is it stars? When he surfaces again he has a kind of headache, like a sinus headache but pleasant, a feeling of fullness; Davide calls that "rapture of the deep," nitrogen narcosis, not possible here. A bird flies overhead, its blue leathery wings distinctly reptilian, what bird makes a cry like that? and he kneels in the sand to write with one finger, watches the waves erase his words, writes again, watches again, writes—

—until a new figure appears on the shore, blurry as if seen through heat, bright silver splashes following his feet, hair blowing back in a self-created breeze. As that Ari avatar approaches the crest of the dune, other figures occur one by one: he sees Clara in her mushroom-style DaVinci cap, the purple flower one is Meghan, the other three must be the funders.

###

They want him to stay and celebrate: Clara uncorks champagne and Action soda, Davide blasts the theme from some other game, a screenful of flying screeching women, and Meghan displays her new, jewel-red Aztec lilies, flowers already in place for a celebration, all of them as excited as the funders had been—the philanthropist and her museum director friend, the jug-eared man from the video and the Fraktur mural, his name is Leland Cardenal, someone should tell Derek Ferris—all cheering the way he handled the jargon, talked the talk for a walk not his own, dazzled and convinced those funders to see the game as much more than a game, as a piece of pure experience art, a way to re-experience the world . . . He hoped Max would make an appearance, waited for it, but Max did not; can Max hear them celebrating, now, from that quiet room upstairs? his own old hiding place, but Max is not hiding, Max is very busy being Max.

He makes the toast, hugs Clara, blows a kiss to Meghan, then shares the extra good news of his official separation from Your Own Eyes, just in time though "I had Devon prepped," Meghan says, meaning her attorney, they were ready to fight Ines on his behalf, a fight as brave as it would have been futile. But "Genie saved us from that," he says, so they all toast again, to Genie, lifting glasses as Davide solemnly hoists a pink plastic jug; he has not asked Davide about the t-shirt episode, what difference does it make now, that loose cannon never his worry anymore.

Then glass down, "I need to go," he says, "and finish up," they think he means the loft but the loft has already been emptied under the apologetic eye of the friendly concierge, whom he tipped outrageously, then asked *Has anybody come looking for me?* And the concierge said yes, in fact, late last night though the man who came would not leave a name, only said he would stop by again, and *Short guy, long arms, right? If he does come back, don't tell him I'm gone. And can you have my stuff delivered? Here's the address.*

He had left the Hechman phone on the empty kitchen island, that phone already triumphantly wiped by Burk, his ID log-in blocked from the YOO offices, the countersigned separation sent; had Ines meant to let him twist in the wind before she fired him? or was she distracted, diverted from her allergy getaway to her sister's funeral instead, at some gated family stronghold in Bonn. Felix has been downcast about Genie—they had talked last night, while he packed up their things—Felix with shadows under his eyes and a new frown, new lines beside his lips: *"Private funeral" really means "fuck you, Genie's friends." We can't even go!*

Nobody can go.

I didn't even say goodbye to her.

Genie wasn't mad at you—

I'm mad at myself. I should have said something, it was the last time—

—Felix with more time for that grief to compound, stuck in Barcelona listening to the sounds of the sea, the rustle of the leaves of the Judas trees, the street dancers' pop tourist beats, while Alaine negotiates some extended push-and-pull with the church people, because *They might yank the permission, she says. They don't like Silver Landings, they don't like the horns—*

You mean the mask? You didn't even wear the—

—they think it's the devil or something. So now her aunt is involved, the aunt's a bishop . . . The acoustics really are unbelievable, in that church, basilica, Felix sent shots of the crisscross stone ceiling and windows like rainbows, shadowed alcoves of hanging saints and blessed ladies and candles burning in tall glass jars. *But maybe it's better this way, better not to do it—*

What? Why?

Because, one hand held palm-up like a saint's invitation, or warning, *we don't know what it's doing, we don't know what it wants—At AltFest we had them, I had them, I could have made them do anything! When Alaine fell over she had spit coming out of her mouth, drool, it scared the fuck out of me—And what if I had that?* the mask just out of screen range, like the silent third in the conversation. Then *Why do you have to stay there?* as Felix leaned closer to the screen, his exhaustion more visible still. *If you can access the game from anywhere?*

So he had explained again, this kind of thing is always less a process than a conjuration, some hands-on magic might still be needed, and *Anyway*, pointing to the packed boxes, his bags, *two days, the walk-through and I'm gone—*

What about that fucking thug?

—because he had shared the story of his escape from the hotel, trying to make it sound like an adventure, part of the Julian encounter: knowing that Felix would want to know about Julian but would never ask, *I trust you*, so *Julian was in town to play, he played some beats for me*, but that news was not happy-making either. So *Two days, and I'm gone.*

Two days, as the screen jostled, Felix leaning back into shadow, the apartment blinds made stripes across the wall, like a jail, or a cage. *I'd feel a lot better about all of this shit if I was with you.*

And so would he, these days have felt impossibly long, and since that call he has not been able to reach Felix again, ***absent subscriber***, Felix has not posted either, so what does that mean? He tries not to catch that oddly doomful vibe, by tomorrow morning he will be on a plane, his last use of the Hechman corporate card, *Ines can pay for some fun,* Genie would totally approve. But between that flight and right now, as he tugs shut the office door, exits the building's front entrance for the first time and the last, what to do? besides smoke and wander through the city, a kind of farewell tour because *you're done with all that, this time we go for good, no more Genie, no more games—*

—with a stop at a curbside flower vendor, green and pink and defiant against the afternoon's returning cold—"Three of those, are they gardenias?"—then into a doughnut shop for a chocolate roll, then a Kaffee Kart's long impatient line, where as he waits Dodi messages, ***come drink, the rough beast wants to dance—***

—Dodi holding court in some dour basement bar, deep-scratched tags on its metal streetside door, and on the stairs a faded line of posters for bands and parties long passed. Descending, he can hear Dodi's loud complaint, "All the real dive bars are closed, where are we supposed to meet the muse?" so "Buy me a shot," he calls, "and I'll tell you."

So they drink, he and Dodi and slippery little Michael who has sheared off his braids, and Alix and Katya and Katya's friend Ed, and Ed's friend Placebo who arrives in a long black scarf and a wraparound cape; all of them are wrapped up in something called Horny Nights, has Felix heard about this? some underground knock-off of Silver Landings where people hop around naked in costume shop horns, they dance to his recorded beats, and fuck and spar, sometimes even fight, but "Ours," Dodi lifting his shot glass, "will be *much* more authentic. Authentic as a Maenad!"

"We wanted to have it by the river," Alix says, as Katya nods, "where they do the holiday marts, but the cappies are really cracking down. No public assembly over fifty bodies, unless it's commercially sponsored—"

"And absolutely no public nudity," Placebo rolling his eyes, "can you believe."

"If I still had *my* empire—"

"I know where you could do it," Ari says. "If you want to keep it real."

Then everyone is buying takeaway rounds—no Club-Mate, but they have club soda, he gets a bottle of that and a half-liter of Modska—and everyone is piling into a Hopper, two Hoppers, neither of which will go far beyond that former squat street, Lady of the Lake its one safe and busy oasis. So from there they walk, they follow as he leads them—

—to the paper mill site—Weir Paper, Mr. Weir the unseen husband of Ines? Genie would approve of this too—where a half-dozen shouting young women play cutthroat soccer on the sundown side of the buildings. Inside, everything is still broken, ICKI is still there but his bagger friends are not, or not in this building with its rusted mezzanine ladder and still-growing trees and pile of pallets that Dodi immediately spots, Dodi clapping hands, twice and sharp, a gunshot echo—"Our stage!"—and Katya climbs, to twirl her white-bright lanyard flashlight like a disco ball while Michael starts some beats on his phone, bubbly and bland, but "Play Mister Minos," Alix calls—

—as Ari scavenges a grimy plastic dish tub with holes punched ragged through the sides, to set the club soda bottle carefully atop it, the white flowers below to glow in the dimness, not gardenias but they still *symbolize lasting friendship,* here at his own private

funeral party for Genie: *super scummy but I liked it,* all the trespass and decay and clinking bottles, and Felix's beats like dandelion seeds, a risky flight into a hurricane of beauty, maybe Genie is flying somewhere now, he raises the Modska to her in a toast—

—and Katya romps with Alix and Placebo, while Ed circles, shooting video, and other bodies approach from the falling light outside, the curious soccer players, one of them pulls at Michael and laughs, while two scrappers wander out of the building's deeper shadows, to set aside their magnet sticks and collection bags, nod to the beats, share out a smoke—

—and his phone goes, Felix answering, finally: ***At the loft, where r u?***

wtf? at the loft? the Hechman loft? ***ur here??!***

I couldn't wait, where r u?

@ a party

Where?

@ papermill

JFC! Don't move, I'll come get you

—and he laughs out loud, how strange and perfect that Felix should somehow arrive, *you're playing, I'm here!* for Genie, and for him too: feeling the Modska and espresso and champagne, lighting another Club, drifting toward the entrance to wait—

—and nearly full dark when he spots the slowing Hopper's headlights, another car not far behind, who is that? killing its lights as Felix climbs out of the Hopper, unmistakable and swift across the plain of dark weeds and glittering glass as "Over here!" he shouts, waving into those lights. "I'm here—"

—and from that second car a passenger, a shadow detaching from darkness, a squat figure, man's figure, who is that? on a purposeful convergence course with Felix—And suddenly he knows, he runs, he runs so fast he can barely feel his body, *party with us party boy*—

—but by the time he reaches them everything is already over, Marko's man doubled up on the ground, covering his face, as Felix locks arms around Ari to bundle him into the Hopper's backseat,

Felix's body thrumming, muscles bunched, the sharp smell of sudden combat sweat as "Go," Felix pants, "drive, drive—Baby, what the *fuck,* baby!"

"That's the goon," Ari says, breathless himself. "He was looking for me—"

"This," the driver says, as the car bumps and slews, dried mud ruts to gravel to pavement, picking up speed under pale green streetlights like spotlights or faraway stars, "*this* is why no one picks up out here—"

—and Felix's kiss tastes like raspberry lip balm, he wears the pink cap from the café, the white letters on the brim spell out ASTER BAR and "I got you," Felix says, "it's OK now . . . Fuck, I think I broke my thumb."

13

The forest air carries a flower scent, generic floral: Max has lobbied for at least a few harsh odors, wet vegetable rot, or blood, the sour whiff of trash, *why does Y edit out the pain,* but so far Clara's answer has been no. Clara has also said no to a new NPC Davide wants, Davide calls it the Roamer, a ceaselessly moving figure half-greenwood and half flesh, Clara said *Why not just call it the Grim Roamer and be done with it? We've got the skulls, that's enough.*

Enough for who?

Davy, jesus, leave it.

Max has a custom avatar now, one Davide designed, a more minimalist version of himself, eyes and hands and a mobile scribble of body, the flesh made Y . . . He has spent the last few hours, half-day? day? roaming too, through this forest that will eventually be as deep and expansive as the water, and as he walks, he writes: with a stick, with his finger, with a stub of something that looks like a rock and works like charred charcoal—a sentence, a word, a question, a quote, today's is *Split the stone and I am there*—like the Factory graffiti wall, like *breadcrumbs, dirt crumbs,* if all these words were assembled would they make a path? or a story? Will anyone read it? Davide keeps asking if he is comfortable being in the game, but he has no useful answer; sometimes it feels as if he has never been anywhere else, never lived anywhere but here.

Now he follows the quincunx path made to lead the players,

like feeder veins to a beating heart, from the various entry points up to the build site, to choose their play trajectory, to stay or float away, the one irreversible choice in B of P. At that site, he sees a tree carved with a crossed-X sigil, sees another, what does it mean, who did it? There are new visitors in this garden, he never sees them but he knows they are here, *they're going to get in anyway, it might as well be through us,* so has Davide opened the back door to those Kunstfarm students? and who else? Does Clara know? Clara had said no to that too—

—as from down on the dunes comes a tinny shout, "Max? Max where are you?" and emerging, he sees it is Marfa, Marfa using a stock avatar, an earnest-looking castaway that in no way suits her. "Max, hey—Come out, I don't want to puke—"

"Clara says that shouldn't be happening," though what Clara really says is *No way Marfa's getting Y spins, not possible in here*, but "Clara's wrong," Marfa calls, "again. Come on—"

—back into the office room that seems more stuffy and disordered with Marfa in it, Ari's boxes and the mask still piled in the corner, his own improvised clothing rack and small stack of essentials, books and notebooks and bike in the corner and "When's the last time you saw the sun?" Marfa says, tugging at the blackout curtains.

"Yesterday. Monday. I need to use the lav a second," so she waits in the hall, on her phone, talking to who, Meghan? As he pumps the chemical toilet, he hears Davide's name, Lukas's name, he hears her say, "No way, not if I can help it."

Outside the afternoon is hot, the sky a deepwater blue, wind enough to send a scuttle of trash from curb to curb. They pass through a knot of transit cappies checking backpacks and bags, onto the train then off again, in the early crush of office workers and slouching uni students, a handout team in pineapple print t-shirts pushing free smoothies, past a cluster of chrome trikes outside a delivery depot, when did he last ride his own bike? *when's the last time you saw the sun?* A line of sweat grows at his neck in the old BurnOut henley, plastic sunglasses on a logo lanyard, as Marfa slips on beetle-green shades through the windy mess of her hair, its deep brown shine, and "The pub's not far," she says, as they cross the avenue against the indignant skirl of a Hopper horn. "You good with a walk?"

"I'm not," wry, "an invalid. I walk all the time, I go to the launderette, I go to the co-op—"

"That's not what Davide says."

"He's talking to you again?"

"Yelling at me. About Lukas."

He was present for the start of that schism, eating lukewarm pizza at the cemetery table with Marfa beside him, watching Clara and Davide argue onscreen with Meghan, Clara agreeing in principle that Lukas should be taken off the game, Meghan insisting on removing Lukas entirely from Fantastic Fantoms, earning Davide's instant enmity, *You can't do that!* and Clara's seesaw disagreement, *Meghan, Lukas is Lukas. He overstepped, but he means to help—*

Help? He has no authority to speak on our behalf, and the people he's "consulting" with—

It's murky, I'll admit—

—none of them are people we would in any way choose to work with. And all of them seem to be involved with Mathias Bergeron, whose profile is still toxic. As your producing entity, Meghan absolutely firm behind her frail desktop flowers, *I can't risk that sort of liability, Clara, I know you understand.* So Lukas was gone.

Now Marfa pushes at the pub's door, a friendly, mostly empty space of old green leather seating and a blurry flat screen showing soccer, and "Two pints," Marfa says to the lean white bartender. "How's it going, Danny?"

"Could be busier. Want a banger plate?" that arrives with the drinks, flatbread garlic sandwiches and a small mountain of hot oily fries, and "This is good," Max says, glad to sit beside her in this quiet place, their knees just touching, sipping the pale ale; he almost never drinks now, smokes a little but not much, Davide has none to share or sell, Davide in a drought, in pique—*All the best shit is from Lukas's roommates, so back to the fucking candy corn!*

Maybe sometime he will walk and smoke again with Ari, he misses Ari more than he expected, Ari has not come back into the game.

Finally "What did you want to talk about?" he asks. "That you wouldn't, in there?"

"I wouldn't in there because Davide is always in there. And Davide says that Bergeron is straight up hiring Lukas."

"He told me that too."

"He didn't tell me, I found out. Look," pushing the plate aside, showing a jumbled string of chat from Davide to someone called Sister Sting, ***pikkin up his badge L-boy is reddy!!*** then a new profile piece on Avant Gamer, *Mathias Bergeron Still Wants to be Your God*, and "This," Marfa tapping that profile, "this says that Bergeron was at AltFest9000, he had an 'enlightening' time. The guy's got serious fucking money, and toxic or not, people are going to work for him. Lukas isn't exactly a top of the line coder—top of the line anything, have you ever actually listened to that guy? Or smelled him?—so why would Mathias Bergeron want to hire Lukas, except as a conduit to B of P? And to your little side project—"

"Side project—"

"Max, come on," dropping her voice, "I know Davide's trying to end-around the game. A red mod."

Red for danger, red for stop, useless to try to deflect her, and he will not lie. "How did you find out?"

"It wasn't all that hard, believe me. Clara must know, maybe Clara even thinks it's not the worst idea ever, gamers are weird. But once Bergeron's involved, there go the brakes! Did Davide tell you about those soldiers in Idaho? Eight of those soldiers are still in a fucking fugue state, a full blown dissociative—"

"He showed me," those reams of dev research, redacted UX interviews with the beta soldiers in that prototype of dual existence, Project Cloudburst, the set-up brutal but *Doable,* Davide said, *or it was until shit went bad. Then they picked up all the pieces and made Maven, then Maven 2, the military's always got the funding and the warm bodies to throw at things. You ever hear of Jill*

Strunk? Or BEEP? They're trying to do it, too. "But nothing's happened since then."

"There's a lot of talk."

"It's still just talk."

"Then," her hand briefly on his, a warm enclosing pressure, "why don't you talk it over with Ari."

"We already did," behind the dumpster in the smoke, their talk his anchor in the sea of Davide's plans, *this is the story, whose story,* this game is even bigger than Davide thinks it is, Ari knows that too—

—and she looks at him the way she had on the roof, tugging him back from the edge, *Max be careful!* then "Why," she says, "do you want to do this? Isn't it enough?" is what? the ale and food, her presence, the world, his body? and "It's not like that," he says. "Our interview, remember?" like all her interviews, all those Factory confusions and exaltations, all part of the story, just like everything is, he is, she is.

They finish the plate, he starts to suggest they get another ale, but her phone buzzes, and "I have to jump," she says. "The plumber's there to fix the kitchen spigot, didn't you ever notice that that spigot barely works?"

Truthfully, "No," and she shakes her head, a pained dismay that has nothing at all to do with Sugar Shack. They leave together, back out into the breeze and the heat, down to the bus that she boards with a tiny wave, and he waves back and keeps walking, not aimlessly but without conscious direction, his body's meat reality of sweat and breath and heartbeat, his shadow another avatar below this moving and changeable sun.

###

"You're a member here?" Ari asks, and Ilias winks: "No, but Gussie's girlfriend is," Ilias Karagiannis, Ilias the host of this afterhours party at the members-only hotel, black bungalows and barrels of bougainvillea around a white-tiled pool, a table of champagne and lemon vodka, chilled cucumber rolls and black and white cake. So far Ari has met a festival producer, a guerrilla ballet dancer, a pair of Y directors who laugh at each other's jokes, and half a dozen DJs, while Felix stands at the far end of the pool, eating cake. At the other end sits an older woman in a deck chair, a chic bandanna like Annelise in thirty years, smoking a black cigarillo and watching everything; when Ari smiles at her she offers him one from the packet: "Black Canary, the nicotine's like heroin. Who's that striking man over there, do you know?"

"That's Mister Minos," as he bends to take the light, a fuming old school silver Zippo, "he's a DJ. And," with a sudden rush of pride, "he's my," boyfriend, partner, "my man."

"He looks like a god," so matter-of-factly that Ari has to smile, not a compliment, a statement of fact. "I'd like to take his picture. I'm a photographer, my name is Miriam."

"I'm Ari."

"Would he agree to being photographed?"

"I can ask."

Together they consider Felix, Felix who has been very quiet since Barcelona, that gig canceled with a curt email from the church, though Alaine seemed philosophical, almost detached—*My aunty did her best, they wouldn't listen*—Alaine in a white mechanic's jumpsuit and Felix in black, their brief yin and yang embrace as Alaine hurried off for a retreat with some dancing monks called dervishes, and Felix and Ari left again, bag and duffel, invited by Ilias to come to this party, stay at the hotel as his guests. . . . This morning, Felix still in bed, Ilias appeared on the restaurant patio where Ari sat with fierce coffee and a black bowl of pale green figs, Ilias in a vintage Treacleman t-shirt and gold aviator shades, careful to reference Ari's Factory rep, to insist that he does not want to batten onto Felix's celebrity, wants only to offer Felix whatever he needs to make his work: *I told him and I'm telling you, Indigo would be thrilled to have him. And it's not only about the beats. Mister Minos is totally unique—*

He is. And this is totally his decision.

But you're a big part of it. I know that, I respect that. Why don't you guys come out to the studio, after, and hang for a little with us?

And now "Attention, hey," Ilias calls, champagne in one hand and tablet raised high in the other. "Time to drop that 'Oyaboya'! Augie, Gussie, you there?" two onscreen faces appearing in a backlit studio, two big smiles, the poolside speakers boom a new Das Augie track as the crowd lifts its glasses and applauds. Felix skirts that crowd to reach Ari—"You ready?"—and Ari nods, then remembers Miriam waiting, steers Felix her way, "She wants to meet you, take your picture—"

"You're a photographer?" Felix asks, looking down at Miriam in the deck chair, the small pyramid of cigarillo butts beside her.

"Yes. You're a DJ?"

Something flickers in his eyes. "I play music."

"Can you swim?"

"I can. He can, too—"

—so they do, nearly naked, the water as warm as their bodies, the pool's underwater lights cycling tropical greens and blues. Felix strokes back and forth, Ari floats, while Miriam shoots from the pool's edge, her attention a felt and physical thing, like a hovering raptor or a single-minded angel. And when they climb out, dripping, "Send me one?" Ari says, and Miriam nods.

Back in the snug poolside bungalow, Felix draws the black matchstick blinds, and "She reminds me of Mrs. G.," he says, "my piano teacher. Mrs. G always said that we don't choose our gifts, they choose us," shrugging off his damp shirt, skinning down the wet briefs, the bone bracelet a white curve at his wrist. "Come here, baby."

Yet afterward Felix does not doze in pleasure, lies staring at the stuccoed ceiling as Ari watches, head nestled on his shoulder, until "I'm going to sign with Ilias," Felix says, "it's the right thing to do, for us. So you never have to do what you did with Ines, you can just—do what you do."

"You want to play, you don't need them—"

"I need to play," still staring straight up, those new lines at his lips again, that new frown. "But things are different, now."

"Different how, you mean the hum? You hear—"

"I hear everything. Remember what the tattoo guy said? 'You must be mystics'? When I was in that church—" shaking his head, as if no words exist for what he heard there, only sounds. "But the people, the priests, whatever, they were acting really weird around me, like I shouldn't even have been in there. Since Silver Landings, people look at me differently, but since AltFest they treat me differently. Even people I know. Even Alaine! You're the only one who hasn't changed."

"Is that why you came back to get me?' a gentle joke, but Felix shakes his head again, closes his eyes, then rolls to his side so they lie face to face, and "We should get married," Felix says.

"*What?*"

"Marry me."

"You want—"

"Will you marry me?"

"Yes!" on a laugh, *boyfriend, partner, my man,* my husband, "*yes,*" and Felix holds him close, so close he feels the doubled beat of their hearts, like rings of joy expanding, and blinks the sweet heat of tears, more amazed by this moment than by any possible miracle. Then "What do we do?" in blissful confusion, "do we tell people?" thinking of his father, when has he last talked to his father? and Max, he should tell Max, as "My mom would kill me," Felix half-laughing, "if we did it anywhere but at home. You'll like my mom . . . Let's sleep for a little," twined together as the party fades out, the beats stop and the birds call, one bird right outside their window, four quick notes ascending, repeating, as dawn gives way to day.

Instead of rings, they choose new ink, for Ari three small stars across his wrist, for Felix a green daisy behind one ear. The tattoo artist, a lanky woman with pink surgical gloves and a multicolored angel wing sleeve, promises that headphones will not irritate the skin's healing: "I'll be careful, believe me," her gaze on Felix speculative and bright. "You're a DJ at that music studio, right? Are you going to play out here? People would come from *everywhere*, believe me."

And "Do you want to do that?" Ari asks, as they climb into Gussie's borrowed black Jeep: no buses out here or trains, only one long mostly-paved road to and from this little commercial outpost, the tattoo booth tucked inside a catchall clinic and pharm, beside a pizza and curry place, a grocery that sells takeaway liquor and a bar called Outpost that does the same, though no Bushmills here, only cheap and potent Red Rose. "Play in the fields?"

And Felix smiles, curls still pulled back by the throwaway paper hair band, palming the wheel—"You tell me—" Felix released somehow, relieved, no more frowns and no more silence, Felix settling at once into that studio compound, the space manned by Gussie the other Indigo partner and Karim the engineer, they work together for hours, pausing only for beer and pizza and sleep; Ilias wants to do a five-track 12-inch, Felix says only *Wait till you hear* . . . Last night, long past midnight, Gussie came to the guest artist's rooms, a bedroom suite retrofitted from what was once an office, bulky metal shelves, old blue linoleum under the fuzzy throw rugs, and invited Ari out to the yard to smoke, where *With 'Oyaboya,'* Gussie said, lighting a sweet palm leaf blunt, *we got a lot accomplished in the studio, I mean Augie's got a good work ethic. But working with Felix—It's like time stops in there. Karim said to tell you thanks* and *Thanks for what,* though he had smiled when he said it, he knows they think he has influence over Felix, that he is somehow behind all of this.

While Felix works, he wanders that compound—the meticulous studio is in the main building, repurposed from the oily ruins of what Gussie says was once a machine shop, *We got it for cheap because it was mostly falling down. But Illy loved the vibe out here*—ramshackle brick in an overgrown field, spruce and scrub and crabapple trees, a few old strange metal behemoths still rusted in place behind the buildings, a doorless truck chassis and a charred bonfire pit, the same netherworld beauty as the paper mill; he almost pointed that out to Felix, then thought better and did not. When he walks, he lets his mind float, what will it be like to be married? and *at home,* where will that be? where will they go from here? *There's so much we could do together, was that really your dream,* what is his dream? to dance, while Felix plays for the whole world.

His world has been watching him, Nightlifer and Beat Buzzer and Kickchat posts wondering what is happening with Ari Regon, no events made or announced since the fail and bail at Karbon, Felix's no-show at the basilica noted too, ***No Majiic at that church, Ari Regon's as quiet as his DJ bf, the Dark Factory site is slated 4 a hotel reno??? Ari Regon shuts down more than he opens lololol!*** even the Dreamtime failure got hauled out again. No one knows about his involvement with the game, but that seems stalled too, when he tried to log in he was kicked back again and again, his password denied, why? while his messages to Max produce nothing but silence.

And silence now in the green fields they speed past, only a plane's faraway doppler drone, the changing voice of the road as it drops from pavement to gravel, this is the quietest place he has ever been, but Felix says he hears the hum clearly here, *I hear everything here.* And "This new thing," Felix says, pulling into the circle of driveway dirt, parking behind a muddied white motorcycle. "It's almost done, I think you'll like it."

"He says it changes time," pointing to Gussie outside by the double door entrance, Gussie with his bleached fade and blueberry blue half-glasses, waving at them—"Hey, Suze's here, she brought us some food—" then into his phone "Illy, yeah, tonight for sure."

Inside, beside the main room's refectory table, black oak scarred with decades of burns and careless bottle rings, is a woman, biker's leather and a rope of blonde hair, thumping down a bag of something pink and knobby beside the bottles of plum rakia and wine. And "I'm Suze," she says, with the faintest accent, less of country than of class, she sounds like money. "Gus said everyone is getting bored of pizza. I hope you like radishes."

"I'm Ari."

She shakes his hand, her grip warm and surprisingly callused, but her gaze is all for Felix still at the door: "Mister Minos, Felix, I've been wanting to meet you. When I saw Miriam DeFebvre's photo, I said to Gus, *This* is your new talent? It's more than a coincidence—I'm a sculptor, and if you would be willing—"

"I'm here to play," Felix polite but only polite, opening the outer door—"Gussie, you good?"—to lead the way into the studio then close that door, the red light a bright visible refusal, and "I like radishes," Ari says, as Suze makes a dry half-smile.

They end up eating together on the back slab steps, cold concrete and waxed cardboard plates, a fresh ragout of radishes and ramps and tiny green peas that roll everywhere, and Pinot gris they drink from mugs, as Suze shows him her art studio: a big white room full of big white statues that look like they came from the holy Roman empire, blind-eyed faces like Deborah's Seneca, and "This is Artemis," she says, "mother of the hunt. This one is Hermes, the messenger. I've wanted to do the Minotaur for a really long time, he's an extremely potent symbol of—"

"Yeah, I know."

"Your dance club event," raising her mug in acknowledgment, "Ilias showed us. So when I saw Miriam's portrait on Eyeball—" Miriam who is apparently a fairly big deal in the art world, Meghan's funders probably know her too, and a lot of people seem to love that picture of Felix in mid-swim, water flying, wet hair flung out like branching horns, mouth wide for air. But the one he loves is the one Miriam sent only to him, ***merci Mr Ari, outtake for you, DO NOT SHARE***, of Felix head down and climbing from the deep end, fully beautiful yet somehow profoundly remote, outside of any time, *Mister Minos is unique* but unique means only one—

"—would pose for me? I'd gladly pay for his time. I work from life, so this is a perfect chance."

What does she mean, how could anyone not work from life? but instead of speaking for Felix, whose answer would anyway be an instant no, he says, "You ever see these?" pulling up some images of Horny Nights, including a few from Dodi's paper mill party: battery lanterns hung above the pallet altar, a DJ crowned in green branches, but that party barely started before the cappies rolled in, scattering the dancers, *cracking down*, Dodi has a legal fund link on his MePage now. As Suze stares and swipes, he drinks the wine, his wrist warm and smarting from the new tattoo, three stars to go with the triple whorls, are they falling or rising? and looks out at that empty landscape, the sun has nearly set, the crickets are calling, they might be the only people left in the world.

Then the steel creak of the back door, the quick orange snap of a lighter, and "Getting dark out here," Gussie says, then lightly bumps Ari's shoulder: "Hey congratulations, Felix just told us. We need to throw you guys a party—"

Like Dodi's old shows, but with no experience boundaries, and out here there are no boundaries at all, no cappies, nothing but a road and the trees and the crickets, the black hillocks of brush, the dark—and in his mind that very first flash of Felix masked, horns against the sky, *a forest king, you owned it, you must be mystics, people would come from everywhere, call it Dark Park* and "Do you," Ari asks, "ever do shows, out here?"

"A party," Suze says, still staring at the images on his phone. "A big party."

###

SOLVE 4 X, they call themselves, those anonymous gamers and students, who run the trails and leave sly breakage in their wake, leave the crossed sigils on the trees, the ones who came for more than just beta. Davide has not explicitly acknowledged their presence, but he keeps sending Max teaser notes, *X to emphasize duplicity/duality, crosses = crossed meanings, left = right, yes = no,* Davide in his cockpit supervising his daylight coders, dialing up the volume on the new Rixia track, low lurching beats with a chittering insectile vocal, the Solve for X soundtrack? as trees twine and choke with vines on his largest screen.

And on Clara's screen, "We're pushed back for how long?" Meghan's tone tense, tugging at her golden earbead lines as if they are the source of her discomfort. "Two months? six?" tugging, tugging. "That gallery wanted to feature us at the LOOP fair. Now what can I tell—"

"Tell them we're dealing with it," Clara giving Davide a sharp sideways look. "It's not a permanent issue, I promise you that—Max, stop blinking!" distracted as Max bends to the scanner beside her workstation, staring into the eyepieces until the sensor beeps, another layer of useless new security; then escaping for the door, away from this space hemmed in by that three-way tension, it feels smaller than his room upstairs, unbelievably small compared to the game—

—but waiting on the stairs is Marfa, she puts a finger to her lips and follows him up: to close his door and prop one of the folding chairs against it, to keep people out? or keep him in? And "I hit you four times since noon," she says. "You should check your messages sometimes."

"I do check. I'm just slow."

"Never mind. Here," her phone out, "here's a link. Someone wants to talk to you."

"Who?"

"I wasn't sure I could make it happen, that's why I didn't tell you first," as the link appears on his phone, a shiny line of cartoon animal faces, CHOOSE ONE so he picks a bird, yellow and beaky—

—then sees a panda waving at him, and "That's me," Marfa says. "Just follow me," through a parklike setting as quaint as the games he played as a kid, blocky and deliberate old school primitivism, until "This is his," Marfa says, the panda pointing toward a little blue cave. "He's the cat thing," as HELLO TEZCAT pops up on his screen, then HELLO FRIDA.

"What game is this? Who is this?"

"It's Mathias Bergeron—"

"What?"

—as a round black bearlike cat emerges from the cave, HELLO CANARY!!!! CANARY IN THE GOLD MINE HA HA HA and "What the fuck?" Max turning to Marfa—but the cat, or bear, is still talking, a thick scroll without punctuation or context, until Max suddenly understands that Mathias Bergeron is talking about the Aztecs, the extraction of hearts, GO IN BWTN THE RIBS THATS ME, as the bear cat does a little hopping dance. BUT GOD IS A GAME NOT AN ARMY THATS WHAT THOSE WRATH FUCKS GOT SO WRONG.

TEZCAT, the panda says, CANARY WANTS TO HEAR YOUR THOUGHTS ON B OF P.

CANARY PPL SAY IM A BAD GUY HUBRIS NOT TRUE!!! I LOVE GOOD GAMES I WANT YOUR GAME TO HAPPEN DIVINE INTERVENTION THX FRIDA! the bear cat hopping back into the cave, and THX TEZCAT, SEE YOU SOON as the panda disappears, the bird is left alone in paradise—

—and "Intervention," Max says, "what does that mean? Is he talking about Lukas?"

"Not Lukas. You. I sent him our interview, he said you two were 'simpatico,' he says he'll help—OK," nodding at her phone, "here it is, the meet code's good for sixty minutes. But we can't do it here," pointedly pointing to his screen and the floor, both too close to Fantastic Fantoms—

—so they decamp to Sugar Shack, where he sees again the plywood bed, her high-top work boots beside it now, and a gaudy Big Solomons t-shirt hung to dry by one opened window, a bag of shwarma takeaway on the red-topped table, where they sit together over her tablet. And as Marfa inputs the meeting code, "The animal thing was a test," she says. "This will really be him."

"Really him how?"

"Real time, I mean, wherever he is. Maybe on his own little island. Maybe that's where he got that fancy tooth—Tezcat, hi," as a face appears, Mathias Bergeron pudgy in a collarless button-down shirt, a razor cut to disguise an early-balding head, and a smile with, yes, a prominent green tooth, a jade inlay, is that a Mayan homage? Behind him is a ferocious and detailed projection of the endlessly swarming armies of Fear of God, the martial red and gold ziggurat of the launch screen—

—as for a moment Max feels an existential vertigo so overwhelming he needs to grip the table's edge, how many worlds are operating in this room alone? this space that briefly was his and now is Marfa's, her life a palimpsest over his own ghost tenure; and Mathias Bergeron's play fortress cloaking his own geographic meat reality; and B of P where they all will meet, with the real world surrounding everything, which world is the most real? or is that the void—

—while Mathias talks, not about B of P or Fear of God or any game, but how he taught himself to use his nondominant hand to write: "It gave me an entirely new perspective, a new neural perspective. Just like when I went to AltFest9000. You weren't there, were you, Canary?" using that name as if they are old friends, as if they talk all the time; yet Max feels it too, a strange dismaying familiarity, not that they are close but that in some other world he could have been just like Mathias, could have been Mathias. "I need to talk to Minos, but I want to approach him like a friend, personally. Frida says you know him personally."

"I know him. Mostly I know Ari."

"Ari's the boyfriend, right? the producer? I heard Minos got barred from a church venue in Barcelona," as a jarring bright blue square pops up, a music site news tidbit, *New DJ partnership already parts ways.* "But 'this is my body,' the Spanish church is fine with *that.* Religion has always been a shuck," while as if in planned synchronicity the storming army is repelled and flung silently shrieking from the ziggurat, the perspective zooming in on its priests in their ornamental sacrificial skullhats. "Fear of God was supposed to clear the decks for enlightenment, but those loser terrorist fucks—Anyway. Tell Minos I want to set him up to play, and I'll be in touch—"

"Tezcat, wait," Marfa leaning forward, one hand out as if she will physically reach through the screen to detain him. "What about Birds of Paradise? What about—"

"Canary and I will talk about all that, we have a lot to—Wait," with a green and sudden grin, "Canary, what's your tattoo?" as Max, with a mounting sense of inevitability, another kind of vertigo, slowly lifts his forearm toward the screen. And "Simpatico," Mathias's crow, "I knew it! Talk soon," then he and his temple massacre click to gray and gone—

—and Marfa's instant frown: "Your tattoo?"

"It's Tezcatlipoca. The avatar of—"

"Of being simpatico. 'Tezcat,' jesus, OK. OK, make *absolutely* sure he gets you off that beta brain list. I already told him you weren't part of Lukas's little gang—"

"You talked to him about me?"

"Why do you think I sent him our interview? What did you think this was all about?" brusque to the sink to fill one glass of water, two, from the useless spigot now made useful: because Marfa made it useful, made sure it was repaired, Marfa fierce and competent as a heat-seeking missile, no more skyrocket, no more burn and fall, Marfa who made sure to contact Mathias Bergeron,

I want to do this for you, I wanted to be your girlfriend, what can she possibly see in him, what can she want? Yet in that interview, *our interview,* they were together in a way he has never been with anyone else, not even Ari, for certain not Mila, would anyone but Marfa have asked the questions she asked, what is that but love? *Love is a wonderful thing,* love is a game coded in secret, she offers him the second glass—

—but instead he takes her hand, feels the snake ring cool between their joined fingers: he could tell her that sometimes it seems to move, its minuscule winding coils and black winking eye, the same way his tattoo seems to yawn, Tezcatlipoca the jaguar god of the night sky and the void, Tezcatlipoca who sees everything in his obsidian mirror, all the follies and wants of humankind: but instead he only looks up at her, he only says "Thanks."

And she holds his look, until "De nada," she says, "this live-in-a-game shit is nuts, but you should at least be able to live," and takes back her hand, sets the glass to the table, takes a drink from her own. "'Enlightenment,' with a guy like that it could mean anything. What are you going to tell Felix?"

He examines his glass, clear glass and clear water, remembering CHEAP BREAKFAST, *no made environment can be seamless, you come fucking close* and "Ari," he says. "I'm going to talk to Ari."

Bonus Content

One of the monster's names was "Asterion," star

The asterion is an anatomical landmark on the lateral aspect of the skull, formed at the junction of the occipital, the temporal, and the parietal bones.

An Ear for Bliss: Ilias Karagiannis of Indigo

Interview by Shawn Hessen for HEY LISTEN!

reprinted from *HEY LISTEN!*

An A&R rep is a music lover, a Beat Buzzer addict, a metrics wrangler, and a determined club hunter, always searching for the tightest sound. For this week's Insider Interview, Indigo's Ilias Karagiannis talks about finding Mister Minos.

Indigo has always been about Gussie [August Burns] and me putting together the deepest projects, the ones that will resonate.

Working with an artist means respecting that artist commercially, making sure they have the representation they need. On a first-look level, an artist is the analytics, the data, image, visuals—what is this artist about as a personality?—so Mister Minos had a ton of stuff out there already, obviously. And he was on my radar because of Blaze [booker Marc Blasey], even then you could hear that this is someone with his own direction.

His beats are so tight, and he's in a class by himself for audience response. And also, people don't really know this yet, but he's a classically trained pianist, he plays piano on "Balcony," that's going to drop real soon.

But in the end, everything—support, product, image, everything—for us it all comes back to, why is Indigo getting involved? And Mister Minos is everything we want to be part of.

Because his music literally changes people.

In one word? I would have to say "bliss." Not ecstasy, we all know that has multiple meanings, chemical, and sexual. But bliss exists in your spirit. Gussie says Mister Minos's stuff is an infinity pool that's actually infinite, the blue just keeps stretching out in front of you—lapis lazuil, that's the color I see in my mind when he plays, this super deep blue. It could actually be indigo! So maybe it was fate, to make the infinity pool where everyone swims together forever.

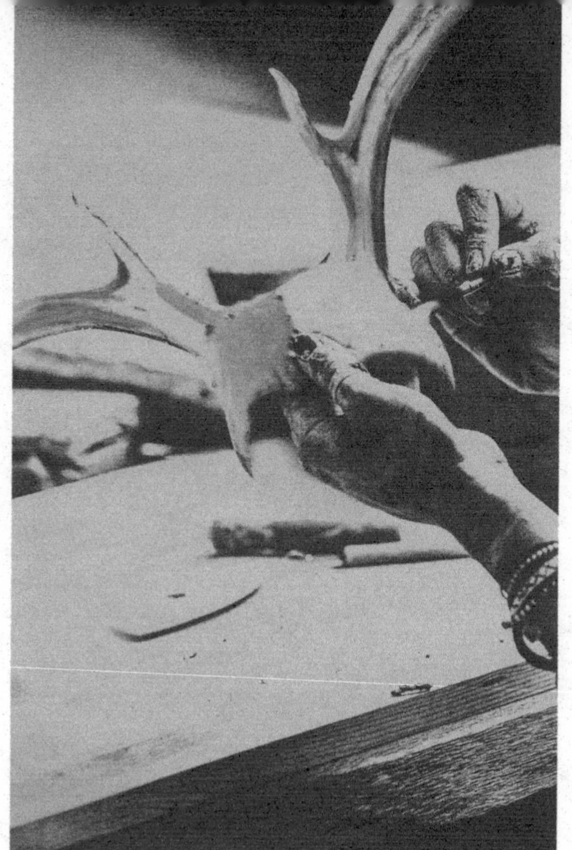

14

Noon, and outside warm and cloudy, but the guest room with its bare brick walls is cool, almost chilly. Ari sits alone, propped in bed with the sheets swirled around him, coffee in hand and answering Meghan—

BB's sparking about Dark Park, need a co-producer?

??? u out of the game???

Gallows humor, but Meghan is clearly upset, upset enough to alert him that B of P has been infiltrated by squatters, she and Clara now allied against Davide who says one thing then does another, because ***Lukas is Davide's friend, Lukas let those people in*** to scramble and infest, he does not understand exactly what those squatters are doing in the game, or to it, but ***We'll miss the LOOP deadline***, Meghan adding an angry-face, ***jeopardize funding! wish you were here but glad you're not.***

ppl r saying i close shit down

—but not here and not now, Dark Park already begun in Felix's instant smile—*You mean do our thing here? This new thing? Baby, absolutely*—this one night only event, Felix playing for as long as he wants, playing in the yard past the buildings in whatever moonlight or starlight the night provides, the fields and trees behind and a crowd to listen and dance, and if they want to dance in glitter or horns or naked, they can. And all of it coming together so swiftly it seems unreal, he has seen it before, this domino fall, but never with so many welcoming swerves: the legal availability of the outlying land signed off by the mayor over Outpost lagers, *Culture tourism, bring the people in here, that's what we need!* and Suze volunteering her formidable abilities onsite, she knows exactly what to do with a two-man build crew and various power tools, *Scaffolding and air hammers, that's how I work.*

But the real surprise is the gamer guy, the ex-Fear of God guy, Mathias Bergeron coming from nowhere with his offer to stream the show on his own site: Bergeron is apparently a large fan of Felix, though Felix is a lot less engaged by Bergeron, *Tell him I'm working, baby!* so Ari handles as best he can the long baffling messages, several times a day—***resonant body theory = AltFest 1000%! Tactile dimension is key, but Y is over, don't know how much a GOD player you were ha ha ha***—Bergeron seems to want some kind of affirmation, or blessing, from Felix, for what? And Bergeron knows Max somehow, he used Max's name as a password; Max would know all about the God game, could likely decode those messages, should hear about Dark Park . . . He wants to talk to Max. He needs to talk to Max.

Now the guest room's creaky door creaks open, Felix yawning, scuffing off his shoes, so ***c u***, Ari says to Meghan, ***in b of p if i cd get in***

Sorry, security roulette. C will send you a new pw

c u here come & dance im serious♥

♥ I do need a vacation

And as Ari sets his phone aside, "Suze," Felix says on another yawn, "built an altar out there, or what's it called, a pulpit?"

"She tried those horns on you again? They fit?" this new version of the mask not a mask at all, but a sprouting rack made from wire and plaster, bone white like the bone bracelet, beautiful, imposing, potentially dangerous, they could be antlers or branching coral or something utterly else, Suze had labored over them as if she were carving them from marble. Though if she hoped this effort might make Felix willing to pose for her, she must be disappointed: Felix is polite but has not thawed, Ari thinks he knows why, yesterday he made Felix laugh by saying *Genie would eat Suze in two bites.*

And "You," Felix says as he slides into bed, tugs a share of the sheets, "you look like a butterfly in a cocoon. You really missed all this," and he smiles, because Felix always knows, because he has missed it: missed the making, the chatter and speculation on Beat Buzzer and Kickchat, the endless messaged questions, the assembly of energies like a circuit feeding into itself: it feels like the Factory and Silver Landings and the nights of the Holy Roman Empire, feels like nothing he has ever done before, like a crown and an open door and "Look," he says, showing a link, a ZPO prediction, *Is Dark Park Ari Regon's big comeback?* and "'Comeback,'" Felix murmurs, head in the pillow, "you were always here. Always will be . . . Remind Ilias, the piano," then is gone into sleep as Ari watches that quiet face, feeling his own heart alive and glowing like a saint's in a church window, like the basilica pictures, a red and sacred heart.

As quiet out of the bed, he slips on a shirt and heads downstairs, more coffee and a plump plum from the refectory table, out into that warm unseen sun where Karim is running cable, Karim in a royal blue sports jersey and fat black bracelets of gaff tape, and "Tomorrow's going to be blast," Karim says. "My mate Josip wants to rig up a wine fountain by the fire pit, that cool?"

"Can he make it champagne?" perching on the rough wooden platform to eat the plum, its curling skin and tart juice, and run through the stream particulars one more time with Bergeron's supremely efficient tech contact, her handle is TopDoggieGurl—

Haptic resonance like bass in the chest, your onsite engineer's been really helpful

gus is blast

Here's preview final on the opening, sending for approval

—of a visual, the blue-green earth in a clear rotating globe, it looks like a snow globe, it looks peaceful until the focus pulls back to show the intense and choppy sea of space surrounding, comets and bullets of space junk, galaxies neon and remote, magenta white and gold burning cold against the void, that globe less than a champagne bubble in a boiling midnight sea—

Approved to use?

yeh

And "Ilias says," Suze leaning over his shoulder, canvas work shirt and hair in a twisty gold bun, a cigarette pulled from behind her ear, "Felix needs the piano outside? Why can't he use the keyboard?"

"He wants the real piano."

"This platform won't take weight like that."

Wiping his fingers on a spiky patch of grass, "Can we set it on the ground?"

"In the mud, you mean?" annoyed, he offers her a light but she marches off into the studio building, where after a few moments Ilias exits, just ending a call: "Can't wait to see you, for sure—Know who that was?" jubilant to Ari. "Upsetta! She's already on her way, she heard about it from Bergeron's feed," Ilias awed by that connection, *Fear of God's got a fuckton of followers, to have Bergeron support us is miraculous. That's down to Felix, and to you.* "And the journo's on his way for your shadow interview."

"Felix wants to move the piano."

"For 'Balcony'? We can do that, sure," nodding like a man who will move a mountain if necessary. "And I just heard from the mayor, he's fucking thrilled, a charter bus showed up and they're all in the Outpost drinking Bloody Marys."

In the studio, Suze and Gussie stand in hushed and heated conversation, so he detours around them and into the tiny one-chair office, to sit and quickly scroll: a new club app called Zwank with the tagline "Zwank Your Night," Your Own Eyes hyping a "Wine & Wonders" cocktail event, and a jarring eight-second video of ***Sunset Partner Siegler Charged***, what the fuck? Jonas in a baggy gym t-shirt and cheap blue trainers, head down and escorted by cappies: the link says Sunset Entertainment is involved in investment fraud, does Sunset Entertainment mean Marko? *I'm fucking drowning, who are you to judge . . .* Jonas's dogged walk and expressionless face, *your ass better have an exit strategy,* he watches that video over and over—

—until the new password pops up from Clara, ***sorry, here you go***, and he digs out a clunky old tiara from the desktop gaming rig, and logs in: to marvel at all the new details, the shining fence of concertina wire, the wet purl of the waves, the sand as brown as almond butter against the background riot of flowers, purple orchids, birds of paradise; the sky seems darker, as if some clouded god decided to hide the sun. Max is nowhere visible, so he climbs the dunes to the forest, the green secrecies of the trees, and walks, walks—

—until from the farthest curve of the path he sees Max, waving, approaching, moving faster than he ever has in real life, Max shaking his head when they finally meet: "Where's your Ringer? You look like a little kid's drawing."

"It's like going bare at the Factory," noting that Max's new avatar looks more completely like Max than meat Max ever has, all the inessentials finally pared away. "You didn't see my messages? Any of them?"

"I'm—in here a lot. It's good you're here, come on—"

—heading side by side down that smooth trail, so different from the muddy, rocky, rooted path where they had first walked and smoked together, Ari remembers thinking then that Max was a crank, a stubborn visionary to open like a nut, and harvest a kernel of vision for the betterment of the Factory, was he wrong? Yes. And no—

—as Max recalls their first night's trek across the Factory floor, his own dazzle and bewilderment, that feeling of impending crescendo, is what he feels right now the same? No; and yes—

—and pausing to point out "A Phoenician palm," with carving on its trunk, twisty *X*s like the symbol for DNA, more carving on another tree, another, another. "Davide planted them. A lot of them."

"Davide's been busy. Meg said—"

"Wait," with a brief headshake, checking a player tally that Ari cannot access, until "Davide's logged out," Max says. "We can talk now."

"What's Davide's problem?"

"He's pissed off. He thought Mathias Bergeron was going to help him—"

"Help him do what? And Bergeron, he says he knows you. He's got some weird theories about Felix—"

"He's got weird theories about B of P, he thinks it's like the Mayans and the Aztecs," *they weren't wrong, Canary, you sacrifice good to get best!* though Mathias apparently cares not at all about Davide's ambitions or the Lukas Solve for X crew or Maven 2, *Even the fucking military knows you're not going to jam total meat reality into any kind of Y, not for the foreseeable, that's why they stopped trying!* "He says he's going to talk to Clara and Meghan, some backdoor money thing so no one knows it's him. So things are about to get bigger in here. A *lot* bigger."

"Bigger out there too, he's streaming Dark Park. But it's still Felix's beats, and still your game—"

"With a reach like his," *anybody could play it, everybody could play it,* "that's how you get to mycelium. Full mycelium—"

"Well, is that a bad thing? People like to dance, people like to play—"

"Mycelium's not a human thing."

"Is *that* a bad thing?"

"Jesus, Ari!" *I'm not a theorist, I'm a realist, I'm done!* but even then he knew they were just getting started, even before then, *you make your own heaven, I believe that.* "I don't fucking know, nobody knows . . . Maybe it's the end of the world."

Ari says nothing. They walk on, walk down the dunes, down to the water where the foam curls at their feet, repeating, insistent, and Max crouches to write in the sand, *DUM VIVIMUS VIVAMUS,* until "Did you know," Max says, "I was scared, before?"

"I know you ran, before."

"Because I knew you would do it. 'Shit to do,' remember?"

"I remember," the feeling of wanting to make things happen, things bigger than his life, bigger than his world, how big is the world? *We made it happen.* Looking from the words to Max, that distillation of Max, "It feels different in here now, doesn't it. You're different. You like that?"

“Yeah. I do.”

“Felix is different, too. Wait till you hear him play.”

“You’re not different, you’re just—more,” on this beach, in this world, how big is Ari’s world now? “Did you ever find out about Krishna?”

“You know I didn’t,” bending for a handful of foam, splashing Max, splashing again until Max splashes back, like boys playing on the beach. Then “Want to be my best man? Me and Felix are getting married.”

“Wow,” and Max smiles, wide and pleased on that narrow avatar face, “wow, congratulations,” offering a handshake that turns into a hug, serious, bodiless, a hard threshold embrace as they hold to one another, Ari wondering what Max will look like when he sees him next, Max wondering if he will ever see Ari again.

Then “Good luck with, with all of it,” Max says. “And tell Felix break a leg at Dark Park. Or *merde,* whatever.”

“You should come,” with the sudden echo of that true and radiant, immensely Ari smile. “Best date ever—”

—and Max recedes as Ari dissolves, back in the crowded little office, tiara off and motionless in the rolling chair, as if he has traveled a long way. And “Hey,” Gussie’s voice in the other room, loud over the jostled twang of a piano, “watch it, watch it! Hold that door—” as his own phone tings, tings, Ilias, ***Journo’s here 4 the interview, Jake Ulrich, says he knows u?***

Bonus Content

EVERYTHING WILL BE OK JK

Ari—

These are bare bones summary notes, but the points are key. I tried to keep it as concise as possible.

Reality recreates itself

Everything starts in darkness. All creation myths begin in chaos and the void:

- Unkulunkulu the reed
- Nyx, the black bird who lays the golden egg
- PanGu with 2 horns and 2 tusks
- the Ogdoad
- the hidden deities of Japan
- the Hebrew ruach moving over the waters
- etc

Being in the dark is defined as being left out or kept apart from needed knowledge, but the dark is where everything ultimately exists. Humans consistently search for/reach for light, and the primal definition of that light is the numinous. There can be religious aspects to the search, but the numinous is nonreligious/areligious. It's not an "answer" to or opposite of the void or chaos, if anything it might intensify that chaos.

Humans have been in the dark for a very long time.

We live in a self-curated reality

Humans can't create reality, but we constantly attempt to curate it by our choices between available circumstances.

Outside events can change this curation, or disrupt it, or destroy it, but we keep choosing some things, and excluding other things—in school, work, friends, etc, including our social identity, beliefs, theories and ideas—then call the things we choose "reality."

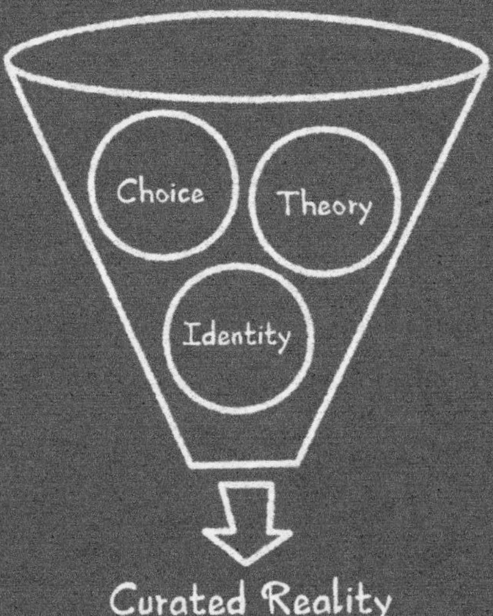

Reality persists in all circumstances

To a kid playing a game, the game is the real world.

To a student in art school, the school is the real world.

To a director making an event, the event is the real world.

All of these "are" discrete segments of reality, but each one feels like a full reality in itself. Then that reality cycle ends/is left behind, and a new cycle takes its place.

When you brought me into Dark Factory, a new cycle started.

Reality reveals itself more fully as we evolve to experience it

After our first nights at the Factory, I started to see things. I went back to define the nature and cause of those "visions," make notes, and potentially make them stop/return to my baseline sight. [I never expected to work there. I never actually did "work" there.]

When I gave you the Fuck the Factory notes, I expected you to have a definition/explanation for what was happening. You said, You're seeing real life like it's Y: meaning that those things were not "visions" but <u>a visual apprehension of a greater reality landscape that is present at all times and has always been present.</u>

I researched all the possible or probable causes—psychophysiologic, psychobiochemical, psychodynamic—that could cause me

continued on page 276

continued from page 275

to see that way, but none of those causes were present in my case [drug use, brain tumor, lesions, dementia, psychosis, etc]. So if all other causes were ruled out, then your meaning was/is correct.

This has strong and ongoing implications beyond my own visual/mental state.

When you put me with Clara, and she put me with Davide, another new cycle started. Felix had started one too.

Reality may be catalyzed

A catalyst not only causes a reaction, a catalyst <u>increases the rate of that reaction.</u>

I believed that I stopped writing/working on the game to force you to come back and deal with whatever human problems might occur from that level of reality access, or at least acknowledge the potential for those problems.

What I subconsciously wanted was for you to <u>catalyze the game's creation.</u> I wasn't sure that it could even be completely realized without you physically being there. [I didn't understand this at the time.]

Once we talked, another cycle started.

Reality is answerable only to itself

Davide believes people could be inside games physically to a much greater degree than they are now. He has graysite research that claims to have repeatable results [can share that if you want to read it] and he believed we could incorporate—literally: *corpus* means *body*—these extremely high levels of player presence into B of P. That would begin as the players explored the game, and trigger a response that would mimic the way I see, and the way Felix hears. That was why he wanted me to create the game's story, and Felix to create the soundtrack: to impose our way of engaging onto the players' engagement/experience.

Meghan was against the idea of heightened corporeal presence even hypothetically, because of long-term safety and liability issues. Clara was willing to consider it in the future, with an industry partner and more funding. Davide wanted to try it immediately, but he didn't have the resources. Then Lukas talked to a friend who worked on Fear of God.

[Fear of God is a very popular RPG that was removed from all major platforms until Mathias Bergeron was purged from the game, because a terrorist group was using it to recruit and train new members, and MB made statements saying that was immaterial, because "all religion is bullshit." Unsure how much of this you already know?]

Let reality be reality. —Lao Tzu

We made up stories to keep from falling apart:

We as in humanity, *homo ludens*, may be the last evolutionary step before whatever comes next, whether it's another version of us or something completely other, maybe better than we ever were at managing itself, managing life, "real" life, across all striations of reality. Clara believes this is the whole point of all games and all Y.

We made up stories to keep from falling apart:

Stories made from Y, or words, or music, or tree branches, smart pens, vitamin water, street garbage, white blood cells, neurons, neutrinos, literally anything, because anything and everything is already part of the same story.

Falling apart = falling away = falling into the void = falling so far into the self that it seems like there is no way out. Then we see the light at the end of the tunnel, and the light is the void, and we fall from apocalypse to paradise, and back into the caves, around the campfire, on the beach, always in the story.

This is the story. You said that.

➔➔*Dark Factory*➔➔*Birds of Paradise* + *Dark Park*➔➔*???*➔

Curiosa felicitas. You were right about the theories, too.
Come and walk around sometime. I'll be here.

Your friend,
Max

15

"OK," Max's murmur to himself, thumbing ***To read whenever*** as he sends to Ari his last notes, the last thing he needs to do in this room before the stream starts; the sun outside glows as it is going down, night is coming on. He has already tidied the room, carried the trash downstairs, pumped out the toilet, tidied himself too in a clean shirt, he even had the urge to shave, why? Marfa noticed, he saw her notice when she walked in, but she said nothing—Marfa wearing cherry red earrings that look like buttons, they match her red t-shirt that reads FOREVER WAS YESTERDAY, and her lipstick, is that lipstick? when did Marfa start wearing lipstick?—Marfa here after her stop at Fantastic Fantoms, to confer with Clara and bolster Meghan, and ignore Davide—

—who is already militantly ignoring everyone, sullen and mutinous because *Matty B,* Davide's cockpit mutter to Max in passing, *used me as a passkey, used Lukas too. Tell Matty B I twigged to that, tell him we still know where all the trapdoors are . . .* Davide presumably does not know that Mathias has been messaging Clara, Mathias adding Max to those messages too—***Molecular ≠ experience personalization, leverage player engagement w/serotonin receptors, more squish more gunk, get their hands dirty!!***—though to Max, Mathias shrugs at those details: Mathias stationed crosslegged at the shady center of the quincunx paths, using one of the stock avatars, a square-shouldered explorer in a black safari hat, and *None of that* *stuff really matters. If you're doing it right, they're not living in the game, the game's living in them—*

How many people will stream this? How many—

—and that's what's so great about you, Canary, and Minos too. Absolute bodhicitta! It's too bad you didn't make it to AltFest. But at Dark Park you'll see.

And now "What happens tonight," Marfa asks, "when the stream goes live?" looking not at him but at the mask balanced on the boxes, as if sighting blind from the edge of a cliff. On his screen the sidebar image of a horned man's body falls upward, black trees below, and below that the countdown clock clicks toward the stream, not backward but forward, *DARK PARK 21:20:00, 01, 02*. "Felix plays for a cast of thousands, while you do what?"

"I'm just there. For—whatever happens."

"'There,'" one-finger lifting a Ringer tiara, letting it drop. "Well then, I'll just be here."

"In the game?"

"No," sharp, but the sharpness is not meant for him, Marfa is unsettled, why? "Riding shotgun. If shit 'happens,'" slapping open one of the folding chairs, setting it beside his table, "to go sideways, I'll be here."

He remembers that Factory night, ***Shit's going sidewise up here***, Marfa showing up there too out of the blue, out of the dark . . . Before he puts on his tiara, he looks once more at her and this little room around them, feeling not fear but a kind of mountaintop hesitance, as if once he logs back in, some greater world, with all its unknown parameters, will thus be ratified, and begin: for her, for Clara and Davide and Mathias, the squatters and the streamers, and for him too, *instead of being the first humans, we're the last.* And in that last pause, that plunge, "Our interview," he says, "did you upload it?"

"I will," she says. "Tonight."

And then he is inside, where the first thing he sees is new faraway lightning in the sunset sky, white and gold, who put it there? Davide? the suggestion of a storm, or the start of a storm itself?

but no thunder, everything is quiet, the Rixia track is gone so the only sounds are the waves and the birds, looped and calling. He breathes in the smell of salt and flowers, and a wet new vegetal reek, someone finally took his advice and edited in the pain. And here comes Mathias, rolling down the shore like a pirate, still the stock black-hatted avatar but with a new mouthful of neon green teeth, curved and sharp as a cat's as "Canary," Mathias shouts through that Cheshire grin. "You ready to play?"

From the guest room window Ari watches a pair of sparkler rockets' gold and white trails in the sky, their spent sticks falling invisible to the weedy yard, no need here for haptic moss, everything is already alive, the brambled fields, the windbreak line of trees animated by a small storm of birds come to roost as the sun goes down. And the yard is filled with people, talking, laughing, in the mingled smells of blunts and cologne puffs and cigarettes, squashed crabapples and spilled lager: the Mister Minos fans, the Silver Landings veterans and former Factory power users, the local and curious, the Indigo contingent led by Das Augie in pink sunglasses, chatting up London goddess Upsetta; even Dodi showed up in a rusted sleeper van with Katya and Michael and black-caped Placebo, all four of them wearing fantastical horns handmade from wire and fabric and drooping flowers, *Did you imagine we would miss out on this!* And his phone tings continuously, journos, friends, Meghan's message from the Outpost, ***everybody @ this bar knows who you are!*** before she arrived in an AWIP t-shirt and a neon green orchid boutonniere, just in time to be their official wedding witness—

—because Felix wanted that, Felix said as he dressed in white, all white, to match the horns, *The mayor can marry us, I already asked,* as Ari sat startled on the bed. *We can do it now.*

Now? What about your mom? And I told Max—

We'll do the church thing for my mom, this is for us. Baby, come on, with such a yearning smile that *Let's do it,* he said, he pulled on black jeans and a jacket and they did, there beside the fountain sputtering pink champagne, Ari wearing the bright boutonniere, Felix with a dandelion tucked in his hair, they held hands and said to each other *I will.* Gussie played a two-finger wedding march on the piano as Ilias led the applause, and Meghan thumbsigned the civil document, then cried because *It's so lovely,* she said.

Now from that dark window, he knows without seeing that Felix is ready to start, feels it like a hum, yes, in his own body, feels light-headed too, as if all of this is a waking dream, the marriage ceremony, the sparklers in the sky, the flower over his heart. Grabbing his cigarillos, checking his phone for the streaming cue, he sends a message to Max, who knows when Max will see it? 💣 ***its ON*** 💣

—and Mathias shouts "We're live, Max! We're live right now, Minos is playing!" as the lightning becomes an *X*, a rough inexpert rendering as if drawn by an angry child, is that Davide? Mathias stops as Max stares, as the lightning eclipses the sun's horizon, then races through the black water, branching, crisscrossing, a thousand Xs heading for the beach—

—as Ari hears the piano's chords and a rising vocal, not Felix, a voice repeating *Meet me on the balcony, meet me*—startled to recognize his own voice, is this a recording from the Fraktur flat, a lifetime ago? or from the Hechman loft?—*meet me, meet me*—

—and "Jesus christ," Mathias pointing, greenly laughing, "here it comes!" retreating to the dunes but Max does not move, though his body braces upright in the faraway chair as that light strikes the shore in a giant glitch explosion, a swarm of white Xs, *solve for X*—

—as the chords storm and the beat drops, Ari drops his cigarillo in the fire pit and starts to dance, pulse already pounding, joining all these bodies in the yard, the field, still arriving from the road, how many more are in the stream? and all of them dancing, Gussie is dancing, Dodi and Katya, the tattoo artist flapping her arms, Meghan is dancing with him now, she loops an arm around his neck—

—and Max sees nothing, his eyes as empty as the void, but when his dazzled vision clears he sees the jagged fissures where the power struck, the way heat turns sand to glass, those Xs have turned to other letters, many letters, words, what words? filling the beach, still twisting and branching—

—as the beats and piano entwine, Felix a white reed vibrating in the light, one bright spotlight on the green uneven ground, Felix with mud smeared already on his white pants, the horns as white in the dark tangle of his hair, Mister Minos the god of this new church—

—and Max on his hands and knees in the sand, writing as fast as he can as the words multiply, everywhere, exponential, mycelium, as Marfa takes his hand that wears the ring and Max, she cries, Max can you hear me! And he can, because the paths have finally crossed, his world has made itself, he hears her and he says Look Marfa, look at this! Marfa shouting MAX MAX MAX so he writes her name too, MARFA MARFA, his hands are different now, he hears Mathias yelling Jesus fucking christ—

—and Ari keeps dancing, *number one guy on the floor, meet me meet me on the balcony, you want to do everything, everything that's yours* and everything is already here, Felix and Max and the paper mill feeling, the trees rising, green and black and white and whorled like his wrists, like the stars, the stars in the sky, the sky is falling, falling, he is falling like a star as the ones closest pull at him, to hug and stumble and crawl and he calls out to them, the ambassador, Dance with me, meet me, meet me—

because the world is the factory and this is what it makes, what it was made for, a joy nameless because it needs no name, resistless, beautiful, absolute

we don't know what it's doing and we don't know what it wants
we're the seams

curiosa felicitas

Is this place about games? Ari asked. *Because I really wanted to dance.*

But he said it with a smile, and that smile was more than enough for Sandor, Sandor who insisted that *They get good DJs, let me just ask who's on tonight, want a vodka shooter?* So while Sandor conferred with a tall woman in a shiny red Jamarama jersey, the DJ? the club manager? he drank the vodka shooter and observed the club's boxy, empty dancefloor, the motionless clumps of other drinkers, the looping bounce screens that no one was watching, no one here seemed to be having a good time—

—especially not the pair just entering, arguing, one of them was arguing anyway, ratty black denim jacket and waving his arm like a teacher, a preacher, the only one alive in this whole place—

—and *She says,* Sandor reporting back with two more shooters, *the DJ's going to start in just a minute—*

Who's that guy over there? You know him?

Him? as Sandor peered, then shook his head. *He's the guy no one likes. He went to Kunstfarm, he makes these weird shows—*

No one? on a laugh. *That's kind of an accomplishment. What's his name?*

—as just inside the door Max stood debating with Jake, Jake who had insisted they come out to this amazing video bar, but one look around told Max he would not be amazed, had just wasted half an hour on the bus and one of the four swipes left on his bus pass, though *Come on,* Jake urged. *Have a lager at least, give it a chance—*

A chance to do what?

—as the music started, a serviceable beat, Ari tossed back his vodka and *Come on,* to Sandor, *let's dance*, joined in a few minutes on the floor by a few determined girls who looked like art students, bungee pants and shiny blue eyeliner: but the vibe remained dead,

continued on page 284

continued from page 283

after that first dance he knew he was done. And on the way to the exit they passed the black denim jacket guy, the unlikeable guy, and Ari could not resist, he flashed him a smile, his brightest, most amused and winning smile—

—and *Who the fuck was that?* Max asked, as the outer door opened and closed. *That guy in the purple shirt?*

Him? That's Ari. He's everywhere, he's a big party guy.

A big party guy, and he shook his head, not at Jake but at that departed and provoking smile, as if he and that guy, Ari, already knew each other, were in on some joke together, something personal and hilarious and vast. *Well that's all we fucking need.*

I wrote Dark Factory for you: to read, watch, listen, add to it, make it yours. This is for you.

Dark Factory is an ongoing playground, and so many people came to play! My special thanks to:

Publisher and creative force Tricia Reeks, and agent nonpareil Christopher Schelling

My supportive Patreon Backstage patrons: Isa Arsén, Carmen C. Curton, Zita Gillis, Debra Knealing, Kevin Lovecraft, Sony Murphy, Alice Phelan, and J. Daniel Stone

Beta readers Charlie Athanas, Laura Bailey, Carroll Brown, Maryse Meijer and Carter Scholz

Sofia Ajram of Sofia Zakia Jewelry, Antechambre Design, Charlie Athanas, Quinine Hours, and Kobie Solomon, for artistry above and beyond

Denice Brown, Diane Cheklich, John Collins, Johnny "Thief" Di Donna, Ann Stirling Griffin, Rachael Harbert, Cornelius Harris, Josh Malerman, Max Manoogian, Henrik Möller, Isabella Ness, Kevin Peterson of Sfumato, Keith Rosson, Martha Gibiser Shea, Chad Stocker, Kat and Gregg Thacker, and everyone who continues to share their creative energies and knowledge

Unique thanks to Rick Lieder and Aaron Mustamaa

—Kathe Koja

BIOS

KATHE KOJA

Kathe Koja writes novels and short fiction, and creates and produces immersive performances that cross and combine genres. Her work has won awards, and been optioned for film and performance. kathe@darkfactory.club

ARI REGON

Ari Regon works at Dark Factory, making sure every night is a totally fulfilling experience. ari@darkfactory.club

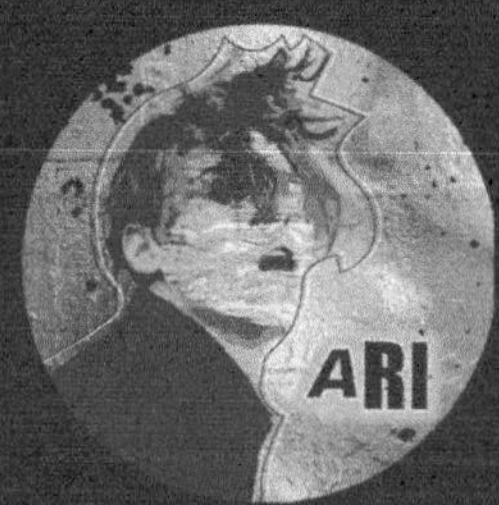

MAX CASPAR

Max Caspar is a reality artist, concentrated on site-dependant, durational installations. He holds an MFA from Kunstfarm. He also writes. max@darkfactory.club

MARFA CARPENTER

Marfa Carpenter is a freelance culture journalist whose profiles and articles have appeared in *BlogOut*, *Daisychain*, *Excelsior*, *Artfetish*, and *Journal of Daily Pop*. Her current project is Making It Real: The Dark Factory Interviews. marfa@darkfactory.club